PENELOPE DOUGLAS is a *New York Times, USA Today*, and *Wall Street Journal* bestselling author. She grew up in Dubuque, Iowa, and attended the University of Northern Iowa, studying political science. She then earned a graduate degree in Education from Loyola University New Orleans. She's the oldest of five, lives with her husband and daughter in New England, and loves breakfast, gin, and Hannibal Lecter. She does not drink gin for breakfast, but she might eat breakfast at Hannibal's. *shrugs*

Her books have been translated into more than twenty languages and include *The Fall Away Series*, *The Devil's Night Series*, and several standalones.

Instagram: https://www.instagram.com/penelope.douglas/
Spotify: https://open.spotify.com/user/pendouglas
TikTok: https://vm.tiktok.com/TTPdSskp6R/
BookBub: https://www.bookbub.com/profile/penelope-douglas
Facebook: https://www.facebook.com/PenelopeDouglasAuthor
Goodreads: http://bit.ly/1xvDwau
Website: https://pendouglas.com/
Email: penelopedouglasauthor@hotmail.com

And all of Pen's stories have Pinterest boards!
https://www.pinterest.com/penelopedouglas/

ALSO BY PENELOPE DOUGLAS...

Stand-Alones
Misconduct
Punk 57
Birthday Girl
Credence
Tryst Six Venom
Five Brothers
Midnight Curfew (TBR)

The Devil's Night Series
Corrupt
Hideaway
Kill Switch
Conclave
Nightfall
Fire Night

The Fall Away Series
Bully
Until You
Rival
Falling Away
Aflame
Next to Never

The Hellbent Series
(Fall Away Spin-Off)
Falls Boys
Pirate Girls
Quiet Ones
Night Thieves
Parade Alley
Fire Falls

QUIET ONES

PENELOPE DOUGLAS

PIATKUS

PIATKUS

First published in the US in 2026 by Penelope Douglas
Published in Great Britain in 2026 by Piatkus

1 3 5 7 9 10 8 6 4 2

Copyright © 2025 by Penelope Douglas

The moral right of the author has been asserted.

*All characters and events in this publication, other than those
clearly in the public domain, are fictitious and any resemblance
to real persons, living or dead, is purely coincidental.*

All rights reserved.
No part of this publication may be reproduced, stored in a
retrieval system, or transmitted in any form or by any means, without
the prior permission in writing of the publisher, nor be otherwise circulated
in any form of binding or cover other than that in which it is published
and without a similar condition including this condition being
imposed on the subsequent purchaser.

A CIP catalogue record for this book
is available from the British Library.

ISBN 978-0-349-43578-7

Printed and bound in Great Britain by
Clays Ltd, Elcograf S.p.A.

Papers used by Piatkus are from well-managed forests
and other responsible sources.

Piatkus
An imprint of
Little, Brown Book Group
Carmelite House
50 Victoria Embankment
London EC4Y 0DZ

The authorised representative
in the EEA is
Hachette Ireland
8 Castlecourt Centre
Dublin 15, D15 XTP3, Ireland
(email: info@hbgi.ie)

An Hachette UK Company
www.hachette.co.uk

www.littlebrown.co.uk

PLAYLIST

"All I Want Is You" by U2
"Bother" by Stone Sour
"Cradle of Love" by Billy Idol
"Drive" by Britta Phillips
"Far From Home" Five Finger Death Punch
"Hats Off to the Bull" by Chevelle
"My Demons" by STARSET
"Numb" by Linkin Park
"Raise the Dead" by Rachel Rabin
"Say Something" by A Great Big World, Christina Aguilera
"Stronger" by Through Fire
"The Boys of Summer" by The Ataris
"The High Road" by Three Days Grace
"You Don't Own Me (feat. G-Eazy)" by SAYGRACE
"You Stupid Girl" by Framing Hanley

In addition to playlists, all of my stories
come with Pinterest
(https://www.pinterest.com/penelopedouglas/
quiet-ones-2025/) mood boards.
Please enjoy *QUIET ONES*'s board as you read!

AUTHOR'S NOTE

The Hellbent series is a spin-off of the Fall Away series. These are the kids' stories.

Reading the Fall Away series is helpful but not necessary. The parents do appear a lot, as well as references to their past storylines, so if you wish to read those first, the order is *BULLY, UNTIL YOU, RIVAL, FALLING AWAY, AFLAME,* and *NEXT TO NEVER*. (*The Next Flame* is simply *Aflame* and *Next to Never* in paperback form together.)

If you don't want to read the Fall Away series, but you do want to read all the times the characters in *Quiet Ones* appeared before this book starts, go here. (https://pendouglas.com/2022/02/28/get-ready-for-hellbent/)

FALLS BOYS (Hellbent #1) and *PIRATE GIRLS* (Hellbent #2) are also **strongly encouraged** before you read *QUIET ONES* (Hellbent #3). There is an ongoing mystery playing out in the background. I do try to bring you up to speed in this story, but you'll have the best experience reading *both* previous installments first.

Enjoy!

- A. HAWKE'S HOUSE
- B. DYLAN'S HOUSE
- C. KADE'S HOUSE
- D. TBD
- E. HIGH SCHOOL
- F. EAGLE POINT PARK
- G. FISH POND
- H. CEMETERY
- I. THE LOOP/FALLSTOWN
- J. MINES OF SPAIN

*This map is a loose representation of Shelburne Falls to give you a basic idea of the placement of homes and points of interest. There are more streets and businesses than what the map includes.

K. SKATE PARK
L. BLACKHAWK LAKE
M. JT RACING
N. QUINN'S HOUSE
O. QUINN'S BAKERY
P. BLACKHAWK SUMMER CAMP
Q. BOWLING ALLEY
R. MOVIE THEATER
S. RIVERTOWN
T. THE DIETRICH HOUSE
U TBD
V. TBD

"You have to fight twice—once against your fear
and once against your enemy."
— Carolyn Keene,
Captive Witness (Nancy Drew Mystery Stories #64)

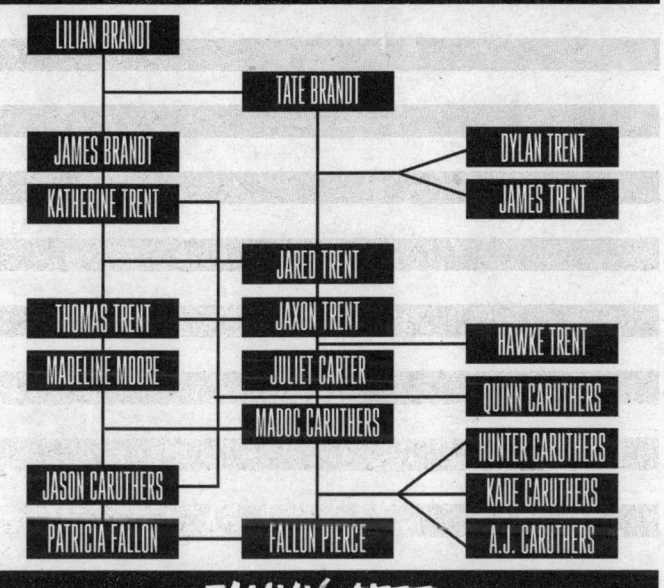

"Was it a threat, or a well-meant warning?"
— *Carolyn Keene, The Secret of Shadow Ranch*

WESTON

PROLOGUE

Quinn

Nine Years Ago

"We don't have to find you, you know?" he calls out.

I step from one rafter to the other, and then kneel down and peek through the slits in the ceiling beneath me. My niece and nephews are below, searching the great room of the main lodge of our family's summer camp. At only ten—a couple of years younger than me—I don't think they know that the ceiling above them is false, the rafters I stand on hidden away up here by the previous owners decades ago to conserve heat.

I'm so close to them and they can't even see me.

"If we turn off the lights," Kade goes on. "You'll come to us!"

I drew the short straw, so I have to hide. If they find me, then I'm the one who has to steal the keys to the ATVs for a no-parents' midnight ride this weekend.

I really don't want to steal anything. I'm not good at breaking rules.

"Quinnnn..." Hawke sings in a calm tone, and I watch him look from left to right like a cyborg scanning for heat signatures. "I know you can hear me, and I don't have to shout. Where are you?"

I smile. Hawke is actually only a year younger than me, and I don't usually stump him.

I never really felt like the oldest out of the kids. I'm still wondering where I fit. My older brothers are their parents, and since the age gap between my brothers and me is more than twenty years, they act more like *my* parents too. Their kids grew up more like my cousins, but not in the same way that they're cousins with each other. I never understood *why* it felt different, but I just knew that someday it would be.

Maybe I liked that I'd be treated more like an aunt to them when we grew up. Or maybe I didn't. All I knew was that something separated them and me, and it was more pronounced when we were all together like this, because that's when I noticed the couples. How everyone broke into a natural pair. Dylan and Hunter. Kade and Hawke.

The babies, A.J. and James, would also grow up together.

They didn't exclude me. But none of them gravitated to me like they did to each other.

Even the adults were all in pairs.

"Quinn!" Dylan yells, searching underneath lunch tables, dressed in her Chucks and hoodie.

Kade's twin, Hunter, follows her. Always within reach of each other. "Quinnie!" he calls.

"Quinnie-bean!" I hear Kade tease from farther away.

I hate those names. I should tell them, but everyone teases each other in this family, and I don't want to make it awkward.

Hawke stalks slowly, out of view, and I plant my hands on the rafter under me, pushing myself up. I leap from one beam to another, following their voices in the faint light streaming up from below.

It's a little dark up here, but it was the only hiding place I suspected they didn't know about.

They trail through the lodge, and I don't peer down to see which rooms they search. The kitchen, the pantry, the offices...

Taking out my compass, I flip the lid, finding north. I turn to where the needle points, knowing the lake is ahead of me—out of the lodge, across the lawn, and to the beach. Then I pivot to the left, knowing the way out is that way.

"We're coming for you, Quinn!" Hunter threatens.

Followed by Kade, "I just hope we find you before *sheee* does."

She...

I glance over one shoulder, then the other, looking above me and all around.

Undergrove.

That's what they call her. The spirit who lives on the tiny island in the middle of the lake. A summer camp urban legend. I scan the far recesses of the dark corners, the walls of the attic disappearing into a black void. She *could* be there.

But I shake it off and kneel back down. He's just trying to scare me out of hiding. I don't believe in ghosts.

And I don't know why I'm even playing hide-and-seek. I don't want to steal the ATVs for a secret ride in the woods, either. One of the many other things about me that made it feel like I never really fit in with my family. They all love to drive things. Especially the adults. Cars, motorcycles, drones, boats, side-by-sides...

Lowering myself, I peer through a small hole in the ceiling.

They all love speed, and they're all in pairs.

My brothers and their wives...

My parents...

"Can I help you?" I hear my mom through the peephole.

I watch her pick up the other end of a table, helping my brother's mom—my dad's first wife—clear the room. The whole family is gathered this weekend to help my brother Jax and his wife, Juliet, clear and clean the lodge and cabins for renovations that'll happen over the fall and winter, before next summer's campers arrive.

Madeline, my dad's ex, tenses. "No, I've got it."

"It's okay." My mom walks backward, leading the table out of the room.

But Madeline drops her end, snapping, "Katherine, please."

I narrow my eyes. Madoc's mom has always been nice to me. Why is she being mean?

My mom freezes, her expression timid. She looks like Jared, a little. And like me when I don't know what to say. We all have the same eyes. Brown, like chocolate, is what everyone says.

My blonde hair is my dad's, though.

I curl my fingers into a wooden beam. I don't like Madoc's mom talking to mine like that. Madeline didn't yell, but she sounded like my brothers when they're scolding their kids.

My dad appears in my view. Dust covers his khakis, and there are green paint marks on his white T-shirt. He doesn't say anything to his first wife, cupping my mother's face, instead, and looking at her softly. His fingers thread through the wisps of long dark hair that've escaped her messy bun.

I lean down more, watching carefully. I'm not supposed to know why my dad's first wife doesn't get along with my mom, but I do.

My mother pulls back from my father. "I'll see what they're doing in the kitchen," she tells him, trembling.

My mom leaves the small room—once a little old library, I think—and my dad turns to his first wife. "It's been years—decades," he points out. "How long are you going to make her pay?"

"I'm not trying to hurt her," Madeline tells him. "But we'll never be okay."

My mom was my dad's mistress. For a very long time, I think.

Madoc's mom, while kind to me, doesn't visit much. She lives in New Orleans with her husband, and Madoc and his family go there to visit most of the time. They even took me once.

My dad lowers his voice. "It's me you should be mad at."

"I am."

My father steps closer. "She was young."

"And then she wasn't," Madeline replies quickly.

There's a five- or six-year age difference between my parents. He was in his twenties and already married with a kid. My mom was a teenager with a baby of her own. It's weird to me that someone hates them, but I love that my dad only worries about someone hating my mother. It hurts him to see.

Madeline sighs. "I'm not going to get into this with you." She squares her shoulders. "You're married, you've been married for fifteen years, and I know you're happy. So am I," she tells him before dropping her voice to almost a whisper. "But I can still feel it, you know?"

I tilt my ear to the peephole.

"Being forgotten," she goes on. "The nights I was alone, knowing where you were, and wondering what the hell was wrong with me that you kept running to her." Her tone grows harder. "And it doesn't change the pain that your daughter is beautiful and kind and Madoc adores her, but she's going to get you at your best when he got you at your worst," she growls, a sob thickening her voice.

I want to defend my dad. And my mom. They're good parents and good grandparents and they don't do anything wrong.

"All that pain because you couldn't stop fucking her," Madoc's mom says.

I wince.

She continues, "You don't get to demand that I forget simply because you perceive that an acceptable amount of time has passed."

My dad drops his eyes and part of me understands the sadness on his face. I guess I'd be mad if I were her and it were my husband.

"I'm sorry," he whispers.

"Would you have done anything differently?"

He doesn't say anything at first. Maybe he'll say he shouldn't have married Madeline in the first place. I mean, if he didn't love her, then...

But instead, he says, "I would've...left you sooner."

I flit my eyes to Madoc's mom, and it's brief, but I see it. The flinch.

He would've still married her.

To get Madoc.

I can't help but wonder what their wedding day was like. Celebration and laughter and dancing. Does it hurt her how much she hates him now? Could that happen to my brothers and their wives? Could it happen to me someday?

She leaves the room, and my father barely has time to run his fingers through his hair before Jared's wife Tate walks in. "Can I help?" she chirps.

He flexes his jaw, struggling to find his words. After a moment, he exhales and forces a smile. "Thanks."

They pick up the table and move it out of the room.

I watch them disappear from view and inhale through my nose as if pushing everything I just heard down into my stomach. Hiding it away. Keeping it to myself.

I don't know why. Maybe because no one talks to me about the past. They don't want me to know things.

Maybe it just feels good to know more than the other kids. Everyone acts like I don't have a clue because I'm quieter than they are.

Or maybe it's just fun to see and listen to what people say when they're not around children.

"Just give us a clue!" Kade bellows, pounding walls.

"A bird chirp," Hunter adds from the distance.

"Or a knock!" Dylan offers.

I grin to myself.

But then I hear the booming voice that knots my stomach. "Quinn?!"

My oldest brother Jared. There's no reason to be scared of him, but I am, because I can never seem to stand up to him. It's like my brain leaves my body, and I forget English.

"How long have you guys been seeking?" he asks them.

"A while," Hunter gripes.

"But I'm not forfeiting!" Kade immediately yells loud enough for me to hear.

Me either. I slide over to another beam, about to slink down for a better view, when a knock echoes through the blackness of the attic.

I pop up straight.

I jerk my head, scanning the dark corners of the loft. *What was that?*

Another knock, and I jump, feeling a scream rise up my throat. I clamp my hand over my mouth to stop it.

But maybe I should just yell. I don't want to be here anymore. I watch the black voids, waiting for something to emerge.

Three more knocks vibrate through the attic. I think they're coming from the kitchen area.

Heading from one beam to the other, I crouch down, spotting Lucas Morrow through a sliver in the panels. Hunched over the steel work table, he makes notes on his blueprints, and my stomach does that thing where it spins, like an ice skater pulling her arms in close to her body to go faster and faster.

Is he the one who knocked?

His light gray T-shirt is streaked with dirt and patches of sweat, the fabric a little tighter on him than it used to be. I don't really like it.

I know he's twenty-four—always have his birthday on my calendar like the rest of the family's—but he's looking more and more like my brothers. The way you can kind of see his body underneath his shirt. How his arms have little hills on them, up and down, up and down... And the veins in his hands and neck are always pushing up through the skin. Girls are always looking at him now. He had girlfriends in high school, but it's all the time now.

He pulls off his light blue Chicago Cubs cap, slides a hand over the long strands of blond hair on top of his head, and fits it back on, backward this time. I don't know what Jax had him doing today, but he glows with sweat, the stubble on his jaw glistening.

Lucas was only eight when Madoc took him under his wing as part of the Big Brothers Big Sisters program. He'd lost his dad not long before. As my brothers' honorary little brother, he's been a part of the family since before I was born.

"Are you sure she didn't go outside?" I hear Madoc call out from another room.

"We're all supposed to stay in the great room," Hawke shouts. "That's the rule."

"When's the last time you heard from her?"

I sigh at Jax's question. What does he think? That I stuffed myself in the deep freezer in the kitchen? Got kidnapped? Their kids climb trees taller than my house, but I can't survive without wearing bubble wrap. Why do they worry more about me?

"Quinn!" Jared growls.

Followed by Madoc's bellow, "Quinn Livia Caruthers!"

I straighten my spine. I'm in trouble now.

But Lucas moves under me, standing up tall.

"Quinn?" he says in a low voice. "I know you're there."

I keep my lips locked together, but I can't stop the smile rising. He did do the knocking.

"I didn't tell them where you were," he tells me, his head still bowed to his blueprints as the rest of my family searches the other rooms.

It's not like it was hard for him to find me. He showed me this was here in the first place. They found it when Jax was planning the renovations, but it won't be here for long. He's tearing down the false ceiling to open up the room.

"You could at least say hi to me," he says, probably unsure if I can see him through the cracks. "It's Lucas."

"Yeah, I know." I sniffle, the dust up here tickling my nostrils. "I always smell you before I see you."

A laugh escapes him, and he hops up onto the table and comes at me, opening the latch. A square door big enough for a person to climb through opens up right under my head. "Hey," he chides, pulling out the collar of his sweaty T-shirt to take a sniff. "Your sister-in-law bought me that cologne."

And why are you wearing cologne to the lake?

But I don't ask out loud. I like how he smells, I guess.

He jumps back down, and I slide to the opening, peeking my head out.

He pours over the blueprints. There are lines and numbers—measurements or something—and I can see several sheets for individual buildings. But he inspects one that has a layout of an entire ski resort. His dream project.

He probably brought them with him today to get Fallon's advice. Madoc's wife is an architect, and also Lucas's mentor at the architectural firm where they both work.

"What are you going to call it?" I whisper, glancing around and not seeing anyone else.

He sharpens his pencil. "I've tried not to think about it," he replies. "If I plan too far ahead, it'll jinx it."

"Don't you need a mountain first?"

It's a ski resort. He'll need a lot of land.

He nods. "I'll need investors for that."

"We have mountains here," I tell him, hopeful.

He tosses a smirk up at me. "No one flies here for skiing."

But they could. We have a small ski place about forty minutes away. My parents like it. It has an inn and restaurant and stuff, but I don't think it brings in people other than locals. Maybe if we were closer to the city, we'd get some tourists.

Unfortunately, I'm not very good at skiing. The other kids are, though. Everyone else loves speed.

I float my eyes around the papers, trying to make out how it would look in real life. There are buildings, ski lifts, chalets...

"Why do they call it the bunny hill?" I ask, remembering that slope being the only one I was good at last winter. And the winter before.

He leans over his blueprints. "Sounds like a question for your journal."

My journal. Juliet gave me one when I was little and told me to put all of my questions in there. Then, we could work on researching the answers.

I never did, though. I mean, I use the journal, but by the time my family and I sit down to look something up, I don't care anymore. I just have other questions by then.

"Have you ever tried snowshoeing?" I inquire next.

I don't like skiing, but maybe if there are other winter activities, I can go to his resort too.

Lucas shakes his head. "That just sounds like work to me."

I twist my mouth to the side. Does everything have to be fast to be fun?

I point to the chalets dotting the areas around the ski slopes. "Why are the roofs shaped like that?"

They're like tall, upside-down Vs.

"I don't know."

I sneer. "Yes, you do."

He looks up at me. "And so do you if you think about it for a minute."

I dig in my eyebrows.

But sure enough, I look back at the houses, ponder if the shape of the roofs help keep in the heat before I remember that chalets are commonplace in mountains. Mountains get a lot of snow. And the steepness of the roofs lets the snow fall off easier.

"Did you figure it out?" he presses after a few moments.

"No."

"Yes, you did."

I try to keep my smile inside at the twinkle in his blue eyes, but it starts to peek out. "Maybe."

I see his cheeks crinkle with a smile as he leans over the table again.

"Quinn!" Jared growls.

I sigh. I guess I should forfeit, but it's either get into trouble for hiding too well, or get into trouble for stealing ATV keys.

"All right, let's go outside!" Jared barks. "Spread out. You guys, stay in here and find her. Search the pantry, the closets..."

"Would she have gone into the lake?" Madoc asks as they leave.

I can't make out Jared's grumble, but no, I wouldn't have gone into the lake. I'm not allowed to go alone.

"You're not going to give them a hint?" Lucas asks as the boys and Dylan shout and slam doors below. "Kade's going to shut off the lights on you."

My eyes dart left to right, and for a second, my heart speeds up. I don't believe in ghosts, but it's harder to not believe in them in the dark.

"Your brothers are worried," he points out.

"Why?"

"What do you mean?"

"Why are they always worried?" I ask him. "About me, I mean."

They worry about their own kids, sure. Madoc is always dragging Kade away from one kind of trouble or another, and Jared is constantly telling Dylan 'no.'

But I'm not their kid.

"Is it because I'm a girl?" I inquire.

The way they tell it, they were running around town unsupervised, even at my age. Why treat their sister differently?

Lucas looks up at me. "I think..." He hesitates. "I think it's because they didn't have the best experience with your parents growing up, Quinn."

I lower my eyes, anything I was going to say lost on my tongue. Lucas is the only one who tells me the truth.

I share a dad with Madoc, and a mom with Jared. My parents are great with me, but they weren't around for Madoc and Jared as much when they were younger.

And Jax never had parents. Not really. His and Jared's dad was a monster, and Jax's mom left him when he was little. Mine and Jared's mom took him in when he was a teenager, and she's a good grandma to Jax's son Hawke now. Very different from how she was when my brothers were young.

I've put the pieces together from overhearing things in my life. I guess it's just hard to imagine they used to suffer when I didn't see any of it.

"They want to always be there for you," Lucas says. "And to make sure you know you're loved."

They still don't trust their parents. Not…completely.

But still, I clear my throat. "Well, you can tell them to stop now."

He just chuckles. "They won't ever stop. Your first boyfriend is going to be in for it someday."

"Not if I like somebody they already like."

"That might work." He shrugs. "Or not."

It'll work. It's my only hope.

"You'll learn how to drive in a few years anyway," Lucas points out. "You'll be able to escape them any time you want."

"Not likely." I wring out my hand, whipping off a spiderweb I picked up. "Half of my family races something motorized."

Like I would get very far.

Lucas just laughs—the first time, I notice. He hasn't laughed in a while.

"Well, then you will too," he assures.

"You know I won't."

My tone is final. I don't feel that need for speed that the Trents and other Caruthers do. I like walks. And bicycles. And being a passenger.

But he continues, "You could change your mind. When you were eight, you thought you were going to marry me too. Remember that?"

"Oh my God." Every follicle of hair on my head electrifies, but I force a scowl. "Gross. Shut up."

He laughs again, but I can feel the blush on my cheeks. When I was eight years old, I declared my devotion for him, but now I just feel embarrassed.

Even if butterflies are taking flight in my stomach.

Right now, I feel like I belong.

I only feel like that when he's around.

Tilting his head back, he peers up at me. "How do you—"

But his voice is cut off as Kade bellows, "Quiiiinn!"

I round my eyes. He's close. Is he coming to the kitchen?

"I'm turrrning off the lighhhts!" he taunts.

I suck in a breath, turning my head side to side. My skin crawls at the thought of the things that come out in the dark. Bats and spiders and clowns.

Lucas puts a knee on the table below again and pushes himself up, about to close the hatch.

But something on the little door catches on his shirt and he hisses. "Shit."

He jumps down, the nail nearly tearing the T-shirt off his body.

Long, jet black lines fall down the back of his right shoulder. Like an upside-down V but curved like branches, arms splitting off from the main limb.

"Lucas, what is that?" I burst out.

I've never seen him with a tattoo. Did he have it this summer when we were all swimming? I would've noticed.

He slips out of the shirt and yanks it down off the nail, causing it to rip. He turns, his back to the wall. "It's nothing."

He avoids my eyes, inspecting the shirt in his hands. Shooting back up, he closes the hatch, but he gives me a wink as he hides me away again. "You got this," he whispers.

I smile.

"Quinn, come on!" Kade bellows.

But Dylan barks at him, "Just forfeit."

"Well, why don't you?"

"I'm bored," Hawke mumbles.

A door creaks open downstairs and several pairs of feet hit the floor.

"Where is she?" Jared growls. "Now!"

"Ugh," someone groans.

"Fine, we give up!" Kade shouts. "Come out! I forfeit."

I release a breath and race to the attic door in the great room, whipping it open. Climbing down, I hop onto a long dining table and dust off my clothes, everyone turning to look at me. Not Lucas, though. He's gone.

"What the…" Kade runs over.

Dylan smiles. "Hey!"

"What were you doing?" Madoc and everyone else follows, all of my brothers' brows etched with aggravation.

But Hunter pushes past his dad and climbs onto the table. "I didn't know that was there! Let me see!"

Kade, Dylan, and Hawke rush over as I jump down and out of the way.

"We're tearing it down to open up the room," Jax tells his brothers. "There are yards of rafters up there."

Madoc peers up through the opening. "I wondered if there was a second level or something."

Jax shakes his head. "Just empty space."

"Who told you that you could play up there?"

I look up at Jared. His voice is curt.

Before I can answer, Dylan speaks up. "Oh, Dad. Leave her alone."

"Do you know how thin these boards are?" Madoc gripes at me. "What if you fell?"

"Then I would've gotten hurt," I point out. "And Dad would've blamed you."

Madoc steps in. "Why you little—"

Jax pulls him back, clamping a hand over his mouth.

Dylan giggles, and I fold my lips between my teeth. I can't believe I said that.

"Let me up!" Hawke yells as Hunter pushes Kade through the opening.

"I want to see next," Hunter says.

But Dylan takes my hand, and we run as Jax grabs the twins by the waists of their jeans. "You two, come here."

Dylan and I race outside onto the porch and down the steps.

I did it. I didn't forfeit!

"Kade has to steal the keys now," Dylan brags.

It won't be hard for him, unfortunately. But I'll admit, it's nice to see him lose. He never does. Especially against me.

The lake ripples with the light breeze, and I spot Lucas's torn shirt on the beach. Dylan runs, joining her mom on the sand as she bounces James, Dylan's baby brother, in her lap.

Where's Lucas? I walk down the dock, scanning the water, and then I turn my head left and right, looking down the beach. I want to tell him I won.

Of course, that means I still have to go ATVing, which sucks.

Sliding off my sneakers, I sit down on the dock and dip my feet into the water. I study the island out on the lake. Maybe a little smaller than a football field, it's filled with trees and large boulders trailing up the hills. There's a cliff you can jump into the water on one side, and I even heard there's a small cave somewhere. A canoe sits on the beach. Is that where Lucas went?

But just then a phone rings, and I look behind me, seeing a couple of people in the parking lot. I squint through the sun in my eyes and put my hand over my brow to see. Lucas?

The next thing I know, something grabs my ankles, pulls, and I'm flying forward off the dock. "Ah!" My heart leaps in my throat, choking my cry just before I hit the water. I flail, screaming, but it's just bubbles coming out of my mouth underneath the surface.

I kick, but I'm hauled backward and quickly lifted up.

I cough and sputter as Lucas holds me by the shoulders.

"You big…" I struggle for breath. "…jerk."

He presses a finger over his lips. "Shhh…"

I wipe the water out of my eyes, both of us crouched down and hidden underneath the dock. He casts his eyes upward, completely drenched himself.

"That wasn't funny," I whisper-yell.

He murmurs, "It was kind of funny."

Footfalls hit the dock, and he goes still.

So do I.

"What?" I mouth.

But he just gestures, "Shhh!"

Are we playing hide-and-seek again?

The dock creaks under the footsteps, and I think I see two figures through the slits in the wood. Madoc and Jared, maybe?

They don't say anything, and I try to move to get a closer look, but Lucas keeps hold of me. I gaze up at him, his golden hair and long lashes over blue eyes.

There's two of them up there. And two of us. A pair.

Finally, they retreat, but Lucas waits another minute or so. Eventually, he releases me and swims backward out from under the dock. "Later, gator."

My hair is plastered to my cheeks. "I hate you," I gripe.

He grins wide. "But you're making me pizza tonight back at Madoc's, right?"

"Yes."

But I pout about it, not sure if I'm mad at him for getting my clothes wet, or mad that I'm never really mad at him.

He beams. He loves my pizza.

I wish we could play hide-and-seek as a team, but...

We never get another chance.

A year later, he's gone.

Leaves town. Doesn't text. Doesn't call.

He's grown up, and I'm not. I guess we weren't a pair, after all.

WESTON

CHAPTER ONE

Quinn

Nine Years Later

I peer out the little window in the kitchen door, seeing the man still finishing his coffee. He sits at the table in front of the tall wall mirror, and he's been there for two hours. I hate kicking people out, but...

Oh, who am I kidding? I've never kicked anyone out.

I usually rely on them seeing me switch the sign on the door and start cleaning up for them to get the hint that I'm closing.

Here I am, though. Dishes are done, counters cleaned, trash taken out, dough prepped for tomorrow, and floors swept and mopped. I only have to pack up the leftovers for the day and count out the register, which I refuse to do when I'm alone in the shop with a customer I don't know. Hailey, my cashier, and Noel, my barista, left hours ago.

But as if he can hear my thoughts, the lone guy rises, buttons his suit jacket, and tucks in his chair. *Aw*. Nobody does that. I smile as he pushes through the door, leaving the bakery.

"See you soon," I call out.

He doesn't reply, simply turns his head slightly, showing me the side of his face, and nods once.

Once he's gone, I lock the door behind him and shut off the light. Heading to his table, I pick up his cup and saucer and swipe up his napkin to find a phone sitting underneath it.

I look to the windows, then to the phone, grabbing it as I set the dishes down and run to the door.

I open it and peer out. "Sir?"

I look both directions, but all I see are diners sitting outside to my right, at Rivertown Grill, and some cars driving by. He's gone.

I lock the door again and inspect the phone, finally noticing how old it is. The gritty texture leaves patches of black on my hand, and I bring it to my nose, noticing the scent of fire. I flip it open, pressing buttons, but it's dead. No one uses these anymore. What a strange thing to even carry.

I shrug. He'll come back for it.

Swiping up the dishes again, I walk into the kitchen, set the phone on the counter, and place everything in the sink. I turn and move all the remaining pastries from a tray to a box.

But no sooner have I started than Dylan comes bursting through the swinging door, from the front of the shop.

I jump as she rushes me. "No, no, no!" she cries, running for the chocolate coconut donuts. "I need them!"

Hunter laughs, trailing in behind her, followed by Hawke and Aro, Hawke's girlfriend.

Dylan barrels into me, and we take turns shoving each other with our hips for supremacy over the remaining baked goods.

I snatch one out of her hand before she takes a bite. "No, you need to take them to the senior center and help me out."

I'm doing a test run for the summer to see if I can be a bakery *and* do some light fare for lunch too. Sandwiches, flatbread pizzas, soups....

I'm staying open way too late, though, and trying to be back here at three-thirty in the morning to bake is making it difficult to find time for exercise, my family, or any kind of sleep.

QUIET ONES

If I don't get into a groove with my business soon, this trial will be a fail. I thought going to business school would teach me more practical applications, but I'm still struggling on time management. I learned marketing and accounting, and I've easily mastered things like strategy, taxes, and communication. But leadership? It would've been better for me to apprentice before jumping into my own bakery. Jared would tell me that real work experience trumps schooling every time. I don't believe that, exactly, but I'd be better off if I'd slowed down.

Hunter stands on the other side of the counter, plucking a donut off the tray and handing it to his girlfriend. "We'll take them," he tells me, kissing Dylan on the temple.

"How'd you guys get in?" I look around at them. "I locked the front door."

Aro won't meet my eyes, Hunter gives me a tight smile, and Dylan leans her elbows on the counter, shrugging. "No, you didn't."

I cock an eyebrow as Hawke snorts, pulling a chocolate milk out of the fridge.

Hunter glances to him. "It's time to tell her, man."

"We'll tell her when she's ready to use it," Hawke replies as if I'm not here.

Dylan stuffs her mouth with the pastry as she looks up at me with glee.

I point my finger around the room. "You know I'm older than all of you, right?"

They all laugh.

They've been hinting about something for a while now. I know there's some urban legend they're researching, and I know they're in here after closing hours and off-season too. I gave them all keys because I might've needed any one of them to have access, in case a pipe burst while I was away at school, or if they were in need of extra space for holiday cooking.

But something is going on, and the only reason I don't press harder about it is because I don't want to know. If I know, then I'll feel like I have to be the responsible one, because I'm the oldest. I'd rather not ruin their good time.

I shouldn't feel like that, but I know I'm not fun. I'm the inexperienced one compared to them, and it sucks. I've got a college degree. My own business. I'm disciplined, punctual, and a taxpayer. Why do I feel younger than them?

"Come on, we've gotta get back." Hunter dusts off his hands. "Lights out in thirty minutes."

They're all working at Camp Blackhawk, like last summer. They get a couple of hours of free time while the kids have campfire jamboree at night.

I hand Hunter the two boxes to drop off at the senior center. "Where's Kade?"

"Tending to needs." Dylan cleans her teeth with her tongue. "Whatever that means."

"Even I know what that means," I say as I lead the way to the back door.

Like Dylan, Hunter, and Aro, Kade is nineteen and would prefer to spend his summers doing one thing and one thing only. So suffice it to say, he makes the most out of his two hours of free time before lights out.

"Hey, what's this?" Dylan asks.

She picks up the phone that the customer left, turning it over in her hand.

"Someone left it on a table," I tell her. "I'm going to put it in the Lost and Found."

"It looks like the one that was in my desk when I stayed in Weston," she explains. "I forgot about it."

A look passes between her and Hawke.

"Did you see who left it?" Hawke asks me.

"Some guy." I take the phone out of Dylan's hand and set it back down. "I didn't get a good look. Why?"

Hawke's quiet before he draws in a deep breath and shakes his head. "No reason. Just leave it in the Lost and Found. Someone will come for it, I'm sure."

Aro throws him a look as I push open the back door, nudging them out. Not that I don't love them, but I have exactly two hours before I need to be in bed.

Dylan takes another bite, groaning. "Quinn, seriously. You should go global."

"Mm-hmm."

"At least domestic shipping!"

I smile, giving her a little shove.

But then she spins around. "Or enter that baking contest!"

"Right!" I feign enthusiasm. "The Shelburne Falls Festival of… Reindeer…Chestnut…Silly Sweater Dasher Dancer Ice Miracle Angel Fest!" I tease. "Will do!"

Hunter laughs his ass off because I'm a baker in a small town, and I've heard all of the Hallmark jokes.

They wave, Dylan blowing me a kiss, and I catch it, closing the door and locking it.

I adore them all. I love how happy they are. They deserve it.

But I feel like the odd one out more than ever now.

And Kade doesn't count. He loves being unattached.

I shake it off, needing some fresh air. And my earbuds.

Changing in the bathroom, I don a pair of black leggings, sports bra, and white tank crop top with a black jacket over it. I braid my hair and pull on the light blue Chicago Cubs cap before slipping my ID and shop key into the pocket on my leg and fit my earbuds into my ears. Tuning to my favorite list, I leave through the back door, locking it behind me.

It's only after eight. Dark but not late. The streets will still be alive with activity. Especially on a warm June evening.

I leave the alley, heading onto First and turning onto High Street. I roll my shoulders, stretch my arms above my head, and let the breeze wash over my body as the scent of potted flowers on the sidewalks lingers in the air just a little.

I double-knot my tennis shoes and start jogging, passing my shop, Rivertown Grill, and the bowling alley. I take a right into the neighborhood, and feel a burst of energy in my legs, free at last. I sidestep trees and mailboxes, swerving around cars parked at the curb. Then, I cross the street and dive between houses.

Mr. Zellers sits on his back porch, and I wave as I descend the small grassy hill to the fenced-in community pool. I race past it, inhaling the chlorine and remembering the first and last time I swam here. I had a pool at home growing up—still do—but if you wanted to be seen as a teenager, this was the place. Turned out, I didn't really want to be seen.

I pound the pavement, sweating already, and curving right onto Main Street.

A truck comes up behind me, passes, and I see the red paint and the JT Racing emblem on the tailgate. I hold my breath, dread setting in, but I keep running, even when I see his taillights brighten. *Oh, no.* The vehicle halts in the middle of the street and I square my shoulders, continuing on.

Jared steps out of the driver's side. I don't slow down. "Don't worry. I'm staying in lighted areas—"

But my brother swoops me up and throws me over his shoulder.

Damn him! I grit my teeth together, but only kick my legs once in frustration. It's no use fighting more.

Jared carries me around the truck, and Jax hops out of the passenger side, opening up the back door for him.

Jared deposits me inside, and I try to jump out, but Jax slams the door in my face. I yank out my earbuds and pound my fist against the window.

I don't believe this.

I kind of loved it when I was six. Started to resent it when I was eleven. I'm twenty-one years old now.

"Run in the morning," Jared says, climbing into the cab.

"My business is open in the morning!" I'm louder than is helpful. "This is the only time I have."

He shifts the truck into gear and hits the gas.

"Shelburne Falls is a safe place," I point out.

"Until a traveler comes through one night and slaughters a family," Jax argues, "and people start saying 'it was such a safe town, we used to leave our doors unlocked...'"

I drop my head back, locking my hands on top. "I'm in prison."

"No." Jared turns down his music. "You're our little sister. And beautiful. A born target."

For what? Men who might want to talk to me?

I meet his eyes in his rearview mirror and actually laugh. "Do you have any idea what your daughter," and then I point to Jax, "and your son, for that matter, are getting up to at that camp with their significant others?"

"Don't piss me off," Jared bites.

"Don't gross me out." Jax scowls.

This is part of the reason I feel younger than my niece and nephews. Jared and Jax are well aware their children are in love—and acting upon it—but I'm too fragile to go out at night.

For a minute, I think he's driving me back to the bakery—or to my parents, where I still live since I just finished school and haven't had time to rent an apartment—but he stops a block over, in front of the new gym that popped up a couple of years ago.

Which I was interested in checking out, but again, haven't made time for.

They drag me inside where a young woman is smiling at the counter. "Hi, welcome to Astrophysics. Can I help you?"

"Look, Quinn, a track." Jared points above, and I see runners circling the building on the second floor.

Jax slips his hands into his pockets, nodding in approval. "Indoor, cameras, proper lighting…loving it."

I give the girl a tight smile as Jared slaps down his credit card. "Set her up."

I should fight it, and I have every intention of being quite the handful for my brothers when I have more time, but I'm just too tired. It takes twenty minutes to fill out my information and sign some papers. I bypass the tour, schedule a fitness test for another day, and grab a towel, heading through the lobby.

Jax works on his phone at a small round table near the doors. Jared sits with him, elbows on his knees as he peels a complimentary orange.

"You're just gonna sit there?" I ask. "The whole time?"

Like he doesn't trust me to get home on my own?

He just tips his eyes up at me but says nothing, and I remove my jacket and head into the gym. I wish Madoc was here. He's a lot more reasonable. He'd get them to leave.

Sticking my earbuds back in, I restart "The Boys of Summer", leaving my towel and jacket on a bench. I step onto the three-lane track, wait for another jogger to pass by, and quickly follow. An arrow on the wall dictates the direction we're running, accompanied by a sign letting runners know that eleven-and-a-half laps equals one mile. I dig in my heels, loving the slight cushion of the ground, easier than pavement, and I pass under a digital timer above our heads that keeps minutes and seconds if we want to pace ourselves.

Not a bad set up, actually. I just want to go, though. There are mirrors on the outside wall, sporadically interrupted with windows, the inside walls occasionally giving way for people to leave the track and head into the workout areas. Two-dozen weightlifting machines sit on the oval floor at the center of the track, and I look around, seeing a few women, but mostly men. One huge guy with a long silver beard lifts a massive dumbbell over his head with one arm as he sits on a bench and watches himself in the mirror. Another props up his phone to film himself doing squats.

I float my eyes over the room, seeing a man in black track pants with a white hoodie doing pullups. I let my eyes linger for a second. Long, lean, broad... Blond.

A wall cuts off my view, and I blink, my heart suddenly pulsing a mile a minute.

I try to swallow, but I can't. The wall breaks again, and I jerk my head, looking back into the workout area. He keeps going, pulling his chin up over the bar, and I stare at the side of his face and the back of his head...but it's too far away to be sure. His hair is wet with sweat, and he has earbuds in like me.

I lose sight of him again. I can't get a look at his face. Another wall, and then I enter the other side of the gym giving way to a different workout area. I try not to, but I find my legs moving a little faster to circle around again to the other side.

It's been eight years since he left town. If he were back in town, Madoc and Fallon would've made a big deal about it. I would've heard.

The Cubs cap feels tight. *His* Cubs cap. I keep going, my braid bouncing over my chest, but when I come up on his weight room again, he's gone. Runners pass me, and I scan the room twice out of the corner of my eye.

Then...

I see him.

My stomach flips. He lies on a bench, holding a bar over his body before bringing it down and pumping it back up, again and again. His long legs are bent, his shoes on the ground, and even though he's wearing a lot more clothes than the other men here, I can't stop staring at everything but his face. Built chest under the hoodie. Narrow waist. Toned shoulders and strong arms. The muscles on the top of his thighs bulge just a little under the black pants.

The wall separates us again, and when there's a break, I glance quickly, seeing him replace the bar and sit up. He rises, grabs his towel, and lifts his head, meeting my eyes.

My heart plummets into my stomach.

Oh my God.

Lucas?

I look away, disappearing behind another wall and entering the other side of the gym.

My chest hurts. I stop, tapping my earbud to pause the music as I step through the entrance to another workout area. I stagger a little over to the water fountains on the wall and bend over, pressing the button. I drink, wetting my parched throat.

What the hell?

How can he be here? How can he be here for even an hour without me hearing it from someone?

But he's just working out like he's been here for days.

I stand upright, wiping off my mouth. Did he recognize me?

I should say 'hi,' I guess. I grew up with him, even if I was way younger.

After college, he worked with Fallon as an architect before transferring out of the country all those years ago to build skyscrapers in Dubai.

I was thirteen when he moved abroad, and his baseball cap is all I have left. I traded him my compass for it on his last night in town. Does he still have the compass? I guess he wouldn't be wearing it. I dip my head down to hide the hat, my cheeks warming with embarrassment.

But I catch myself in the mirror behind the fountain. My hair's a mess, makeup's gone, and I'm sweating already. Thankfully, my tired eyes are hidden under the bill of the cap.

No, it'll be awkward. This isn't how I imagined seeing him again.

I walk to one of the Pelotons and climb on. Starting a Lanebreak workout, I mute the music and just follow the designated pacing and resistance while I absently read the headlines floating across the bottom of the TV screen above. Through my earbuds I hear barbells clanging and feet pounding the treadmills, and I almost settle into a pace until he passes behind me with a friend.

"Come on, cardio," his buddy says.

His friend jumps on the treadmill on my left, Lucas taking the one on the other side of his friend. I pedal hard, glancing at them both in the mirror on the wall in front of us. His friend turns his head toward me, his short dark hair falling over his brow. He wears black shorts and a gray, sleeveless T-shirt with the sides cut out, showing off his tanned muscular arms and pecs.

Is that...Lance?

He turns to Lucas on his other side. "I fucking hate working out at night," he says. "What do you do with the endorphins when you leave?"

Lucas doesn't reply. Guess it was a rhetorical question. I keep facing forward, minding my own business.

Lance is an old friend of Lucas's from college. I saw him maybe once or twice growing up, but Lucas kept his friend group largely separate.

"I need my wife," his friend remarks with a smirk as he jogs. "Thank God, I married a woman with as much energy as me."

"Girl," Lucas corrects him. "You married a girl ten years younger than you."

"I had to cast a wider net to find my soulmate."

They obviously think my earbuds are on and that I can't hear.

And if he's the same age as Lucas, then his wife is older than me. That's not a girl.

His friend is right, though. I hate working out at night. It takes longer to calm down when I go home and try to sleep.

Lucas taps his earbud. "Lucas Morrow."

My stomach swims up to my heart, hearing him say his name. My hands almost slip off the handlebar, but I wipe the sweat from my palms onto my shorts and refasten my fingers around the bike. I hide my smile.

Why didn't I know he was here? He didn't stay in touch, walked away from us as if he just wanted to keep his eyes forward and the past in the past, but...we were all so close once. Wouldn't he want to see me?

Why would he, I guess. I was just a kid. He'd probably be more interested in looking up an old girlfriend first.

His friend continues to run next to me, Lucas listening to the other end of his call.

"I won't be away long," he tells whoever he's talking to. "Retrofitted? No. That boat's fifty years old. He's not paying for that."

I watch him, his squared shoulders outlining the wall of his chest that's bigger and broader than the last time I saw him. It would feel like I was in a cocoon if he wrapped his arms around me. I lick my lips, my blood warming at the thought.

He just told whoever he's talking to that he won't be away long. Would he just leave, without me ever knowing he was in town?

"He can have his dock outside his office building as long as the city sanctions it," Lucas says. "Blame the timeline on them."

His voice is deeper, and I try to see his eyes in the mirror, but they're cast down. He hasn't noticed me at all since he's been on the treadmill.

He nods. "Bye."

And he ends the call.

He jogs, taking a drink from his water bottle. His brow is pinched, and I don't like that he still has that look on his face. One he didn't have when he was in college but certainly developed before he left.

"You should stay longer," his friend says.

"Come to Dubai more."

"They look at me funny when they search my luggage."

His friend grins over at him in the mirror, Lucas looks up, and I dart my eyes down.

"Stop traveling with handcuffs," Lucas says in a low voice.

My mouth falls open a little.

But then his friend asks, "And use rope instead?"

My mouth is dry again. What the hell?

His pal smiles at Lucas in the mirror. "I guess it won't set off the metal detectors."

I slow my pace, the room tilting a little. I blink a few times to refocus. I remember the first time I learned that Lucas had a whole life outside of whatever he let me see.

His jaw flexes, and then as if he knows I've been here the whole time, he lifts his chin, meeting my gaze in the mirror.

I can't catch my breath as my heart knocks against my chest.

"Lucas!" a familiar voice yells behind us.

I startle, seeing Madoc behind me through the mirror, opening the door to a court with two rackets and a ball in his hand.

"Racquetball," he calls out.

He doesn't seem to notice me yet.

And now I know. He knew Lucas was here. Maybe that means he just arrived today then.

Lucas hops off the treadmill, grabs his stuff, and whips his towel at his friend. "See you tomorrow."

The guy nods once. "Tomorrow."

Lucas and Madoc disappear into a court, and I don't even notice that the guy next to me is gone until my ride ends. I didn't pay attention to my speed or resistance at all. I was lost in thought the whole time.

He said on his call that he wouldn't be away long. Which means he's not staying.

I should've talked to him.

Maybe I'd look into his eyes and see him smile at me, and all of a sudden, realize that my stupid childhood crush was better in my memory. Maybe then I'd be free from this fantasy I always had of him.

I spend another half hour weight training before I drift to the snack bar for a smoothie. I can still see Jared and Jax out of the corner of my eye, waiting, and I hold up my finger, telling them I'll only be a minute. I tie my jacket around my waist, pulling down my cap, but then I hear Madoc's voice.

"Fallon is excited to see you."

I glance up and then back down, Madoc and Lucas, showered and back in their suits as they stand in line in front of me.

Madoc swipes his card and hands Lucas a straw.

"Ran into her today at the office, actually," Lucas tells him. "She didn't tell you?"

"She told me to convince you to stay with us."

My heart starts pounding again. This would be the perfect time to speak up.

"That's nice." Lucas's voice doesn't sound right. "I'll think about it."

"You like your alone time now, huh?"

Lucas shrugs a little. "I'm used to it."

I could ask for my compass back. That was the deal we made. He had to come back; if nothing else, to return my compass and get his father's baseball cap back.

"Stay the summer," Madoc suggests. "Almost anyone can work remotely now, and she could use you here."

I see Lucas turn and glance over his shoulder at me. "Uh..." He shifts back to Madoc. "I have to get back as soon as possible, actually."

No.

He turns a little again, and I know he's staring at me. I raise my eyes, locking with his.

"Sorry." He laughs at himself a little as he stares down at me. "It's just... I used to have a hat like that."

I can't talk. I can't blink. I just peer up at him.

Madoc takes his drink. "You had *that* hat. That's Quinn, dude."

Lucas's face falls, and Madoc hooks an arm around my neck, planting a kiss on the side of my head. I can't seem to remember my own language, all of a sudden. I thought maybe he recognized me earlier when he stared, but judging from the look on his face, he's surprised.

"Hey, guys," Madoc calls to Jared and Jax, leaving to go talk to them.

I stand there, managing to hide how hard my heart is beating.

Lucas blinks, and here—now—I know that nothing was better in my memory. I loved his longer hair as a young guy, and his lazy clothes when he loved rock climbing and being a lake bum, but I can see his blue eyes better now, striking with his hard jaw and sun-kissed skin. I drop my gaze to the crisp white shirt and tie wrapped tightly around his neck.

"I can't believe I didn't recognize you," he says.

I swallow. "It's been a...a long time."

He doesn't have social media. The only pictures of him I've seen are from events posted to their company's socials or news sources.

He breaks into a grin, shaking his head as he comes in. "My big brother's little sister." He hugs me. "How are you doing?"

I rise to my tiptoes as my eyes fall closed. He smells like one of the stores my mom takes me to that has a dress code. It's been so long since I've felt his arms, and tears spring to my eyes, I missed him so much.

His hands rest lightly—appropriately—one on the back of my shoulder, the other wrapped around my waist. But his neck presses into my cheek, and my lips part on their own, wanting to feel the smooth, warm skin too. I almost tighten my arms around him.

But I quickly pull away. "I'm...sweaty. Sorry."

I lick my lips, hearing my brothers chat, and I know he can see how nervous I am. All the times I envisioned his return home, I can't believe the moment is now.

I clear my throat. "So, how long are you around?"

I know the answer. I heard him tell Madoc and someone on the phone.

But his smile drops, and he thins his eyes a little, gazing at me. "I don't know..."

The vein in his neck throbs steadily, and I take it back. I don't really like his suit. I liked him with messy hair and no shirt, like that day at the summer camp.

"Uh, how old are you now?" he asks. "Twenty-ish?"

"Twenty-one."

"In college then?" he presses.

I open my mouth, but then Madoc is there, with his arm around me.

"Our little Quinn finished at Notre Dame in three years," he says proudly. "Runs Frosted over on High Street now."

Lucas looks from my brother to me. "The bakery."

"Yeah," I reply.

He smiles again. "I remember your cooking. Missed your pizza."

My whole body warms. It warms too much, and I'm boiling.

"You okay?" Madoc asks me.

"Yes," I say, but it comes out as more of a pant. "I need a ride home. Since I'm not allowed to ride my bike or run in the dark."

Madoc laughs and Jared and Jax walk up.

"We got you," Jax says.

Yeah, I know. In the far recesses of my brain, maybe it would've been incredible for Lucas to give me a ride, but I know that wouldn't have happened.

They start to walk out, and Lucas takes his drink but drops his straw. I bend down, but so does he, accidentally hitting the cap off my head. The long pieces of hair not secured in my braid fall out, and we squat there, only inches between us. That afternoon at the lake comes back as clear as day when we were under the dock. I look at him through the locks hanging in my face.

He's not smiling anymore. And I can't breathe again.

I pick up the cap. "Here. You said to hold onto it until you got back."

I hand it to him.

But he shakes his head, gently pushing it back to me. "Hang on to it for a little while longer. I'll get it before I leave."

So, I'm going to see him once more before he goes?

I rise and so does he. "Goodnight," I say.

He doesn't reply, just looks at me like he's lost. His gaze lingers on me before his brow deepens and he swallows.

"Quinn?" Jax calls.

But my shoes sprout roots, keeping me locked in front of Lucas for another moment. Then two. *You could give me a ride like you used to*, I want to say to him. He could tell my brothers we need to catch up. Tell them he wants to see the bakery.

I don't wait for him to say it, though. I turn and leave, resisting the urge to look back, because my brothers are watching, and I already know what they'll think.

Lucas Morrow and I are too old to play together now.

SHELBURNE FALLS

CHAPTER TWO

Lucas

The muscles in my arms burn as I stare up at the ceiling of my old bedroom. That same branch outside scrapes against the window pane in the wind, and the scent of the vanilla candles my mom used to burn linger in the air.

I always remember stuff like that. The little things.

They stick in my memory more than faces or conversations.

More than any holiday.

More than my dad's funeral. That was a blur. But I guess it would be. I was only eight.

I remember how the seatbelt smelled in his old Buick. The sounds of the heavy doors clicking shut. The argument he and Mom had over whether the light above the stove was a nightlight or not, and the crusty feel of my bath towel when I left it on the radiator to dry during a snowy December night.

I remember Madoc.

How I was so scared to meet him that first time, and how he smiled all that day, and how I didn't realize how much I needed all of those smiles.

How he sat and talked to me after I got beat up in eighth grade, even though I have no recollection of what he said. I just remember that he was there.

How he taught me to drive when I was fifteen, and when he put his cufflinks on me before I left for prom—the ones his father gave him. He just stared at my sleeves as he worked. Wouldn't even look me in the eye, because he was probably afraid I'd be embarrassed by the pride on his face and the love he had for me.

The pride...

If only he knew.

I unclench my hands, liquid heat spreading across my chest as I throw off the sheet and swing my legs over the side of the bed.

I drop my elbows to my knees and squeeze my eyes shut as I run a hand through my hair. *Fuck*.

Picking up the compass from the bedside table, I flip it open and point the needle, my head following just slightly to the right, finding north-northwest.

It points out of the house, to the street, beyond the old neighborhood, toward the deserted country road, and into the woods. Toward the one thing I always point it.

Snapping it shut again, I set it on the table and wipe off the sweat on the back of my neck, my palms gritty with grime that's not really there anymore. *The little things...*

The grandfather clock downstairs chimes three, and I rise. I won't get back to sleep.

Descending the stairs of my mom's old house, I leave the lights off and head into the kitchen, past the empty living room and the boxes of photo albums from the closet. I fill a glass with water and swallow it down, filling it again.

And as I turn north-northwest, I pause for a moment, feeling the tug of that invisible string. I know if I walk forward—across the kitchen, through the wall, past the fence—and straight for six miles, from this spot, I can put an end to it. I can stop dreading the disappointment I'll cause and start enduring it.

Instead, I drift into the living room, the hardwood floors glowing in the moonlight streaming through the bare windows. The cleaners left the house in immaculate condition yesterday, and aside from a few remaining belongings to dump into storage, the house is ready to be put on the market. My mother left two months ago, thriving in a senior community in Arizona, but she made sure to leave behind the one remnant of our family that she knew I'd never let movers or some realtor throw into the garbage. It was her way of forcing me home. After eight years.

I smile at my father, gazing into his gray eyes. "I'm taller than you now," I tell him.

His Coast Guard dress jacket and cap hang on the bracket where the curtains were attached. His favorite chair that they used to hang on sits in the storage unit I rented yesterday. I haven't decided where I wanted the coat and hat yet. Take it with me back to Dubai or leave it in storage here? I'm still deciding.

"Nothing has changed, though," I continue. "Just like you said it wouldn't. I knew you were right."

I swallow hard, staring down at my glass of water. His eyes burn into me, and I almost shrink.

"I'm still not telling anyone, though." I swirl the water. "And I'm still going to leave in a few days."

My dad was a lot like Madoc. But my dad is dead, so he never has to be ashamed.

Flicking my eyes back up to his picture on the wall, I study the cap over his light hair and the smile of a hero that makes him look so much younger than me, even though he was the same age as I am now when he died. He smiled a lot too. Just like Madoc.

I loved playing racquetball with him today.

And seeing Quinn. *Jesus.* The way she looked up at me from under the bill of that hat, the same big eyes... I noticed that about her a long time ago. It was the way she looked only at me. As if waiting for something.

A painful swell fills my chest. "God, I miss them, Dad."

All of them.

And I can't wait to leave. I'd forgotten how small this town is, how everyone notices everything, and how slowly things move. I like the city. The busyness of Dubai is addicting. There's always someone to meet. Things to see. Places to be. Food, music, work...

Shelburne Falls is a fucking fish bowl.

My dad stares at me but says nothing. He stopped speaking to me years ago.

Setting my water down, I climb the stairs, throw on some joggers, sneakers, and the white hoodie from the gym last night. In a minute, I have my earbuds in and my phone snug in the pocket of my pant leg, playing "Bother" as I lock up and leave the house.

I scan the street. Empty, except for an old, white Malibu that's been sitting there since I was in college. Most of the houses are dark aside from a couple of porch lights. I look around again, awareness rising up the back of my neck, before jogging down the steps and onto the sidewalk.

He's not in town anymore. I'd felt easier about returning once I knew that, but no one knows where he is and…

Others did take his place.

The longer I stay in town, the higher the chance they'll find out.

I'll leave as soon as the house is listed and the things my mother left for me are safely stored.

I pass a few overgrown lawns interrupted by the odd manicured yard, but nearly every house needs a paint job and roof or gutter work. The McKeltys still favor that ugly chain link fencing, but…they did replace it, at least. No more rust.

It wasn't a bad neighborhood growing up, and I can't say it's bad even now, but it's not Madoc's neighborhood. And it's not Fall Away Lane. We kept our property up, even without my father—or rather, my mother did. The house could be very easy to sell.

Or it could take forever. It's not close to schools, and the neighborhood is too old to change its ways, most of the homes inherited or owned by an aging population that won't be ideal for new families.

Either way, it means nothing to me. It can take a lifetime to sell as long as I don't have to be here for it.

I jog into town, past Jared's shop, Astrophysics, and the store where I bought all of my bicycles growing up. E-bikes now sit among the others in the window display.

Coming to the end of the street, I pause, ready to go right to the high school, but the tiny stubble on my cheek hardens like needles, awareness surrounding me.

I don't have to look to the left to know where that road leads.

Into the country, the path darkening as it courses farther from town and deep into the woods.

Pushing off, I run straight, instead, but I make it no more than a block before Quinn's shop comes into view on High Street. I tap my earbud, silencing the music.

Frosted.

Crossing First Avenue, I jog down the opposite side of the street from her shop, and I notice a light through the windows. There's a warm glow way in the back, through the kitchen doors.

A figure moves past and disappears again, and I draw in a long breath, remembering last night at the gym.

"So, what is she...?" my friend Lance whistled behind me as I watched Madoc drive off with Quinn in the passenger seat of his car. "Ten years younger than you?"

He was teasing me for the shit I gave him over his wife's age.

But something swam in my chest as I watched Jared and Jax barreling after them like a fucking convoy was necessary to make sure their sister got home.

"I wasn't looking," I told him.

He just laughed and moved to his car at the curb. "She was."

I'd forgotten how perceptive Lance could be. When I got into town, I wasn't even going to call him, but I see him often enough when he travels abroad, and he just got married. He would've been pissed if I didn't contact him after not returning for the wedding.

And Quinn is twelve years younger than me. His wife doesn't seem so young now.

I really should've recognized her last night. Instead, I watched her watching me and thought maybe I could get through this visit with a nice distraction like her in my hands for a few days.

Shit.

I stare at the shop, seeing a glimpse of her again in the kitchen. She wasn't looking at me last night. At least not like that. I was just important to her once. I'm sure it was weird to see how I'd changed.

I jog across the street, around the side, and into the alley. Coming up on the delivery door, I see a bicycle locked to a drainage pipe. I knock on the door.

Unfortunately, I'd lied to Lance. I had been looking. Before I knew who she was and saw her running around the track.

And I'd really liked looking.

She was staring at me, continually catching my eye every time I turned her way. I'm so fucking stupid. She was looking because she recognized me. I was looking because…

"Who is it?" a light voice calls through the door, sounding just a little timid.

Yeah, a young woman working in here alone in a deserted downtown? She doesn't want mysterious knocks on the door in the middle of the night.

"Quinn, it's Lucas."

She doesn't answer, and the door doesn't open.

A few seconds pass, and I lean in closer, amused. "Lucas Morrow," I clarify.

Another second passes and still nothing.

I open my mouth to say something else, but I have no idea what.

Then the lock clicks and the door swings wide. Quinn stands there, holding the door handle. "Sorry," she says, sounding out of breath as she slips a hand towel into her back pocket. "I was…yeah."

She shakes it off, peering up at me from under the bill of my cap. My smile falters, lost for a moment in the lamplight reflecting on her lips. I should've recognized her last night. She has the same brown eyes. Everyone always grouped her in with her mom and Jared, and liked to describe the shade as chocolate, but Quinn's were different. They held a hint of gold, like chestnuts.

And she seemed to have the same inability to hold people's gazes for longer than three seconds. Or maybe it is just mine.

She takes in my clothes. "Exercising again?"

"Jet lag." I walk in as she holds the door open for me. "Saw your lights on and thought I'd check out your place."

I stop just inside the door, facing her as she locks it again.

"Before you leave, you mean?" she asks as if finishing my sentence.

Something about her tone is curt. I look down, watching her lick her lips as she pulls the door a few more times just to make sure it's secure.

"Are you mad at me?" I ask.

I grin a little, teasing, but her wide eyes just gaze up. Not really hurt or challenging, but...she doesn't answer me, either.

She wears jean shorts and a pink and white Raglan T-shirt with an apron around her waist. A braid hangs over the front of her right shoulder, my old cap on top of her head. Again.

Does she wear it every day? I gave it to her the last time we saw each other. We were at the Loop. Madoc and Jared were supposed to race, but her dad showed up and took her home. She was thirteen, and I gave her the hat to ease the guilt, but then she traded me her gold compass to make sure I'd return someday. The weight of it sits against my thigh inside my pocket.

She moves past me, gesturing around her shop. "Last time you were home, this was empty, huh?"

Home...

I gaze around at the old building. After all the years I passed by it when I lived here, it doesn't look as old inside as I thought it would.

She leads me through the kitchen and into the shop. "I bought it right after I graduated high school."

"How'd you afford that?"

She pushes past the counters, turning to face me among the tables.

I breathe out a nervous laugh, realizing. "Sorry, rude question."

How quickly I sink back into the role of someone close enough to her to pry.

She shrugs. "I got an investment from my mom. And my dad owned the building, so I got a deal."

She presses her lips together, though, and avoids my gaze as if there's more to the story.

The display cases are empty, trays not yet put out for the morning rush, while baskets hang from hoops, covering an entire wall that probably offers an assortment of breads and rolls, loaves and buns. The front of the shop is almost entirely covered by windows, and I can see the sidewalk across the street where I stood a few minutes ago.

Several tables sit around me, and there's more on the sidewalk outside, and I know she didn't do all of this alone. I can picture her family—minus me—spending a whole day together, painting, wiring, and moving in furniture and sacks of flour. Three Days Grace or Five Finger Death Punch blasting over a speaker. Jax probably brought pizza. Madoc, the beer.

"It was strictly a summer business while I was in college," she tells me, letting her eyes float around the room, "but now that I'm done..."

She runs a hand down the counter, and I notice a lock of hair spilling out of the cap and down her cheek.

She goes on. "I can do more seasonal confections—apple cider donuts, pumpkin hand pies, peppermint fudge for Christmas. Soon, I'll be adding some light lunch fare..."

"Pizza?"

She smiles. "Yes."

But the way she says it, almost an intimate whisper but filled with joy, like a...like a kiss.

I don't know what happens, but it hurts to breathe, and I'd love to hear her say it again like that.

I blink, swallowing and turning, looking for anything to distract myself. I gesture to the sidewalk out the window. "Picnic tables in the summer?"

She nods, and I can see the delight in her eyes. She loves what she does.

"Would love to rent the place out for kids' baking birthday parties," she explains. "Book club meetings..."

"You'll need a liquor license for that one."

She laughs, and I look anywhere but at her. The floor-length mirror on the wall catches my attention, my reflection staring back at me. It's the size of a door, the ornate gilded frame chipped and worn. But stunning.

And confusing. This building is wider from the outside. I'd love to see the blueprints. This room seems like it should be bigger.

"How's Dubai?" I hear her ask.

I blink. "Humid." I sigh. "But...it's good. People are a little nicer there."

"Yeah?"

"Well, the penalty for being rude is heavier," I point out, remembering that even vulgar language and finger gestures can lead to fines or jail time in Dubai. "So is the penalty for crime." I wander a little, taking in the wrought-iron light fixtures and beautiful butcher block counters. "With the way your brothers still act around you, I'm guessing the penalty for crime is steep here too."

Laughing, she slides her hands into the pocket of her apron. "Oh, you caught that last night, huh? When I hung out with you, they'd loosen the leash," she jokes. "But after you left... Suffice it to say, I didn't have many dates in high school."

She stands to my left, that side of my body warming to the point of burning. *Good*. I mean, not good. She should've had a normal high school experience, but how many dates does she need? Maybe prom? That's about it.

What about college? She had to have boyfriends in college.

I clear my throat. It's none of my business.

The silence stretches, and I still haven't looked at her.

"So, you like it?" she finally asks. "The shop?"

I nod. It feels like her. But most importantly, she gets to run the show. The Quinn I used to know would've loved the independence this place would've given her. Does she still feel that way?

"Let me show you my favorite part," she says, excited. "It's still a secret."

She leads the way back into the kitchen, and I follow her around a large steel rack, down a short dark pathway with boxes stacked on both sides.

I stand behind her as she flips a latch, and all of a sudden, two dark green shutters swing open. The early morning air hits me, and I move around her, my hand grazing her waist. A jolt spreads up my arm, damn near stopping my heart.

I yank my fingers away, trying to steady my breathing.

Looking out onto the sidewalk of the side street, I notice plenty of room for curb parking. First Avenue was never very busy. Foot traffic would be easy too.

Backing up, I spot the cooler behind her and empty shelves behind me. There's a wide counter at the window for customers to order.

"Ice cream stand?" I guess.

A gleam hits her eyes as she leans out the little doors. "Tables all the way down on this side." She waves her hand to the right, then to the left. "But not on this one because there will be a line."

She nods so assuredly and completely confident that I can't resist teasing. "For sure," I tell her.

"An awning here for the rain," she says, looking overhead before spinning around, too excited to stop. "Sprinkles and sauces, and other than cones and cups, I'll have two signature sundaes which I'm still working on ideas for."

I don't know if it's the way she talks with her hands, showing me where everything will go, or if I'm just remembering how much of a planner she always was. I have this memory of her sitting by herself on the floor her dad, Madoc, and I had just built that would become her treehouse. She sat up there for hours with her notebook, drawing up a floor plan, and making a list of items to move in. I had to go retrieve her when it was time for dinner.

"I love how my shop smells." Her voice is nearly a whisper. "Every scent is good. But nothing smells like ice cream."

"What does it smell like?"

She draws in a breath, leaning on the little counter as I gaze down at her.

A ghost of a smile plays on her lips. "Like no school and no homework and no..." She exhales. "...no one telling you what to do. Like summer and a hot day of getting lost on your bicycle." She meets my eyes. "No matter the flavor, it always smells like freedom. But especially butter pecan."

I breathe out a laugh. And for just a second, I feel like I'm really home. I remember those summer days. Popsicles, crickets buzzing, and the smell of hot grass and chlorine. I'd always find her in the park or the cemetery, somewhere quiet where she could ride her bike.

Who do her brothers send to keep an eye on her now?

I push the thought away, not liking the irritation climbing the back of my neck. It was always my job.

My eyes drop to her lips, and she parts them, inhaling a quick breath.

"So..." She clears her throat and swallows. "Um, Jax told me last night that you're back to put your mother's house on the market," she adds. "I was sad when she decided to move to Arizona. But I understood." She looks back out the shutters. "Not much here for her."

No.

Not much here. No family. No grandkids. After I left eight years ago, I never came back. I bought my mom tickets to come see me, and I met her in various cities I might've been working, but...

No sense keeping a house for just one person. She's happy out West. She has friends, a community, and manageable weather.

A timer goes off, and Quinn spins around, returning to the kitchen.

"With all of our technology," she calls out behind her as I close the shutters again, "it seems you should've been able to handle everything from Dubai."

I watch her remove a pan of croissants and slide in another, setting the timer again.

I wouldn't have had to come back if my mother hadn't purposely left my father's things in the house. If I didn't want them trashed, I had to come back for them.

I'm not going to tell Quinn that, though. I don't want her to know that I wouldn't have returned if I didn't have to. I would've continued to act like they all didn't exist because it was the only way to not miss them so much.

I veer around her worktable and snatch my cap off her head. "Aren't you glad I'm back, though?"

"Hey!" Her hair comes tumbling down in front of her eyes.

I work on resizing it for my head. "You should be wearing a hair net anyway," I tell her.

"But…"

I pluck a hot croissant off her pan. "Gotta go."

"Hey!" she barks louder this time. "That's two sixty-five."

I pull apart the pastry and take a huge bite. "For flour and water?" I tease, knowing croissants are mostly butter.

She doesn't miss a beat. "It's cheaper than Starbucks."

She has her hands on her hips, and I almost can't help but smile again. It's like old times.

The savory, soft texture damn near melts on my tongue. "It's really good."

I start to leave, hearing her behind me. "What about my compass?"

"I'll see you later."

I don't know why I just don't tell her that she can have it back. A deal is a deal.

But I'm not ready. I've carried it with me every day for eight years. I never leave my apartment without it, much less the country.

I unlock and push through the back door, stepping into the alley before she can yell at me more.

"Good morning," Isobel chirps, pushing her rectangular frames up the bridge of her nose.

I stand in front of the kitchen counter, tightening my tie as I glance at my assistant on the laptop screen. "Good evening," I reply since it's the end of day in Dubai where she is. "Shoot."

She sets a file aside and looks at the screen, but not at me, as she reads away. "Al Mazrouei & Rao approved the suggested changes, but want a tour of the progress so far," she tells me. "I scheduled them to meet you at the site on Monday."

I nod, grabbing my suit coat. "I'll be back."

"It's in your calendar." She fingers a pen as she continues. "Also, Generation Industries is on board for the plumbing and mechanical for the Stewart multi-use."

"Send me—"

"I already got with legal and finalized the contract," she says. "The client has it."

A text rolls in, and I pick up my phone.

Gym tonight? Lance asks.

"Julia Khan"—Isobel goes on—"called about her son again." She looks at me point-blank. "Are you absolutely sure you wouldn't like an intern?"

I start tapping out a reply to my friend. "I am absolutely sure you would like an intern," I retort.

Eight PM, I tell him.

My assistant tsks. "I resent that. I was only aiming to help by adding to his view count."

I throw her a smirk as I set my cell down, both of us remembering her being very interested in his social media when we first received his résumé.

Isobel Chen has worked for me the past five years, and while she's impressive on paper—born in Shanghai, educated in Britain, speaks five languages, well-traveled...—I was nervous about being a single man and hiring a woman. I didn't want her getting any ideas.

But I quickly realized I was too old for her. At only twenty-eight, even men her own age are too old for her, apparently. The girl is a hunter.

She goes on, "I finished the expense report and emailed an outline of the research."

I click through my mail. "I see it."

"Bill needs you to call him sometime tomorrow...or today"—she corrects herself, given the time difference—"and South Korea has decided the downtown lot is the best."

I bring my mug of coffee to my lips. "Well, they'll have an excellent view of the Burj Khalifa."

"Prestige by proximity," she sings in her posh BBC lilt.

"Precisely."

"It could be worse." She stacks another folder. "Their board could've decided on a glass curtain building."

I chuckle. "I would quit."

She smiles, knowing me about as well as anybody now.

I scroll messages, seeing if there's anything I need to address with her before she leaves the office for the night. It's already after seven there.

But then she inquires, "Why are you in a suit?"

At her accusing tone, I look up. I only brought suits. And exercise gear.

"You're home," she scolds, her eyes gentle like she's talking to a kid. "I Googled it. Middle America, baseball, apple pie... Relax a little."

"Yeah, I'm done talking to you now."

She grins. "Have a good day, Mr. Morrow."

"Keep me in the loop." And I end the call.

Closing the laptop, I note the thumbs up from Lance to meet tonight at eight and start to text Madoc back. He wanted me to meet him at Jax and Juliet's summer camp today, but I can't imagine why.

Or rather, I know why, even though he won't admit it. He wants to reacquaint me with the town. I haven't been around much yet, but I can tell a lot is different. More restaurants, bigger homes, a bustling downtown area... Shelburne Falls is a quaint little stop for food and shopping while people are on their way to the lake or Chicago. I half-suspect he and my mother are in this together, some plot to make me fall in love with home all over again.

I never stopped loving home. I just resisted thinking about it. Every time my mind drifted away from the sun and the desert sand to the summer rain and black soil of the Falls, I'd stop myself. It was hard at first. The bad memories were forefront—the stress and worry. But now, it's easy. My work has taken its place, and that's my home now. My life has a routine.

Carrying my mug, I walk to the window and slip my phone in my pocket, the text to Madoc still not sent. Branches sway in the morning breeze, the cloud-covered sky dark and threatening, and I slow my breathing, trying to calm my heart. It's been pounding off and on since I left the bakery this morning, and I'd love to believe it's the three cups of coffee since.

Quinn.

I'd thought of her over the years. Every once in a while. I'd brush my teeth and think, with a small laugh, about the time she asked how the stripes got in the toothpaste, or I'd look into the koi pond of the restaurant I'd taken a client to and remembered how she once wondered if fish get thirsty. So many questions.

I shake my head. I should've searched the family's accounts and social media posts, even discreetly, just to check up on them. At least I would've known what she looked like last night.

So even then, at Frosted this morning—fully aware of who she was now—why did I still want to look at her?

And I can't be the only one. This town is packed, summer traffic heavy, and someone's going to be interested in her if they aren't already. I guess that's good. She should have someone. She seems on her own a lot. At the shop this morning and at the gym last night.

Guilt creases my brow, thinking about how I seemed to always be her other half when the family would go to theme parks or movies back in the day. I don't want to think that no one has taken my place in the time I've been gone. That she's been the odd one out.

I want her to be happy. She deserves all of it.

But...romances at her age rarely last, of course. Let her concentrate on her business. Life is a shitshow in your twenties anyway. She doesn't need assholes, and every guy in his twenties is a dick. I'm glad her brothers look like they're on top of it.

I set the coffee down, take out my phone, and send a text to Madoc.

Be there by noon.

Slipping my phone away, I pick up the mug again and lift it to my mouth, but then...I notice it.

A Traverse parked across the street.

I stop, tightening my grip on the mug as I study the dark figure in the driver's seat. The army green SUV was there yesterday too. With a frozen figure lurking inside. I'd thought maybe they lived on the street, but...

Windows tinted, parking lights on... I charge for the front door, dropping the mug on a little table nearby, the cold coffee sloshing onto my hand.

The moment I step onto the covered porch, the car races past me, my heart stopping mid-beat as I watch it peel around the corner, giving me no clear view of the driver. I can't even tell if it's a man or a woman.

Illinois plates. 7Q6...

Shit. It's gone before I lock in the rest of the number.

"Dammit," I murmur.

It could be nothing.

But it's not. Why would they speed off otherwise?

I breathe in and out, staring after the SUV with the pulse in my ears too loud to hear anything else.

I wince at the pain in my chest. Was it him? He's supposed to be gone.

Was it one of his thugs? How would they know I'm back already?

Fuck.

"Lucas Morrow?" someone says, nearly shouting.

What?

Finally, I blink, noticing the man standing on the sidewalk. About my height, he stares at me, dressed in a gray suit with a white shirt and black tie. His jacket is slung over his arm. I don't recognize him. Was he driven here in the Traverse?

"Are you Lucas Morrow?" he asks, enunciating his words like he's said it more than once. He proceeds down the path to the porch, holding out his hand. "I'm Paul Devney. How are you?"

I swallow to wet my throat. *Paul Devney.*

The real estate agent. Right.

I glance at the midnight blue Cadillac parked opposite the SUV that just left. That must be his car.

I exhale. "Nice to meet you." I shake his hand. "Please, come in."

I hold the door open for him.

"Thank you for the pictures," he tells me. "I should have the listing up today. I understand you're anxious to sell?"

I toss a glance back to the street, searching for any more sign of the Traverse. "Almost enough to let it go for free," I say absently.

Paul Devney got busy, touring the house, taking some measurements and a few more pictures, scribbling down a record of past renovations. The carpet was ripped up a decade ago and replaced with hardwood. There's new paint, a fenced-in backyard, and only a slightly dated kitchen and master bath.

I told him I'd let it go for well-below asking price. If it came to that. My mom might have an opinion, but she has me to take care of her if she needs.

A couple of hours later, I'm on my way to Camp Blackhawk, satisfied the listing of the house is in good hands.

My phone rings, a number I don't recognize popping up. But I see the local area code. Anyone here I want to hear from is a contact I have saved. I toss it back down on the passenger seat. *Two days. Just give me two days, and I'm gone.*

I take a left on *the* road, feeling like my tires are on fire, but I veer right before too long, exhaling when I'm off that particular highway. The hairs on my arms rise, feeling the pull behind me, both of the road and of the bakery. I'd love a glimpse of her face right now. Just for a second.

Pulling through the arch, the words Camp Blackhawk overhead, I slide into a space to park, overlooking the manicured green lawn and lake fifty yards beyond.

Kids race back and forth across the grass, while others swim laps in the lanes stretching between the two docks. I see Jaxon Trent carrying a canoe to the water, while a guy who looks a lot like Madoc, only younger, works with other counselors to inflate a bounce house. Is that Kade or Hunter, maybe? I haven't seen the kids in years.

The main lodge sits to the left, through the trees, and I step out of the car, coming around the front. I lean back on the hood. The first time I came here with Madoc and Fallon when I was little is still so clear in my head. There had been cabins down the beach, remnants of the old camp and a boarded-up lodge, but they've developed it beautifully since. So much so, it's almost a shame. I don't miss how quiet it was, but I do miss it being private. A place anyone could enjoy.

I'd caught Jared and Tate making out in his car that day. Or, now that I'm grown and understand more of what I was seeing, they were probably doing more than that.

There was something about it, though. A mystery or danger I didn't understand.

But I remember thinking about how I'd grow up and get a girlfriend and be able to do what he and Madoc were doing. I wanted to be like them so much. They always had women around, seemed happy partying and living the life. And then they found the loves of their lives, and everything got even better, and I thought life was really that easy.

It wasn't.

I got older and fooled around, but never here. By the time I was ready, the summer camp got developed. Too many people around.

Now, I'm too old.

"Hey, Junior."

I look up, seeing Fallon cross the lawn toward me.

I smile. *Junior?*

"What?" she teases, knowing what. "You look exactly like him."

I tilt my head, spotting Madoc still on the lawn behind her head. He has one leg in a potato sack, partnering with some kid in a three-legged race along with other parents and their campers. His jacket is discarded, and his light blue tie is loosened around his neck.

"I'm grown up now." I straighten as she leans on the hood next to me. "I have my own style, thank you. I wouldn't be caught dead in a pastel necktie."

"Bet you can still tell when a woman is wearing a thong, though."

I snort, unable to stop the rumble of laughter. Shit, I forgot she knew Madoc taught me about that years ago.

I shrug. "Well, he made sure the most important lessons stuck."

We watch him do the three-legged race as he grins his ass off, and while all the parents and counselors probably think it's so nice of the mayor to stop by and spend time with them. Fallon and I both know he loves it as much as the kids do. I have no doubt he wishes he could do the Color War and food fight too.

He keeps everyone around him young. I will him to look over and approach because Fallon has fallen silent, and I know she has things to say.

"Lucas—"

I bow my head. "I'm happy there," I tell her. "Nothing is wrong. I love you all. I just..."

I draw in a breath and glance over at her. Her head is turned toward me.

"I just...moved." I nod. "My life is there now."

That's all I ever say. It is what it is. It won't change.

She chews on her bottom lip, only the faintest of lines around the corners of her eyes. Other than my mother, she's the woman who nurtured me the most. I even followed in her footsteps, studying engineering and architecture.

"You know, Madoc was always the better parent," she says in a quiet but firm voice. "I've always known that. He's strong. He knows when he shouldn't say things, and he can control the urge to get angry." She looks at me. "He's patient. I'm not."

The softest smile curls one corner of her mouth.

"I've struggled with that far more than I want to admit," she tells me. "I don't like waiting for people to come around because it wastes time."

It always amused me how different Madoc is than his wife. A woman he fell in love with when they were just kids, back when she was his stepsibling.

And when their parents separated them, he latched on to a best friend who was exactly like her. Jared is temper and fire, just like Fallon. It takes more work for them to control themselves than it does Madoc.

"Your life isn't there." She narrows her eyes on me, accusingly. "Do you think I don't talk to the firm? You work seven days a week, you haven't taken a single vacation in eight years, and I've seen your calendar."

I clench my fists. "What?"

My company is under the same umbrella as hers. We communicate a lot and report to several of the same people, depending on the project.

"Every waking moment is planned," she tells me as if I don't know. "Your meetings, your meals, your exercise routine. Even..." She exhales, looking away. "Dinners that last exactly two-point-five hours."

I run my hand through my hair. "Jesus."

That is far more personal than she needs to know about. Goddammit.

I'm a thirty-three-year-old man, and I'm busy. I'll consider a relationship when I have the time. And I don't have the time right now for more than a nice meal and a couple of hours in a hotel room every so often with a woman who's also busy with her own career and doesn't want any more than that, either.

"You don't live," she says. "Not there. Not anywhere. Don't lie to me."

I arch a brow and turn my head away, wanting to rage.

But I won't. Not with her.

I like my life the way it is. I'm good at my job, I have friends, and I don't want to bring a woman into it. What if I transfer to Berlin or Sydney?

And I like my privacy. I know she means well, but she's holding on too tightly.

"Fallon?" I look over at her, my voice as gentle as possible. "You're not my parents."

I swear she doesn't move. Not even a flicker in her eyes. But there's pain there all the same.

I sigh, putting an arm around her, and tug her into my side. She's so small next to me, like I used to be next to her.

"I'm sorry," I whisper.

I don't think I regret saying it because I think she needed to remember that I have a mom. And I had a dad. She and Madoc don't have to take on that burden.

I guess I get it, though. They helped me grow up.

"Let me enjoy my time while I'm here," I tell her. "Let me try some of that Irish whiskey I hear Madoc is so good at making."

A smile spreads across her face, but she still doesn't look at me.

I hear a command. "You're staying through the weekend."

But it's not her who says it. I lift my gaze to Madoc strolling up, his jacket hung over one arm as he rolls his sleeves back down.

"I have to be back Sunday."

He doesn't say anything, just tosses his wife an unreadable look before meeting my eyes again.

"But you know what I want to do?" I stand up straight. "Before we get plastered later…I wanna drive."

Then, he smiles. "That's my boy." Digging out his keys, he tosses them to me and leans in to kiss his wife. "Wanna come?"

"No." She turns and watches us walk to his old silver GTO, the car I first learned to drive. "You go. Show him what Fallstown has become."

I defer to him. "Fallstown?" I ask. "What happened to the Loop?"

He just chuckles, climbing into his passenger seat while I get behind the wheel.

WESTON

CHAPTER THREE

Quinn

"Thank you." I hand a small bag and coffee to the customer, a woman dressed in straight-legged white pants and a blue pinstriped shirt. "Enjoy your day."

She leaves with a smile, and I watch her go, admiring her work clothes. I can't dress like that here, but I could look more professional, I guess.

I dust off the flour on my T-shirt and move away from the counter, removing an empty tray from the case. I hand it to Hailey, the cashier with two perpetually messy buns sitting on top of her head like horns. "Can you take that?" I slide out another, stacking it on top. "And that too. Thanks."

She backs through the kitchen door, spinning around with the trays in hand. I slide behind Noel, who works the espresso machine, his thick silver rings glinting in the sunlight.

I approach the next customer, and she opens her mouth to speak, but then Mace is there. She butts in. "Emergency."

"Mace," I scold, throwing a glance to the young woman she entered with. Mousy brown hair hangs in her eyes. I don't recognize her.

The darker-haired one, Dylan's age and dressed like a rocker with the body of a sexy Marine, grips the edge of the display case between us. The Green Street tattoo is dark against her tawny neck. "I need two-dozen brownies," she tells me.

"No."

I take a step, trying to tend to the customer she pushed out of the way.

The woman's mouth twitches in a nervous smile as her eyes flit between Mace and me.

But then Mace is there again, and I sigh. "When? How soon?"

"Eight seconds ago."

I shake my head, craning my neck to the customer again.

Impossible. I can't just drop everything.

Quickly, the customer blurts out, "Two loaves of bread, and please tell me you have more of that garlic dipping oil." She winces a little. "I didn't see it out on the shelves."

I hold up a finger. "Yes. I do. Just a moment."

I twirl around, rushing into the kitchen, and dive into the pantry to grab a box. Mace follows on my heels, her friend following her.

I plop the box down on the table and reach behind me for the scissors on the high shelf. "You can have—I mean, buy—two dozen of whatever I have left," I growl to Mace.

"But Hugo wants brownies."

I slice open the box. "I'm creeped out that your gangster boss even knows who I am. I really wish he didn't." I dig out a jar of the garlic oil. "And what kind of criminals like brownies?"

"They're for one of his associates." She folds her arms over her chest, the black leather jacket grinding. "Their kid has a potluck at school or something. I promised I'd make it happen."

Hailey carries a tray refilled with goodies back out to the front, and I catch sight of the shallow box on the work table, the old cell phone I'd put in there last night missing. Did someone—

Ugh, never mind. Too busy.

"Mace, I'm swamped."

"I know!" She grabs the girl next to her by her shirt and hauls her closer. "That's why I brought you help." She gestures to the kid. "She'll work for free today and tomorrow."

I eye the girl, seeing her light brown hair pushed behind one ear as she sports a faded navy sweatshirt two sizes too big. Is she even sixteen? Or even consenting to this?

I lift an eyebrow at Mace, and my lungs constrict as she pulls a knife out of her back pocket—her last resort. She flips open the blade, gripping it at her side as she stares at me.

It only takes me a moment to calibrate. "Are you serious?" I almost laugh.

Maybe I would've felt threatened when I first met her a month ago. Dylan and Aro had been sneaking their Weston friends and little Green Street criminals into the Falls on a regular basis by then. But I know better now. She colored my fingernails with Sharpie after I fell asleep at a party last week. She's a marshmallow if she likes you. And she likes me.

She hoods her eyes, closing the knife again. "Okay, I'm kidding," she mumbles. "But just so you know, I could make you my brownie slave if ever I decide to."

I hesitate a moment and then shake my head, because I can't seem to ever want to disappoint anyone. "They will be boxed on this table in two hours," I tell her. "That's the best I can do."

"Awesome." She breaks into a smile. "Didn't need them at his school until two anyway."

Of course, you didn't. Emergency, my ass.

She takes out a cigarette and starts to light it, but I grab it out of her mouth. "Gross." I crush it in my fist and fling it into the garbage. "Now let me work."

I push her out the door, back into the bakery, and quickly turn to the young woman she brought to work. "I'm Quinn."

No time for handshakes.

"Codi," she nearly whispers.

I try to catch her eyes, but I can't even see what color they are. She wears baggy jeans, rolled up at the ankle, and her nails are painted with chipped pink polish. Her heart-shaped face makes her seem so young, but the trim waist visible just above her loose jeans makes me wonder if she hides herself on purpose to not get attention. In any case, she looks old enough to work legally.

I point toward the store. "The shelves out there all have labels," I instruct, gesturing to the storeroom behind me next. "Would you be able to grab whatever you need from here to restock them for me?"

She nods about four times in quick jerks.

"When you're done, please clear and clean whatever tables inside and outside need it." I grab the jar the customer asked for and call out behind me. "Sixteen an hour, plus you get to split tips," I tell her.

I don't know if I can afford the help, but I can't *not* pay her. And it's only a couple of days.

It takes another hour before I can free myself from the morning rush to get Mace's brownies in the oven. While those bake, I get the soups going for lunch and start prepping the pizza pans with dough. I typically prefer to stay in the kitchen as much as possible because the summer crowd always brings in old classmates who want to talk when I'm busy. Or my dad, who always winks at me when he insists on paying for his coffee like this is my lemonade stand.

He's just trying to be supportive. My whole family makes me nervous, though.

My brothers only stop in to check that everything is running smoothly, to make sure no one is fucking with me, and whether or not I have a ride home. And their wives are too afraid to order birthday cakes, thinking they're taking advantage of their relationship with me to get a last-minute order in. Don't they understand? I want them all to rely on me. To bum a coffee, a cake, or a donut. It feels good to be needed and treated like an adult with something to offer.

The only family members I might like to see paying for their treats are my niece and nephews. They take stuff because they think I'm too gutless to stop them. It's different.

However, today, I keep fighting an urge to leave the kitchen and go back out front. Every once in a while, I'll hear a male voice and my pulse will quicken, or I can't help myself from glancing out the windows on the off-chance Lucas wanders by.

It's been hard to stay focused.

Where is he right now? What's he doing?

He doesn't show up, though. At least to my knowledge.

It was bizarre, being alone with him this morning. I was afraid he could see me blushing, or how I could barely breathe every time he looked at me. What did I seem like to him? I keep replaying everything I said in my head, thinking about what I *should've* said instead.

The girl, Codi, works quietly as she lugs in tub after tub of dirty dishes, straightens shelves, and walks around with a broom and dustpan. She even restocks napkins, finding more by herself in the storage room, and tucks in vacant chairs whenever she finds one. I don't hear her speak more than one word, but I know she can. A fellow teenage girl was leaning her chair back into the wall mirror, and I don't know what Codi said to her, but she stopped and planted all four legs back on the floor. They must have the same superstition in Weston. We don't lean back into mirrors here.

I don't know why. Something about them being doorways or some other such supernatural nonsense. Hawke knows. He studies all the urban legends. There's another one Weston and Shelburne Falls share, as well. *Pay to pass.* Throwing a coin—an offering—over the bridge between our two towns. I don't know where that tradition came from, either.

There are others, none of them ever concerning me. I've leaned into mirrors and crossed bridges without paying, and maybe been followed by a car with its headlights off here or there... It's just fun to think it's real.

Well, not fun, maybe.

Comforting. We need our traditions. It adds hope that the world still has mystery.

But it doesn't. That's why we have books. And movies and theater and video games to escape into. Many people between our two towns love distractions like that.

Like racing. Around and around and they're never going anywhere. What's the point? I just want to go forward.

The scent of pizza fills the shop, and I prop open the front door to let fresh air in. Grabbing two more empty platters from the case, I throw a glance at the mirror again, smiling at the idea of tempting fate some night and seeing how long I can lean before I scare myself and run. Maybe I believe a little.

Pushing through the kitchen door, I hear dishes clank and look over, seeing my mom at the sink with one of my aprons on.

"Mom, what are you doing?" I drop the empty trays on the worktable.

My mother stands with her hands in dishwater because she thinks it's faster than using the machine and wastes less water. Which it doesn't. I know what I'm doing.

"How else am I going to see you?" She looks over at me, taking the faucet hose and spraying one plate after another clean. "You get home after dinner—sometimes not even until I'm in bed—and then you're gone before I wake up."

I come to her side and shut off the faucet. I tuck a piece of her dark brown hair back up into the clip she used to pin up the rest.

"I'll get into a groove." I hand her a dry towel for her hands. "Things will slow down."

"When?" she fires back. "January?"

I pause, instantly seeing the flinch on her face. She knows the last thing that would be helpful is making it sound like I'm disappointing her. I'll just think I need to work harder.

Finally, she smiles, blinking a slow apology, and I'm almost irritated by how fast she can switch gears. By the time she became Katherine Caruthers, though, she knew how to handle my father, three teenage boys, and addiction. I kind of wish I'd gotten more inexperienced parents, but they knew all the tricks by the time I arrived. They were home for dinner every night and pancakes on Sundays. And while they took my phone at night to force a good night's sleep on me, they pretended they didn't know that I had a tablet and a laptop.

She takes a plate, using the towel to dry dishes, instead.

"Are you complaining that people like my bakery?" I ask, but don't wait for a reply. "I'm busy. This is a good thing."

Yes, I'm busier than I would like, and I'd love to manage time for maybe a social life—and sleep—but I'm handling it. We knew this would take time to figure out.

"It *is* a good thing," she says. "I'm so proud of you."

"I can do this on my own." I gently take her towel and dry the dishes myself. "I have a staff."

She lowers her gaze, her warm eyes filled with worry and things unspoken. Things she still feels guilt over with my brother.

"I know you're there if I need you," I tell her.

It's the best I can do to ease her mind. I know she's there, even though she wasn't for Jared.

We're quiet, and I dry some more plates and put them away as I feel her attention on me.

I glance at her, seeing her mouth slightly open like she wants to say more. "What?" I ask.

She doesn't seem to breathe for a moment, finally shaking her head. "Can you be free Saturday after two? For the rest of the day?"

"Why?"

"Madoc and Fallon are having everyone over." She takes more plates from me, stacking them on the shelf. "Lucas's flight is late. They'll have a cookout, some fireworks..."

I unplug the sink, not hearing the water drain over the sound of my heart in my ears.

He barely stayed.

Once he sells the house, there'll be no reason for him to return. Ever.

I swallow the lump in my throat. "I'll try."

If he's leaving, then I don't think I want to see him. What's the point? Giving him a whole evening when he'll never spare five minutes for us again?

My mother moves behind me, starting to leave, but she stops and turns.

"I'm not trying to overcompensate," she clarifies, as if she'd read my mind.

I look over at her, the solemn look on her face telling me she's aware of the baggage her boys still carry.

Her brow pinches together in sadness. "I just want to see you having fun."

I shake out the towel, flexing my jaw. "I am." I offer her a grin. "I love this. Promise."

She's quiet but doesn't move, and I finish stacking dishes onto shelves.

"You're just always so busy," she tells me. "The studying and extracurriculars in high school. Finishing your college degree a year early, culinary classes in your spare time, this shop in the summers... Like you were always rushing to be thirty or something."

The world in front of me blurs.

She's not wrong. I'd just been hoping no one would notice. Or if they did, they would say I was "motivated" or "a hard worker." But the truth is, I was never excited to be in college. I was excited to be done. I never wanted to go on Spring Break with friends. There were better ways to spend that time.

I was always racing to a finish line.

To be grown up.

I turn my face back to the sink, rinsing the suds out before she can see my chin tremble.

I *think* I'm having fun. I'm finally done. I finished school and started my business. Now, I'm ready for...

I don't know. What do I want now?

My own life. Not a life away from my family, but one where I'm in the lead. Where I make my own decisions, have privacy, and don't feel like I'm always following someone.

She doesn't press further, just touches her hand to my cheek. "I love you."

"I love you, too."

But I don't look at her because I don't want her to see my face. In a moment, she's gone.

I accepted a long time ago that my mother is the smartest person I'll ever meet. In terms of street smarts. More than my dad, Madoc, Jared, or even Jax, because my mom has made nearly every mistake imaginable. When she speaks, it's from experience. Not anger or power or trauma.

After boxing Mace's brownies, I set them on the table and take the extras to the front. I load them into the case, but a customer stops me.

"Can I buy those, actually?" he asks. "They look great."

"Sure."

Boxing the rest of the brownies and setting them on the counter, I glance up, seeing Aro and Dylan through the windows. They stand right outside, next to one of the patio tables on the sidewalk.

They wave through the glass, Dylan using two hands.

What the hell are they doing? I toss a quick wave back as I direct my attention to the customer and the guy he's with.

"Anything for you?" I ask the second gentleman as he browses the options.

Aro passes a stack of large white posterboards to Dylan. She holds them up for me to see through the window.

I'm mad at you, it says.

Mad? I glance around to the customers in the shop to see if they notice her.

"I would love something," the young man replies with a sigh. "Anything for diabetics?"

Huh?

I turn back to my customers. *Oh, right.* I smile at the guy, noticing Dylan throwing the board over her shoulder, letting it fly onto the sidewalk.

Guess who we saw at Camp Blackhawk today? the next board reads.

My heart thuds. Aro grabs the stack, flipping to the next poster.

Oh my God... it says.

Then, she fans herself.
My stomach somersaults. *Lucas.*
The customers stand there, and I let out a single, nervous laugh, dropping my eyes. "Uh...how about...chocolate chip blondies?" I ask.

Moving down the case, I take a square of parchment paper and reach into the shelf. I raise my eyes as Dylan snatches the cards back.

Jax says you saw him last night. She lets that card fly. *And you didn't text me?*

She and Aro both throw out their hands, little snarls on their faces.

Great.

I hand the blondie over the counter to the man. "One hundred percent free of refined sugars."

The dude takes it. "Are you serious?"

I nod like a caricature, more because I'm trying to hide how distracted I am with what the girls are doing outside. "They're sweetened with dates," I explain.

I'll meet you at the gym tonight, Dylan announces.

"Try it," I tell the guy.

She reveals another sign. *Eight o'clock.*

The pulse in my neck knocks against my skin.
The man chews a bite, freezes, then lets out a moan of satisfaction. "I'll be damned."

Aro is covering for me.

I glance to Aro, seeing her grin. And wiggle her eyebrows. She doesn't ever do that. *Oh, God.* What are they planning?
"Can you make anything else naturally sweetened?" the customer asks.
I glance at him, swallow, then look at Dylan and Aro.

Dylan gives me her biggest, brightest smile. *He's not leaving Saturday because you're going to make him want to stay!*

I lick my lips.

You know how?

And then, right there, on High Street, on the sidewalk in front of my damn shop, she and Aro start dancing, thrusting, and moaning in ecstasy as they flip their hair all around like strippers.
Snorts go off in the shop, and I let my eyes fall closed, holding in something between a growl and a laugh. *I'm going to kill them.*
I'm...
I'm...
I'm really going to kill them.

"I'm...um..." I clear my throat and look at the customer again. "I'm willing to...try." I grab a business card from the slot on the counter and hand it to him. "Feel free to email me a request, and I'll see what I can do."

He smiles, taking the card. "Thanks." And then gesturing to the case of blondies, "I'll take all of them, actually."

His friend laughs, and I get busy packaging up the rest, glaring at Dylan and Aro through the glass case.

Try it! Dylan holds up one more sign. *Sex is soooooo super fun!*

Then they both give me all their thumbs up.

My forehead dampens with sweat, but then I realize my hair and shirt are sticking to my neck and back too.

Are they really allowed to just leave the kids at the camp during the day like this? I'm texting Jax.

Unfortunately, work doesn't keep me at the shop as long as I would like. I stayed open a little later than usual in hopes of some stragglers, but by five, the door is closed. By six, leftovers are dropped off at the fire department this time and the deposit is made at the bank. By seven, the dough is prepped for the morning and the place is clean. Emails are answered. Inventory done. Shipment of coffee stocked.

I check the lock on Frosted's door, then glance at the clock on the wall.

7:58.

Blood warms as it flows down my arms.

I didn't tell Dylan I would go to the gym.

But she is expecting me.

I walk to the floor-length mirror, trying to ignore the little way it feels like my lungs aren't taking in enough air, or how I can't think of anything else other than how I'm expected somewhere right about now.

I brush a few strands of hair out of my face.

Staring at my reflection in the mirror, I take in the pizza sauce staining the canvas-colored apron wrapped around my waist, and the flour on my forearms that I missed when I washed up. Everything went well today.

Almost.

I always worry if customers can tell when I'm frazzled. While I'm turning a profit, even with all of the menu additions, the higher utility bills from staying open longer, and the new equipment I ordered for the ice cream stand, I still haven't figured out the part I promised my mother I would. My time.

I need to start delegating responsibilities and training Noel or Hailey to run the shop so I can have a day off. I'm not sure what I would do with one, though. I abandoned most of my hobbies years ago, and I don't have friends. I mean, ones not named Trent or Caruthers, at least.

I love Dylan, of course. I feel good around Aro. Hawke is one of my safe places. And Kade and Hunter would never fail me. Other than that, I think I should want friends, but I really don't. Maybe I just find family easier because they have to accept me. With anyone else, I don't like half the shit that comes out of my mouth, and I go home feeling like I spent hours trying to make a relationship happen that I didn't want anyway. I could've spent that time cleaning something. Or researching flavor combinations. Or exercising or sleeping or reading or peacefully walking and getting lost in the breeze while listening to music in my earbuds. Every single one of those things more enjoyable than dying slowly at some lunch or movie outing that just ends up feeling like something else I had to fit into my schedule.

Maybe I'll just go jogging tonight, instead. Ride my bike to Eagle Point Park and run through there. It's closed to everything but foot traffic at night. Jared won't find me. He still hasn't learned that he can track everyone he loves on an app on his phone. God help us when he does.

Pain strikes in my stomach, and I exhale. I haven't eaten since before noon. I pull my ponytail out, fluff my hair, and tie it back up again before removing my apron.

Lucas probably isn't even at the gym. Or maybe he was and now he's gone. Or perhaps he won't work out till later. Who knows...

Several dark spots spread across the mirror, some in clusters and others splattered out like stars in a sky, and I use the apron to brush at them. They don't come off. I tsk. The mirror is deteriorating. I wish we could get the damn thing off the wall.

I check the clock again. *8:02*.

I sigh, turning back to my reflection. Hawke was certain that removing the mirror would damage the brick, not to mention the nightmare we might find in the walls, like rats or mold. I can only hope he was teasing me. I want to be aboveboard and have a clean place, but a discovery like that could destroy my business.

And...I also feared finding something I couldn't afford to fix three years ago when I opened the place, either. Like a structural problem.

I don't really want to potentially damage a wall now that I'm open full time. Construction would hurt the traffic trying to come in here when I'm just getting going.

Fingerprints dot the edge of the mirror on the top right. I lean in, narrowing my eyes. It's four fingers, minus the thumb. As if someone clutched it from behind. I frown, the images of various horror movies making me shudder.

I wipe the prints off too.

Moving into the kitchen, I toss the apron into the laundry and grab my backpack. Stepping into the bathroom, I change, slip my earbuds into a pocket, and push any long bangs back over the top of my head. But as I reach for the cap, I stop, realizing it's not with me. He took it this morning.

I frown. I have others at home, but...that one was nice and broken in.

He still hasn't given me my compass back, either. Does that mean the hat is still technically mine? I smile to myself and dash back into the shop. Maybe it would be warranted to go to the gym after all and take it back.

I charge through the door of the kitchen to grab my phone, but as I pick it up, I see the empty Lost and Found box again. I forgot to ask Hailey or Noel who came in for it. I thought I would've noticed—it's a small shop.

Just then, ringing pierces my brain, and I gasp. *Dylan* appears on the screen, and I exhale, swiping. "Hello?"

"Are you coming?"

I switch off the kitchen light. "Maybe."

"Well, I'm waiting." Chatter and music play in the background. "And I have to be back by ten."

"I didn't ask you to work out with me tonight."

This was her idea.

But she just goes on, not hearing me. "Can you bring some leftovers?" she asks. "Hunter snuck me away behind the archery range, and I missed dinner."

I hang up on her. *Unbelievable.*

Then, it occurs to me I could've asked her if Lucas was there.

I'm glad I didn't. I don't want her thinking that would have made my decision for me.

A text rolls in. *Hurry!* she writes. *I'm so hungry!*

I growl. "This is stupid." I slide my phone into my pants. "Go exercise so you can go to sleep."

I start to leave, mumbling to myself, "Your brother paid for a membership. You're allowed to use it."

But then I circle back and throw some leftover croissants into a paper bag and stuff them into my backpack.

In three minutes, I walk through the doors of Astrophysics a block away.

Heading up to the counter, I tap the device with my membership card.

"Welcome." The same young woman from last night greets me. "Towel?"

"Please." She pulls one from under the counter, and I take it. "Thank you."

After I secure my backpack and jacket in the locker room, I fit in my earbuds and climb the stairs to the track with the bag of croissants. I glance around for Dylan, but try to keep my shoulders relaxed so it doesn't look like I'm looking for someone else.

Noah Van der Berg lies on a bench, pressing a bar up and down above his chest. He exercises with Dylan sometimes, part of their race training. Where is she?

Then, Farrow Kelly rises off a leg curl machine far to my left. He stares at me.

I glance back at Noah, who drops the bar back into his cradle and sits up, meeting my gaze too.

Unease settles into my stomach, and I stop breathing for a moment.

Oh, no.

Quickly, I tap out a text to Dylan.

Where are you?

The hair on my neck rises. Darting my gaze up, I see Farrow and Noah walking straight toward me, one from the left, and one from my right.

"No, no, no..."

A notification pops up.

Oh, I'm at camp, she writes. *I sent my associates.*

My chest caves. "Dylan," I whimper under my breath.

Trust me, she says next.

And just as both men close in, I spot Lucas breezing past on the track, his chin lifting in greeting. My heart thuds, and he almost looks like he's about to smile, but his gaze flickers to the boys, and casually, he turns back to the track, disappearing.

I blink slow and hard. *I'm gonna kill her.*
I'm going...to kill her.

When I open my eyes, Noah is there, and I'm pretty sure he speed-walked to beat Farrow. "Hi," he says, stopping in front of me.

Noah Van der Berg is about my age, maybe a few years older, and the star of JT Racing, my brother's company. Jared recruited Noah after he met Noah's father, who constructs custom motorcycles for the Motocross circuit. My brother makes engines, so JT Racing and Van der Berg Extreme are just short of being married to each other.

And Noah, I hear, leapt at the chance to leave his secluded childhood home in the Rocky Mountains to come race for my family.

That's about all I know—other than I've seen him with at least two different girls on the back of his motorcycle since I returned home a month ago. We haven't formally met.

I search my brain for how to make them go away, but Farrow finally steps up to his side. "Take off, Van der Berg." He throws the other guy a look through hooded eyes. "I'm working out with her." Then to me, "Dylan sent me."

"Yeah, she sent me too," Noah retorts.

Farrow steels his spine, looking away and grumbling, "Fuckin' Dylan..."

Yeah, pretty much. This is her plan, because she thinks two good-looking men at my side will make Lucas jealous.

Or it could make him not talk to me at all! Did she think about that?

I throw the croissants into the nearby trash can, avoiding both of their eyes. "What did she tell you?" I whisper.

Farrow shrugs. "She said you just moved back home, and that we should be friends."

Noah adds, "And I'm not allowed to make a pass unless—"

"*Until...*" Farrow interrupts him before looking back to me. "Until it's very obvious that you want me to."

I feel my face flush, and I almost roll my eyes to distract from it, but I resist.

Farrow Kelly might be only twenty, but there's something in his eyes that tells me his game level far exceeds Noah's, and it's not even in regards to women. The Green Street tattoo—simply the word RIVER etched with a line stricken down the middle—stretches vertically on the left side of his neck. Like Mace's.

Green Street is a gang in Weston, the dilapidated mill town across the river that's been hanging by a thread since a flood drove most of its citizens away more than twenty years ago. Houses sit abandoned, businesses remain closed, and whatever law does exist is only for hire. I don't know what goes on at Green Street, but I do know Farrow has a seat at the adult table and his blond hair, a shade lighter than Noah's, is often under a black ski cap at night. Light hair doesn't disguise the blood splatter, does it?

But they both have eyes that look like they're constantly smiling even when they aren't, and I don't think that's fake.

"She also said I should give you a ride home," Noah continues, ignoring Farrow, "so your brothers know you're safe."

"A ride home on your motorcycle?" Farrow teases him.

"Jared likes me," Noah points out to him. "In fact, all of her brothers do. And all of her family."

"Nuh-uh," Farrow barks at him. "Dylan and Hunter are mine."

My gaze flies to Noah.

"No, you don't get Dylan," he continues to argue. "I share a bathroom with her."

"Fuck off, Stoner Mountain Boy."

"I don't smoke weed, you little shit!"

"You're from Colorado," Farrow bickers.

I can't help it, but my eyebrows are up by my hairline, amusement taking over.

I've seen them both around, been in rooms they've been in and heard them talk to Dylan, Hunter, Jared, et cetera, but I've never dealt with them personally.

I'm not really intimidated, though. They remind me of my brothers.

And Kade, Hunter, and Hawke, for that matter. I don't know about Farrow, but Jared obviously trusts Noah enough to let him live under his roof with his teenage daughter, when she's not at college or the camp, that is.

"You guys can stay if you want," I tell them, veering around Farrow, toward the track. "Or you can go. I'm just exercising, and I don't need a ride home, but thank you."

Noah sidles up to my right. "I'll stay," he tells me. "In case you change your mind."

"I'm here anyway," I hear Farrow say just behind me.

"Wanna jog?" Noah gestures to the empty lanes.

I take a quick glance, not seeing Lucas. Did he get off the track?

He might not talk to me if they're hanging around.

But...at least this way, it doesn't look like I came here looking for him. Noah and Farrow give good cover, I guess.

I nod, and Noah walks with me.

"Ah, shit," I hear Farrow say. He stops, staring at his phone. "I'll catch up."

"You mean at the weights, because mafia meatheads can't do cardio?" Noah taunts.

Farrow doesn't respond, just shoots Noah a look as he grabs himself between his legs and jerks once before spinning around and walking away, his phone to his ear.

Lucas breezes past, casting us a sideways glance, and then he's gone again.

Goosebumps spread up my arms, into my hair. He doesn't look happy. Maybe Dylan does know what she's doing.

Noah holds out his hand, formally introducing himself. "Noah Van der Berg."

I look back at him just as I see Lucas glance back at us.

I smile, shaking his hand. "Quinn Caruthers. Nice to finally meet you."

SHELBURNE FALLS

CHAPTER FOUR

Lucas

She's laughing. Why does it bug me?

He smiles, she blushes, they talk, and I run a little faster, so they don't pass me. And they smile some more. And talk and talk and talk.

I thought I might see her here tonight, but I don't know why I assumed she'd be alone if I did.

I guess it's just a reminder of how the world keeps moving without you. Quinn used to want me around.

She has other people's attention now.

I jerk my head to the side, cracking my neck. It's good that she has people around her. He has a kind way about him, at least. Easy eyes that look at her like he's seven and she's carrying a plate of cookies. Not like the other one who looks at her like he already knows how this night will go, and it will end entirely in his favor.

I exit the track, swipe my hand towel and water bottle off a bench, and wipe the sweat on my forehead that isn't really there. I'd only been jogging for a few minutes, trying not to think about how I timed my arrival when I thought she might show up.

Madoc was here last night too. I just wanted to catch up with them both some more before I leave. I haven't seen him yet, though.

I head for the bottle filler and see them jog past, her running partner trailing her just a couple of inches, his eyes dropping to her ass.

Noah Van der Berg.

Madoc told me about him today at the track—the family's new honorary addition. He's on Jared's racing team, lives with him and Tate, and acts as a pseudo-older brother to their son, James. Good friends with Dylan too.

Actually, all of them, I hear.

Saw him for a beat at the Loop, straddling his bike and talking up some girls. I can spot a young guy, new to town, and enjoying a playing field of fresh new faces a mile away. They don't mind him having fun, but they will mind when he's having fun with Quinn. I guarantee it.

Tipping up my bottle, I take a drink.

"Is he coming tonight?" I hear a voice ask.

I swallow a little more water and then stop. I think it's the other kid Quinn was with.

"What time?" he asks.

He's on the phone.

"What time?" Again, but sterner.

I take a step, then two, and spot the other blond around the corner, his back to the towel station. He holds a phone in his hand, an ear piece is in his ear.

"You think I want his job?" He grins. "I'll be taking yours first."

He slides a hand up under his black T-shirt and rubs his stomach.

"And then Reeves will fucking find out how short-lived power is when you have no people."

I pull back just behind the wall again.

Reeves.

Drew Reeves?

"I won't be late," I hear him say. But then his voice softens. "Well, I might be late. Kind of like what I'm looking at right now."

I take another step, seeing him follow Quinn with his eyes as she runs with Noah.

"Don't wait for me."

He ends the call, tucks the phone into the pocket of fitted gray sweatpants, and then he turns.

And that's when I see it.

RIVER inked vertically down the side of his neck, a line stricken through the word.

My chest caves. *Fuck*.

I stand there, watching him walk back to Noah and Quinn as they stop running and move to the machines. Something coils in my stomach as I clench my teeth.

The tattoo. The fucking tat.

Green Street.

He had said "and then Reeves *will* find out…"

…*will*.

As if he's still here.

But he's gone. I checked. He was driven away two years ago. The crooked Shelburne Falls cop who ran the Weston Green Street gang and was caught siphoning confiscated goods for his own benefit and conning a bunch of kids into doing his dirty work. He fled, and an underling took over.

But eight years ago, Drew wasn't a cop. And he wasn't alone.

I'm not welcome here anymore, under any condition, but I couldn't exactly tell my mother that when she forced me home. Even Lance doesn't know what happened.

And Madoc will never know.

Does Green Street cause him any trouble? If I'm seeing someone with a tattoo after only two days here, the group has to be thriving.

Neither of these fucking guys should be around Quinn.

Lance sidles up to my side, done with the treadmill. "Legs?" he asks.

I'd forgotten he was here.

I watch Quinn move to the shoulder press as her friends circle her.

"Upper body." And I shoot off.

"But we did that yesterday."

I don't stop, and he doesn't argue.

Climbing on to the lat machine, I glance at Quinn in the mirror, seeing her about twenty feet behind me with the guys. She starts her reps, Noah next to her on a weight bench while the other one lingers behind her. What's his name?

Quinn doesn't look at me, her chin down.

But then...she lifts her head and locks on my gaze in the mirror. She flashes a small smile, my heart jolting.

I'd forgotten how her whole face brightens when she does that.

"So, what did you think of Fallstown?" Lance hangs in front of me, his hands gripping a bar over his head.

I shake my mind clear, trying to hide the pounding in my chest. "It was fun." I let the bar rise and then pull down again. "Nice tracks."

Fallstown. Thank goodness I'm not going to be here long enough to learn that new title.

Madoc let me do a few turns in his car. And then showed me how I was *supposed* to do it. Amusement pulls at the corners of my mouth, remembering how it felt when he taught me to drive when I was fifteen.

Actually, thirteen, but I'm not supposed to tell anyone that.

"It was fun, *and*..." he teases.

I almost chuckle. My friend knows me. "And I'm glad they changed the name because it's not the Loop anymore." Quinn glances at me, followed by Van der Berg, no doubt overhearing. "Clean, scheduled, and corporate." Instead of wild, chaotic, and exciting. "The Loop is gone," I say a little louder than necessary. "It's a shame."

My ego takes over, and for some reason, things that never even occurred to me are now pissing me off. Like how she has people in her life who don't even know who I am. And how I know more than they do about everything in this town, and I don't like how they're just fucking walking around without permission.

"Yeah, nothing like it used to be," Lance offers.

I know I'm not thinking clearly. I'm being stupid. It's just me feeling threatened and possessive of a life I no longer have, but I can't shake it.

And I don't care. Not really. It's just possessiveness of my history here, which isn't nearly as good as my life is now overseas. Things just always seem better than they were, in retrospect.

Quinn moves off the shoulder press and takes Noah's place at the weight bench, Van der Berg and the other one helping adjust her weights.

"But we do have other things to offer," Lance adds.

Noah moves behind her. "I'll spot you."

"Oh, I remember," I reply, tipping my eyes up at my friend. "Small-town privacy, speed traps, and pancake suppers."

Hard to avoid the interest of such a close-knit community.

"No, I can hear you," Quinn says, and I watch the boys smile down at her as she listens to them over her ear piece.

"We have mystery." Lance moves in, lowering his voice. "Every appetite can be satiated in a city, and no one cares. A small town is where you're afraid to get caught. That's where the fun is. Who's having an affair with who? Who's the secret love-child of the police chief?"

Who's hiding a body...?

Yeah, I get the picture. I shake off the aggravation weighing on my shoulders.

"It's the relationships in a small town that make everything messy..." he trails off.

"Thank you," Quinn says, and I glance over, watching Van der Berg take the bar as she sits up.

"It's the people you see every day that make your secrets more dangerous," Lance tells me. "And more worthwhile."

An earbud tumbles to the floor. Quinn sees it but continues her set.

I release my bar, replying, "Maybe I would've thought so before I came back and saw how developed the town is now."

It's not quiet anymore.

Bending down, I swipe up the ear piece and blow off any dirt or dust.

Approaching, I gently take Quinn's ear and slide it back in. My fingers tremble at the feel of her soft skin and the strands of hair caught behind her lobe. I don't touch too hard, almost like she's fine china.

"The Loop used to be wet and dirty," I tell Lance as I ignore the boys and feel Quinn go still as she clutches the bars in her hands. "Illegal and dangerous. What made it fun was that we were doing something we weren't supposed to."

She lifts her eyes to mine, the young men with her like statues in the corner of my eye. I can feel them watching us, and I hold her for another second—and then another—amplifying every moment she doesn't shove me away, showing them that she knows me. Showing her that I'm still the closest man to her outside of blood.

"But the more the town grows, the more people fear losing what they have. The mystery dissipates in favor of shared preservation."

Backing away, I have a seat at the machine next to her and start pumping, despite my heart racing more as the seconds pass. Lance takes the rope on my other side and pulls down again and again, exercising his triceps.

I don't check Quinn, breathing slowly and calmly as if nothing happened.

"So," I ask Lance, swallowing. "Am I going to meet your wife?"

Quinn resumes her arm curls, and I exhale slowly.

"Sure." He nods. "When you get one for yourself. I'm not letting her around you when you're unattached."

I force a laugh, trying to act like Quinn isn't the only thing I'm aware of. "Like I would ever…" I joke.

"But she might."

I shake my head. "Bring her on Saturday. The more the merrier to the Caruthers."

I didn't want a party. But I can give Madoc one night.

"Will *she* be there?" he murmurs in a low voice, gesturing to Quinn.

I was hoping he wouldn't notice her or how she was the same young woman who worked out next to us last night.

Gripping the bar, I climb off the shoulder press, keeping my voice down, "As she's Madoc's sister, I'm sure she will be."

He rises too, and lingers close as I take over his machine. "Want me to make sure they're not?" he teases.

Van der Berg puts on a show for Quinn, curling his biceps as he lifts a bar. The other one leans into her ear, whispering something from behind. A glimmer of amusement curves the edges of her mouth.

I release the handle, the sound of the weights clanging against each other making the others in the room startle.

I turn to my friend, teasing, "Just don't send one of our old buddies after her for a young wife of his own to match yours after I leave, okay? She's a kid." I grab a weight bar. "And leave them alone." I indicate the boys she's with. "You've settled into calm, domestic bliss. Keep it that way."

I should've been as smart as him back in the day, and then I wouldn't be in the mess I'm in now.

He circles around my other side. "You saw his tattoo?" he asks under his breath.

I dart my eyes to the Green Street guy with Quinn. "Yes."

I'll ask Lance about Green Street later. It'll save me from asking Madoc. I was hoping to avoid any mention of the club altogether, but I see now that it will be impossible.

Lance and I get busy lifting, one of my eyes staying on Quinn through the mirror in front of us.

"Sit ups." Noah gestures her to the floor. "Wanna race?"

She breathes out a laugh. "No."

Quinn moves to the pec machine, straddling the seat and sitting tall with her back arched. I shift my gaze away from her hips in her tight leggings.

"Leave her alone," the other one chimes in. "You can't fit her into your schedule anyway, Van der Berg."

The latter just smiles at him. "Wanna race?" he repeats.

"Not really." Green Street shrugs. "We already know I'm a better rider."

"Can you even get into a bar?"

"And when I can," he moves in closer to Noah, "what are you going to do then?"

"Take Quinn to a different one."

She snorts, quickly folding her lips between her teeth to stop from laughing.

I scowl.

She rises from the machine, grabs a free weight in each hand, and raises both arms over her head. But she stops before she even starts, pivoting toward Green Street, who lurks behind her.

"Come around the front," she instructs, pointing.

He smirks. "Yes, ma'am."

He moves to the area in front of her, not at all embarrassed that she knew he was ogling her ass.

Quinn lifts both arms into the air, again and again. "So I hear you leapt at the chance to move here," she tells Van der Berg. "Is this you living the good life?"

Why am I not talking to her? And if I'm not talking to her, then why don't I move-the-hell-on to another area?

Noah puts his foot up on a bench, leaning his shoulder onto a machine as he smiles playfully at her. "You mean, is it fun not waking up at four thirty in the morning to shovel snow with a hangover because the Internet has been down for a week due to a storm, and the only thing to do is remain consistently drunk?" he retorts. "When you get to wake up every day and know that not one hour will be spent being unhappy, yeah, that's the good life."

To that, she smiles. Soft, genuine, and it stays there.

Fucking little shit. He sure knows how to talk to women. He's sensitive, personable, wise... I don't like him.

"Touché," she breathes and then turns to the other. "What about you? Living the good life?"

He doesn't miss a beat. "The only way out is through." He shoots Noah a look. "I don't leave *my* people behind."

Noah's eye twitches, but he doesn't argue.

So, they both live here. Or close, anyway. Green Street Guy is younger than Quinn and Van der Berg. But probably only by a year or two. I gathered that much.

Noah drops to the ground, does one pushup, but then the other one drops down in front of him, eye to eye.

"Last one to twenty goes home?" Green Street suggests. "Now."

He might be a little younger, but he's bigger. Maybe an inch taller, but broader too. Like he was an athlete.

As a Motocross racer, Noah would try to keep his weight down.

"You sure?" he grins.

"I'm sure. You ready?"

"Almost." Noah looks up. "Quinn?"

I find her in the mirror.

"Lie down on my back," he instructs her.

Excuse me?

She stops mid-exercise, and I think I see her gaze dart to me, but it was too quick to tell. "No."

"Please?"

He says it so fucking gentle, and even after all this time, I know Quinn hasn't changed. She finds it hard to disappoint people.

My muscles burn as I watch her set the free weights down, lower to him on the floor, and press her chest into his back. The tips of her shoes rest on his heels as she layers her forearms across the back of his shoulders.

"Like this?" she asks, and I wait for her to look at me again. She doesn't.

Noah smiles. "Perfect."

"Set?" the other one snips.

"Go," Van der Berg announces.

Everything tenses as I watch both young men dip and rise, pushing their body weight—and in Van der Berg's case, Quinn's too—up off the ground.

Again.

And again, both bobbing up and down with damn near the speed of a bullet.

Quinn smiles, her stomach probably flipping because that's what happens when we ride rides. *What the fuck...*

Looking across to Green Street, her eyes shine. A few people stop to watch, one taking out his phone and filming.

"Hey," Lance blurts out at my side. "You've been doing that same exercise for about a hundred reps."

I pause. Huh?

I remember the bar in my hands and drop it, just noticing how hard I'm breathing. My arms are on fire.

I turn my head over my shoulder, watching with my friend as Noah bounces and she starts to slip.

"Hold tight!" he shouts, excited.

She clutches his shoulders, squeezing her eyes shut and laughing, even as he slows around number twelve. The other one outpaces him and Van der Berg winds down more and more, losing strength, but he and Quinn beam anyway, even knowing they'll lose.

Smart kid. He didn't need to win, and Green Street knows it as he finishes first but isn't happy. Van der Berg didn't need to prove his manliness. He created an experience with Quinn. His own. His and hers.

Other people will make her happy.

"I win," Green Street says as they all rise.

"Did you?" Noah dusts off his pants. He takes Quinn's hand, helping her up.

"Better not let the mayor see his sister riding your back," the other one warns. "Or…maybe he should."

I grab my towel as he gestures to the security camera in the corner behind Van der Berg's head.

"I'd be more worried about the other half of her family tree," I interject, taking a seat at the arm press again. "One Trent will kill you both, the other will hide it."

I didn't mean to say it—or insert myself—but she's not getting a quality workout with these two dipshits anyway. I know, in the basement of my mind, that I'm full of shit, but it's a good enough excuse. She's busy, and she's here to workout.

Lance takes his cue, stepping off to make a call, and I begin my reps, not looking at either kid.

"Who are you?" Van der Berg asks.

But Quinn responds before I have a chance to say anything.

"This is Lucas Morrow." She stands at the lat machine, elbows pinned to her waist as she just moves her lower arms, pushing the bar down. "He used to babysit me."

Babysit?

I dig in my brow. Why would she say that? As if I'm so much older.

And these dickheads don't need to know my name.

I rise and lean down, changing the pin on her machine to add more weight. "It wasn't babysitting." I lift the corner of my mouth in a smile. "It was my pleasure."

"Morrow…" someone whispers.

I stand up straight, eyeing Green Street. He zones in on me, brows pinched together, and I can see the wheels turning in his head. My pulse throbs in my neck.

"How's everything coming with the house?" Quinn asks me.

Noah touches her shoulder, giving her a nod as he takes his loss and leaves.

When he's gone, I reply. "It's going well."

"Do you think it will sell quickly?"

Her eyes shine, wisps of hair falling around her cheeks and shoulders from her ponytail. I intended to give her the hat back, but...it's nice to see her face.

"Why?" I ask. "Anxious to be rid of me?"

She moves to the next machine. "I'm just starting to wonder if I need a place of my own."

As in buy my parents' house? I go still for a moment, letting the thought sink in.

That would actually be nice.

I'd know it was staying in the family, so to speak, and she would take care of it. I never intend to return to the Falls, but that house was where I met Madoc. Made some good memories. Came of age. I'd love to know it was going to someone who would respect it.

But she doesn't need a place of her own. I glance at Green Street. *Where she can have a personal life...*

I inhale a hard breath. "Stay with your parents," I tell her, moving to the pull-up bars with my towel and water. "For as long as you can. Trust me."

No need giving herself a mortgage, especially when Madoc says she's at the shop eighteen hours a day anyway.

I slide past Green Street, staring him in the eyes a few inches from mine. "You can leave, too," I nearly whisper, not bothering to ask. "I'll see her home."

He swallows, quiet for the first time tonight.

And that's when I know that he knows exactly who I am.

Clearing his throat, he says, "I'll see you later, Quinn." He looks at me, though. "Gotta run."

"Bye," she calls out.

And he leaves, disappearing down the stairs.

I shouldn't have done that. He'll tell someone whose attention I don't want.

But Quinn already told him my name, and now I know... They remember me in Weston. All I can hope is that I'll be gone before anything goes wrong.

I look around for Lance, spotting him on the treadmill again. He's keeping his distance because he thinks I'm about to get laid.

I stand next to Quinn's machine. "I recognized Noah Van der Berg," I tell her. "Madoc mentioned him. Who was that one who just left?"

Green Street...

"Farrow Kelly," she replies. "Graduated from Weston a couple of years ago, I think. He's friendly with Hunter and Dylan."

Does she know what his tattoo means? I open my mouth to tell her that she should stay away from him. Even if he's nice and means well, trouble surrounds him. And it will surround everyone he cares about for the rest of his life.

I don't want to talk about him, though.

At least I'm here to give her a ride tonight.

I take a drink of water and smile down at her. "That croissant this morning was really good."

Her eyes light up. "What did it taste like?"

"Like...bread?"

She stops just short of rolling her eyes. "What did you think of when you bit into it?"

"Ugh, your questions..." I sigh, but I smile. "Some things don't change."

She stands up, grabbing her towel. "Croissants remind me of a sleepy, old attic," she says in a dreamy voice. "Warm light spilling through the windows, casting an antique glow onto some forgotten, old, dark green chest. They taste like a whole day of rummaging through little treasures. And the flakes and crumbs?" She nearly bounces on her feet. "Sounds like wrapping paper when you sink your teeth into it, right? It's like biting into a present."

I stare at her, caught between wanting to cover her in bubble wrap so she's protected forever and ever and ever and never changes, and wanting to know if she's still only playful like this with me. Like she used to be.

With everyone else, she was the quiet one. The quiet Caruthers. The quiet sibling. The quiet daughter.

Instead, I just chuckle and squeeze my black bottle, squirting water into her face.

She jerks. "Hey." But she laughs as she wipes it off.

I push her toward the cage. "Go stretch."

We're done working out. I need to be up early for a call, and I'm not leaving her here alone.

She takes one side of the cage, I take the other, and we hang on to the bars, stretching our arms and legs. She hooks her foot on a bar behind her, working the front of her thigh, and for a moment, I can't take my eyes off the toned legs, bare in her short black shorts.

Her long-sleeved black and gray camo Under Armour shirt covers her stomach and goes up to her neck, but it's tight, every curve accentuated. I hugged her last night, but I only held her loosely, around her shoulders. How would it feel to wrap my arms around her waist?

I blink long and hard. *Jesus...*

But I quickly see a man on a machine behind her, taking in her figure, as well.

I grit my teeth and move, putting myself between him and her.

Gazing down at her hair, I inhale the scent of her shampoo. Last time I saw her eight years ago, she stopped at just about where my heart sits. Now the crown of her head is at my mouth.

Yet, it's more than that. I can talk to her like an adult. And God, part of me wants to. I want someone to talk to. She's connected to me, like Madoc, but unlike him, she's not pressuring me and constantly looking with a question in her eyes, or holding back anger at the time I cost us when I left.

She needs to stay the same, though. I don't want her to ever change.

I almost touch her hair. *Stay like this.*

I grab the bar instead and draw a deep breath, blinking away the thoughts.

"Twenty seconds," I say, pushing her head back down and keeping her bent in half to stretch.

She grunts, her ponytail dragging on the floor. "You're not my babysitter anymore."

"I'm still older." I keep my hand on the back of her neck as I take a swig of water. "I'll always be older."

"So, when I'm twenty-six and you're thirty-eight," she argues. "It'll still be like this?"

Twenty-six.

Thirty-eight.

When she's twenty-six, how many men will have loved her by then? How many will she have loved?

"Lucas?"

I let out a breath. "No," I tell her. "You get full autonomy by then. Promise."

But the truth is, she'll belong to someone by then. Much sooner, by the looks of things. Men don't want other men around what's theirs, and they won't like me around her. Even if I'm just a family friend. If I'm not blood, I'm a threat.

I let my gaze fall; possessive of the time I was a part of her life. Someone will come along who doesn't know that I meant anything, and it'll be like I never existed. He'll get more years than the thirteen I had with her.

I knew that, though, didn't I?

We turn in our towels and make our way out of the gym to my rental car in the back lot.

"You need to get a license." I unlock the car and open her door. "And a car."

She climbs in and waits for me to open the driver's side door. "I understood that argument when I was thirteen," she calls out as I climb in, "but we have Uber and Lyft now."

"It's safer to own a car and have the option." I close the door and fasten my seatbelt. "And not be at the mercy of men looking for an in by offering you a ride home, right?"

I start the car and slide my phone into the console, but before I pull away from the curb, I look over at her. She stares at nothing, a solemn expression on her face.

"What?" I ask.

She just shrugs. "I have a license. I *can* drive," she admits. "There was no way my brothers were going to stand for anyone in the family not being able to drive stick, either, but..."

"But?"

She twists her lips to the side. "Bicycles are quiet." Her voice is timid as she turns to me. "Walking is quiet. And there are no seatbelts. I like the air."

My heart softens, Quinn's appreciation for the little things flooding back like she's a kid. She always took it a little slower than everyone in her family. Liked walking and feeling the wind and admiring people's yards as we passed.

I want her to ride her bike.

But not in the snow, and not in the dark.

"Driving is a skill," I explain. "The more skills you have, the stronger you are. Right?"

And I don't want her bumming rides from horny little pricks with arms and abs and stamina and shit.

"It's dark. Let's go." I shift into Drive. "Or I can call Jared or Jax to take you home, if you prefer."

She scowls at me, and I almost laugh. "Your threats are vicious," she says.

I press the gas, smiling. "Seatbelt."

WESTON

CHAPTER FIVE

Quinn

Dylan was right.

Lucas was only friendly after Noah and Farrow left the gym last night. Was he annoyed? Why would he be? He didn't know them. And if he's leaving, severing his last tie by selling the house and not planning to visit, just like he didn't for the past eight years, then he shouldn't have really cared about not being able to talk to me. What would be the point, right?

He didn't even know for sure if I was going to be there last night...

Unless...

I lie in bed, looking up, the soft glow of my parents' lanterns around the driveway outside dancing on the ceiling of my dark bedroom. It's a little before four, but I've been up for half an hour, replaying in my head the moments at the gym last night.

Could he...have been jealous?

I entwine my fingers where they lay on my stomach. I could barely resist looking at him constantly last night.

When Noah and I ran together. When the guys helped with my machine.

When I laid on Noah's back.

I hope Lucas didn't notice how I was stealing glances at him.

At first, it felt like we were strangers, because I didn't say hi and he didn't say it, and the longer neither of us talked, the more awkward it felt, but damn, I loved it. My heart beat so fast. I always wondered if I would still have my crush if I saw him again. Now I know. Steam had covered my skin and fire had filled my chest, and he was all I was aware of.

And even more, as the minutes went by, because he stayed close. He didn't leave to go play racquetball or bench press with his friend.

I release a breath, a light layer of sweat coating the back of my neck.

A fantasy flashes in my head of Lucas in a suit, like the one from two nights ago, picking me up at the gym and *not* taking me home.

I blink slow, clearing my head. *No*. To him, I'm like his kid sister. He'd never forget all the years and see me as any other woman.

He wasn't jealous. He was protective. Like my brothers.

But two things are certain. When we were alone in the bakery yesterday morning, and at the gym last night, it felt like it used to in all the best ways. I'm easy with him like I'm not with anyone else. I thrive in his presence.

And...I still want him.

As much as I did when I was sixteen and thought about him and missed him. And when I was eighteen and twenty and ready for it all and remembered him shirtless in his car after a day at the lake.

He gave me his number when he dropped me off last night, in case I needed a ride home again.

Maybe tonight...

My T-shirt sticks to my chest, and I breathe shallow. Sliding my hands down, I rub between my legs, over the sheet, the sudden urge to strip off everything almost scorching. I'm throbbing so hard.

I sigh. "I need to get my own apartment."

I'd lived in the dorms my entire three years at Notre Dame, but I opted not to have a roommate. Plenty of privacy. Not that I'd never touched myself with my parents in the house, but maybe I don't want to be quiet anymore. Or have to stick to my bedroom.

I'm late anyway. I need to get to Frosted.

I groan and sit up, throwing off the bedding. Grabbing my phone, I swipe and log in, seeing two missed calls from Hawke.

What does he want? I check the time of the notifications. 12:08 a.m. The last one was 12:45 a.m.

And that's why I put on a Do Not Disturb, Hawke.

If someone's hurt, they'll call my mom down the hall. The little amount of sleep I can manage is crucial, and my younger family members like to send me reels at one o'clock in the morning, or wait until 11 p.m. to invite me out on a weekend night.

Dropping the phone back to the nightstand, I head downstairs. The house is silent except for the grandfather clock that chimes four. Not even the stairs creak because our house isn't very old and my mom has carpet on the steps. They built this place just before I was born; Madoc getting the house he grew up in just a little way down our same quiet street. I'm not sure why my father gave up his home only to build another in the same neighborhood. It's one of the family secrets I still haven't cracked.

But I loved growing up here, outside the main part of the town. Sleepy, clean, and it smelled good. The surrounding forest made a great space for hikes, nature walks, and animal-watching.

There's not many people my age around here anymore, though.

Swinging around the banister, I head toward the kitchen. My parents usually wake up around six-thirty, and I think it's one of my favorite things about my profession. Having the house to myself for a little while before I head to work. It's different than staying up late. By then, I've had a full day, I'm tired, and not good for much other than Netflix and snacking. I have the energy to enjoy my alone time in the morning.

Rounding the corner, I head to the coffee machine, but as I scoop some beans into the grinder, dark forms loom in the corner of my eye.

I glance, seeing four men sitting in the dark at the kitchen table.

I gasp and jerk, dropping my spoon as I spin around. "Geez!" I gape at my brothers all sitting at the circular table with Lucas standing to the left, behind Jax.

What the hell?

What are they doing here? And in the dark, not talking?

"What are you guys doing?" I blurt out, leaning back on the counter to catch my breath. *Nearly gave me a heart attack...*

My pulse jackhammers, echoing in my ears.

But then I pause. Hawke had called in the middle of the night. And they're here now. Was he trying to warn me about something?

I float my eyes over all their faces, lingering on Lucas's for a moment longer than the rest. "What?" I ask them.

Did something happen?

Jared sits between Jax and Madoc, his back to the window. I can't make out his eyes, but he opens his mouth.

Madoc stops him, telling me instead, "We would..." He hesitates as if searching for words. "We would *prefer* that you not hang out with Noah Van der Berg or Farrow Kelly."

I falter. *Huh?*

"And definitely not together," Jax chimes in.

Madoc nods. "Yeah, definitely not together."

What?

I dart my eyes to Lucas again, who draws in a long breath before shifting on his feet.

That's why they're here?

"It's four o'clock in the morning," I point out.

Jax sits up. "We—"

"Four o'clock..." I bite out, swiping up my spoon again. "In the morning." Do they have any idea how crazy this looks?

I snap my gaze to Lucas. "You told them?"

How else would they have known I worked out with Noah and Farrow last night?

His eyes go wide. "I—"

But Madoc interjects. "*Everyone* knew except us," he barks, shooting out of his chair and bringing me his phone.

He hands it to me, and I see Farrow, Noah, and me online, doing pushups. Lucas and his friend hover in the periphery, lifting weights but watching.

I cock an eyebrow at Madoc. This is what drove them to my house in the middle of the night?

I click on the comments, the first one saying *#foreplay*. It has eighty-nine likes.

I grit my teeth, recognizing the username. *Dylan...*

And everyone has seen the video. Everyone in town, anyway.

Customers seeing me splashed online in my tight clothes, seemingly flirting with two young guys...

I shove the phone back at Madoc. Turning, I grind the beans and start the coffee maker. "Hunter is very close to Farrow," I explain calmly, "and Dylan is very close to Noah."

If they're good enough as their kids' friends...

"Noah and Farrow aren't trying to sleep with them," Madoc points out.

I clench my teeth so hard my jaw aches. "I can make competent decisions."

"And men like them," Jax snaps, "are very good at making sure they're the decisions beautiful young women make."

"Good thing they weren't in high school with you guys," I choke out, but don't look over my shoulder because Jared is being unusually quiet, and I'm afraid of why. "The competition would've been fierce."

"Cute," Madoc sneers. Then he moves away from me. "And what were you doing? Watching the whole time?"

I watch him charge for Lucas, who frowns. "Who brought her home?" he retorts. "I got rid of Farrow, didn't I?"

He got rid of Farrow?

He's why Farrow left all of a sudden?

But Madoc just keeps going. "I'll deal with him." Then he jerks his chin at Jared. "And you set Noah straight."

I dig in my heels, coming around the island. "Don't talk to Noah about anything!" I fire back, but my chin still trembles. "I mean it!"

Noah loves Jared. I won't have him feeling like he did anything to disappoint him.

They sit there, and I resist the urge to look at Lucas. If he sees the little amount of water in my eyes that always happens when I get upset, he'll pity me.

I gaze around at them, one by one, not really remembering when I first learned that Jared and Madoc's lives sucked as kids because of my parents. But I do remember the moment I felt that I wanted to be a good sister. That I wanted to be worth it.

Opening my mouth, I try to think of what to say to get everyone level again. To calm the situation, get them to trust me, and make them happy all at the same time, but... I just shake my head. "I have work." I exhale. "I'm not interested in Noah or Farrow."

I twist around, back to the counter, and dig out a coffee cup. I slam it down on the counter, more frustrated with myself than them now. What do they think they can do if I want to date someone they don't like? Ground me?

But I'm always the one to end the tension because I don't want them mad at me.

I know they want the best for my life. They wanted me to be the one sibling who had the charmed childhood, so they could live vicariously, but don't they see? It was in all of the trouble where they found out what they were made of.

My throat grows thick with tears. I barely know who I am. I always do what I'm told.

Jared still hasn't spoken. He feels a million miles away right now.

I wait for the machine, not bothering to turn around when I hear them slowly leave the table and traipse down the hall to the garage. They close the door, and seconds later, I hear their cars start.

Someone moves at my side, and I eye Lucas as he reaches into the cabinet behind my head.

I guess I was right, after all. He didn't stay close last night because he wanted to. He did it because he still sees me as a little girl.

"You used to be *my* friend," I tell him, braver with him than with my brothers. "You used to have my back while I was growing up." I jerk my chin toward the hallway where my brothers just disappeared. "Now you take their side?"

He trusted me more when I was a kid.

"Because they're right," he says in a stern, but quiet voice. "Noah Van der Berg and Farrow Kelly have reputations."

I shake my head. "Young men with reputations? Scandalous."

As if he, or my brothers, were angels at that age.

"I'm not kidding, Quinn," he says, setting down a coffee cup. "Noah is a womanizer, and Farrow is dangerous. They don't want to be your friend. They want one thing."

"That's not true," I spit out, gripping the counter behind me. But then I soften my voice, playing. "I'm such a good cook, I'm sure they'll want a hot breakfast when we wake up in the morning too."

He slams the cabinet closed next to me, and I jump. But I almost smile for the first time since I came down the stairs this morning. My heart is racing. I like talking back.

"You're not my brother," I tell him, and then mutter to myself, "And my brothers are not my parents."

I'm an adult.

He stares down at me, and I tighten my jaw.

"No." He shakes his head. "I'm not your brother, your father, or your uncle." His voice falls to a whisper. "And I'm asking you to stay away from them."

Something swells in my chest as his rises and falls, almost flat against mine. I can just feel his breath on my hair.

I drop my eyes. "But you leave tomorrow night," I remind him before looking back up. "Right?"

If Noah's my workout buddy or Farrow gives me a ride home, what's he going to do about it?

I walk away, feeling his eyes on me as I go.

Hours later, and I'm still riding my emotions, the embarrassment turning to anger. Not that it's been a bad thing because I've been moving my ass and chewing through little jobs—one after the other—since I arrived at the bakery this morning. My multi-tasking skills have broken a new record, I'm sure. The self-talk and rehashing the entire argument with my brothers and Lucas kept my legs fully charged and my awareness at an eleven.

I shouldn't have given in so easily with Madoc and Jax. There were so many things I could've said, like reminding them that I'm a grown woman, but as usual, I think best when it's too late.

I stuffed a glazed strawberry donut in my mouth for lunch without even the slightest bit of guilt. I worked it off before I even ate it.

"Thank you, everyone," I call out, putting chairs back down after Hailey mopped. "Good job today."

Noel and Codi slip out the canvas bags that line the bread baskets on the wall and take them to the laundry while Hailey finishes cleaning the case and counters.

"If you're working tomorrow, we're out of here by two," I tell them.

"Yeah!" Noel shouts, whipping off his apron that's stained with coffee.

I check the lock on the front door and head to Hailey at the computer. "Were you able to submit that order?"

"Done," she chirps.

One more accomplishment today. Delegating. I taught her how to order more inventory, and both her and Noel how to prep for lunch. I'm glad I had kept the menu simple and devised a grab-and-go section to alleviate the number of orders. They all learned quickly. Maybe now I can start staying in the back to bake more during the day so I'm not here so late.

I stick a few more things into the cabinets, watching Codi as she vacuums out the baskets and wipes the gold rings that hang from on the wall.

I smile to myself. As good of a job as these kids do, she's the only one who treats this place like it's hers. Meticulous, helpful, attentive...

Her light brown hair hangs in her eyes, the ends matted, and her navy-blue short-sleeved T-shirt stained with patches of flour. The same stains she got yesterday. I look down at her rolled-up jeans and flip flops. Everyone has to wear close-toed shoes here, for safety purposes, but she was already wearing them yesterday when Mace brought her, and today is her last day, so I didn't see the need to make it complicated.

I like that she's quiet, because I am too. But she could talk a little more. I don't think the others have spoken to her much.

Hopefully, she enjoyed spending time here. People are usually happy when they come into a bakery. They're always happy to see us.

Heading over, I take my cloth out of my apron and help her. "Just remember, everyone gets a shift treat," I say. "If you want a pastry or something to take home."

She nods but doesn't make eye contact. "Thanks."

They get a free meal if they're working a full shift, but Codi's been here all day. Essentially two shifts. And she hasn't eaten a thing. We did offer.

"What year are you at Weston?" I ask.

"I just graduated."

"College?" I press. "Any plans?"

She shakes her head, the matted locks swinging over her shoulders.

How does Mace know this girl? They're opposites in every way.

I look at her, trying to catch her eyes. "Do you have another job?"

Again with the headshaking, and I end it there. She doesn't want to talk.

I clear my throat, stepping away and touching the tip jar. "Can you split up the tips?" I ask her.

But before she can answer, Hailey grabs it. "I got it."

I glance at the redhead, assuming she's just being nice, but I see the glare she shoots Codi's back as the kid still wipes off the rings.

Hailey looks as if she doesn't trust her.

I inhale a deep breath. Weston versus the Falls. Things haven't changed. The people here still think Weston is all drug dealers and thieves.

But...I noticed last night that Farrow had that tattoo, and I know it's not a social club he belongs to. Mace has it, as well.

And Codi was with her. She might not be a criminal, but she knows some.

Everyone gets busy grabbing their backpacks and jackets, and I see Codi slide a brownie off the tray in the kitchen, quickly wrapping it in parchment before hiding it in her sweatshirt pocket. As if she's stealing something when I already offered it.

I should've made her eat today.

Hailey splits the cash, and everyone starts to leave.

"Codi?" I call before she disappears through the door.

She stops and turns, her eyes lifting to mine and then down again.

"Are you by any chance free in the morning? I could use you for another shift, if you want?"

She swallows, her eyes wide, and then she nods again.

"Five a.m.?"

Another nod.

"Thanks," I tell her. "Have a good night."

She leaves, giving a half-hearted bob of her head, and I lock the door behind them. I shut down the lights in the front of the shop and turn on some music, getting busy with preparing for tomorrow.

After tying up the bag of towels and aprons for the laundry service, baking three batches of brownies, and preparing dough for morning pastries, it's well after nine, and I have three missed calls from Dylan.

I saw her call. I let them all go to voicemail, but she didn't leave any.

I know what she wants. She's got some free time at the camp and wants to gossip. And more than likely see if I'm going to the gym again tonight.

I'm not.

He'll be there, though. If nothing else, just to chaperone me and cart me home afterward on my brothers' orders. I don't know how to explain it, but I don't want to make it easy on him. If he wants to talk to me again, he can come find me.

As the minutes tick by, I stick to my guns no matter how desperate I am to see as much of him as possible. In twenty-four hours, he'll be gone.

My stomach hollows out, and I lean into the counter, closing my eyes for a moment. He'll leave, having seen me as a woman like I waited for him to and having talked to me as an adult. And that will be it. He's not drawn to me.

I growl, pushing away the pain in my chest, and keep moving. I dig out some paperwork for Codi to fill out as I assume she's open to being hired as a formal employee—at least for the summer—and then I finish up the last of the dishes. Turning off my Bluetooth speaker, I head to the front of the shop and switch off the battery-operated lanterns on the tables that Noel forgot.

The space behind me creeps up, and the hair on my neck rises. I jerk my head, feeling someone behind me.

But there's nothing. The only thing there is, is my reflection in the mirror.

I let my gaze float to the left and right, a shiver coursing through me.

I was never scared of the dark, but I'm hyper-aware tonight. I shake it off and move to the bathroom, changing into my running clothes. For some reason, I feel safer out in the dark night than in here, and I hurry to dash outside and lock the door behind me before I jog out of the alley.

Sliding my phone into my pocket, I stick in my earbuds and start the playlist. One of my mom's favorites, "Cradle of Love" plays.

I jog, taking a right down High Street and then another right, into the same neighborhood I ran through a couple nights ago. I pass the pool and Mr. Zellers's yard, race up Fall Away Lane, and around the high school just as lightning flashes across the sky. I realize I've done a loop leading me back to Pine Street and Astrophysics. I don't turn in there. I glance, trying in the barest of moments to not look like I'm looking for his car, but turn back away before I can tell if he's there or not. He crossed a line this morning, and I'm not letting him get away with it like I do with my brothers.

I keep climbing up Hill Street, past Finch, and take a right on Lake, the area less populated.

And a little darker.

Lights from houses spill into their yards, and I see kids roasting marshmallows around a firepit, the adults with drinks in their hands.

Such a good town. Such a nice way to live.

I guess that's what I should think.

Yet, all I can think about are Jared, Madoc, and Jax. They lived here and grew up in nice houses, but they didn't always have nice people inside. My dad was rich and young and entitled with his first wife.

And my mom took her pain and drowned it in bottle after bottle.

None of this I'm supposed to know, but she made sure I knew exactly what her mistakes cost her.

She wrote her memoir and slipped me a copy years ago. She wanted me to learn through her.

All of them so scared of mistakes, so why am I dying to make one? I'd love to have a secret they'd all disapprove of because I'm tired of being quiet. No one hears my heart beat, least of all me.

I'm so lost in thought as I run that I hear the engine behind me rumble for half a minute before I actually register it.

I glance back, seeing a dark car coming up. Do they know their headlights are off?

I'm on the gravel, off the highway, but I inch over a little more to let the car pass safely.

Seconds pass, then thirty, and I look behind me again, still seeing it back there. Traveling slowly on an empty road, a lone figure in the driver's seat.

I breathe faster, my mouth going dry. I take out my earbuds and cut right, back into a brighter section of town.

I beat the pavement, my legs burning as I hear the car speed up.

Shit. I glance behind me, seeing it there again. It's following me?

Running, I make a sharp right down Pine toward Astrophysics. It's the one place I know is open twenty-four hours.

I charge ahead, reach the gym, and then stop, watching the car tread slowly down the lane I turned. It passes me, and I look, but the windows are tinted enough that I only see the silhouette of someone driving. No one else appears to be in the vehicle.

An old, black two-door. I spy the make on the rear, not needing to read it to recognize the font. My brothers tested me on every family road trip.

Dodge. It's an old, dark black Dodge. Maybe '70s model.

It takes another right when it hits the corner, heading back up Hill Street, and I dash over one more block until I hit my shop. I really don't want to be alone—I should've just gone to the gym—but I can't bring myself to call my brothers for help. I'd never live it down.

What if I lived in a city with no family? Or I find myself in a situation with no one to help me? I have to deal with things on my own.

I scurry down the alley, unlock my shop as I jerk my head every other second to check for sight of the car, and dive inside. I twist the lock.

I walk across my kitchen, through the door, and into the storefront, looking out the window for any clue that I was followed.

What the hell was that?

I heave breath after breath, feeling like I have a basketball bouncing inside my chest. What would I have done if someone had cornered me alone?

Air pours in and out of my lungs until finally, every muscle it takes to breathe is too tired to keep up the pace, and I force myself to slow down.

I don't think I should ride my bike home. It's too far. I could try for an Uber, but this town doesn't have many. They mostly operate on the weekends.

Shit. I wish I had an e-bike. Jax suggested it last Christmas when he was thinking about what to get me, but I resisted. They're so expensive.

Dammit.

I could crash in Dylan's bed since she's at camp. Her parents' house is only a block away. I'm sure Jared would love to know I'm tucked in safe behind his locked front door.

I turn to leave—to make a run for his house—but I look up and stop dead in my tracks.

A scream lodges in my throat as I gape at the wall in my shop. Thunder rolls overhead.

The mirror… *It's open*.

WESTON

CHAPTER SIX

Quinn

Rain hits the windows like darts, and I jolt, coming out of my trance.

"What the hell..." I breathe out, gaping at the wall mirror that's open like an actual door.

I pat my leg, feeling for my phone. Quickly, I snatch it out of my leg pocket.

Between this and the scene with the old Dodge, I can't catch my breath.

I unlock my screen, thinking. *Jared? Jax?* I could call them. They're closer.

They'll overreact, though. There has to be a better option. Dylan? One of my nephews?

But I scroll my phone, lingering over Lucas's name.

He would come. Immediately.

I try to push away the suspicion in the back of my mind that it's just a reason to see him, but it's not that. I... I just don't want to ask my family for anything. Before I know what I'm going to say, I dial Lucas.

I hold the phone to my ear, hearing it ring, but as if I'm waking up, I quickly jerk it away from my ear. "Shit."

I hang up before he answers, even though he's going to see that I called. I don't want his help, either. Not after this morning.

Taking a step, I start to move toward the kitchen, but I stop. Someone could be in there. Someone had to open the mirror. Were they going in or coming out?

I could go out the front door, but the car could be out there.

I dial Hawke. He's the one who made me keep the damn mirror in the first place.

But as the line rings, realization swirls in my head.

He made me keep the mirror...

Actually, he was adamant about it. *It's beautiful...it adds character...a great Instagram shot for customers...*

And you have no idea what problems are behind it. Deal with it down the road, he'd said.

My heart pounds in my ears, drowning out any other noise.

He knew about this.

They all knew about this. Kade, Aro, Hunter, Dylan...

Memories surge of the times they just seemed to show up and I hadn't seen them enter the shop. Or when food would go missing overnight, but I hadn't gotten a notification of anyone entering on the exterior security cameras.

My mouth falls open as shock and rage flood my chest and head.

The ringing stops, Hawke picking up the line. "You're up late."

I just stand there, words on the tip of my tongue, but they're the wrong words, and I don't know how to be sly. I'm not like them.

Do I want to call him out?

"Y—yeah," I stutter. "Sorry."

I'm not sure a fight is the way I want to go yet. I need to be certain he lied to me.

"Just wanted to touch base before I forget," I tell him, swallowing to wet my throat. "You seemed to love the mirror in my shop. Do you want it before I donate it? I'm having it removed tomorrow—"

"No, don't..."

Heat instantly courses through my muscles, and I exhale.

Oh, he knew all right. The whole damn time.

I open my mouth to yell at him, not just because I should've known about a secret entrance to my business, but he lied to me. They all lied to me. For how long?

My mind races, going back over the years and knowing they were in and out of the shop while I was away at school, but I just assumed they were being protective and checking on things for me. Or having some fun with the kitchen.

Why didn't they tell me?

My eyes sting. They didn't trust me.

"Why shouldn't I get rid of it?" I ask him.

"It's..." He pauses, then continues. "It's a surprise. Your birthday is coming up, so be patient."

A surprise...

I approach the open mirror, the ache in my chest steeling hard and cold. "Sure."

He's quiet for a moment, then asks. "You won't remove the mirror?"

"Nope."

There's a tense silence, and I don't think his mind is eased. Once we hang up, he'll probably call Dylan to panic. I might smile if I weren't so pissed.

I stop at the entrance. "Goodnight," I say.

"'Night."

I hang up, Hawke forgotten before I even take the phone away from my ear. If they've been in here, then it must be safe.

Heading to the opening, I stop myself just before I put a foot in and peek inside. "Hello?"

A long black tunnel lies before me, and I think I see an opening, but I can't make out much else. Black walls, dark floor, and it smells like a cave. Wet rock, earth, deep...

I open the flashlight on my phone, shining it inside.

The tunnel is bare and empty, the long walls a black or deep gray. I step inside and spin back around, pulling the door closed and seeing my shop through the two-way mirror.

"Those little shits," I grit out under my breath.

It's not a mirror from the inside. It's a window. I can see everything in the shop. Who comes and goes, who's working, what's stocked on the shelves, the register with the cash... But no one out there would be able to see me in here.

Raising my phone, I find the latch on the upper left and secure it, now knowing why the fingerprints I found last night looked like they were made from someone gripping the mirror from behind.

I unlatch it again and open the mirror, making sure I know how to get out. I close it again, just in case one of my family members with keys come in. I turn, light from my phone showing me the way.

My running shoes squeak on the floors as I step down the long corridor, the faint light at the end getting bigger.

I stop at the end, spinning my flashlight to the hallway to my right and back again to the room that spreads before me.

All at once, everything looms—the expanse of the massive space. The ceiling as high as three floors, bigger and taller than my parents' foyer. The high windows, wet with rain. The rusted, spiral staircase to the far-left corner, leading to a door in the ceiling. The kitchen with half-eaten bags of chips on the counter, and the living room beyond with the massive TV, couches, PlayStation, and liquor bottles on the coffee table. I run my eyes over some Latin words drawn in thick white paint on the back wall. *Vivamus moriendum, est.*

'Let us live, since we must die.'

It's an inscription on some statue at City Hall. I feel like I've seen it somewhere else too.

There's also some diagram with documents, pictures, and writing posted on the brick. Yarn links one idea to the other, creating a web, as if mapping a story.

I don't know how long I stand there, but it must only be about four seconds because I press my foot to the floor, realizing I stopped mid-step.

But still, I take all that in, fire spitting from my eyes. "Little. Shits."

They've been crashing here.

Hiding out to party and drink and have sex, and they were doing it in high school! I charge into the kitchen, whip open the fridge, seeing all the food. Sandwich stuff, condiments, leftover pizza, beer...

In a matter of minutes, I walk down the hallway, through the workout room and the two bedrooms, seeing clothes, a tube of Aro's red lipstick in one room and one of Kade's baseball caps in another. Not to mention a nightstand with at least five empty condom wrappers. I cringe. "Goddammit!"

Barreling out of the room and charging back into the great room, I head up the spiral staircase, open the hatch, and peek out onto my roof.

Or Rivertown's, I don't know. I need to find blueprints and see who actually owns this hideout.

I take in the scope of the space and the escape routes, and I descend the stairs, noticing another door. I peek inside, taking in another hallway. At the end is more light, and I make out Rivertown Bar & Grill through a window that I know before I even get there is another mirror just like the one in my shop.

So…

There are three entrances. Two mirrors and a roof hatch.

Is only my family using this space, then? They moved in the exercise equipment, the beds, and the TV. I recognize most of this stuff.

Heading back out to the great room, I scan the event map-slash-timeline they're puzzling together.

Carnival Tower…

Rivalry Week…

Winslet MacCreary…

I knew Hawke was researching the urban legends. This must be home base. I shake my head, turning my eyes away.

I start to walk out. I'm not sure what I'm going to do. My gut wants to react. Call them all and start screaming, but then what?

I pass the kitchen counter, heading to the hallway that leads back to my shop, but I put my hand on the cover of a book I don't remember seeing when I passed by here just a minute ago.

The brown leather is soft and flimsy, like a journal, and I can tell before I open it that the paper is old. The edges are yellowed and tattered. I pick it up, seeing a thin gap inside, as if something is stuck between the pages.

I look around the hideout again. I remember smoothing my hand over this counter when I came in. Was this sitting here then? Shit, I don't remember. I was high on adrenaline.

"Hello?" I call out. "Hello?"

No answer.

Flipping it open, the pages immediately spread to where a photograph sits. I lift it out, staring at a young blonde. She sits on the edge of a bed, I think. The headboard rests behind her, her bare arms stretched in front of her, just covering her naked torso. I can't see anything else of her. Long locks drape in her eyes, and a pink neon light casts a glow on her hair from somewhere behind.

I narrow my eyes, studying her. She kind of looks like me. I turn the picture over.

Don't look at me like that. You make me wanna die.

-*M*

Who's M? Not Madoc.

I fan through the pages, looking for a name, but there's so much writing, it's so small, and I can't make out anything. The writing looks different in the journal versus on the back of the picture, though.

I stick the photo back inside, but her eyes catch me before I close the book. I stop, gazing at her hair too long until I feel my own tickling my cheek. And the soft lips as if they're mine, swollen from a thousand kisses.

For a moment, I'm there—sitting on the edge of that bed, my body alive, and goosebumps spreading over my body as he takes my picture.

I peer closer, studying the headboard. There's a crack in the wall behind it. I remove the photo again and hurry back down the hallway, dipping inside the bedroom with Aro's lipstick. I flash my phone behind her and Hawke's bed, darting my eyes between the break in the wall and the one in the photograph. Sweat dampens my body.

This photo was taken here.

Different bed, but same room.

Who is this girl? How old is this photo? "M" isn't Kade, Hunter, Hawke, Dylan, or Aro. It's not Noah or Farrow. Who—

My phone rings, making me jump.

I clear my throat as I glance at the screen.

Lucas.

Then someone bellows, "Quinn!"

I spin around, running back to the hideout kitchen and slipping the picture between the pages of the book. Leaving the journal on the counter, I return down the hall. Lucas stands in my shop, his black track pants and white T-shirt soaked and dripping on my floor. He was clearly at the gym and ran here in the rain. Shit, I shouldn't have called him.

He looks around. "Quinn!"

Turning back and forth, he holds his phone to his ear. Patches of his wet hair look almost brown as he runs a hand through it, droplets of rain glimmering across his face. My cell vibrates in my hand, and I scramble to ignore the call before it rings. Then, I mute it.

He can't see me.

I ball my fists, feeling nerves fire underneath my skin because he's six feet away, and...

He can't see me.

I bite my bottom lip to keep the smile at bay.

Letting my eyes fall down the T-shirt that sticks to his taut stomach, I imagine my hands running over the dips and muscles. What does his waist feel like? His arms?

It's nice to just look at him.

Without being caught.

"Quinn!" someone else shouts.

I flit my eyes to the left, seeing Madoc push through the kitchen door.

He's dressed in sweats and a hoodie. They must've been working out together.

I turn off the flashlight on my phone.

"She didn't leave a message?" Madoc asks Lucas.

He shakes his head. "No." Then he disappears to the left and I hear a knock as he checks the bathroom.

"Well, her phone's here." My brother clicks away on his. "Somewhere..."

I tighten my fist around my cell. I forgot we can all track each other.

Lucas appears again, rubbing the back of his neck. I memorize the veins in his hands, the cords in arms, his long, tan neck...

He leaves tomorrow night, and I drink him in one last time.

"Her bike is still outside," he tells my brother.

It only takes Madoc two seconds to heave a sigh. "Fuck, she went jogging," he states. "Probably got caught in the rain. And without her goddamn phone."

Because I make irresponsible decisions all the time, right, Madoc?

My brother starts to leave. "I'm gonna jump in the car and go pick her up."

"Wait," Lucas barks. "I'll stay in case she shows up, but leave me the key in case you don't come back."

If Madoc finds me, he'll just take me straight home. Lucas will have to lock my shop up.

Madoc hands my key to Lucas before heading back through the kitchen. After about fifteen seconds, I see my brother's silver Audi cruise down High Street.

I watch Lucas, every inch of my body coursing with heat as sweat cools my neck. This reminds me of that day hiding in the attic at the summer camp. There's something about watching people. We might be afraid of what we'll see, but it's also the only way to find out what they're so desperate to protect you from.

Lucas approaches the mirror, and a breath lodges in my throat as he stares inside. I freeze as he stops inches from me, and I look up, only one step from his mouth.

He fixes his hair. Brushing wet locks back off his forehead, he breathes hard before lifting up his shirt and wiping down his face. My mouth falls open, gaping at his stomach, his chest…

I touch my fingertips to the glass, inching my body closer as if I'll feel his skin.

"Lucas…" I whisper.

He backs away, and so do I. My family stood here and watched each other and me just like I'm watching him now. All the times I thought I was alone, I might not have been. It's not right.

But maybe now I understand why Hawke and Dylan kept this a secret. There's power in this. To being right under people's noses.

They were worried I'd stop it.

I unlock my phone and call.

Lucas's phone rings a short distance away, and he glances at the screen, answering immediately.

"Quinn?" His voice sounds panicked, and I watch his eyebrows pinch together in worry. "You okay?"

What am I doing? Why did I call him?

But I know why. I needed to see what he looks like when he's alone and thinking of me.

I can't come out until he leaves. I don't think I want Madoc, Jared, or Jax to know about this hideout yet, and he would tell them.

"Yeah," I reply, keeping my voice low in case he can hear me through the mirror. "I'm okay."

"Where are you?"

"I'm safe."

He digs in his brow, his jaw flexing. "Where are you?" His tone is harder, suspicious.

Does he think I'm with someone I'm not supposed to be? I smile to myself. "I don't want to tell you."

"You don't want to tell me?"

His chin rises, his shoulders squaring. "Tell me where you are," he orders. "I'm coming to pick you up."

I know what will happen if he picks me up. He'll take me home. I'll sleep. Then, I'll get up in the morning for another day, and he'll leave town.

I'm not ready to go home yet.

"No need," I say in a light voice. "I'm having fun."

He paces, turning around, and I see the ridges of his back muscles through his soaked shirt. The picture of the girl in the journal sits in my head. She looked like the remains of a love that was too passionate. Too consuming.

It doesn't sound at all healthy, and I want it.

"Games were cute when you were a kid," Lucas chides.

But I simply say, "I don't play the same games I did as a kid."

He stops in his tracks, inhaling and exhaling for a moment. He's turned to the side, so I can't see his face until he pulls out one of my chairs and drops down. "I'm not enjoying this."

He sounds tired. Breathless.

"Quinn?" he presses when I don't say anything.

I study him. I don't want to talk about my family or Dubai or learning to drive or keeping away from the wrong boys. He's been talking to me like I'm still a child.

"What do you enjoy?" I ask.

He lowers his eyes, his chest rising and falling. I'm not a kid anymore, and I don't want him shielding me from his life or sugar-coating anything. I want to *talk*.

"Do you remember Ava, your college girlfriend?" I ask him, but I don't wait for an answer. He had a lot of girlfriends, and I don't care if he remembers her, because I do. "Madoc and his family were out of town, and you were supposed to come over to water the plants and feed the fish, but you brought her one night and got her naked in my brother's pool."

I lean into the mirror, taking my eyes off him only long enough to blink.

"I had seen your car pass and made you some pizza," I explain. "I rode my bike over with it so you could take it back to your dorm."

His gaze stays down on the table, his body barely moving. He never knew I saw them. No one did. It's not like sex was a secret to me, even at that age. I'd walked in on Jax and Juliet in Madoc's liquor storage. Jared constantly had his hands on Tate, and Madoc didn't hide anything, boasting that practice was the best part of baby-making.

However, as soon as I saw what was happening, I hightailed it out of there, only happy when they broke up.

Until the next one came along, that is.

"Boys get to have all the fun, don't they?" I challenge.

A small smile finally curls his lips as he picks a little flower out of the vase on the table. "I think Ava had fun."

Prick.

"And how old was she?" I argue. "About the same age as I am now?"

Maybe even a year or two younger?

I narrow my eyes. "What did you do to her that night?"

"I get where you're going with this," he bites out. "I know you're ready to feel things. And it's normal."

"How do you know I haven't already?"

He cocks a brow. "Have you?"

Amusement pulls at my mouth. "I'm twenty-one."

He curls his fist, crushing the flower.

I laugh to myself.

Oh, I like watching people. They don't always tell you who they are, but they show you.

Why would he assume I'm a virgin? I went to a Catholic university with a hell of a lot of people who grew up in Catholic schools before that. When sex is such a taboo subject, the allure and mystery surrounding it only make everyone sex-obsessed when they get away from home.

I mean, I am a virgin, but it's a leap for him to assume I didn't have one night of poor judgment away at school.

"I'm going fall in love with someone here," I tell him.

"It won't be one of them."

"Like you had plans to marry Ava when you had sex with her," I try to reason. "Why can't I—"

"Because you matter more than she did!"

I halt, the words on my lips fading away. What did he say?

It's like sparklers are fizzing and popping under my skin, up my chest, and down my arms.

He closes his eyes, and I'm afraid to move. To speak.

"I didn't mean that," he whispers. "Of course, she mattered."

But I matter more? I still matter to him?

His Adam's apple slides down his throat. "Quinn, I don't remember a lot from when I was a kid, but I remember you," he explains. "I grew up, knowing what it was to care for a girl—someone's sister, someone's daughter. It made me a better man."

His mouth opens, then closes, his eyes looking conflicted.

"At least, I thought it did," he murmurs.

I don't have time to ask to him to explain before he continues. "I didn't have any siblings or cousins," he goes on, "but with you I got to learn…to set an example and to be invested in someone's happiness. Someone smaller and more vulnerable in the world. You affected me in a way no one else did." He falls silent for a moment. "Quinn, sometimes people just want to connect and not be alone and have a good time. Blow off some steam. You're not built like that."

What does he know? He doesn't know me anymore. Why can't he see me like he sees everyone else? I'm not an angel. Or superhuman. I want to be touched and kissed hard and breathless, just like everyone else.

I don't realize that my eyes are filled with tears until one spills over. I swipe it away.

And why the hell did he leave for so long if I was important to him?

"I think I might be," I say, my throat so tight it hurts. "Built like that, I mean."

I'd go somewhere with him right now and not be alone, just the two of us, and I don't care if he's leaving.

But he asks again, "Where are you?"

So much like my brothers in his duty to keep me away from bad guys. He doesn't want to open up to me more, because if he did, I'd open this mirror, come out of hiding, and ask him to take me to practice driving tonight. Just the two of us.

I wipe my eyes. "Home," I lie. "It's raining. I got a ride from my barista. Tried calling you for one."

He looks skeptical. "How are you calling me from your phone? Madoc says you left it at the bakery."

I shrug. "I don't know. Tell him to update his app."

He falls silent, looking like he has more to say, but then asks, "Will I see you tomorrow?" Because he wants to leave on good terms with me remembering him well.

"Yes."

He nods. "Goodnight."

I hang up without replying and wait for him to leave. I guess I could sneak out through Rivertown, or the hatch in the roof, but I need my bike. I'd risk running into him.

He rises from the table and tucks in the chair, but he doesn't leave. Walking to the windows, he stands and looks out at the night rain. The strain in his eyes is visible from here as he folds his arms over his chest. The storm outside dances across his face in the lantern light from the sidewalk, and I raise my phone, snapping a picture of him. The only picture of him that's all for me.

Don't leave.

Is his life there so much better than us?

But then a vehicle passes outside, and Lucas lets his arms fall as he shoots to the side, out of view.

I freeze. What was that?

I glance out the window, thinking I might see the old, black Dodge, but I catch the tail end of a dark SUV—a Traverse, I think—go by. I don't recognize it.

Does he know that car?

He looks like he was hiding from it.

His phone rings, and he stares at the screen for several seconds before ignoring the call.

What's going on?

He leaves through the kitchen, the back door slamming shut, and I wait about two seconds before I flip the latch and climb out. Closing it back up, I run through the shop, spotting his car at the curb out front before I dash into the kitchen, hearing the lock click.

I wait until I hear his car start up at the front of the building before I dash out into the alley, locking up the bakery again. Then, I jump on my bike to follow him.

He could be going home. Or maybe he's going somewhere I need to see.

Desperate for answers, I pedal to the end of the alley and peek around the corner, his rental car appearing. He takes a right, as if heading to Madoc's house. Or mine.

As he approaches the curve, about to disappear, I take off, pedaling as fast as I can. Water sloshes under my tires, and rain soaks my hair, but I stand up and pump faster, just enough to stay in view. He cruises faster, speeding by the turnoff for Madoc's and my neighborhood, climbing into the forest.

Trees loom on both sides, darkness surrounding me, and I look behind me, keeping an eye out for the old car with its headlights off from earlier. And for Madoc who might still be out looking for me if Lucas hasn't texted him to tell him I'm home.

He continues to ascend the hill, disappearing around the corner, and I groan, my muscles on fire. An e-bike was a fantastic idea. Why did I resist it?

The road splits in two, but you can't go to the left. It's a one-way exit for the other highway, only for oncoming traffic. I veer right, continuing on, but as I reach the top of the incline, I don't see him. There are no cars. Nothing on the long stretch ahead.

I look around for turnoffs and then behind me, in case he pulled off, but he's gone.

Where the hell did he go? There's nothing for miles.

But I can't stay out here, and I'm not riding down some dark, lonely, gravel road. I got braver tonight, but not that brave.

Turning around, I head back into town, my head swirling. Where was he going? Who was in that car that he recognized? Who was in that damn car that followed me?

Why don't I tell him to stay?

So many questions, but as usual, I'm the last to answer them. I'm always the one who knows the least, the one no one trusts to be up for a little fun. Or even better, to lead.

There's only one thing I want more than Lucas Morrow, and that's my freedom from him. My freedom from everyone who loves me, in fact. From everyone who thinks they know me.

I park the bike in the alley behind the bakery, take my chain lock, and head inside. Once in the hideout, I climb the spiral staircase, loop my bike lock around the handle and the latch, securing the door tightly from the inside.

One door down, two more to go.

The hideout is mine now.

SHELBURNE FALLS

CHAPTER SEVEN

Lucas

I envy Farrow Kelly and Noah Van der Berg. For their youth. For their proximity to everything I love.

Unease has been chipping away at my mind like a pickax, and talking to Quinn tonight on the phone made it worse.

I want to go home. To Dubai.

I miss the restaurants. I miss the pool at my gym. I miss coming into my office building and hearing the music Isobel has playing because she's already been there for two hours and loves having the place to herself before everyone arrives in the morning.

My mind calms there.

But I'm dreading every minute that passes too. Every second that takes me closer to my flight leaving. Why?

The time on my phone reads 1:36 a.m.

The party still goes on. Sitting in my car at the curb, blending between two SUVs, I can't take my eyes off the firehouse about thirty yards down the street.

Green Street. The name of the road, the firehouse, and the people inside. The headquarters of Weston's racketeering, which according to my research, includes crime that isn't as petty as I'd hoped it had become in Drew's absence. Hard drugs, weapons, embezzlement, thievery, prostitution...

Hugo Navarre runs it now, and I guess that's who's been trying to call me. It's a local phone number that I didn't have saved, and with the car parked outside of my house a couple of days ago, it's a safe assumption they know I'm back.

Green Street wasn't always bad, and Weston wasn't always rundown. The faded red brick firehouse still stands three-stories tall, surrounded by a parking area overrun with grass and weeds, unmanicured trees, and a quiet road, dilapidated from years of neglect. The town is a quarter of what it used to be. Maybe two-thousand people now. There are no police, and barely any businesses to service the community.

This mill town across the river from Shelburne Falls was once an eclectic place, I'm told, with hiking trails, restaurants, and community gatherings like carnivals, car cruises, and bingo nights at the VFW. Always a little poorer than Shelburne Falls, but it had its own character.

Unfortunately, a flood more than twenty years ago instigated a mass evacuation, and most of the citizens never returned. There's a spot in the forest full of cars that had to be moved off the streets when they were abandoned in traffic because no one could get out, and people needed to find higher ground quickly.

Many houses were destroyed, but the buildings downtown still stand. The massive warehouses, mills, and anything made of brick. The thousand or so windows that once had lives and stories playing out behind them are now just views into rooms of silence.

I glance down at my shoes, the ones I wore to the gym when I tried not to look for her, or wait for her, when I was there earlier. Caked in fresh earth, I shouldn't have worn them out to the forest tonight. They'll leave easily identifiable tracks.

With the rain, I'm hopeful my prints are already gone, along with any other evidence of my visit to the grave. I shouldn't have driven out there at all, but I needed to face it one time before I left.

It's such a lonely place. Dark. And cold.

Forgotten.

Engines zoom past, and I count four motorbikes speeding to a halt in front of the firehouse. My elbow rests on the door as I rub one of my fingers over my lips, watching Farrow Kelly climb off his bike. No helmet and his hat on backward, he swings open the door that I put on that fucking place twelve years ago. Three others follow him in.

Quinn won't have the future she deserves with someone like him. I don't want Green Street to touch her at all, and if that means I can't be in her life either to ensure my past doesn't spill over onto her, then I'll continue to live without all of them.

Even though it feels like it's going to hurt to leave this time a little more than it did the first.

I was so desperate for something of my own back then that I sold my integrity for nothing.

It didn't seem like it at the time. Young and excited, we only saw life getting better and better. Remembering that first day, it's amazing how little I anticipated what Green Street would become.

Or how shit would change for me.

"What are we doing here?" I griped, climbing out of Lance's 4Runner.

"I've got something to show you," he called out, running for the old building. "Come on."

Drew Reeves jumped out from the back seat, leaving his black ski cap and buffalo plaid button-up on even though it was clear we weren't hitting the slopes. At least, not yet.

Lance broke his arm last week falling wrong on a black diamond run, and I thought he insisted on coming today so he could sit in the lodge and get drunk, watching us have fun.

Instead, we were in Weston, or what was left of it. This town had been dead since I was a kid.

Following him around the side of the building with its door missing and all the windows broken, I winced at the stench that hit me as we entered. Damn, did an animal die in here?

The water line from the flood more than a decade before rose up the walls about two feet, and various pieces of furniture sat broken, ripped, and decaying. I wandered deeper in, the large cement floor and closed garage door to my right allowing for one fire truck, or a few smaller vehicles, to fit inside. I let my head fall back and gazed up at the fireman's pole.

"It's the old firehouse," Lance explained, "but it's got a kitchen, bathrooms, and a shitload of space."

"For what?" I asked.

Drew kicked a piece of wood out of the way, hands in his pockets as he strolled.

"A hangout." Lance grinned.

Drew and I stared at him.

Like a biker clubhouse? I laughed to myself.

"I mean, it's the deadfuck of winter," he pointed out, gesturing to his arm. "I'm useless on a snowboard, and I know you two won't have any fun on the slopes without me, so what do you think?" He held out his arms like we were eleven and he'd found us a treehouse. "By summer, we could elevate the hell out of this place. Clean it up, a little paint, a bar..."

"Someplace away from girlfriends..." Drew chimed in.

And Lance added, "...with our other girlfriends."

I shook my head, knowing exactly what would happen in this place, and all of it with the express purpose to fuck something.

Might be fun for a night, but...

I don't know. *Maybe we could put in a pool table. A gaming system. Could be cool, I guess. Someplace to hang out—away from family and school—where we could relax. Maybe that was what I needed. A home of my own with a family I made.*

Madoc never made me feel like an outsider, but it's been a long time since he didn't have to stretch his attention. Fallon, his brothers, the kids... I've wondered for a while if I should still be one more person he has to tend to.

Maybe it was stupid that I still hung around? I was an adult, after all. And they weren't my family.

"Do we rent it?" I asked.

"We can buy it," Lance told us, lowering his voice as if he was telling a secret. "The bank that owns it is out of Chicago, and they consider the real estate here a non-starter. If we get approval from the remaining city council, it's doable between all of us."

Or Lance and me, anyway. Drew didn't have any money, but Lance was trying to be nice. I wouldn't have to use all of my inheritance from my dad for college.

But still... "Why do I want to own a run-down, old building before I own a house?"

"This is a house."

"It's *our* house, Lucas." But it wasn't Lance who said it. I glanced at Drew, his hands still in his pockets and his shoulders relaxed.

He approached and gripped my shoulder where it connected to my neck, squeezing with a light in his eyes.

I'd known these two since we started college two-and-a-half years ago. Now, here we were, last half of our third year, and we'd kept our circle small and close. I liked my friends, and for the first time, I had people I chose rather than people who were obligated to care about me. Not that I'd ever felt like a burden to my mom, but it was nice to create my own circle. Madoc would never tell me I wasn't welcome anymore, but his life was very different from when it was just us. I was a responsibility he didn't need anymore.

"What do you want to do here?" I teased.

"Oh, I plan on being my own worst enemy," Drew replied with a smirk. "And you can handle security."

Security?

I pinch my brow. "You want cameras outside?"

I'd installed them for my mom a few months ago.

"And in my room," he added.

Lance snorted, and I just drew in a breath that felt heavy already. He said shit like that to make me nervous, but I knew he wouldn't film girls in his bed.

And definitely not without their knowledge.

Drew headed to the back, toward a staircase, and spun around. "First dibs!" he called.

Lance darted after him, and I followed, joining them in exploring and daydreaming of the possibilities. My mom would freak if she found out I spent money on something like this. Madoc, on the other hand, would want in. He never really grew up, in all the right ways.

Staring out an upstairs window, I spotted a little girl, maybe eight, with a ski cap covering the top of her head and dressed in an oversized hoodie as she carried a backpack. She trudged through the snow in what looked like broken Doc Martens and stopped in front of a darkened shop window. Quickly surveying the area, she jammed her elbow into the glass. It broke, and she reached in, unlocking the door before she opened it and disappeared inside.

Drew and Lance were in another room, no one but me seeing her. And to my surprise, I didn't move. Didn't call the police. Didn't run to stop her.

Madoc has showed up for me for years. Made sure I was seen. Remembered.

No one in the Falls remembers that Weston is still here. It's my turn to show up for others.

Weston became my cause, like I had been Madoc's. I had the best of intentions, but in the end, my intentions weren't the legacy.

Hours later, and I wake up in my teenage bed for the last time. Tonight, I'll be on a plane.

I check my phone. *9:48 a.m.*

I haven't slept that late in years, but I blame the jet lag. And the fact that I didn't get to sleep until almost five. Quinn was already at the bakery. I saw a small light on when I passed by. After our conversation on the phone last night, I couldn't sleep. Even when I got into bed, I struggled.

It wasn't so much her words, but her tone. Playful. Inviting.

Promising.

Like she had a world of adventure in front of her, and she finally realized it. What I wouldn't give for that feeling again.

She was toying with me, but fuck, if I were Noah or Farrow...

Where would I take her? I'm lost in my head, dreaming a pointless dream where I'm younger. A different man with a different life and a pretty young woman like that is talking to me.

Heat rushes to my groin, and I shut my eyes. *Shit*.

Climbing out of bed, I grab the compass off my nightstand and walk to the window. I find north-northwest.

What would my life be like if Green Street never started? If I'd never met Drew Reeves, or fucked up in a way that altered my life in one moment?

I would've stayed.

The summer looms ahead, warm rain and lake days and eating outside on Madoc's patio...

I had it good.

My phone rings, and I jerk my head, on alert for Hugo Navarre. I'd ignored the call last night, too worried about Quinn, but I wanted to talk to him.

He's not worried about the trouble that sent me away. He's worried, because I still own that building. After a while, Lance hadn't wanted any part of it, so I bought his half. I should've went with him.

I don't give a shit about the building. I want nothing to do with any of it.

I pick up my phone, seeing the real estate agent's name, instead.

I answer. "Paul."

"Good morning." He drags out the last word like a musical note. "Good news. I have someone who'd like to see the house."

"Already?"

"Today, if possible," he says.

That was fast. Of course, it doesn't mean an offer, but the listing just went live yesterday. Selling a house can take years in some cases.

"Would you be able to leave it available to us?" he asks. "Around noon?"

I'd love to know who's interested in the house. Could it be Quinn?

She mentioned craving a place of her own, and she certainly has all the co-signers she could ever want for a loan in her own family, but I have a hard time believing that she'd ask them.

"Okay," I tell him. "Sounds good."

What else can I say? It's probably not even Quinn. If it is, I can talk her out of it before she signs.

"We might have an offer today," he tells me.

"Yeah." It would be perfect to get this settled before I fly away. "That's great."

"Talk soon."

After we hang up, I throw on my workout clothes before getting busy tidying up the house. I make the bed, knowing whoever buys the house gets that too. I have no idea what else to do with it.

I start boxing up my father's memorabilia and pack my clothes into my carry-on, removing the laundry I threw in the dryer. I put away my laptop and chargers, and make sure the food and drinks in the fridge are thrown away.

My old Cubs cap sits on a radiator, and I turn to toss it into a box, but I stop, staring at it. I'm supposed to give her the compass back now that I have the hat, but she's barely asked for it. Maybe she'd rather have the hat.

I still can't believe she was just wearing it—eight years after I gave it to her—when I saw her the other night at the gym. She didn't know she would see me. Pinching the bill between my fingers, the memories come flooding back from the last time I held it like this.

When I was giving it to her...

Dropping my gaze, I saw Quinn looking at me again, but once more, she quickly turned away.

I let out a sigh, starting to feel some of that guilt Fallon talked about. Quinn had known me her entire life. Thirteen years. I guess I could muster up a 'goodbye' even when all I wanted to do was leave.

Walking over, I stopped next to her and knelt down. "I'm going to miss your croissants, you know?"

Her frown deepened as she continued to stare at her paper. "They'll probably have better food and restaurants where you're going anyway."

"But they won't be made by you."

I was trying to soothe her, but she wasn't having it. I didn't want her to be mad at me, but I knew it was hard for a kid her age to understand.

And there were things I couldn't explain to her right now. She was too young. She should be happy and excited without a care in the world, and I hated that she was wasting even one minute of her time thinking I was going to be worth missing.

"Well, stay trained up, okay?" I nudged her shoulder with my hand. "I might be back to visit soon, and I'll expect to try some of your new recipes."

"You won't be back at all," she mumbled, still not looking at me.

"How do you know?"

"Because everyone lies to make people feel better."

I narrowed my gaze, studying her. Where the hell had she come up with a thought like that?

She finally lifted her sad, brown eyes. "You'll find new friends and forget about us."

I shook my head, no clue what to say next. Would I make friends where I was going? Probably. Was I sure I'd be back? No. Right now, I never wanted to come back here.

But I wanted her to feel better, so, without thinking, I took off my cap and fit it over her head, chuckling when the visor part fell over her eyes.

"I will be back," I argued. "I'll have to get my cap back, right?"

She plucked the hat off her head, her eyes going wide as she studied it.

"You can't give me this," she breathed out, stunned. She knew it was my father's and how much I loved it. But for some reason, I didn't feel like I would miss it if I knew it would mean something to her.

"I already did," I shot back. "So take care of it, okay?"

Standing up, I cast her one last smile before turning around to head to my car. I needed to get out of here. I was lying to her. I was lying to everyone. I had no intention of returning, even for the baseball cap. I just didn't want her to hate me. She was the only person who thought I was a hero.

"Lucas!" I heard a yell behind me.

I spun around just in time to see Quinn dig in her backpack and pull out something small. Rushing over to me, she handed me the circular metal case.

"Now you have to come back." She smiled and then dashed off, back to her seat on the ground.

Pinching my eyebrows together, confused, I opened my hand, immediately recognizing the compass her mom gave to her one year for Christmas.

Shit. *This was vintage and an heirloom. If she didn't want it back, her family would. I couldn't keep it.*

I flipped it over, studying the piece, and saw the words inscribed on the back. "Happiness is a direction, not a place."

She was wise, even then. She knew that no matter where I ran, I'd bring my shit with me.

I set the Cubs cap down next to my keys to take to the party tonight. I want her to have it. If I can't be here, my heart can.

I clean out the sink and wipe down the counters, hearing the doorbell ring. I toss the cloth down and head to the door.

A FedEx driver stands on the porch. "Lucas Morrow?"

I nod. "Yes."

He hands me a phone with a stylus. "Sign here, please."

I scribble my name and swap him for the package, closing the door.

I inspect the box, recognizing the Dubai address. I sigh, wondering what emergency I missed that my assistant needed to overnight a package from across the world.

But as I peel open the tissue paper, I don't see a tablet or documents inside. A small white box sits on top of a soft, white twill button-down, and I pick it up, rubbing the fabric between my fingers.

My stomach sinks. *What is she up to?*

Setting the shirt down, I open the smaller package and take out a bottle of cologne.

I cock an eyebrow as I swipe up a card with my assistant's writing on it.

Leave three buttons open.

And wear the cologne. It's lethal. I want to impregnate every man who wears it.

Have fun tonight.
-Isobel

Impregnate. A laugh catches in my throat.

And what does she mean, *tonight*? To the cookout at Madoc's? How does she know about...?

But then it occurs to me. My calendar. I'd put it in my phone. I box the shit back up, ready to get it out of the way for the real estate agent and potential buyer.

But...

I do need a clean shirt tonight.

Quickly, I remove it from the box and hang it up in the closet, setting the box on the floor.

Taking my laptop case, I walk to my car at the curb, sweeping the street for that Traverse I've seen twice now. I want to see it. I want to know who's inside and that Madoc and the others are safe if I leave.

The street is nearly empty, though. I climb into my car.

I'll kill time at the gym, catch up on some emails, and maybe get some lunch before I head back here to shower and see Madoc for the last time.

It would be better to blow it off and leave now.

But I know I'll go to the party, and I know why, even if I push the thought away before it can take form.

I just want to make sure she gets the hat back. That's all.

A breath stuck in my chest, I drive to Madoc's.

I go through the list in my head. *Say goodbye to Tate, Juliet, and all the kids. Madoc and Fallon will be last. Don't forget Jason and Katherine.*

Farrow Kelly and Noah Van der Berg will probably be there as friends of the families. I don't need to address them.

And give Quinn the hat. Assuming I can keep the compass.

What if she's not there? I punch the gas, telling myself it's better if she's not. I'm a little worried about looking into her eyes and saying goodbye again.

It'll be good to get back home, though. To the salty sea air. The spices and sunbaked desert. The sounds of the music pouring out of shops and the feel of my sheets.

Unable to stop the image before it comes, I see Quinn in my head, on top of me and barely shrouded in the shadow of the drapes over the moonlight that streams through my window in my apartment. The sheets fall down her legs like water as she presses her body into mine.

My mouth falls open. What would it be like to have her out there with me, all to myself, for a visit? I could. No one would think a thing if I looked out for her while she travels. And we wouldn't be here, so I wouldn't have to be on guard. I mean, why not?

All to myself...

Another image flashes through my mind, her in my bed, every night...

Her moans hit my ear, and my groin swells and aches, making me groan. The car swerves, and I jerk the wheel, tires screeching under me.

My chest caves. *Fuck.*

What the hell? Sweat breaks out on my forehead, and I breathe hard, trying to keep the car straight.

It's Quinn.

Quinn!

Dammit.

I pull up to Madoc's house, halting quickly, and leave the Cubs cap on my passenger seat this time. It's the last business I have with her. *Later*. If she shows.

I grab the bottle of top-shelf Scotch whisky instead, unopened and left over from my father's things, that I want Madoc to have.

The massive, circular driveway has nothing in the center—no fountain or flowerbed—just a basketball hoop on the far left where I played with Madoc a few times. I loved being here, and in my memory, I still hear the ball bounce and the leaves blow on the crisp fall days.

The space is now filled with cars. I take inventory of Jared's Dark Horse, Jax's McLaren, a couple of JT Racing work trucks, several others I don't recognize, and three motorbikes.

Quinn's bicycle isn't here.

Madoc opens the door as soon as I reach for the handle.

I smile, holding up my bottle. "Brought the good stuff." I step inside. "Let's compare."

He takes the liquor out of my hands. "Happily."

Fallon had warned me he distilled some of the worst Irish whiskey her father had ever tasted, but Madoc made sure to also add that her father drank it every time he visited. I've never tried Irish, so cheers. I just hope I stay sober enough to get myself on a plane tonight.

He closes the door, and I walk with him through the foyer. "You invited too many people, didn't you?"

"Psh..."

I cock an eyebrow. That wasn't an answer. He knows I don't like to be the center of attention. He has Kade for that, unless that kid has changed.

Jared's wife Tate approaches, followed by Fallon, Jax, and his wife Juliet. I glance behind them, taking in the patio full of people. Music vibrates against the sliding glass doors.

I embrace Tate. "Hey."

She squeezes me and then pulls back. "Oh, you smell good."

I chuckle. *Good call on the cologne, Isobel.* But I look around, making sure Jared wasn't in earshot of that.

Dylan, who I'd seen briefly at the camp a couple of days ago, pushes through and wraps her arms around my neck, giving me a quick hug. "Lookin' good," she says, pulling back and surveying me. "But the boys are gonna mess you all up. They want to play football." She tilts her head side to side. "Well, Kade wants to play football."

Quinn isn't here. I almost ask where she is, but it'll seem like it's the first thing on my mind.

Everyone trails outside, and I spot Lance with a young brunette, as well as some locals I vaguely recognize who probably work for the Caruthers and Trents. Others appear to be college kids, friends of Dylan, Hawke, and the others.

"What time's your flight?" Madoc asks.

"Not till eleven."

We stop at the bar, and he turns to face me. "I wish you were staying."

"I have a meeting first thing Monday," I tell him, fighting the regret in my voice. "No place to stay for long anyway. I have some interest in the house already."

His eyebrows dart up, and I glance around the patio, searching.

"That was quick," he replies, but I see his expression falter. "That's... good, I guess."

Yeah.

"And you always have a place to stay." Fallon passes by, placing a tray of fruit on the patio table.

Madoc pours us a couple of drams of each other's whiskey, and we sip each, testing the Scotch versus the Irish. I blow out a breath, the Irish burning a bit more. But not bad.

I pour another two fingers, the last of his bottle, as he laughs. Victorious.

"I'll be right back," I tell him with a smile.

I walk over to Lance, taking another swallow and letting the liquor warm my nerves. The early evening breeze carries the scent of lilacs and grass, and a memory washes over me of how fast summers went when I lived here because I looked forward to every day so much. All of the outside activities everyone enjoyed—swimming, canoeing, concerts, picnics, ice cream runs, yard work, barbecuing, roasting marshmallows, and dining al fresco.

But the pull of north-northwest, where my dread is buried in a shallow grave in the woods, slides up my neck. I wouldn't love the summers here anymore. Not like I once did.

I step up to Lance, forcing a smile as I look down at his companion who wears a rock on her finger that glints in the torch lights set up on the grass.

"Marie?" I shake hands with his new wife. "I'm Lucas. Nice to meet you."

Her lips spread in a bright smile, drawing attention to the freckles on her nose. Quinn's are fainter. I wonder if they still become more prominent in the sun. "You too," Marie says.

I gesture to her husband. "He making you happy?"

"For now," she jokes.

My friend scoffs, she makes a face at him, and he grabs her around the waist and hauls her in for a kiss. I smile to myself, wishing that was my life for a moment.

One little decision. That was the only difference between him and me. One decision charted very different courses for us.

She inches away, walking backward toward the pool and winking at her husband.

We watch her sit down next to a friend and sink her feet in the water.

"I'm happy for you," I tell him.

But he doesn't reply, just looks down, takes a drink, his brow troubled.

"You okay?"

His chest rises with a big breath. "I keep feeling like the shoe's going to drop, you know?" He gives me a nervous smile. "Like something will creep up and take her from me or she'll just wise up."

I see the pulse in his neck throb, and I flex my jaw, completely fucking jealous. He doesn't think he deserves to be this lucky, but he does.

"I guess that means I'm fucking in love with her, doesn't it?" He lets out a small laugh.

"It's nice to have a life you're afraid of losing."

Maybe I should tell him everything. Everything that happened all those years ago that he never knew about because he was gone from Green Street by then. Maybe then he would know how lucky he is and be present in every moment possible.

"You made some good choices," I tell him.

But his face falls anyway. "I keep feeling like if I hadn't taken all of us to that building in Weston, you'd still live here."

"No," I tell him, forcing my tone to stay even. "It went to shit, but that wasn't the reason I left."

Why don't I just tell him? Tell someone?

But if I don't talk about it, then I can pretend it's not the reason for nearly every decision since.

His lips twitch. "I *know* something's wrong, and I don't know what else it could've been."

I swallow the rest of my drink. I need to change the subject. "Well, I'm a little lonely," I tease. "Should I stick around? I can scoop up your girl when she finally leaves your ass."

He laughs, moving toward her. "Well, then I better have my fun with her while I can." And he flips me the middle finger with a smile.

I watch him go, feeling like we're twenty-two again for a split second.

He sidles up to her side, dropping his hand to her hair, and I set the glass down, moving around the deck, past Madoc. "I'll go get another one of your bottles," I tell him. And I veer for the side of the house.

Heading down the small hill, I make my way toward the basement entrance, but I catch sight of something massive and colorful and utterly ridiculous far out on the lawn.

It moves as people jump in and out of it, and I narrow my eyes, trying to remember if it's someone's birthday or something.

Is that a bounce house? Or eight of them, maybe? It's huge.
What the fuck?

A collection of inflatable jumpers sit attached like a small city out on the grass, every single one in motion as kids—and teenagers—bounce around. There's a long, interactive one with a slide and climbing walls, as well as two castles, a couple of obstacle courses, and ones with tunnels. Kade springs down a slide, doing somersaults.

And the scent of pizza hits my nose, goosebumps spreading across my arms.

Slowly, I turn and see Quinn behind the counter of the outdoor kitchen, the pizza oven behind her. My heart leaps in my chest.

She wears a canvas-colored apron, her swimsuit strings tied around her neck.

"I know what you're thinking," she says before I say anything.

"Yeah?" I ask, playing along.

She nods. "What the *fuck* is that?" she recites, jerking her chin at the inflatable city.

I just laugh, walking over and taking a seat on a stool at the counter as she places pepperoni on a pie. "That's Madoc," I explain. "You forget. I've known him longer."

With her brother, no one is too old for toys.

"Do you think he knows he just invented a whole other meaning for 'bounce house' once his son gets Dylan in there?" she jokes.

I shake my head, amused. Yeah, the party will be going long after the parents have gone to bed. That's for sure.

Madoc had told me the whole story of Dylan and Hunter, and how he almost lost his life to his best friend.

But he was laughing his ass off the whole time explaining it to me too. Apparently, I missed a good fight.

Still, though, it's hard to think of Dylan and Hunter as old enough for love when they were like eleven the last time I saw them. And Quinn's older. I can imagine being surrounded by couples will have her dying for someone of her own. I trail my eyes over her bare shoulders, her slender neck...

Why did I come down here?

Her hair is tied back in a high ponytail, flyaways around her face, with the apron covering her swimsuit-clad body. Thank God.

I glance through the clear basement doors, not seeing a soul watching TV or gaming. She's alone, just the distant laughter of everyone playing and the music above.

"Are you hiding down here?" I tease.

"Yes."

Why is she cooking? There's plenty of food on the patio, and she worked all day.

But the thought creeps in... She knows I love her pizza. Maybe she's making it for me?

She takes the pizza and turns, sliding it into the oven. Her back, bare except for the strings of the bikini top and apron stretches long and slender, looking soft.

And tight and smooth...

My body stirs, heat rising up my neck.

She wears red shorts over the bottoms.

Pulling out a finishing pizza, she rolls a cutter through it, slicing up eight pieces. Everything except mushrooms. My favorite.

She slides a piece onto a plastic plate and hands it to me. My stomach immediately growls. I've barely eaten today.

I pick up the scorching hot slice and take a quick bite. Sucking in air, I move it around my mouth so I don't burn, but the cheese won't break. It stretches eight inches from my mouth, and I laugh, pinching it off with my fingers.

I chew, the seasoning like a goddamn party on my tongue. "Shit," I groan.

She leans her elbows on the counter, picking off a piece of pepperoni from one of the other seven slices and pops it into her mouth. "The cheese or the sauce?" she presses.

"Both."

She grins. "I started putting a pinch of red pepper in the sauce."

I take another bite despite my tongue being burned. "Don't make this for either of those dipshits, okay?" I warn her. "I don't want to wake up in Dubai to your wedding announcement."

This would put any man in the palm of her hand.

But she doesn't smile at the joke, just softly holds my eyes in a way that makes my heart stop for a moment.

I bite off another piece, then stuff another in my mouth. "Something wrong?" I ask.

She shakes her head, chewing. "No."

"Something good?" I inquire instead.

"Maybe." She rises up. "But you seem to be on my brothers' side lately, so I don't know if I can trust you."

She can trust me to want what's best for her.

"Don't you think they'll find out anyway?" I ask, curious now.

"Sure," she whispers. "They'll find out after they can't stop me."

I square my shoulders. So she's buying my house? Is that the secret? I should tell her not to, simply because it's an expense she doesn't need at her age, but I don't. Not tonight. She'll probably change her mind anyway.

I watch her lift a beer to her mouth, and for a moment, I freeze, entranced as her lips take the bottle.

She's drinking. Alcohol.

Because of course she is. She's twenty-one. A woman.

"Excited to go home?" she suddenly asks me.

I wet my lips, replying in a clipped voice. "Yeah."

"Packed?"

I clear my throat. "I'll leave for the airport around eight-thirty."

I check my watch. My bags are in the car.

My heart pounds, a brick settling in my stomach.

She stares at me, and I force myself to hold her gaze.

"Do...do you have someone there?" she broaches quietly. "Someone who makes you happy?"

I don't know if I'm imagining it, but she looks like she's holding her breath.

"Sometimes." The pain in my chest grows. "You don't have to worry about me."

I check my watch again, the seconds barely passing. The next two hours will be hard, but they're going to be harder around her. I need to move. Talk to someone else.

"That smells fucking amazing," a deep voice blurts out, coming downhill from the front of the house.

I turn my head, seeing Farrow Kelly in jeans and no shirt, carrying a motorcycle helmet.

Without missing a beat, he invades Quinn's space behind the counter and wraps an arm around her waist, diving in and taking a bite off the slice she holds in her hand.

"Farrow Kelly," she scolds as if they fucking grew up together.

"Stop," he mumbles over the food in his mouth. "You know what 'teacher voice' does to me."

I narrow my eyes, glaring, and I don't care how it looks. What the fuck is going on?

Releasing her, he picks up the rest of the pizza—my pizza—and folds the whole damn thing in half, eating it like a taco.

She throws him a look, but he just shrugs. "You owe me," he states, throwing me a sideways glance. "I had a bunch of shit to do today, and what did I end up doing? House hunting with—"

"Take the pizza," she barks.

House hunting...

With Quinn? He went with her to my house?

Or...my parents' house. Whatever. Why would she bring him?

Sweat dampens the back of my neck, my heart starting to thump against my chest.

"See you soon," he coos, leaning into her. "We're going to have so much fun."

Excuse me?

He leaves, heading for the lawn and the bounce houses as he chows down on *my* pizza.

Quinn lifts her eyes to mine, and I open my mouth to say more shit I shouldn't. There's no reason she needs to be enlisting any male's help, except mine or her family's. Why would she trust Farrow Kelly, of all people?

But someone interrupts us. "Quinn, come on!" Dylan calls.

Quinn hesitates a moment, our eyes locked and my moment to act presenting itself, but I don't take it. She removes her apron and circles the counter.

"I'll see you before you leave," she tells me.

I think I see her chin tremble, but with the fire in my chest and the fog in my brain as I try to decipher what all just happened, I can't think.

I'm paralyzed as I watch her go off with Dylan and some brunette, heading for the bounce houses where Farrow Kelly just disappeared.

Noah Van der Berg jogs after the girls, their little group trailing off like I'm already gone. She just left as if she wasn't always looking for me when she was a kid.

She never walked away from me.

Every muscle is tight, and my jaw hurts from clenching.

I'm in the wrong. I know I am. She's happy. She has people her age close to her. That's good. That's great. Everything's as it should be.

I place my hand on my chest, rubbing the pain over my heart.

WESTON

CHAPTER EIGHT

Quinn

I put my hand on my stomach hoping that will curb the queasiness. *Just keep walking,* I tell myself, feeling his eyes on my back. If I hang on his every word until he leaves, I'm scared I'll cry. It's better this way.

"I have thirteen minutes." I stroll across the lawn, Dylan and Aro at my sides. "Pizza's in the oven."

Plenty of time for him to get back to the party and start making the rounds of goodbyes.

"Plenty of time to make him nervous," Dylan teases instead.

Noah hauls himself up over the side of the first bounce house and disappears inside. We start climbing a ladder of plastic stairs. "Make who nervous?" I ask, still keeping up the charade that every decision I've made since I was thirteen hasn't been with Lucas Morrow in mind.

Dylan looks down at me from above. "Quinn."

"Dylan," I mimic but more curt.

I want to be left alone, and my family is about as skilled at reading body language as they are at reading ancient Greek. The steel in my eyes better be clear. Are they really so dense that they can't imagine how I'm feeling right now? That I'm dreading every passing minute, and I'll wake up tomorrow without the hope he'll ever come home again? What would she be feeling if it were Hunter?

Not to mention, I'm still pissed about them keeping a secret hideout right under my nose, too. Other than locking it up, I'm still deciding whether to confront them just yet.

I won't take anymore meddling where my life is concerned, and that includes Lucas.

"It was a crush," I state, downplaying it as we all climb up to the top of the slide. "When I was thirteen."

"And when you were twelve and eleven and ten..."

"Just stop," I tell her, looking behind me to Aro too. "And I don't appreciate you two thinking it's fair to use Noah or Farrow to make him jealous, either."

Sending them to Astrophysics, putting them in my path, and not telling them why?

But Aro retorts behind me, "I promise you they are *only* interested in being used by you."

"Fu..." I toss my head back, letting the swear word die on my tongue.

I find it hard to say "fuck" in front of others.

Dylan chuckles, and I can feel Aro's smile at my back.

We reach the top and jump down, into the obstacle course. "Everything is better in hindsight," I explain.

I don't need to be twenty years older than them to know that.

"Lucas has changed." I shrug. "He's not very friendly anymore. Almost snobby, actually."

I don't admit to them that some things are so much better than I remember. His eyes on me and how they linger. His body and how much stronger he looks. The electric current that races through my blood when he's close.

Other things have turned sour. He never acted like he was raising me, and it's too late to start now. He treated me more like an adult when I was a kid.

I go on. "It's like any connection I manufactured as a teenager never happened. It was all in my head." I realize my brow is pinched and relax it. "He's a stranger now," I tell them, hoping I sound convincing. "And old."

"And hot as hell," Dylan blurts out. "Men get better with age. Did you smell him?"

I glance back and spot Hunter approaching behind her. Scowling.

"His body feels like he was made in the most elite factory," she says, completely unaware her boyfriend is right behind her.

He reaches around and gently grabs the front of her neck, hauling her back into his chest.

Tilting her head back, she looks up at him, her eyes widening. "Well, I wasn't trying to feel—" she stutters as he twists her around and backs her into the wall. "...feel him up. I just hugged him, and it was hard not to notice."

"Notice what?"

She presses her lips together because she's about to smile. "How. Hard. His. Body. Was."

Her voice is filled with mischief and laughter, and Hunter bites her bottom lip. I suppress the gripe rising up at the sight of my niece and nephew. No, they're not blood-related—their fathers are stepbrothers—but it's still an adjustment. I grew up with us all being family, and I haven't been around much the last twenty or so months that they've been together to get used to seeing them maul each other.

She breathes out, blushing up at him. "I forgot what I was going to say next."

I leave them to it, climbing the blow-up rock wall with Aro. We descend the little slide and start making our way through the maze of columns.

"Dylan's just trying to help you get what you want," she says behind me. "She means well."

"I know."

I know that's what they think. They *all* mean well.

"But you are unhappy he's leaving," Aro says matter-of-factly.

"I'm unhappy my younger family members, including you, for all intents and purposes"—I throw her a look—"see me as pitiful and unhappy because I'm not in love."

"Are you happy?"

"That's not the point!" I scold. "It's invasive!"

I didn't mean to yell, but I want to put them all in their place once and for all. I'm not a failure just because I won't play games to seduce my childhood crush on his last night in town.

Even though I am trying to avoid thinking about what I would do if he was sticking around. At least for another night.

I should've stayed with my pizza back at the oven. I was just angry. Didn't want to give him the satisfaction of having all of my attention as if he mattered. When we clearly don't matter to him.

"You're right," Aro says softly. "But family is like that, I'm learning." A smile touches her eyes. "They're the only people who ever get to see your true colors. But that also means you see their no-filter, advice-when-you-didn't-ask-for-it, beautifully suffocating colors too."

Yeah.

I close my mouth, remembering that her parents weren't there for her. Not many people were, and she obviously prefers her new life full of interfering parents and people to count on. Am I out of line? It's hard to think clearly now.

I climb the next ladder, and she follows.

"If you did want Lucas," she broaches. "Where would you take him?"

"Aro..."

"Come on." She sounds playful. "I know you haven't thought about it *at all*, but where would you do it?"

I reach the top and look to my right, seeing him in his white shirt that fits him perfectly. It's not hard to see what's underneath. He stands on the patio, but his head is turned toward the bounce house.

I draw in a breath, murmuring, "His place, I guess."

"He's selling his place."

True.

My mind whirls, thinking about how it would happen.

Uncontrollable. That's the word that springs to mind. He wouldn't be able to control himself, and neither of us could stop.

"His car," I say quietly.

She smiles. "Ah," she sighs, looking lost in a memory. "I took Hawke's virginity in a car."

An unwanted picture of the two of them in some cramped back seat, sweat making their skin stick to cracked leather, floats through my head. "Ugh..." I grunt. Seems so uncomfortable, and I'm not even talking about the car so much. This family overshares.

We leap down, bouncing out of balance and crashing to our stomachs. I laugh for the first time.

She turns on her side, and we continue to rock with the motion others make in the obstacle course. "You need a place of your own," she says. "Maybe it's time we help you with that."

Hawke's words from a couple days ago drift through my head. *We'll tell her when she's ready to use it.*

They were talking about their hideout. That's what Aro's referring to. A place where I can screw around like they do.

"I might have a place." I sit up, the wall we just leapt from swaying and jerking with someone else ascending from the other side. "I put in an offer on a house today."

She shoots up. "What?"

"Don't tell anyone." I lower my voice, but I can't keep the joy off my face. "I don't want to deal with my brothers until there's no turning back."

"Why are you telling me?"

"Because I think you're the best at keeping a secret," I explain, "and I'm too excited to keep quiet."

She gapes at me, and I feel even happier about that. I surprised her. I don't surprise anyone.

I called Mace, who called Farrow, who helped me take a look at my very own house. He had his own place, knew the area, and I trusted him to keep quiet, because if he knows something the ruling elite of Shelburne Falls—my brothers—don't know, then that might amuse him.

I'm still nervous, though. What if it's a huge mistake? It would take damn near the last of my safety net in the bank, and it needs renovations. At least the mortgage wouldn't be bad.

I see myself standing at my new living room window, looking at the street outside in my new neighborhood, and I can't stop feeling this incredible warmth inside my chest and down my arms.

My brothers are going to be so pissed.

"Then I'm excited for you." She climbs to her feet and helps me up. "A new place to party."

Oh, that's right. Jared, Madoc, and Jax won't worry at all if they're at my house because Quinn never has parties.

I stop to think. Will I have people over? I'm sure I will, but I can't say the thought of an alcohol-infused bash with a bunch of people, many of whom are younger than me, is enticing. Images of small get-togethers hit me, and that might be nice. Girls' nights. Intimate chats with friends. Suddenly, goosebumps break out across my legs, the idea of my own space solidifying in my head. I love it. No more constant questions. *Are you home? When will you be home? A little early for work, isn't it? Who was on the phone?*

I draw in a huge breath, so large I didn't realize my lungs could hold so much. Soon, I'll be able to cook in a home kitchen and not have someone who's worried about me or maybe loves me a little too much making a pressuring comment or asking a question that feels like I'm still fifteen. I'll have empty rooms, all to myself, and I can come home whenever I want, because I'm the only one with a key.

We continue through a tunnel, and I look behind me for Dylan, but she must still be detained by Hunter.

Afraid Aro might pry for more info on my recent purchase, I search for a change of subject. "Have you ever seen an old black Dodge around town?" I call out to her.

I wanted to ask anyway, and now's a good time to get information without the whole crew on top of us.

"Old?" She sweeps her hair up into a ponytail. "How old?"

"I don't know cars that well," I mumble. "Maybe '60s or '70s?"

We push our way out and through more inflatable columns.

After a pause, she finally asks, "Why do you want to know?"

Why aren't you answering the question?

"I was jogging the other night," I tell her. "It..."

I don't want to make her worry too.

"I just didn't recognize it but thought it looked familiar," I say, side-stepping it. "You all know everyone with a car, so I thought I'd ask."

She turns, and I can't tell if she bought that or not. Aro's smart.

"There's a '72 black Dodge from Weston," she finally tells me. "An auto-shop car at the high school. Lots of people drive it."

An auto-shop car...

Okay. That makes me feel better, at least. It was just kids pulling a prank.

A crowd comes crashing in behind me, and Aro hops over a little wall to get out of the way.

A blond head rushes me, and a breath catches in my throat, seeing Lucas, but it's just Noah.

"Wanna jump?" he asks, leaping up and down.

My face has fallen, but I quickly soften my expression to answer.

Farrow walks past, interjecting, "You just want to see boobs bounce," he tells Noah.

"Are you talking?" Noah gripes. "Again?"

I drop my eyes, double-checking my breasts are still fully in the top. I wasn't worried till now.

I start to cross my arms over my chest, suddenly self-conscious, but I lower them again, not wanting to be awkward.

Noah must've seen my insecurity because he removes his T-shirt and hands it to me.

I look at it. Then him.

His soft smile reaches his eyes, not a single hint of a hidden agenda written on his face. He's nice, isn't he?

I take the shirt, gazing at his tanned chest and thick arms. Dylan says he used to chop a lot of wood, but I wasn't sure if she meant something sexual.

"Thanks," I tell him.

I slip the shirt over my head and he darts off, catching Codi as she and Mace fall down a wall.

He grips her waist from behind. "Gotcha."

She looks over her shoulder, that same doe-eyed, silent expression fixed on him as on everyone, including me at the shop all day.

He sets her down, but no sooner does he let her go than Farrow grabs the waist of her jeans and yanks her back to him.

"Did you ask for his help?" he growls, his eyes on Noah, his mouth next to her ear.

She shakes her head slowly, and I frown, ready to intervene.

She's Weston. Same as Farrow. I know they're territorial about their people, but...

"You want him touching you?" Farrow asks her.

Another head shake.

Codi stands frozen, not even trying to get free, and although I spent several minutes in Farrow's company today, wondering how he can be a criminal, it doesn't seem like a stretch now. He changes faces quickly.

I reach over to grab her away from him, but in the same instant, he releases her. Following her over the wall, he disappears out of sight.

I realize I'm breathing in short, quick bursts, and I'm more grateful for my new place now. I'll be keeping an eye on her. I don't know if that was for Noah's sake, or if Farrow purposely intimidates her on a regular basis, but I don't like it.

Maybe Noah is exactly what she needs.

"She works for me." I walk with him. "You should stop by."

"I'd rather blow a pinecone than fuck with whatever that was."

I let my mouth fall for a moment before I break into laughter. I guess with Farrow keeping a leash on every Weston citizen, it might be more trouble than Noah cares to invite. Understandable.

He gently nudges me in my stomach. "Hurry."

Then he rolls over the wall, somersaulting into the next section.

I like him. He's easy to be around. Easier than Lucas.

And so is Farrow. He's flirtier than Noah, but I never dreaded dealing with him when we were together today. He never made me uncomfortable.

Except, of course, during the episode with Codi just now.

I need people around me who aren't family. Not that I can't count on every Trent and Caruthers, but for my own sense of autonomy, I need to *not* need them for everything.

Farrow will stay firmly in the friend zone. He's not serious enough. I would never be certain if he really liked me, or if I was just a game.

Noah, though... I don't know.

Maybe...

But...my heart never stops when he looks at me. Not like it does with...

I stop, clenching my teeth. *Stop thinking about him!* Why is he in every other thought? Damn.

"What do you mean 'it's locked?'" I hear Kade snap from somewhere.

I jerk my head toward his voice.

"Carnival Tower!" I hear Hawke grit out. "I just came from there, and it's fucking closed up."

I stop and veer to the makeshift window with netting separating me from the outside. I press myself to the wall next to it, hearing them out on the grass.

"I don't understand," Dylan says.

"What don't you understand?" Hawke sounds out of breath. "I can't get in. Quinn warned me about renovations she's planning, so I went to clear out some essentials, and I was locked out!"

Carnival Tower. So that's what they call it.

I fold my lips between my teeth to stifle my amusement.

"You tried the roof?" Hunter chimes in.

"Oh, yeah," Hawke mocks. "Should've done that. Completely forgot." Then, in a bark, "Yes, I tried the roof! I tried Rivertown too. The phones are in there, and I haven't finished gathering the data from the one left at Quinn's shop!"

I stand up straight. The phone left at my shop? I lock my jaw. Hawke took that phone from Lost and Found?

What the hell is going on? My lungs swell with pain. The fuck?

What other phones? What data? What the fuck are they doing?

"It's Manas or Deacon," Dylan speaks up next. "It has to be. One of them left her the phone, just like they've kept leaving us phones, so we know they're around."

"At least one of them," Hunter adds.

Manas and Deacon... Are they dangerous?

"Why would they lock us out now, after years?" Aro questions.

"Because they're using it now?" Hunter offers.

Someone else breathes out, "Fuck."

Manas and Deacon. Two people they know who have been leaving them phones. For what? Phones like the one that was left at my shop? Old ones?

It's not these two characters who locked them out of the tower, but someone did leave the phone at my shop. That man the other night. The one in the suit who stayed late and didn't speak.

He left it for *me* to find. He has access to the hideout? My chin trembles.

"It's time to tell her," Kade says.

"Manas won't hurt her."

"And if it's Deacon?" he retorts.

"It's not a coincidence that they leave another phone and lock us out right after she returns home," Hawke states.

My mind swims. Have these men been watching me?

Dylan whispers, "She looks like Winslet."

My God. I don't know what to think. It's all coming too quickly.

"And she just asked me about the '72 black Dodge," Aro tells them.

I bow my head, leaning into the wall again. A tear spills over. They're all having this conversation *about me* without me. It's like this secret life they all lived and didn't include me. Why?

Fucking pairs.

"It was following her the other night," Aro goes on. "Who's in possession of it?"

"I have no idea," Hunter tells her. "I haven't seen it in a year. I'll ask Farrow."

"Discreetly."

"We should've told her ages ago," Dylan chides. "She's there a lot and alone. It was never one hundred percent safe."

"We weren't sure they were sneaking into the tower," Hawke argues.

But Kade barks. "Bullshit!"

My mind races with all this new information. Two men they seem to know, but are scared of, sneak into the hideout and leave clues for them, for what? That story they're puzzling together on the wall inside? How could they be so stupid? To put themselves in danger and me, unknowingly. It's like I'm... Like I'm their fathers, whom they didn't trust to not react.

Damn right, I would've. And I did. They're never getting back in there.

Hawke lowers his voice. "It's the Night Ride."

"What?" Aro asks.

"Aro said she asked about the black Dodge," he points out. "Carnival Tower, Rivalry Week, and The Night Ride. The next chapter."

What does that mean?

I stand there, listening for more, but I don't hear anything. I peek out the window, and they're gone.

I stumble into another bounce house, wandering and lost in thought. How long has all of this been going on? Hawke talked me out of removing the mirror years ago, before I went away to college. I can't even begin to list all the reasons I'm pissed. And who are Manas and Deacon? I'll go back into the Tower later, see if I can make sense out of the mystery they have strung together on the wall.

Two strangers concerns me, but if my own family didn't warn me... And who is Winslet? The girl in the photo rises to the front of my mind.

You make me wanna die.

She was pretty. Where is she now?

There's a mystery in the tower and strangers coming and going, and my nieces and nephews don't think I know anything.

I stand there, swaying with the bouncing, and...

They don't think I know anything.

I smile a little.

What should I do?

Minutes pass, A.J. and James fly through, and we bounce. *Maybe I'll pull a prank of my own on Hawke and the rest.* I leap high and race Noah over the rock wall and follow Farrow, both of us somersaulting through a tunnel with a water sprinkler. *Maybe I'll figure out the next chapter he talked about.*

I laugh and sweat and let it go, the promise of new nights in my new house ahead of me, and for a second, I let myself stop counting the minutes.

I collapse in an orange tunnel, hair in my face, Noah's T-shirt sticking to my skin.

The pizza. Shit.

But for some reason, I don't vault up and out of the bounce house. Dreamy images of my—hopefully—new bedroom with the leaky roof and the raw, unvarnished floor consume my thoughts.

You make me wanna die. His whisper hits my lips.

Yes.

That's where I would take him. To my new bedroom floor.

"Quinn?"

And I open my eyes.

Lucas? His voice rings in my head like a dream I'm not sure was real.

But then he calls again, just behind me. "Quinn?"

SHELBURNE FALLS

CHAPTER NINE

Lucas

I stand there, on the grass at the opening of the inflatable tunnel, waiting for her to reply.

She lies there, in the dim light. Is she asleep?

"Quinn?" I call out again.

"I'm here."

Déjà vu floods me, remembering Camp Blackhawk years ago. The last time she was hiding. I'd listened to everyone calling out for her that day, knowing the whole time where she was. I didn't even hear her up there. I just knew how her mind worked. Quinn only plays when she knows she can win. Which is why she rarely plays.

I'd forgotten about that day. How her eyes caught sight of my tattoo, and how I rushed to cover it up. I remember resenting her quietness in that moment. It made her a better listener. A better observer. I knew then that she rarely missed anything, and I panicked that she might tell someone about it, but I didn't feel right asking her to keep secrets.

She never told anyone, though. Not to my knowledge. Madoc has never inquired about it.

When she doesn't move, I ask, "Can you come out?"

"Come in."

I breathe out a laugh and climb inside. As I move toward her, she sits up and leans back against the wall of the tunnel.

"I took out the pizza," I tell her, "but Jared and Madoc are already eating it."

She chuckles. "Thanks."

I wasn't able to get another piece, unfortunately. I'm tempted to smuggle a jar of her sauce into my luggage.

"I wanted to give you something before I leave." I sit across from her, my heart pumping in my ears. What time is it?

I take in a little air, unable to get a full breath. I pull out the Cubs cap from my back pocket and hand it to her. I'd gone to my car to get it, and I'm not sure why I didn't wait till I was about to leave, but...

She looks down at it, her expression unreadable.

But then a voice interrupts us. "Quinn, don't get my shirt wet!"

She darts her eyes up, addressing the voice somewhere outside the tunnel. "Too late!"

I take in the dark green T-shirt she wears over her bikini top that I hadn't noticed till now.

Noah's shirt? Splashes of water are sprayed across the fabric.

I flex my jaw. They became best friends quickly, didn't they?

I hand her the hat. "Its home is here," I tell her.

Her face softens as she takes it. "You mean, I can keep it till the next time you return?"

The next time I return... Something about the way she says it—kindly, but with an air of finality as if she knows I won't be back—leaves a hole in the pit of my stomach. Quinn notices everything.

"It's yours," I tell her.

She doesn't look at me, just brushes her fingers over the red C on the front of the hat. She's had it in her possession a long time. I never expected to own it again.

But she hands it back to me. "Really, it's okay." She sets it in my lap. "I'd prefer you have that part of your father with you. Besides, you're right. I should be wearing a hair net anyway."

She smiles with that same relaxed air again as if she's already said goodbye.

I close my fist around the bill of the hat—a piece of me—that she no longer wants. That she has no interest in looking in the mirror to see. I search her eyes for a falter—a chink in her armor. Is it really so easy for her? It's like I'm disappearing from her past too.

But what do I want from her, really? If she looked sad—cried—what would I do? She was upset the last time I left. But seemingly, not now.

I stare at the shirt she wears, my eyes starting to burn. She has distractions now.

"Take off his shirt," I say through my teeth.

I squeeze at the hat in my hand, feeling her go still.

"Excuse me?" she asks.

I lift my eyes, forcing the edge in my voice to ease up a little. "Before your brothers see." I move past her, climbing out of the tunnel. "It'll set Jared off on my last night here, and you know he's like a bullet. Once shot, you can't bring it back."

I hope I sound convincing. Having Quinn pissed at me is the last thing I want in this moment, but I couldn't stop myself.

She follows me out, and I weave slowly through the obstacle course and up the next wall, jumping rather than sliding down the next side.

She coasts down, still wearing the shirt.

I lock eyes with her.

Peering up at me, her spine straight, she doesn't blink as she finally slips it off, over her head, and her body comes into view in her skimpy bikini top. Her hair falls back down around her, a little wet. Locks blanket her breast, drawing attention to the curve of a tendril as it drapes over her full and supple skin.

Jesus fuck.

Heat pools in my stomach, my body stirring, and it's like she has a hand fisting my collar and is pulling me in. My fingers ache, empty and begging. If... If she were any other woman. God, any other woman, I'd have backed her up into the corner and kissed her.

Goddammit. She knows exactly what she is doing.

Kids I don't recognize run through, jumping high and falling all over the place. Quinn grabs my hand to steady herself, and I draw in a sharp breath, instantly clasping my fingers around hers. I almost let my eyes close, a jolt spreading up my arm.

God, get it under control. It can't happen.

She stands back upright again, but I don't let her go, both of us leaning into the corner for support.

"It'll pass," she laughs, holding my arm with both hands now. I take Noah's T-shirt from her, hanging it out of my side pocket.

The kids bounce over and over, the house underneath us rocking and swaying, and I plant my hand next to her head to steady myself.

She laughs quietly.

I gaze down at her and try to ignore the buzz on my skin at how close she is. By midnight, I'll be gone. Back to where I'm solid. Back to where I belong. What will she be doing tomorrow?

Or tomorrow night? This moment, right now, will be long gone. In an hour. In ten minutes. And in thirty more seconds, I won't be here with her. This close, smelling her and touching her where no one can see us. I turn my head away so she doesn't see how I can barely breathe.

"Why do you like them?" I ask, trying to keep her to myself as long as possible.

My voice is barely a whisper, but I don't mean to sound like I'm telling a secret.

She looks thoughtful and then shrugs a little. "Maybe it would be nice to have someone to talk to, after all."

"You have family."

"It's not the same thing. They can't really talk to me, can they?" she presses. "Do I really want to know what my family members are doing in private?"

More kids race through, leaping and crashing.

"If I share, so will they, and I'm not interested in the mental image of Hunter sinking his head beneath Dylan's sheets, for crying out loud." She offers a little smile. "But then that means I can't tell them private things, either."

I narrow my eyes. Like someone with his head under *her* sheets?

She looks away. "I need someone to talk to."

We rock like we're on a boat, and I open my mouth to say something, but I don't know what. If this was ten years ago, I'd tell her she can talk to me. She used to have that.

And I would've told her she can be friends with anyone she wants. I don't want her to feel lonely.

It's different now, though. Am I really that worried she'll get hurt by some guy? Honestly, it's probably the best thing that can happen to anyone. She'll probably cry over three or four guys before she finds the one meant for her.

Darts of water hit us, and Quinn and I jerk our eyes up, seeing Madoc's daughter and Jared's son shooting their water guns.

"Brats!" Quinn teases.

The eleven-year-olds giggle and come somersaulting over the slide, A.J. barreling toward us.

Quinn pushes into me, squealing, and we tumble to the floor. I start to catch her, but her knee jabs into my dick, and liquid fire spreads. I gasp, squeezing my eyes shut at what feels like fifteen fucking needles impaling my balls, creating a lightning storm down my thighs and up into my stomach.

I grunt, starting to curl up on reflex. "Oh, shit." I try not to cry, forcing it to come out as a pained laugh, instead.

She sucks in a breath and pushes herself up. "Oh my God." She looks down at me, horrified. "Are you okay? Did I..."

"Yeah, you clipped me a little bit," I grit between my teeth, trying to breathe. "Fuck."

I don't know where the kids went, but they're gone, and I just try to manage lying still as the pain gets worse before it gets better.

Quinn's body trembles on mine, and I pry one eye open. Laughter gleams in her eyes, her lips trapped between her teeth.

"Are you laughing?" I burst out.

"I don't mean to be." She winces. "Can I do anything?"

I realize my arm is around her, my hand at the curve of her waist. I move my fingers just a hair, the feel of her skin making my fingertips vibrate.

"Yeah, get off me," I joke, jerking away. "So I can get the hell out of here before you kill me."

But as I rise up and offer her a hand, her smile has fallen, her expression torn. I didn't mean 'get out of here' as in 'the country.' Just the bounce house.

Finally, she takes my hand and I tug her up.

I gaze down at her, easily lost in her brown eyes. Eyes that have seen me as a boy and counted on me when I was a man, trusted me, and looked right through me, the same now as they ever did. Eyes that gravitated to me with all of her questions and kindness and ease.

"You can do better, you know?" I say, continuing our conversation about Noah and Farrow. "You're not the type of girl to go for guys like that. At least, I never thought so."

Her expression falters, pain hitting her eyes, and I don't try to apologize. It was a shitty thing to say, but I want to hurt her feelings. I'd forgotten the kind of man I used to be in her eyes, and I hope I forget again just as quickly.

Before she has a chance to move away from me, we're surrounded. Kade shows up with a backpack, as well as Hawke, his girlfriend, Hunter, Dylan, and Farrow.

"Nice hiding place." Kade looks between Quinn and me as he digs into his backpack. "Let's do a toast."

What time is it?

He starts tossing tubes of something pink, which I can only assume are shots.

Dylan catches one. "Yesss."

I check my watch. *An hour and a half left.*

I should just leave now. Fuck it.

"Want one, boss?" I hear someone say and raise my eyes to see Farrow holding a tube out for me.

Boss...

The gleam in his eyes meets the ire in mine, and I glance around, no one really noticing. Or registering any meaning to his choice in words.

When I don't reply, he pulls the shot back with a small smile, everyone uncapping theirs and raising a toast.

"To no school and no books," Kade announces.

"Oh, you love books," Hunter fires back.

"Fuck off," his twin gripes. "You know I can barely read."

Everyone laughs, but I watch Quinn toss back her shot and pull another one out of Kade's backpack. She's the only one old enough to drink, other than me, but I watch her the closest. She's going to be drunk in fifteen minutes.

"To Fallstown and the lake," Dylan chimes in.

Followed by Farrow. "And a summer of fun!"

"Ow, ow, ow!" Kade and Hawke howl, everyone raising their drinks high and then swallowing them down.

And as Hawke and his girlfriend toss theirs back, extending their necks, I see them. The tattoos, just like Farrow's.

My chest caves, the ink still on my back that Quinn noticed all those years ago suddenly burning.

They're Green Street too? What the fuck is going on?

Quinn tosses the second empty tube back in Kade's backpack and leaves, hopping over a low wall. I should talk to Hawke.

I debate for a moment, but then follow her over the wall and up another one, walking down a small slide. She hits the grass, finds her flip flops, and heads across the lawn, back toward the patio.

I dig in my heels, powering after her and tossing Noah his shirt as we pass. I see him look at me, but I don't stop.

How much has Weston infiltrated Shelburne Falls? Hawke wouldn't be doing anything illegal, would he? Jax raised him better, and these kids have choices.

Fuck.

Everyone is eating, drinking, and laughing, segregated into small groups around the pool as music spills out of the speakers. I make my way straight for Quinn, but then Jared is there, wrapping an arm around her shoulders and tugging her in close.

I halt.

I should apologize. I want to leave her with a good memory of me, at least.

I can't see Jared's face, but he talks to her with a folded piece of her pizza in his hand. She nods, and they seem happy.

Just leave. She probably wants to stop looking at my fucking face anyway.

Gritting my teeth, I turn.

But Madoc is there, beaming at me. "Just in time." He puts an arm around my shoulder and turns me back to face the crowd. "May I have your attention, please!"

Ah, shit.

"I know most of you made sure to be here," he announces, holding a drink in his hand, "because I always have an open bar, but there is a deeper reason."

"Madoc…" I beg him to stop.

The music cuts off, and out of the corner of my eye, I see Quinn and Jared turn toward us.

"When I was sixteen," Madoc tells everyone, releasing me and addressing his guests. "I met this kid who supposedly needed a strong, level-headed, positive, and well-behaved male influence."

Chuckles and snorts go off around the pool.

"But he got me, instead," he teases, throwing me a look. "I tried to be a big brother to him, set an example, give him advice, and show him the ropes, but the more time I spent with him, the more influence he had on me, instead." His tone softens, thoughtful. "I started watching cartoons again, and remembered how good cereal tasted, and I started rooting for the Cubs."

"Go White Sox!" someone shouts.

Others clap and cheer.

But I can't unclench my jaw, everyone's eyes like lava on my skin.

I was so nervous the first time I met Madoc, but I shouldn't have been. He was a pro. It took me all of four minutes to get attached to him.

"He was supposed to be the one who needed me," Madoc says, his voice gravelly. "But the truth is, I was heartbroken when I met him. I'd lost someone very important in my life."

I tilt my eyes up, finding his wife on the other side of the pool. She smiles small through her chin trembling and the tears in her eyes.

Years later, I found out that while I was losing my father, Madoc was a teenager, losing the girl he loved. He was suffering, too, the day we met, not that he let on.

"And I was acting like an asshole because of it," he explains to his guests. "This eight-year-old kid reminded me of who I used to be when I was happy, and I didn't want to be numb anymore. I wanted *him* to be happy, instead." Madoc looks around the crowd, everyone quiet and listening. "My dad once told me that if you're a good father, your hopes and dreams transfer to your kids when they're born. They come first."

Madoc's father is Quinn's too, and he would know. He wasn't an attentive father to his son. But he learned.

"So I cheered for the fuckin' Cubs," Madoc goes on, smiles breaking out around the pool. "And subscribed to *MAD* magazine. And built airplane models and ate hot dogs three times a week, because they were his favorite, and I was grateful for every second of it..." He locks eyes with me. "Because I think I needed all those things more than you did."

My eyes burn, and I know he can see it. I blink, dropping my gaze, and about to fucking choke. They don't know me. Not really. He wouldn't say all this if he knew.

"I came back to life when I met you," he whispers only for me to hear.

I shake my head. *Please stop*.

"I'm not your father," he states, "but I think of you as my son."

My chest shakes, and I almost can't hold it in. *They're not my family*, I tell myself. *They're not...*

As he finishes, I hear the smile in his voice. "And I hope it's not too long before you come home again."

He pulls me into a hug, and I can't help but wrap him in my arms and hold tight. One last time.

A little clapping goes off around the pool, and Madoc finally pulls back, everyone looking to me now.

I have to say something. I know this is where I belong, and I can't tell myself I don't have a home here because this family's track record disproves that. Jared's mom took in Jax when he was a teenager. Jax and his wife, in turn, took in their son's girlfriend and her siblings. This family makes room for everyone.

But I can't be here. If I don't leave, Madoc could be implicated in things I did. I have to go.

I clear my throat. "I..." I laugh. "I actually asked for the hot dogs because I thought you liked them," I announce. "I mean, you'd eat them three times a week, so..."

Everyone breaks into laughter, Madoc shaking his head at me.

There should be more to say to the man who gave me so much. To his wife, who was a big sister and a second mother, a mentor, and a friend.

To the people who gave me a community and a family that would show up for me at a moment's notice. A *moment's* notice.

I meet Quinn's eyes. "I'll miss you all," I tell them.

Quinn's brow pinches together, and I see the tears she's trying to hold back, feeling a sob in my throat. But then she drops her eyes, staring at her drink, and I wait, but she doesn't look at me again.

I don't have anything else to say.

The patio is silent, and I'm a piece of shit, but that's it. It's over.

Madoc's smile falls a little, but he recovers quickly, coming in for one more embrace.

I ignore the eyes of everyone waiting for more. They don't understand, because they can't. It is what it is.

Except Farrow Kelly. I catch him as he stands there like a stone, staring at me and knowing he's probably the only one here who knows why it's best that I leave.

Others approach me—Fallon, Juliet, Tate, Jax, and Jared—some of them hugging me one last time, and others shaking my hand. I thank them for coming.

When I finally lift my head, Quinn is gone.

My heart skips a beat, subtly scanning the pool deck and lawn. She wouldn't leave...

"I'll be back," I tell Madoc.

I head around the house again, to the lower-level patio, but she's not there. Slipping into the basement, I bolt up the steps, enter the kitchen, and head for the front door. As soon as I open it, I see her walking across the driveway, pulling on a white button-up over her bikini top.

"Quinn?" I call.

What the hell? She walks past cars like she's leaving.

She turns, the shirt still open.

"Where are you going?" I ask.

"Home." She won't look at me. "It's just a short walk."

Turning, she continues for the end of the driveway and the quiet neighborhood road beyond.

I bolt. "Wait."

She stops, and I see her exhale before she spins around.

I step toward her, pulling the cap out of my back pocket again.

I start to offer it to her, but she laughs. Bitterly. "I don't want it."

Looking at me now, her eyes are hooded, her fists clenched.

And I see the moment the curtain in her heart closes. No flexed jaw, no softness in her eyes, no anger, no trembling chin...

Just finality.

"You asked if I was mad at you," she says.

I did? Oh, yeah. Days ago. In her shop.

"Yes," she replies. "I am mad at you."

I swallow through the pain in my throat. I don't want to hear this.

She steps closer. "After a while, I started to understand that you didn't just leave all those years ago." She stares at me point-blank. "You ran away."

I breathe in and out through my nose slowly, hardening my stance.

"I remembered little things that seemed like nothing at the time," she tells me. "How you got quieter in the months before. How you would stand in the corners of rooms with your hands in your pockets as if you couldn't wait to get away from us."

A headache spreads up the right side of my skull, and I twist my neck, cracking it.

"How there were phone calls that seemed to agitate you, and how you lost weight."

"Quinn, stop…"

But she continues. "When I got older, I remembered all of this, but I didn't really worry because it had been years by that point, and I'd heard you were doing well in Dubai. Very successful, they said."

Yeah. I am successful. I flex my jaw. The opportunities that arose from living in a major city far exceeded any I'd find here, so…

She lowers her voice, tears in her eyes. "Madoc just told you how much he loves you." Pain is etched across her face. "How much you're a part of him, and you couldn't come up with more when you're never going to see him again?"

I blink, faltering. Madoc doesn't need to be told. He knows I love him.

But she just shakes her head. "I thought I would love seeing you come home, but even now…"

I almost take a step closer. I want to hold her.

"Even now," she goes on, "it's as if we mean nothing to you when you meant so much to us."

"Quinn…"

But she stops me. "There has been a *hole* in every room you weren't in for the past eight years, and I am done," she growls through her tears. "You're not family anymore."

A motorcycle engine fires to life nearby, and pain hits my eyes. She hates me.

I start for her. "Quinn—"

But she holds out her hand. "My compass," she demands.

I open my mouth, then close it, feeling it rest against my thigh in my pants' pocket. "I left it in Dubai."

"Do you remember where you left it in Dubai?" she bites out as if it's not precious to me and I don't know where it is at all times. "Maybe discarded in the bottom of a drawer somewhere?"

I square my shoulders. "Somewhere."

She inhales a big breath and backs away, dropping her hand. "Farrow?" she calls out.

I turn my head, seeing him straddle his bike on the other side of the driveway as she walks over to him.

I don't know what she says to him, but she hops on the back of his bike and he hands her his helmet. They speed out of the driveway, her arms tight around him, her shirt flapping behind her.

I bow my head.

Fuck, I need alcohol.

I hear my phone ring as if it's coming from another room. Absently, I pat my pocket, digging it out. I answer, "Hello?"

"Hi!" the realtor, Devney, replies. "Sorry for calling so late, but I wanted to catch you before you got on the plane."

My plane. What time is it?

"We have an offer." His cheerful voice hurts my ear. "It's not a great one, unfortunately, but it's all cash."

I stare at the end of the driveway where Quinn just disappeared. "Who?"

"They wish to remain anonymous."

Right. She doesn't want more of my invasive opinions, no doubt.

"They're offering—"

"Just give it to them," I say.

"Excuse me?"

I hear the door behind me close and turn to see Noah Van der Berg slipping his T-shirt back on and digging out his keys.

"I don't care what the offer is," I tell Devney. "Let her have it."

Noah climbs on his bike, setting his phone in the holder.

"O–Okay," Devney stammers. "I'll call them and email the paperwork to your mother."

I hang up, not even saying goodbye, and run my fingers through my hair over and over again. I'll feel better once I get home. To my real home and to my office and to my routine.

Far, far away from Quinn and her questions and her curious eyes and her scent. I clench my fists.

Dammit.

"Need a drink?" the kid asks.

I exhale, like air escaping a tire. He read my mind. "Is Jack's still open out on County Road 5?"

I don't know what the hell I'm doing or if I mean it, but the words are out before I can stop them.

"That dive right after Camp Blackhawk?" he asks. "For now."

Fuck it. I've got time.

I dig in my pocket for my keys and head to my car. "I'll drive."

I don't look to see if he follows. I can drink alone. I climb in my rental and start the engine before I see him approach and open the passenger's side door.

He sits next to me, and I put on my seatbelt.

"You're not gonna fuck me up, are you?" he asks.

I break into a laugh. A genuine one that feels fucking fantastic.

I shift into gear. "I leave for the airport in an hour."

I don't have time to get *that* drunk.

WESTON

CHAPTER TEN

Quinn

I told Dylan and Aro not to use Farrow or Noah. Now look at me.

Farrow jacks up the speed on his motorcycle, and I tighten my arms around his narrow waist, resting my head against his back. Tears stream out of my eyes, being blown down my cheeks.

I can't believe I did that. It could be the last time I ever see him.

Everything was just on the tip of my tongue, and I feel like it's been there for years. I couldn't stop it. Was it weird to him that I was so upset? He doesn't know that I've been nursing a crush my entire life. That I've thought about him and dreamed about him.

So attached to the one person I felt a connection to in my life. *Pathetic*.

I'm not mad at him. Not really. He's got his reasons, even if he doesn't trust us enough to tell us, but...

I just...

I don't want to think about him anymore. I don't want to hear his name. I don't want to know where he is or what he's doing.

For the first time ever, I feel like I have everything in front of me. No idea what or who, but the feeling is there all the same, and every second I move farther and farther away from Lucas Morrow and don't retract my words feels like I'm becoming someone else. Someone with possibilities.

We fly past my parents' house, and I jerk my head, seeing my father's car in the driveway. A light burns in the living room window.

Farrow cruises to a *Stop* sign, and as soon as we halt, I dry my eyes. "What are you doing?"

He was supposed to take me home.

"Come to Weston," he says, instead. "We don't have to fuck. You can sleep in Hunter's room."

A small smile is visible at the corner of his mouth.

Hunter lived with Farrow a couple of years ago when they both attended Weston High School. I'd heard he and Dylan still kept his room there, even after they went off to college. Somewhere to do their private things during summers and school breaks when they were out of the dorms.

I almost say no. It's instinct.

But what would happen if I said yes? No one would know where I was. For once, I'd truly be on my own, but not alone.

And something about his offer is endearing. Like he doesn't want me to be alone either.

I keep my arms wrapped around him, the heat of his body making me cold everywhere I'm not touching him. I stare at the side of his lips. "And if I'm not tired enough to sleep?"

Turning a little more, he looks at my mouth, our lips inches from each other. *Sometimes people just want to connect and not be alone and have a good time...*

Isn't that what Lucas said?

Is there anything wrong with that?

I move in a centimeter. Then another. And Farrow parts his lips.

But then he blinks, pulls back, and exhales hard. "Don't do that," he begs. "You'll regret it when it's done, and even knowing that, I'd still go to pound-town with you."

Pound-town? He's trying to ease the moment by making me laugh, but I'm a little frozen. Not because he pulled away, but because I can't believe I didn't.

He looks over his shoulder at me, the bike rumbling under us as he tells me, "I'm collecting Caruthers, you see."

No, I don't see, but he's probably right. I might like the feel of him tonight, but I haven't thought about him like that. I'd be using him.

I clear my throat. "To my shop then. I've got work to do."

I want to take a look in this Carnival Tower while everyone's busy at the party. Look through that murder map they have going on the wall, find these phones Hawke is so worried about, and see if he has any blueprints, as well. Lucas Morrow will be on his precious plane before I know it.

Farrow gives the bike some gas, and I hold on tight as he flies off.

We cruise into town—the sidewalks empty, except for the late-night crowd on the patio outside Rivertown. Soft light spills from the street lamps, and the smell of begonias drifts in the warm air from where they hang from poles, each swaying between two banners advertising the Fourth of July Parade and Picnic. Two days of activities Madoc has planned, including community service projects and a historical re-enactment.

Farrow swings into the alleyway behind the shop, and I dig out my key. "Thanks," I tell him.

His gaze lingers, like he's second-guessing refusing me, but the momentary temptation has passed. I let him off the hook.

Turning, I head into my shop, hearing his bike retreat back for the street.

I lock the door, leave the lights off, and keep my eyes peeled for any stalkers. These Deacon and Manas guys can't get in, but they might try. And that ugly black car from the other night still sits in the back of my mind. It's probably nothing, but it's too much at once to just dismiss, as well.

Pressing the latch, I push the door in and step inside Carnival Tower, closing it behind me. A whisper of light streams in at the end of the tunnel from the streetlights through the windows in the great room, and I turn on the flashlight on my phone.

Finding the padlock I'd left on the floor, I slip it through the hole I drilled in the latch and lock myself in—or anyone else out.

It's the one entrance that remains unlocked unless I'm inside, but since I changed the Frosted locks today, without any help from my brothers, no one can get in the shop unless I'm here anyway.

I quietly step down the tunnel, the same feeling I had before making the hair on my arms rise. The feeling like I'm never alone in here. I come upon the main room, the gaming console still sitting in the same place and the scent of popcorn, old pizza, and chilled brick hitting my nostrils. The long hallway to my right disappears into a black void, and eyes watch me from the empty corners of the great room. It's like that old, philosophical question—if a tree falls in the forest and no one hears it, did it happen? That's how Carnival Tower feels. Like it's still alive when no one's here.

Flipping on the overhead light, the room is awash, and I wince, blinded. Turning it off, I blink my way over to the sofa table and turn on a lamp. A warm glow fills the space, and I let out a sigh. *Better*. If Hawke ever used the big light, I would've certainly noticed from the outside before now.

The words on the wall across the room brighten. *Vivamus, moriendum est.*

Did Hawke write that on that wall?

Maybe Hunter. Dylan and Kade aren't sentimental like that.

Or maybe it was here before.

The outline of the mystery spans a third of the massive wall, and I walk over, taking pictures with my phone. I zoom in, getting a closer look at yearbook printouts, news clippings, and a couple of police reports they've collected. There are copies of text conversations, and as I back up and take in the wide array of evidence, I see it's arranged to look like a map. A city map. Everything is posted on the wall, Weston High School, Knock Hill—a once affluent area of townhouses in Weston—Shelburne Falls High School...

And my shop.

Several clippings are spread over High Street, red yarn stretching from every poignant location to another and numbered in chronological order.

A narrow, winding space of brick is visible between the two towns, representing the river. Something about the shape of it—the lines of water—reminds me of something. Like branches...

I scan the pictures, documents, texts, and accounts of the urban legends, piecing together what my nieces and nephews have learned so far.

Carnival Tower used to be a speakeasy a hundred years ago. My shop was the business front, and Rivertown Bar & Grill next door was a house. Until about twenty years ago anyway.

One night, a young girl was babysitting there, and a thug from Weston came hunting for revenge. She didn't know that his older brother was behind the mirror, hiding in the speakeasy where I am now, watching them have some fun.

Don't lean back into mirrors.

I grew up hearing that. A silly kids' superstition that mirrors are doorways or windows or something. I never paid it much attention. I mean, how often does anyone find themselves leaning into mirrors?

But now I know. Every story starts with something true, I guess. Does Lucas know about these legends, since he grew up here too?

I move over the evidence, inching down as I follow the yarn across the map. By the looks of things, they didn't have as much fun as planned that night because the brothers wanted to carry it out a little longer. They lured her to Weston in the prisoner exchange that happens during Rivalry Week every October between the high schools.

In fact, this more than two-decades-long tradition was their idea, it appears.

I told you she always liked me more, I reread one of the printed-out texts.

My blood goes cold, seeing pictures of the house. *Their* house in Weston. The raw, hard floor of the bedroom where she slept those two weeks.

Winslet MacCreary.

I move back down the map, searching. I saw her name somewhere else too. I spot it, in Hawke's writing, as well as the names Deacon, Manas, and their deceased brother, Conor. Jogging back over to the coffee table, I pick up the diary I noticed last time I was here and dig out the picture of the sexy blonde, her naked parts expertly shielded by her long arms and angle in the photo.

Winslet.

According to the evidence, she didn't return the love—obsessive love, from what it sounds like—of Conor Doran. His twin, Deacon, also a football player for the rival town, Weston, came for revenge on Grudge Night after his brother killed himself over her.

Their older sibling, Manas, was really the one in charge, though.

I peel open the cover of the diary again, hearing the brown, leather spine softly crack.

Turning the page, I see a column of words—some short phrases—written in a frantic script. Some are carved into the paper while others are thrown out like a whip. I stare at the page, trying to figure out some rhyme or reason to the information that looks like a shopping list.

-six nights since you threw me onto the street

I shake my head, confused.
I keep reading.

-warm hands, squeezing my arms like a snake bite
vein in your neck, memory of it against my lips
-porch light flickers
-rain pelts your shirt to midnight blue

Memories? It looks like a female's penmanship, if a little wild, but there are no capital letters or periods. No sentence structure, as if she's narrating.

-flood sirens
-blood streams down your temple
-Deacon in the attic window

-quiet in the street
-door closes
-alone
-quiet

Flood sirens... This could be recounting the night Weston flooded two decades ago.

Who pushed her out of the house? Manas? Deacon was in the attic window, so...

-walking to the river
-no tears
-alone
-hair matting my face like skin
-engine behind me
-white car
-I'm alone

For a moment, I feel wet hair sticking to my cheeks too. I'm there with her. Lost.

Her thoughts are staggered, as if she can't form cohesive thoughts, even six days later. Watermarks dot the page, ink smeared, because she went back and wrote—and re-wrote—words in the margins.

More etchings of *alone* and *quiet*.

-cold hands, squeezing my arms like a snake bite
-more cold hands
-dark
-tires moving through water

She's hearing things. Not seeing them. Is she blindfolded now? Tied up?

-scratching, break nails, stings
-falling, water
-no tears
-alone
-can't breathe
-quiet
-forever, quiet forever
-six nights
-six nights, six nights, six nights...

I push my finger up the page, back to *falling, water*. I'd missed the comma. I thought it said *falling water*.

But she was falling.

Then...there's water.

My chest rises and falls, and I let the wheels turn in my head, but I can't believe them. This has to be a joke. Someone's rendition of what happened that night, but it's not the true story. Winslet MacCreary was not the origin of our urban legend about mirrors.

Or the urban legend about the bridge. I scan the murder map again, seeing mentions of Rivalry Week and the stories about the car still at the bottom of the river.

Pay to pass.

I do know that urban legend and where it came from a little more than the Carnival Tower one. A story about a girl who was packed into a car trunk that was forced over the side of the bridge between our two towns.

I hold the diary, my hands shaking.

Whenever people cross the bridge, no matter which way, they flick a coin into the water. Not for luck. Not out of remembrance.

They pay to be allowed to pass unharmed from her ghost that's still down there.

According to Hawke, Aro, Kade, Dylan, and Hunter's map, she died there.

Six days later... I'd read.

I lower my eyes to the pages again.

-free
-swimming
-air

I breathe out the faintest...weakest...laugh.
She didn't die. At least not there. She made it out.
Has Hawke seen this diary?

-alone, she writes again.

-alone
-alone
-alone

I picture the girl in the photo, breaching the surface of the water. The flowing river around her, surging in the storm, the current carrying her. It's dark, she's alone, worried to call out for help, because those who put her in the car could still be close.

Does the one who cast her out of the house even know what just happened to her? Could he be the one who did it?

I flip through the journal, seeing pages filled with the same lists, scribble marks, some things X'd out, but more like in anger rather than scribbling out a mistake. There are words carved into the margins and some pages written with script so small, it might take me a day to read a single page.

I set it back on the island and move away for a moment.

I don't want to be played.

There's no way to tell for sure if the journal is hers, someone else's, or if it was forged as part of some bullshit story this Deacon and Manas are playing with my younger family members. There's a reason Hawke doesn't have copies of any of its pages on the murder map. As far as I can tell anyway.

But I get an idea, all the same, and head back out the secret entrance and into my bakery. Digging out the memoir my mom gave me more than three years ago detailing her and my father's love story, I carry it back into the tower and set it down next to Winslet's journal.

If it moves between now and my next visit, I'll know someone is still finding a way in here.

But mostly…Carnival Tower seems a place for stories, and it seems like it belongs here.

I sweep the rest of the hideout again, looking for any clues. Underneath beds, around exercise machines, in cabinets and bureaus… Found some handcuffs, which on my first guess might be Kade's, but I half-suspect Aro uses them on Hawke or Dylan on Hunter. I won't ask.

The monitors in the surveillance room all glow with the live feed of High Street, Fall Away Lane, the alley behind my shop, and the exterior of JT Racing. There's a view of Fallstown, some old firehouse I don't recognize, and—I squint, looking closer—the parking lot at the summer camp.

He should have a camera on Frosted's roof. It would monitor that entrance, at least.

Searching the drawers, I don't see the phones they were talking about, but I do find blueprints. I smile, pulling them out. As I spread them open, a memory hits me—that day at Camp Blackhawk and Lucas's ski resort dream laid out on the kitchen worktables.

I lock my jaw together, trying not to lift my eyes to the clock on one of the computer monitors. He must be about to head to the airport.

Why do men think there's one rule for themselves and another for everyone else? Deacon and Manas sought revenge on Winslet for not loving their brother, and then proceeded to use her without giving her their hearts in return. Men in my family have been cruel and uncontrollable in their passion for the women they love, but their daughters—and their sister—need leashes.

What does Lucas do in bed with women that he would think Farrow Kelly or Noah Van der Berg were deviants if they wanted to do it to me? The fucking hypocrite.

Raising my eyes, I see the time. *9:42*

My heart jumps in my chest. It's later than I thought.

He's at the airport now.

It's over.

I set the blueprints on Hawke's desk, pass by the diary and my parents' story on the kitchen counter, and walk out of Carnival Tower through the mirror in my shop. Walking out the backdoor, I lock up Frosted and head out of the alley, sliding my phone into one back pocket and my key in the other.

I've never walked this path. When I pass Lucas's house, I'm always jogging. It felt less creepy, finding a way to visit something of his—some place he lived—if I did it under the guise of exercise.

But it wasn't just a way to be close to him over the years that he was gone. It was something I had to do, like I was visiting a grave.

Lucas's house sits a few houses down from the corner, every window dark, not even the porch light shining. I always loved this house. The neighborhood is something my father would call 'spotty,' but really, it's just old. No HOAs to make sure people mow their lawns or keep from parking on the grass.

I start to turn onto his walkway—a blue craftsman with two massive white columns posted on either side of the wooden stairs sitting ahead—but a low rumble drifts into my ears, and I slow.

Glancing left, up the street, and then right, I don't see the '72 Dodge, but I swear, that's the sound it makes. Chills crawl up my neck, the sound of its engine coming from somewhere.

Jogging up the five stairs, I hear the wood creak as I step up to the door, snatching the lockbox in my hand from where it hangs on the doorknob. There are numbers like a phone to dial in a code to retrieve the key inside. Real estate agents put them on for potential buyers.

Shit.

I drop it and take the knob, giving it an exasperated, half-assed twist, and it opens. I let my mouth fall open. "Nice..."

That was lucky. It's unlike Lucas to be irresponsible like that.

Putting a foot inside, I peer my head in, seeing empty hardwood floors shining in the moonlight. All the furniture is gone and the faint scent of fresh paint and Lysol linger in the air.

I enter the house, closing the door behind me. I haven't been in here since the last time Lucas was home. I would come with Madoc when he picked him up, or get dropped off here on the occasion Lucas took me somewhere on his own, like to a movie only I wanted to see, or shopping for Christmas presents for the family.

Drifting through the house, I take one last look at the kitchen where his mom raced around the table when we were playing tag, and the living room where he let me try on his dad's jacket and hat.

I wander upstairs, find his room, and inhale the scent of that cologne he wore tonight. He stayed so close. Was he that worried I'd fall in love with the wrong guy in a bounce house?

I laugh to myself as I browse the room. His bed is the only piece of furniture that remains, the mattress a stark white. I circle the bed to look out the window into the backyard, but I spot his white hoodie from the gym the other night on the floor. Bending down, I pick it up. He must not have seen it here when he was packing up. I lift it to my nose, inhaling, and suddenly flooded with him. Tears spring to my eyes and a truck sits on my chest at the smell of his skin. And his cologne and the summer air, and it reaches down into the pit of my stomach, taking me back, because he always smelled like this.

And I feel a sudden urge. Hidden in this empty room, in this empty house, in the dark of night, I stop thinking for a moment.

I strip off my shirt and my bikini top and pull the hoodie over my head. It falls halfway down my thighs just before I drop everything else I'm wearing to the floor.

Stepping out of my shorts and bikini bottoms, I pull my hair out of the sweatshirt and sit on the edge of the bed, just like Winslet.

Not naked like her, but goosebumps spread across my arms, down my legs, and into my scalp all the same. I wanted to feel something he wore on my skin.

Tears suddenly fill my eyes as my toes graze the floor. "I've been in love with you since I was a kid, Lucas," I tell his memory, out loud.

The cloth of his hoodie brushes my nipples, the skin of my thighs tingles under the hem. I part my legs just a little, letting the cool air in.

"Everyone in our family has someone," I say as a tear falls. "Madoc has Fallon, Dylan has Hunter, James has A.J., Kade has anyone he wants..." I breathe out a laugh as I swipe a tear off my face. "When I was little, you were the one I looked forward to."

The sweatshirt is so loose on me, I feel his imaginary hands climb inside.

"You were smart and funny and kind." I rub my lips together. "You trusted me to hear difficult things when everyone else tried to shield me. You talked to me. The only one who really talked to me."

Everyone else lied to me. All in my best interest, of course, but Lucas couldn't. For some reason, it didn't sit right with him.

"When I grew up, I thought about you," I tell imaginary Lucas. "I wondered if you'd like what you saw when we met again. And if you'd want to keep looking."

An image of him is in front of me, leaning over and reaching up inside the hoodie, pulling me down the bed by my naked hips.

"I rushed to grow up, so you could find me before you found someone else..." I finally admit. "Finished college early, started a business... In case you came home, I'd be ready."

My mother never knew why I was racing to a finish line nearly all my life. I missed him when I was a kid and knew, even at thirteen, I didn't want him to meet anyone. And when I turned eighteen, I was happy, because even if I was still too young for him, I was old enough. It was one barrier finally out of the way.

I'd never even wanted another guy.

I'm glad he came back. I needed to see him with adult eyes because now I know. He runs, and he'll always run. There are better men out there.

"I'm ready." I rub the insides of my thighs, heat pooling between my legs. "Just not for you."

The ghost of his hand wraps around my throat and pushes me back onto the bed. I lift the hoodie over my head and open my legs.

"Never for you," I gasp.

SHELBURNE FALLS

CHAPTER ELEVEN

Lucas

The vein in my neck throbs, and I can barely take in a breath. I watch her through the blinds in my closet doors, naked and writhing on my bed with her knees spread wide and her hand between her thighs.

What the fuck.

Her long torso arches on the mattress as she grips the inside of her leg with one hand and rubs herself with the other. And while her hand brushes slow and soft, she thrusts and moans, her breasts rocking like...

"Ah," she groans. "Ah, ah, ah..."

...like she's being fucked.

I close my eyes, heat flooding my groin. *You can't look at her.*

She's a kid. She's always been a kid to me, and I can watch this—feel this—with any woman. Far away from here.

Her little whimper of pleasure drifts through my ears, and I open my eyes, trying to resist lifting them up to her.

But I do.

Long, toned legs. Smooth stomach. Round, full breasts. My hands ball into fists, empty. My lips part, nearly feeling her hard nipples over my mouth just before I envision myself sinking my teeth into her body.

I clench my jaw, my dick straining against my pants.

I should've cleared my throat by now. Done something to stop her. If I'd known it was her entering the house, I wouldn't have hid. But it's late, I'm drunk, and there are no more fucking knives in the house in case it was Green Street coming to ambush me. I'm late as hell for the airport, but I couldn't stop thinking about the things she said to me at the party. My heart split in two, hearing how much I meant to her, and it nearly stopped when she said I wasn't family anymore. Drinking with Noah, I couldn't forget it, and I told myself that I just wanted to leave the hat and the compass here at the house for her. She would've found them when she moved in.

But I'd heard the door click shut downstairs and dipped into the closet to see who I was dealing with, when lo and behold, the girl herself wandered in.

"Ah," she moans. "Ah."

She rolls her hips into whoever she envisions on top of her. Me?

Is it me she's thinking of? What does she see? What do I look like? What am I doing to her?

She jerks, throwing her head back again and again, and my face flushes with fire, watching her finger herself like there's a fucking guy nestled between her legs.

I can't believe what's happening.

Quinn?

It's her, but it's not.

Quinn is timid. Gentle. She's not messy. Why is she doing this? She wasn't fucking in love with me. It was a crush that I thought ended when she was ten.

But I watch her lifting her knees back so far I see her...

I drop my eyes, my chest caving. *Quinn*. A quiet kid. A little lonely. Always finding herself at my side. Did she really rush to grow up for me?

"I want my mouth on you," she whispers.

The skin of her nipples is hard and tight, the flesh around them soft and plump, and she starts thrusting into her hand faster, almost growling.

So rough with herself. Quinn's not rough.

I groan, leaning my arm up on the edge of the door and peering at her as I adjust my cock. Blood pumps, making my dick swell harder, and I can't fucking leave until she's done, and I can't stay like this. I push my cock down as it strains against my pants. *Fuck*.

It's almost as if she knows I'm watching, the view is that good.

But it's not true. This is her home now, and she thinks I'm gone already.

I should be, but I don't look at my watch. The hat and compass belong here. I had to bring them back. I didn't say a proper goodbye to Madoc and Fallon, either. That needs to be done.

And Green Street... Should I have known nothing would stay buried forever?

If I interrupt her now, she'll know I watched for several minutes. I can't leave.

And I can't look away. "Say my name," I mouth.

She said she was ready, just not for me.

Who is she dreaming of then, if not me?

"Say it," I whisper, too low for anyone to hear.

But then...

She rolls over, onto her stomach, and bends her knee out to the side. Propped up one arm, with her other hand still underneath between her legs, she fucks the mattress. "You can go harder," she gasps.

My cock hardens like a rock, my gaze locked on her ass.

"Come on," she pants. "Please, Noah. Harder."

I jolt, every muscle hardening like steel. What the fuck did she say? I bare my teeth, watching her rock back and forth. *Noah?*

I grab my cock, ready to burst out of these doors and slice her fucking train of thought right out of her head. *Dammit.* I'm hard as a rock.

I still see her as a girl. Is that what she thinks? That another man will see her like this because I can't?

I don't want anyone else to see her like this. I...

"Come with me," she says so sweetly. Her hair hangs in her face as she looks over her shoulder at whoever she's dreaming is fucking her. "Come with me, come with me..."

A moan escapes me, and I bite the inside of my lip to stifle it.

She throws her hair back, the locks snaking down her back, grazing her ass, and every follicle of hair on my body rises. I can see my hand running over her spine, gripping her hair after I push whoever she thinks she wants out of the fucking way. I can feel my body thrusting into her, harder, as my mouth finds hers.

I take care of her. No one else.

God, Quinn...

I reach for the door, about to push it open. There won't be any turning back.

"Come with me," she whispers, and I watch her. Feeling her on top of me, riding me like she rides the mattress, as I grip her ass and feel her pant on my mouth. *Come with me...* The scent of her skin, the taste of her lips, the slick warmth of her pussy...

My whole body blazes and sparks under my skin, and I close my eyes as I listen to her come, damn close to spilling in my pants. I press a hand over my groin, harder.

She moans and then whimpers in a high-pitched tone.

Then there are soft, little breaths, fading away.

I open my eyes, but I don't look at her. I stare at the floor, the sizzling embers in my brain making everything blurry.

She's all grown up.

A beautiful, passionate young woman who can love a man with that incredible body, and they're going to like what they see.

And feel.

I lock my jaw.

When I finally raise my eyes, she's dressing, her gaze downcast as well.

She picks up my hoodie, and I think she's going to put it on—keep it— but she doesn't. "I wish it was Noah or Farrow or anyone else, but it was you I thought of." She exhales hard. "And it's out of my system. Finally."

She tosses the hoodie into the corner of the room, on the floor, and I narrow my eyes, watching her leave.

She closes the door downstairs, and I walk out of the closet, stepping over to the bed.

Leaning down, I run my hand up the mattress, finding a tiny little spot where she dripped.

I run my thumb over it, still feeling her warmth. Did I know the moment I saw her at the gym that first night that I wasn't getting on any planes any time soon?

I swallow. There's no fucking way Noah Van der Berg or Farrow Kelly are ever seeing Quinn like that. This town is my home, Madoc is my family, and Quinn is mine to protect. She always was.

And I know I'm not out of your system, you little brat.

Jared climbs out of his car—one of the new Mustang Dark Horses—and if I had any energy, I'd laugh. It was only fate that he ended up getting sent Mustangs free of charge by the manufacturer for promoting the brand.

What did Madoc say yesterday? *Yeah, Jared is all about supporting our local tow truck drivers.* I shake my head. Madoc hates Fords, and I was glad to hear the rivalry still stands.

Jared sees me and stops, probably surprised I'm not on a plane right now.

He approaches me, the early morning light warming my shoulders. "What are you doing?" he asks.

I've been here for an hour, my plane probably somewhere over Eastern Europe by now. I haven't called Isobel to warn her I won't be back in the office tomorrow.

I can barely open my mouth to reply. "Honestly, I don't know."

I expect a pinch to appear between his eyebrows. It's what happens when he looks at you like you're dangerously close to wasting his time.

But instead, he chuckles. Breezing past me, toward his shop, he digs out his keys. "I know that feeling," he muses, unlocking the door. "Got me into a lot of trouble back in the day."

Yeah, well, I'm too old for that feeling. Too old to not have a plan.

But I can't get her out from under my skin.

The memory of that gorgeous body moaning on my bed fills my brain, and I go hot everywhere, only a few feet from her most volatile brother.

When he doesn't ask me what's wrong, I speak up. "You're not going to grill me?"

"No." He shakes his head, leading the way into his shop. "You're figuring it out, and I'll leave you to it. You would've gone to Madoc if you wanted a hug."

Thank you.

And yes, people don't come to Jared to validate their decisions.

"I, um..." I clear my throat. "I need a car."

He faces me. "What's wrong with the one you have?"

It's not tinted and everything Jared drives is.

Plus, Green Street knows what I drive. I need to look gone, at least for a couple of days until I figure out what I'm going to do.

But when I keep all that to myself, he gestures out to the lot full of company cars and older ones that various members of the family once used. "I've got a Colorado," he drones on. "A 4Runner. Or Tate's old Bronco?"

I spot one of his old Mustangs under a cover. I could tell that shape anywhere. The Boss 302. It was the car he had when I'd caught sight of him in the back seat with Tate twenty-five years ago. Madoc never let me drive it when I got old enough.

Good summer car.

"Anyone using the Boss?" I broach, chills spreading up my arms and my blood racing already.

He purses his lips, his baby still very close to his heart. Then, he opens a container on the wall and tosses a pair of keys at me. "Don't fuck it up," he grumbles.

I smile. "Thanks."

I start to leave, but I need to say something.

"Noah's not a bad kid," I start.

He and I didn't talk much last night—just had a couple beers.

Well, I had four, actually.

I have every confidence he's a good friend to Dylan and Hunter.

Jared nods, bending over to pick up a socket set laying next to the tire of a Corvette. "If I can keep him from getting any girls into trouble for the next few years, he'll be great," he tells me. "Unfortunately, he's more than his father and I can handle sometimes. He's got a mind of his own."

"So, he fits in then."

Jared smiles.

Yeah, Noah is a good kid. That doesn't mean he's a man, though.

But at least he's not a criminal.

"Farrow," I continue, "*is* a problem."

"Caught that in your short time here?" He looks over at me, amusement in his eyes. "Don't worry. Madoc and I have our attention on it. Unfortunately, Dylan and Hunter adore him and they, too, have minds of their own."

"I meant in regards to Quinn," I point out.

He stops, his smile gone as he sets the case down on a toolbox.

I go for it before he has a chance to panic. "You know girls like her as well as I do, Jared. Kind, trusting, generous—"

"Naïve?"

I smile softly. "Pure of heart," I say, instead. I move in and keep going. "It's normal—and necessary—to make mistakes and fall in love with the wrong people, so you can fall out of love and learn the lessons, but those two guys… They can fuck up her life. It's all guys like that are good for at their age."

There, I said it. I don't hate Noah and Farrow, but Quinn is not cutting her teeth on them.

Jared heaves a sigh, looking everywhere but at me. "Fuck." He runs his hand through his hair. "I worry more about Quinn because she's not resilient. But that's not her fault. It's mine. And Madoc's and Jax's and her father's." He looks at me. "We paved every step she walked."

I know. And now she doesn't have any street smarts, but what were they supposed to do? Not look out for her?

"I'll be around for a while," I announce. "If she needs a ride or you need someone taught a lesson."

He chuckles but looks weary. Reaching out, he shakes my hand. "I think I'm gonna like you as a grown-up."

Good, because his sister doesn't.

Before I have a chance to take my keys and leave, someone rushes through the front door.

"Jared," Jason, Quinn's dad, bursts out. "Thank God."

I move aside so he can get to his stepson, but Mr. Caruthers doesn't come any farther than peeking his head inside the door.

He gripes at Jared, "I'm trying to take your mom to Bermuda for the week and my display is lit up like a Christmas tree. What did you do?"

"Not a fucking oil change," Jared barks back. "I'm not Jiffy Lube. Did you take it into the dealer and have it done a month ago like I told you?"

Mr. Caruthers shuts his mouth, just standing there.

I stifle my smile.

"Jesus Christ," Jared growls, storming toward the door. Jason moves out of the way, letting his wife's son barrel outside, toward their Bentley Continental GT.

Quinn and Jared's mom Katherine steps out of the driver's side, offering her son a little wince of apology. She's dressed for the beach in a thin, white dress with a straw hat.

Jared climbs in the driver's seat, turns on the car, and suddenly his face contorts into a cross between a bear and a disgusted schoolteacher. "Oh, what the f—!"

But he clamps it shut in front of his mom.

Quinn's dad and I stand back, silent and not moving like we share a father who's on a rampage and we're trying not to be noticed.

"Son of a bitch," Jared bites out, walking around and lifting the hood. "Three-hundred-thousand-dollar piece of shit is what you're about to have." A thread of smoke curls into the air from the engine. "Goddammit! Someone just shoot me in the head…"

Jason clears his throat, and I'm trying very hard not to laugh. Jax once gave Jared a book on "responding instead of reacting" and "accepting things he can't change." I wouldn't be surprised if it was still sitting on the corner of Jared's worktable in his home garage with two inches of dust on it.

I pull out the keys to my rental parked three spaces away and hand them to Jason. "Take mine."

He eyes me. "Are you sure?"

I nod. He can return the car to the rental place; otherwise, I would've had to call them to come pick it up.

"Thank you," he says.

I give him instructions on turning in the car, grab my shit out of it, and climb in Jared's Boss as Jason flies out of the parking lot in my rental with his wife.

"I'll see you soon!" I call out to Jared, who's still buried under the hood.

He doesn't reply, and I'm fine with that. Best to get out of his way while I can.

I drive off, still relieved that Jared didn't ask any questions. With luck, Madoc will find out through him and have time to process before we talk. There's a lot to figure out. Do I want to cancel the sale of the house?

I don't think so. I don't know how long I'm home, and I don't want to pull the rug out from under Quinn. I like the idea of staying someplace else while I'm here. A new view.

Then, there's the issue of work. I'll need something to do, but I'm not sure I want to commute to Chicago.

And Green Street…

Lots to tend to.

After showering and changing at my house, I leave through my door for the last time and plan to go to a hotel. I could stay with Madoc and Fallon, but I'd like privacy right now. And I don't want them involved in what I have to deal with.

Stopping at City Hall, I dig up a map of Lake Road and make a call to Isobel to tell her I'll be away a little while longer. What I can't handle remotely, she or one of my partners will.

I walk out to my car at the curb and start to open the door, but I look up and spot Madoc's SUV pulling into the side lot. He exits the vehicle, carrying his briefcase to the walkway as his car beeps locked behind him.

But he sees me and slows. Recognition dawns, a slight smile crossing his face, and to my surprise, he doesn't explode with questions and excitement.

As if he had an idea he'd see me again soon.

"Workout tonight?" I call to him.

I'll need to be ready for Green Street, because once they know I'm still here, they'll act.

He tips his chin at me. "Eight o'clock."

I nod in agreement. Maybe I'll give Lance a call too. See if he wants to come out.

Or not.

I didn't mind seeing him when I thought I wasn't staying in town long, but I need to be severing fucking ties here, not encouraging them.

Getting back into my car, I drive to Frosted and get in line, seeing Quinn shuffle one of her workers out of the shop with a tower of boxes to deliver. I slip my hands into the pockets of my black track pants, my fist curling around her compass as my eyes drift down her body. Skin that was flush with my mattress twelve hours ago. Now, it's covered neck-to-toe in clothes. Good girl by day. She can shift like a chameleon, and some guy is going to be very lucky someday.

I step up to the counter and order, "Small, black coffee."

She lifts her head at the sound of my voice, her chest caving.

She doesn't blink, and all I can think about are the thoughts she was thinking out loud about me last night. Everything she wants to do with me.

My mouth goes dry, and I fight to slow my heart.

In a moment, she turns and pours me a cup, affixing the lid without a word.

She sets it down in front of me. "One-fifty."

I dig out money, her round eyes staring straight at me, her jaw tense.

I slide over a five-dollar-bill, her compass sitting on top.

"Madoc still sees me as family," I tell her.

She tries to take the money and compass, but I don't let go.

She looks at me.

"They all do," I point out.

Whether she does or not.

I'm not going anywhere until I'm ready.

I take the coffee and leave, feeling her eyes on my back as I go.

Sliding into the Boss, I set my cup in the holder and start the engine.

And I smile, suddenly realizing an excellent place for me to stay while I remain in town.

WESTON

CHAPTER TWELVE

Quinn

Why the hell is he staying?

And for how long?

I wouldn't lower myself to ask when he showed up earlier at my counter. I'd been keeping as busy as possible, my commitment to letting him go from the Falls—and my head—stronger than ever.

I won't dwell on how my stomach dropped, or how I could barely hide the tremble racking through my body at the sight of him. I was shaken. And so happy to see him, and I hate myself for feeling that in that moment. Why can't he just let me move on with my life?

I couldn't sleep last night but not because I was upset. I was more numb than anything, but all I kept thinking about was years down the road when he inevitably showed up again for a wedding or a...a funeral. Maybe I'd be married. With kids. Maybe I'd have a home and a whole life with a family of my own, but deep down, I'd know that everything I lived up until then would be in anticipation of what he would think about it when he finally saw it. Would he like my husband? Would they get along? Would that tension still stretch between us every time he looked at me?

Or did I just fantasize everything? The jealousy I sensed from him when I worked out with Noah and Farrow at the gym? The protectiveness he doesn't exhibit with any of the others, only me? The way he kept seeking me out?

The way my body would come alive whenever he touched me?

And even when he's not.

Last night and my little escapade to his old house drifts through my mind, and I feel fire rising on my face. God, he was still in town while I was...doing what I was doing to myself on his bed. I almost shudder, thinking about how easily I could've been caught.

There was nowhere else I could be, though. To smell him there and feel his clothes on me and imagine we were sneaking around, but I didn't care, because he wanted me. It was such a turn on. I thought if I got it out of my system, it would be closure.

But now...

I shake my head. He needs to leave. I won't be happy—and maybe not for a while—but I'll get over it. I need to live for me now.

And I damn-well intend to, despite whatever he's up to. I've got plans of my own.

I drift around the worktable in Frosted's kitchen, the shop empty and dark as I stare at the blueprints I'd found in the tower last night.

Joy starts to swell in my chest. "It's mine."

I survey the layout of the building, which includes my shop and the tower, comparing the square footage to the original deed I'd collected at City Hall this afternoon.

I smile wide. *Mine.*

I'm not sure if my father paid attention when he bought the place years ago, but Carnival Tower is part of Frosted's original floor plan, not Rivertown's. What I could do with that space…

A chair outside tips over in the wind, crashing against the sidewalk, and I rush outside and pick them all up. I must look like an idiot who can't stop grinning at the butterflies in my stomach as I stack the chairs against the storefront.

My low ponytail whips over my shoulder, and I tilt my head back and close my eyes, feeling the sunshine on my face as the rustle of leaves and the gusts of wind fill my ears. For someone who hates speed, I do love a breeze, and now that I'm the proud owner of over a thousand extra square feet, the future holds all sorts of promise. My work, my new place, and maybe some friends and hobbies…

And, in time, I'll start dreaming of another man.

I head inside and close my shop door, locking it. I'm still in my black pants and chef's coat, a uniform I wholly embraced earlier today.

I always felt more of a business person instead of a baker because I didn't attend a culinary academy. I fit in seminars and lessons during the occasional weekend at college, or in Chicago over holiday breaks, but mostly I just got in there and got my hands dirty. Constantly, since I was a kid.

And I watched a little YouTube.

I'm a baker, though, and a practitioner of the culinary arts, and if I want everyone to see me as an adult, I need to stop wearing T-shirts and shorts on the job.

I'm still wearing sneakers, but at least they're clean white Sambas with black stripes. I match, and matching is mature.

A car cruises by, and I open my eyes to see three kids on skateboards and scooters fly past too. I got everyone out on time today. The customers were done by two, the staff by three, and I've been on my own for a few hours.

There was plenty to do with the time. I had three cakes to finish, tarts to prep, ingredients to measure out for the morning, and I needed to update the specials and soup-of-the-day for tomorrow.

Making sure the place is secure, I snatch up the blueprints and glance through the windows to see if anyone's looking before quickly opening the mirror to Carnival Tower.

Heading inside, I pull the hideout closed and walk down the tunnel, flipping on the lights.

My parents' story still sits on the counter, unmoved as far as I can tell.

I cut a right down the tunnel and turn on the lamp on Hawke's desk, although I hate calling it that. It's more like a command center with two rows of monitors, all fired up with live feeds of the town, and one with some website I don't recognize.

I pick up the blueprints and spread them open, seeing a date scratched with faded pencil in the corner.

December 1, '19.

December first *nineteen*-nineteen? Has to be. The pages have a yellowed hue and the paper smells musty, like old wood. Dust and grime cover it too.

Inspecting the layout, images float through my head.

Expansion. More seating, a bigger kitchen, more ovens, a shipping department for online orders, maybe a whole sister store for candy and ice cream, a private party room... The possibilities are endless.

I grip the sides of the papers, my stomach fluttering with joy. "God..."

If I thought I was busy now... I laugh out loud.

But then, my phone rings. I startle. Setting the blueprints on the table, I pull out my cell. Checking the screen,

I brace myself to see Lucas's name, frustrated that he pops into my head again, but...it's an unknown number. Just a local area code. It could be a customer.

"Hello?" I say, holding the phone to my ear.

But the other end is silent.

I wait until finally... I hear a breath in my ear.

I stand up straight. "Who is this?"

It's a moment, then two, and I hear them breathe again before I'm about ready to hang up.

But then he speaks. "You locked the tower," a man with a smooth voice I don't recognize tells me. "Didn't you?"

Every muscle in my body tenses, and I walk out of the surveillance room, keeping my eyes peeled. "Who is this?"

I try to harden my voice, but it comes out with a shake.

"I'm the one who left it open for you."

The smirk in his tone crawls up my spine.

Drifting into the great room, I spin slowly, scanning every corner. "Why?" I ask.

"I wanted to see what you would do."

So he was in here. In my shop too. Is he the one who left the phone that night?

"What *will* you do?" he inquires.

"Are you Deacon?" I press instead. "Or Manas?"

His low, deep laugh curls into my ear, making me uneasy. "You caught up quickly."

"How do you know I haven't been piecing it together with my family since the beginning?"

"Because I hear their conversations too," he retorts before adding. "Quinn."

My skin crawls. He knows my name.

Maybe it wouldn't be hard to figure out. All anyone has to do is look at my website.

But I stifle a shiver anyway. He's watched me from behind the mirror. At night. In the early morning when I was alone.

I swallow to wet my dry throat. "Where are you?"

"On the roof."

I shoot my eyes up to the hatch, seeing my bike chain still wrapped around the handle.

"Don't bother texting for help," he tells me. "I'm better at this than you are."

I back away, ascending the two steps up to the kitchen where I can keep an eye on the tunnel toward my shop and still watch the roof hatch.

"Where is Manas?"

"Still in New Orleans, I'd imagine. But he'll be here soon." Deacon's voice is casual. "It won't be hard for him to figure out where I went."

I wasn't sure which one he was. I simply guessed based off the impression I got from the others at the party last night. Deacon seemed like the one they worried about more.

I can almost feel his breath in my ear. "Open the door," he whispers.

I watch the roof, my heart pounding painfully. "No."

"He watches you, you know?" Without missing a beat. "All the time."

"Who?"

"You know who."

Lucas?

"He might never act on it," Deacon explains. "He's very conflicted, that one. He knows what's going to happen, but he still fights it."

Oh my God.

He's watching him too.

"But deep down inside," he goes on, "he would give you anything you wanted and do anything you asked."

The hair on my arms rises. I'm scared, but I want to know. "How do you know that?" I murmur.

"When he's close to you, nothing moves." Deacon's voice is breathy, soft. "Just his chest. It means his heart is beating faster, and he's trying to hide it."

I close my eyes, sparklers firing everywhere under my skin.

"He's afraid of a lot," Deacon adds.

Is he?

How is he noticing this? No one else does. Or they don't talk to me about it anyway. Not Madoc or Fallon. Not Dylan. No one else seems to notice what I do.

Until now.

I knew Lucas paid me a lot of attention these past few days. He was invasive, protective, almost possessive. Constantly there.

Did he stay because of me?

"What do you want?" I ask.

"I want to watch you."

Watch me do what?

"Were you following me the other night?" I question instead. "In the black car?"

"The what?"

"The old black Dodge."

He doesn't reply for a moment, as if he's surprised.

"That wasn't me," he finally says. "Interesting."

Why's it interesting? He didn't ask what the car did or why I was worried about it. Does that mean he knows it?

"You sound like a popular girl," he offers.

Enough. "What do you want?"

"I want to watch you."

"Watch me do what?"

"Have your own secrets," he replies. "Hawke and Aro were sweet. Hot and sweet to each other. Dylan and Hunter were alive. Volatile and alive."

My stomach knots, and I narrow my eyes. He's been watching us for years.

"But you're the one I've been looking forward to," he says in a breathless tone. "You excite me."

"Because I look like her?"

The line falls silent, and I can't believe the question came out before I could stop myself. I wait as one second stretches to ten, and I can't even hear Deacon breathe.

I shouldn't have asked that. It would be stupid of me not to assume this guy is dangerous, and who knows what will trigger him?

"Hello?" I say.

I check the phone, seeing the call is still connected, but he's not talking. I mean to ask him about the phone he left. What was on it and why did he want me to have it? What about the diary? Did he leave that too?

But I watch the ceiling door, my skin crawling at his silence. I end the call and set my phone down, keeping my eyes trained above.

I've got a lot of men in my life all of a sudden. I can't tell anyone about this one, though. They'll react just when I'm gaining some freedom.

He's been watching my family for a long time without incident, it seems. Should I be more scared?

What's Deacon's goal? It's not me.

It wasn't Hawke and Aro or Dylan and Hunter, either.

In fact, my family members didn't sound like they've ever seen him or his brother. Have they talked to either of them? Have they questioned where these men live, work, or what their endgame is? It's been going on for years, and that's an incredible amount of patience for nothing. There has to be a reason.

He said Manas was in New Orleans? Is that their permanent residence now? I need to make a list of things to find out when—*if*—I talk to him again.

My cell vibrates in my hand, and I look down, seeing a text from Hailey.

Here.

Shit. I dart back out of the hideout, concerned for her as much as me. She's sitting in her car in the alleyway alone. It's one thing to make guesses about my own safety, but the people who work for me?

I need to get rid of Deacon and Manas—whoever they are.

Leaving the mirror, I close it back up and scan the street for anything suspicious before I dive into the kitchen. Juliet needs snacks for the staff in the morning, and I offered to run any leftovers to her. I needed time to sort through everything and close up, so Hailey ran home, showered, and ate dinner.

Grabbing the bags with the boxes of pastries, I shut off the light with my elbow and push through the door, handing her the food.

She smiles, taking everything.

"Thank you," I chirp before spinning back around and locking the door.

I hear her start the engine to her Toyota RAV4, and I throw a quick glance up, worried I'll see Deacon peering down from the roof. I exhale, comforted that I don't have to be back till morning.

Holding up both hands, I catch her keys like a basketball and walk to the driver's side, while she hops into the passenger seat.

I don't drive much, but I do when necessary. Like when I don't want to make my younger employee cart me around, even though I have to mooch off her car.

I suppose some kind of SUV or van for the business would be a good idea. Maybe next year.

I drive us to Camp Blackhawk and grip the wheel, following all speed limits like it's my first time all over again. Since I got my license five years ago, I've only driven a couple of dozen times. When I do, I have to relearn.

The turn-off to the camp is just ahead, and I start to slow, flyaways dancing across my face with the air sweeping through the open windows.

But a figure darts into the street.

I go still, pressing the brake hard as a young girl dashes across the highway and dives into the brush. I cruise past slowly, peering to the right and watch Thomasin Dietrich—the fifteen-year-old local trouble—race into the woods.

Her white ponytail blows in the wind, her body covered neck-to-toe in black pants and a long-sleeved shirt.

The tips of her hair are red now, a change from the black they were last summer and the blue before that.

She looks back at us.

"What is she up to?" I murmur to myself.

She carries a backpack, is not dressed for summer camp, and I doubt she has any business at Blackhawk. Any that's legal anyway. Her father hates my brothers and vice versa. She wouldn't be hanging out anywhere near my family.

She whips back around and disappears into the forest, her house not far down the road.

I turn the wheel, my tires hitting gravel as we approach the camp. I think about calling Dylan or Hawke to come out and take stuff in, but I have somewhere else to be and no time to chat. We drop off the goodies and hightail it out of there, quickly making our way into my neighborhood.

A twinge of guilt hits me even as I purse my lips against a smile.

I don't want my family pissed, but it feels good to set the pace for once. I've kept a secret for a solid twenty-four hours, and it's a big one they're going to care about.

Dylan can pull something like that. And definitely Aro.

But Quinn doesn't break rules. Never Quinn.

Pulling up in front of my house, I see the garages are closed and remember my parents are gone for a week. They'd stopped in while I was busy at work to grab a hug and let me know they were taking off to a resort. It's perfect, actually. I can get moved out in peace.

"Thank you," I tell Hailey as she rounds the car and I hand her the keys.

"No problem!"

She hops into the driver's seat, smiles and waves, and I take out my key, slipping inside the house.

I tap out a text to Farrow. *Come when you're ready.*

I run up the stairs, his reply rolling in. *Cum when I'm ready?*

I roll my eyes and stick my phone in my back pocket.

One more stop before I sleep tonight. I should hit the gym, but I have a full day tomorrow with several Fourth of July orders to prep. I need rest.

After showering, I brush out my hair and pull on some jeans, tucking in a tan tank top. I grab my phone and veer to my dresser, slipping in some gold studs and a little lip gloss.

I start to leave, but I spot a car out my bedroom window that wasn't there when I got here. Drawing back the curtain, I immediately recognize Jared's old Mustang.

My stomach sinks. *Oh, no.*

He's going to have a fit if he sees Farrow Kelly picking me up.

With my I.D., credit card, and cash in my back pocket, I jog down the stairs and instantly smell the cologne Lucas was wearing the other night. I halt.

The legs of a chair scuff across the floor in the kitchen, hot blood coursing through my veins.

I walk toward it, Lucas coming into view as he sits at the table, bent over and tying his tennis shoe. The lights are off, the late day sun dimming, and he's dressed in track pants with a shirt laying on the table.

I don't see Jared.

"Why are you here?" I ask.

My voice is soft but steady. I don't want to be angry at him, but I don't want him here, either.

He doesn't look up as he ties the other shoe. "I sold my mother's house," he tells me. "Your parents were kind enough to let me stay while they're in Bermuda."

So he's staying the week? Or longer?

He must've returned his rental car and borrowed one of Jared's many spares.

"I don't need a babysitter," I state.

There was a time I would've been ecstatic to have Lucas all to myself. If only he hadn't started acting like I was his possession instead of his friend.

Finally, he looks up. "I'm not your babysitter," he says.

Rising, he walks over to me, and I straighten, aware of his naked chest and making a concerted effort not to look.

"I'm sorry for how I've been." He stops in front of me. "You were right."

I was?

"I made...mistakes the last time I was home," he explains. "It was never about you or the family. It was me."

I stare up into his eyes, but my pride won't let me ask him. What mistakes? If I know what happened, I'll understand. Doesn't he know that?

He pulls the blue Cubs cap off the counter next to me.

Slowly, he raises it above my head, and I gaze at him, lost in the moment of standing in front of him like this hundreds of times in my life and gazing into the same beautiful eyes.

He fits the cap onto my head, brushing my long bangs out of my eyes.

He swallows hard. "Please take it," he whispers.

My skin tightens with goosebumps. He stands so close. The kitchen is dark. He could've stayed with Madoc, but he's here. What does he want from me?

I'm not giving the compass back to him.

"I'm meeting Madoc." He searches my eyes, a small smile on his mouth. "Want to go to the gym?"

He's not asking for the compass back. I left it at the bakery anyway.

He just wants me to have the hat.

Do I want to go to the gym with him? God, yes.

I can't say no to him. I never could. I never wanted to.

But that's what women do, isn't it? What my mother did all those years as my father's mistress? She dropped everything when he wanted her close. Because she was addicted to how good his attention felt.

A horn beeps outside, just in time, and I inhale a shaky breath. "Farrow..." I say softly. "I'm going somewhere with him for a bit."

Lucas's eyes narrow, but then his expression relaxes. "Where..." He clears his throat, trying to reel in the agitation on his brow. "Where are you going?"

His tone is gentle, but I can tell he wants to forbid me.

"I can drive you where you need to go," he offers.

My mother only got better when she took responsibility for herself. And my father only claimed her when she showed him that she didn't need him.

I turn to leave, but he stops me. "Quinn."

I look over my shoulder.

His chest rises with a breath that he doesn't release. "Aren't you going to tell me the news?" he asks.

What news?

"You bought a house."

I square my shoulders. How the hell does he know that?

He approaches again. "Aren't you..." He's trying so hard to not be overbearing. "Aren't you worried you're moving a little fast?" he asks me.

Worried? "Yeah." I smile at him. "I'm kind of liking it, though."

I know what being me is like. I'm tired of being predictable.

I leave with my phone and my hat, and Lucas doesn't stop me as I walk away from him and out the front door. Trailing across the driveway, I don't know if I'm imagining his eyes on my back, but I'm aware of him as I climb on the bike. A grin spreads across Farrow's cheeks as I sit behind him, and he cranks up his music as I fasten my helmet. In a minute, we're shooting off down the driveway, cruising at eighty miles an hour onto the highway. The pull between me and where I left Lucas is like a cord about to snap. I just hang on, reminding myself to breathe as my heart pumps in my chest.

We cross the river, and I watch Farrow flip a coin over the side of the bridge. We climb the hills into Farrow's neighborhood, up to Knock Hill—the once upper crust brownstone townhouses that Weston used to boast. Still impressive looking, they've mostly been empty since the flood. I look around at the street, seeing a few cars which appear to be abandoned with missing doors or beer bottles on their hoods, but the trees are all in bloom, casting a nice shade over the lane and spilling a scent into the air of wood and grass.

Fletcher's Barber Shop sits to my right, and I remember Fallon's dad talking about how he still frequented the place. An old-time establishment from back in the day when the town bustled with activity and appreciation for the romance of slowing down.

Farrow parks in front of his place. Technically, Ciaran Pierce's place—Fallon's father. I'm not sure why Ciaran allows Farrow to live there, but he was in residence along with Hunter for a while in high school. Hunter went to college, and Farrow stayed. Loyal to Weston.

I throw my leg off the bike and remove my helmet. Without a word, Farrow takes it, and I look over, seeing a woman in a black pencil skirt and short-sleeved gray turtleneck.

"Did you have a good day?" she calls out, carrying a folder in her hand.

I walk toward her, glancing back at Farrow, who heads up the steps of his own house without a goodbye. He knows he'll see me soon.

I turn back to the lady, her hair blonde like mine, but her eyes are blue.

I smile. "Ms. Doucet?"

She holds out her hand. "Please, Elisabeth."

"Quinn Caruthers." I shake. "Nice to finally meet you."

I turn and look up at the house next to Farrow's, the number 01 in gold on the black plate next to the door. As far as I know, Dylan was the last to live here—for a couple of weeks two years ago—when she was taken as the hostage in the prisoner exchange between the schools. She never told me what happened, exactly, but she said she loved who she became in this house.

Good enough for me.

"And yeah," I reply, remembering Ms. Doucet's question. "The day is ending well, at least. You didn't have to come all the way out. I know it's a long drive for you."

She doesn't reply, just gazes up at the brownstone. She hands me the key. It'll be a little harder for me to get to work now, too, but I'm going to enjoy this for a minute before I decide what to do about the commute.

"I didn't expect it to happen so fast." I stare down at the key.

"We know where to find you if the check bounces."

I laugh. "I promise it won't."

No one's lived here properly in decades, but my loan still hasn't gone through. I would've thought we would have to finalize that first. I guess not.

The breeze flies through my hair, Lucas's hat keeping it at bay.

He'll have some things to say about this when he finds out where my new home is.

Everyone will. Buying Lucas's mother's house would've been better. I tossed the idea around for about a minute that night when I talked to him at the gym. It's a short walk to the bakery, and it's still in the Falls, close to everyone.

But as I look down the street, at the empty porches and no traffic—no Trents or Caruthers—I finally feel like I'm on my own. Even more than I did when I started Frosted.

About ten steps lead up to my new front door, two floors rising above that. A huge house with more bedrooms than I need, but...

Plenty of room to grow.

"01 Knock Hill." Elisabeth stands at my side. "The neighborhood—what's left of it—will be curious about you. As I understand it, the house is part of some local lore."

I'm locked on the attic window, always most fascinated with the high rooms as if things are more secret up there.

What she says finally clicks, and I turn to her. "What?"

"I just wanted to repeat my warning," she points out. "Some consider the house a landmark of sorts. They might not be entirely welcoming to someone else taking possession of it. You understand?"

I catch movement next door, seeing Farrow and some other guy standing in front of the side window, facing me and pinching each other's nipples.

I snort and turn away, trying to cover it with a cough.

"I'm not worried," I choke out.

I've got a powerful friend close who will give me his endorsement.

Ms. Doucet fondles the stud in her ear before ushering me up the stairs. "Let's take another look before I leave you to your new home."

SHELBURNE FALLS

CHAPTER THIRTEEN

Lucas

Farrow's motorcycle rumbles in her driveway, and I stand in the kitchen, frozen like my feet have sprouted roots into her floor.

Make her stay. It's quiet here, just how she likes. It could be just the two of us without any overbearing older brothers or parents or curious eyes. We could make dinner and watch a movie, but...

I listen to her speed away, closing my eyes with my heart in my fucking stomach, because all I could think about with her in the room was her naked on my bed last night. I can't get the images out of my head and how much I loved finding out she dreams of me. Can I be her friend now? Can I trust myself to be alone with her?

Fuck.

She'll be moving soon. I'll be close, but not too close. I need to keep myself under control, so she trusts me again. I don't want her latching on to Noah or Farrow because they have rides.

My house was paid for in cash. Does Quinn really have access to that much money? Without a loan?

Then she can damn well afford a vehicle of her own. Two guys she barely knows, and who won't be there the rest of her life, aren't an excuse to put off the inevitable.

And...they're not going to give her something for nothing.

The next morning, I step into Fallon's workshop, a former chimney service business in a black brick house, far off the road with ivy climbing the wall on the right side of the door. The creak of the screen door sounds like it's from the fifties, and Quinn immediately enters my thoughts again. She probably insisted Fallon keep the rusted, aluminum door because it's louder than a doorbell, but better because anyone just entering your place doesn't mean strangers. She would say it means friends, and the sound would make us smile.

Or something weird like that. Everything makes Quinn feel, and so much of how she associates with the world is rooted in memory. Of which, I'm a part.

I want to laugh with her again. So badly. And I want Madoc and Fallon and everyone else back in my life. As my love of Dubai starts to sink to the back of my brain, and the Falls takes its place, I know that what I gave up here wasn't worth any price.

"Who's there?" Fallon calls out.

I round a glass partition adorned with plants and enter a large room with multiple desks, drafting tables, and a seating area in the corner. Emerald green subway tiles adorn the walls, and I look up, seeing a small conference room through the glass walls upstairs.

Fallon is the only one here. Madoc said she often mentored college students and took in interns, but for the most part, there was no staff. Just her small passion projects. Technically, she's on an extended leave from the company we both work for, which simply means she can have her job back any time. I think the kids and Madoc's building political aspirations were the excuse she was looking for to have some creative freedom again.

She stands in the middle of the room, a VR headset on as she swipes her hands to move through whatever world she's in.

I chuckle quietly as I pull it off her head. "What's this?"

She spins around, startled. "Lucas."

I pull the headset on over my own eyes. A neighborhood spans before me, and I turn, taking in the new world.

"Madoc mentioned you stayed," she says, trying to sound nonchalant when I know she just wants to grill me. "How long?"

"For a bit," I muse, quickly changing the subject. "You didn't answer my question."

"Oh." I can tell she's smiling by her tone. "It's my marketing plan. You know I hate to type."

She puts her gloves on me, and I wave my hands through the air to move the graphics and proceed to the next street. We learned how to design models on a computer, but this really would be a selling point. Being able to put a client into the future to see their skyscraper or home—explore the interiors—before it's even built? Incredible.

But as I move around, past businesses and down streets, familiar landmarks show up. Jared's shop, the gym, the statue of the sleeping fox that sits on a bench in front the tree at the middle school...

"Is this..." I turn in a circle, zoning in on other structures and accents I don't recognize. "Shelburne Falls?"

"Yeah."

But the streets aren't the same. Some of the structures are new, variances in others. "I don't..." I pause, realization dawning. "Oh, I see it." My gaze flits from one thing to the other as I swipe my hands and move the image, taking me from High Street to Fall Away Lane and back to the downtown to City Hall, the police station, and Rivertown Bar and Grill. Windows are bigger, overhangs extended. "Passive solar designs," I say. "Green roofs, rainwater harvesting, the outdoor green spaces…"

This image shows a renovated Shelburne Falls for energy efficiency.

"Walking and bike-friendly streets," she adds.

I look down at the road, seeing that there is a bike lane added.

"The Falls is expanding at a higher rate," I hear her say as I continue to explore. "And now the talk of a train for commuters to and from Chicago…"

I nod, understanding. "Madoc's worried about urbanization. Would that necessarily be a bad thing, though?"

"It doesn't have to be," she concedes. "More people means more jobs and businesses. As long as it's not a McDonald's."

I let out a laugh, removing the headset and handing it to her. "Fallon, the old-timers are never going to agree to this."

"And I would never try to convince them. You know I hate to talk."

She and Madoc prove the old saying that opposites attract. Madoc thrives in a crowd. Fallon detests anything but her small circle. I'm not her kid. But I could've been with the way I take after her.

She sets the VR headset down. "You change people by showing them, not telling them. We start renovating our houses next year."

Renovating…

"You mean…the whole family?"

She nods once.

I can't help but smirk a little. "Jared's never going to agree to that."

"Jared doesn't like to upset his wife even more."

True.

I drift a little, taking in her workshop with its open spaces and a place upstairs to meet with potential clients. All their houses, huh? Fallon's, Juliet's, and Tate's. It's a huge challenge to take on, and it makes me love them even more. That they embrace possibility and lead by example.

"Quinn will love the bike lanes," I tell her.

"She's who I thought of." Fallon grins. "She's always heard music that no one else does, and no matter how much her brothers get on her case about a car, I'm going to help her hold out for as long as possible."

I drop my eyes, feeling guilty. Quinn needs more Fallons around her.

"It's cool." I point to the headset. "I'll have to take that idea back to Dubai with me."

Clients would be able to really see my vision.

"But I am still partial to your old school models," I say. "I used to love staring at them—wishing I lived inside them."

"Well, don't forget your old school model."

She tips her chin up the stairs to the landing. Following her gaze, I spot a few tables, before you get to the conference room, and I can just make out miniatures of homes, office buildings, and other constructions.

My model? And then it occurs to me. The ski resort I used to think I was going to build someday.

I hit her with a bemused look. "You don't still have it."

She beams.

Shaking my head, I can't resist. I jog up the stairs and find it immediately, sitting on a table, the wood and paint and trees a little dusty, but otherwise in the same condition as when I left them.

I study it with more experienced eyes, seeing that the scale is way off. Chalets far too close to the slopes, not nearly enough dining options, and where's the spa? There has to be one.

And for some reason, I thought every skier would be expert level, because I don't see a single green or blue run.

"Well, thank God it was never built!" I shout out to her downstairs. "I think this design would've killed every skier on the mountain!"

I stare at it, hearing her voice. "The only flaw in a dream is if you never begin."

She walks off, back to work, and I gaze at my first model, remembering how I used to picture myself walking through it someday. This was made back when everything was in front of me.

I remove my jacket, loosen my tie, and start pulling apart the model to start over.

Hours later, and I'm finally leaving the workshop. I can't stop the feeling that I'm floating. When was the last time I lost hours like that, caught up in working on something that didn't feel like work?

Fallon still has stuff to do, taking advantage that Hunter, Kade, and A.J. are busy at the summer camp all week. I climb in Jared's Boss, the summer breeze filling my lungs in a way they haven't felt filled in a long fucking time.

I'll be back tomorrow.

I slip the key into the ignition, the engine rumbling to life so loudly that I don't register the doors opening. In a moment, someone sits in the passenger seat. Another person behind me cocks a gun at my head.

I freeze; the nozzle of a pistol pressed into my skull as cologne fills the car. I glance at Fallon's workshop door. *Don't come outside.*

"You weren't a problem for years," the guy in the seat next to me says with a slight accent.

Hugo Navarre.

Head of Green Street. Reeves' successor. Farrow Kelly's boss. It can't be anyone else.

I glance in the rearview mirror at the other guy, but all I catch is his shoulder-length, light brown hair.

"Not because you were banished," he points out. "But because you wanted to leave."

I lock my jaw together, one hand on the wheel and one still on the key.

"You know why you wanted to go?" he continues, elbow propped up on the door as he sits back, fully relaxed. "You couldn't stand your ugly soul and the place where you grew into it. That's the difference between doing bad things in order to eat and doing bad things because you're a fucking coward."

I draw in a long breath through my nose, grinding the wheel in my fist.

He leans in. "Now I permitted you entry out of respect to take care of some family business," he tells me, "but it doesn't look like you're leaving, and if Reeves has to hide, then so do you."

Bullshit. He doesn't want Reeves back. He likes being boss.

Just like he enjoys putting that tattoo on the people close to Madoc. How long before Farrow gets it on Quinn? Or on Hunter or Dylan?

Closing the distance, he nearly breathes on me as he whispers, "I could hide you tonight. Forever." His voice turns sinister. "Unless there's a reason you're still here. I could hide her too."

I whip around, backhanding the kid behind me, his pistol dropping to the ground as I grab the collar of Hugo Navarre's leather jacket.

I glare into his brown eyes, a shade darker than Quinn's as his pal retrieves his gun and points it back at me.

"You *permitted* me entry?" I growl. "Permitted *me*?"

Who the fuck does he think he is? Reeves got me cornered all those years ago because I was a threat, and that hasn't changed. He has no idea if I've told the people close to me everything that happened. He's not going to do shit.

Hugo's eyes gleam, but he doesn't fight back as I press him into the door, squeezing his collar in my fists.

"Don't cross the river again," I bite out. "And don't concern yourself because I own the building you squat in, and I know you do a hell of a lot more than is necessary to eat."

Yeah, I ran. I was twenty-five years old, scared, and ashamed, but nothing I did was for food. I would've rather starved.

Navarre grins. "You forget...I have nothing to lose."

"And no one to mourn your disappearance," I retort.

Anyone who missed him would simply sweep in to take his place.

"You won't hurt me," he says. "You're going to try to stop me."

"Why would I do that?" I narrow my eyes, feigning ignorance. "You'll come after me."

He laughs, but I don't mistake the shaky breaths. "Because Reeves was scared of you."

He wasn't scared of me. He was sick of me.

"And there's only one way to come after you really," Hugo goes on. "I have to find the body."

I hold back the shudder that quakes through my chest.

"Out in the forest, right?" he continues. "Somewhere around the train tunnel, I'd heard."

The train tunnel. The synapses in my brain fire, memories crystallizing.

A wall.

Stone. *Yes...*

I force my voice to stay flat. "I don't know what you're talking about."

But he just laughs. "Luckily, you and Reeves are the only ones who know exactly where it is."

He opens the door, and I don't stop him as he turns and climbs out. The long-haired guy in the back follows him, tucking his pistol into the back of his jeans.

"For now anyway," Hugo calls out and peeks his head back in to look at me. "The Caruthers are having the land out there surveyed for trails and a park ranger station. They probably won't stumble over it." He grins. "But they might."

And he slams the door, both of them walking away.

Heat climbs the back of my neck. I watch them go in my rearview mirror and then glance to the door of Fallon's shop, making sure she didn't see anything.

There may very well be no tracing the body to me, but even so, it would still reflect badly on the town. Especially its mayor and his association with me.

Why didn't I just face it the night it happened?

But I know the answer before I exhale another breath. Because Drew threatened Madoc, and I was in too much pain to come clean so we could deal with it together.

Hugo was right. I was ashamed, scared, and a coward.

I was never a man.

Kids coasted down one of Weston's steepest streets, tumbling and laughing as they tried out my old snowboards in the fresh snow.

"Use your feet!" I yelled. "Press your toes to go left, heels to go right!"

They straight-lined, and I winced, predicting the crash before it happened. Some kid named Wyatt collided with Jorge, both flailing onto the powder that covered the broken street underneath.

It wasn't likely any of these kids could afford a lift ticket, so what the hell. Let them learn to ski anyway.

I held my breath, seeing them both dead on the ground, but then...Jorge started rolling over and Wyatt climbed to his feet. They both threw snow at each other.

Locking my boot in, I cruised down the hill, the club the only thing lit up on the corner with people standing outside like it was a summer night and we were cooking burgers.

I mean, we were cooking burgers, but...

Drew hopped down from his truck, two police officers following him up the snow-covered sidewalk in the otherwise empty downtown.

Why were the police here?

I didn't see Lance zoom in and cut me off. We both hit the ground, my hand sinking through the snow and grating against the pavement.

"Asshole," I chuckled.

He just smiled, whipping a dusting of snow at me.

The kids ran and played, a few parents stood about, and it had been a productive year, making what renovations on the clubhouse that we could afford. We were here every chance we got. We ripped up the floor, sealed the cement underneath, repaired and painted walls, fixed the roof, did a little plumbing, and I installed smart locks and cameras. The address above the door read 8 Green Street. So that was what we started calling it. We paid kids a few bucks to do chores, and we had a makeshift bar others sat at and drank, but we didn't have a liquor license. I wasn't entirely comfortable with it, but there were no cops here.

Until now.

"What the fuck is he doing?" I mumbled to my friend, watching Drew lead the cops inside.

"He thinks he's a gangster," he joked.

Nudging me in the chest, he climbed to his feet, and I did the same, removing my board. We headed down the hill to the club, stepping inside the dark building, couches and TVs spread out where fire engines used to be parked.

Walking to the back of the station, Lance fell in behind me, but I stopped just outside the door to the back room.

"And you can guarantee this supply every week for the rest of the year?" Drew asked one of the cops.

They stood around a table with a large, black duffel sitting on it.

The officer nodded. "After that, you have to find another source."

I peered at Lance.

"Hugo," Drew said to the kid lurking nearby.

Hugo approached him, Drew pulling money out of his pocket. "Go get some beers and tell that piece of shit that if he gives you a hard time, I'm going to be a problem."

The kid couldn't be more than fifteen.

He took the money and tried to slip between us to get out the door, but I grabbed the cash from his hand. "I'll get the beers," I said.

Sullivan's Shop could call the cops on him if he used threats to get liquor.

The kid scowled. "I can do it."

But I barked, "Go play."

I'm not sure why I said that. He wasn't five.

He flipped me his middle finger and disappeared back into the clubhouse. I turned back to watch Drew offer the cops a seat. "Stay a while."

"Drew," I call out, trying to peek around to see what's in the duffel bag.

He looked up just as he was about to sit. I watch him walk over to us, and I waited until he was close and kept my voice low. "What are you doing?" I asked.

"If I tell you," Drew said. "Then I involve you."

"What?"

What the fuck?

I glanced at the bag on the table again. I could only assume it was drugs, and the cops got it from a confiscated bust in Chicago or something.

But he simply burst out laughing. "I'm applying to the police academy," he told us. "Just making friends and trying to get a little favoritism going."

"A cop?" Lance questioned.

To which Drew put his arms around both of us, tugging us in close. "Who's going to watch your mansions while you're taking your families skiing?"

I studied his face, the gleaming blue eyes and half smirk that always gave the impression that he was up to something, but usually it just turned out to be something fun.

He took his seat back at the table, summoning over a young girl with brown hair who wore tight jeans and a crop top. He snaked an arm around her, cupping her ass, while he jerked his chin at another, prompting her to drape her arms around the police officer.

I shot off, but Lance pulled me back. "The age of consent in Illinois is seventeen," he told me under his breath. "He's not technically doing anything wrong."

I glared at Lance.

And when she's almost seventeen? Or he's an actual cop who can get away with anything? Would he do worse?

Madoc would have several words for me if he'd ever caught me hanging around someone who he thought was a bad influence.

But I knew Drew. He was just testing the boundaries. Acting like an idiot. Once the novelty of all of this wore off, he'd focus on other things.

"Lucas, I did it!" Jorge shouted from the front door. "Come see!"

The young woman slid into Drew's lap as he took off his shirt and a tattoo artist started laying out a design on his back.

I spared one more glance at the bag on the table as the cop glided his hand up the second girl's leg.

I drifted away, back into the snow, telling myself that if it wasn't me doing it, then it wasn't my bad to worry about.

I told myself that for a long time.

I drive through town, back toward Quinn's parents' place, lost in my thoughts. I'd wanted to keep my friends, afraid Lance would choose Drew if I walked away, and I wanted to keep the place I'd found for myself, because I was too old to be Madoc's burden. Because having a crew felt safe. Powerful, even.

I liked feeling powerful, even though every day took me further from the man my mother raised and the man my father hoped I'd be.

Turns out, I was more like Drew Reeves than I thought.

I should've stayed.

I should've squared my fucking shoulders and found a way to deal with him, because sooner or later, I would be forced to. Like now.

I need to find the body before Hugo does. I can't protect Madoc without it. And I need to keep Green Street from spilling over onto the people I love.

My childhood home sits dark on the corner as the sun sets, and I slow down, taking in the familiar scents of the neighborhood and my mother's old bedroom window upstairs. It would've been nice to sell this house with a smile, but the door still doesn't feel closed. Like a part of me is still in there.

Quinn will take good care of the place.

I'm about to breeze by, but Farrow Kelly's bike sits at the curb and I hit the brakes.

I glance at the front door, seeing it's cracked open. I look around for her bicycle, but I don't see it. I pull into the driveway and park the car. Is he just giving her rides all the time now?

Stepping into the house, I try not to charge like I have any right to dictate who she comes and goes with, but I'm really fucking regretting leaving a bed upstairs now. Even if thoughts of her and everything she did to herself the other night have haunted me since.

I climb the stairs, pushing open the door to my mother's old room and then my room.

Farrow Kelly stands at the window, looking into the back yard, his eyes turned over his shoulder at me.

I dart my eyes around, looking for Quinn.

"What are you doing here?" I ask him, throwing open the closet doors.

But she's not here.

Farrow turns, drifting lazily to the end of the bed. "I could ask you the same thing, boss. Did the owner give you permission to be here?"

"I'm the owner."

"Grace Morrow is the owner." He smirks and then clarifies. "*Was* the owner."

I take a step toward him. "Where's Quinn?"

He laughs under his breath, and then meets my eyes, smiling like a self-satisfied little prick.

Grabbing him by the collar just as I did his boss a while ago, I haul him up so we're nose to nose and shove him off. "What the fuck are you doing here?" I growl.

He doesn't lose his smile. "Trying to decide where I want my bed." He knocks his knee against the foot of mine, forcing it to bang against the wall again and again. "Maybe a mattress on the floor would be a quieter place to fuck."

Quinn flashes in my head. "Where is she?"

"Quinn?" he clarifies. "At work, maybe? Or at her new place?"

Her new place?

Holding my eyes, he closes his, laughing again. "You thought she bought your house."

She didn't? I retrace the conversation I had with her yesterday. She didn't deny buying a house. If she didn't get this one, then...

"I did," he finally says. "*I* bought your house."

I close the distance between us. "What?"

"Or rather, my father bought it for me."

"What the hell are you talking about?" I'm shouting now. "You live in Weston."

"I do." He slides his hands into his pockets. "But I want a place here too."

"Why?"

He falls silent, refusing to tell me what his game is. I don't want him living here. I would never have sold it to him. His name would be on the paperwork, but my mother owns the house. She saw the paperwork, not me.

"You thought bringing your Green Street shit to Shelburne Falls was a good idea?" I charge.

He just shrugs. "You did."

Yeah, very funny.

"Where is Quinn?" I ask.

Again, he just grins. "I kind of want to tell you that." Mischief hits his eyes. "You'll either handle it badly. Or you'll handle it in a way that brings her closer to you. I mean, that's what you want, right?" he taunts. "Her close to you? Just like you're one of her brothers?"

I feel Quinn on the bed next to us, moaning and swaying as she makes herself come. I watched her. I didn't stop her, and if her brothers knew they'd kill me.

"I remember you," I tell him. He was one of the kids who hung around sometimes. "You were, what, eleven? Twelve? Who's your father?"

Most of those kids were from broken homes. Who's his dad, who lets him run with drug dealers and pimps, but can afford to buy him a house with cash?

He lowers his voice, just loud enough for me to hear. "I remember you too. You installed the motion sensor lights and cameras in the warehouse district. It's how we track movement and create a buffer at Green Street." His smile spreads. "Genius. Whatever happened to that guy?"

Fuck you.

But despite my irritation, pride creeps in. Those sensors were a good idea. You can see from miles away who's moving in the dark and where.

I swallow through the lump in my throat. "What do you want here?"

I left so Madoc, Fallon, Quinn...would all be safe. Being so close now—with his connections to Green Street—is he going to ruin that? Even if I leave?

But to my surprise, he simply says, "I need your help."

My help?

"And you need mine," he adds. "If you want her trust back."

WESTON

CHAPTER FOURTEEN

Quinn

I chew on my pencil eraser. *Crushed blackberries...*

Lying on my stomach in the field off one of Fallstown's tracks, I jot down the ingredient in my notebook and add chocolate sauce.

But then I scratch it out and write chocolate chips instead. *Milk chocolate chips.* Sauce will only overpower the brown sugar and butter, and I want pockets of sweet.

"Oh, he looks like fun," Mace coos.

Pockets. Of. Sweet. I write in my notebook. *I like how that sounds.*

Dylan, Aro, and their friends sit around me with their Bluetooth speaker and coolers, Codi hugging her knees and Mace leaning back on her hands with a couple of other girls whose names I don't remember.

"Who is he?" Mace asks.

What else, what else... An extra egg yolk, for sure.

"Quinn?"

Cornstarch, sugar, salt, vanilla, baking powder...

"Quinn," Mace says sternly.

"What?"

"Who is that blond in the black T-shirt?" she asks me. "The one under the hood with your brothers? Like Farrow, but with more muscles."

The compass sits open on the grass, the needle wavering.

I lift my eyes to the track, seeing Lucas with Jared, Madoc, and Jax, all of them standing around someone's car, smiling and talking about whatever's so interesting under the hood.

My body instantly stirs, taking in his jeans and thick arms crossed over his black T-shirt. Broad shoulders, the lean lines of his chest...

My legs crossed at the ankles, I swing my feet back and forth and bury my eyes in one of my many notebooks. "Lucas Morrow."

I kind of hoped he would've been up when I left this morning. I've never slept in a house alone with him before, and I was barely able to sleep. All I kept thinking about was getting up to make pizza and wondering if the scent would lure him out of bed. A month ago, I would've enjoyed entertaining fantasies about what could happen with a house to ourselves.

Now, I'm too pissed. Still.

"Morrow..." she murmurs. "That name sounds familiar."

"The party the other night was for him," Dylan points out, taking a seat next to Aro.

Lucas stayed in the guest room all night, and he let me leave without any interference, interrogation, or commands this morning.

And without his scent hovering over my shoulder.

I glance at him again, seeing his hands in his pockets now and looking at ease as he jokes with Jax. The pulse between my legs knocks, and I heave a sigh, carving the ingredients into my damn notebook over and over again. *Flour*. How does a baker forget flour?

My phone lights up, and I see a text from my mom roll in.

Do you have a ride home?

I arch an eyebrow. Even from all the way in Bermuda, my parents are tracking me.

I pick up my cell and tap out a reply. *Everyone's here—no worries.*

I have all the rides in the world to choose from.

I'm not even sure why I'm here. Not only does my dad hate me hanging out at the track around groups of traveling motorheads who have girls in every city, but I'm not a fan of the scene, either.

I just couldn't move stuff out of my room with Lucas there tonight, nor did I want to be home alone and pathetic with no social life in front of him, either. I could've gone to the gym, I suppose.

But turns out, he was coming here too. Maybe he was trying to avoid me.

Love you, my mom texts.

I shoot her a heart emoji.

And Dad says he loves you and not to forget the meeting with Tom next week.

I let out a long breath and push my phone away. *Tom Snyder*. Our financial counselor. My dad wants me to start investing.

He won't be happy until I have a cooking show, a magazine of my own, and a Martha Stewart empire. It'll be another bomb to drop, in addition to me moving out, when they discover that I have no money left to invest. I spent it all on the down payment on the house.

I'll call Tom tomorrow to cancel the appointment.

"Is he married?" Mace asks.

Dylan tells her, "No."

I flip the page and start listing half-assed instructions for the blackberry blondies.

"Is he seeing anyone?"

"Do you care?" Aro retorts.

I tip my eyes up, gazing at Lucas again. I saw him kiss more than a few girls growing up. I saw that body on a young woman in my brother's pool. He's not so high and mighty when he's not playing babysitter. Someone—probably many someones—get to see a side of him that no man is allowed to display with me.

"Quinn?"

I avert my eyes, tracing the words I already wrote. "What?"

"Is Lucas Morrow seeing anyone?" Mace asks again.

"I have no idea."

"A guy with arms like that doesn't let them go to waste," she jokes.

I pull on my headphones to get out of the conversation, but I forget to turn on some music.

Dylan chides Mace. "Cool down. He lives halfway across the world. He's only visiting."

"So I'll move quickly."

Why did I think Mace liked girls?

"He's in his thirties," Dylan warns.

Mace flashes a smile. "He knows what he's doing then."

Her long legs stretch out, crossed at the ankle, with her tawny, toned legs bare in black jean shorts.

"And you're nineteen," Dylan continues.

"So I'm old enough, you mean?"

Dylan chuckles, and I try to hold back my scowl, but then Mace pushes herself to her feet, and my heart thunders like it's five times its size inside my chest.

Fluffing her long dark hair, she saunters over in her tank top and combat boots and sidles up to Farrow's side, propping her arm on his shoulder with the other hand on her waist. The one girl in a group of men crowded around some kind of Honda—I have no idea. I'll bet Mace knows.

I lower my eyes but raise them again. And then again, seeing her confidence, easy stance, and how her hands move as she talks.

Lucas and Jax smile, Lucas's gaze on her for so long.

Too long...

I look down. Then back up.

Why wouldn't he be interested? Why wouldn't anyone? She's sexy and can handle herself with anything and anyone. I knew that the first time I met her.

What would I look like with a tattoo?

Dylan reaches over, grabbing a soda from the cooler. "I thought he was leaving."

I draw a picture of my blackberry blondies, pretending I can't hear her.

"Quinn?" she says.

I still don't respond to her, pretending there's music coming out of my headphones.

"Dylan!" Hunter calls, saving the day. She lays the unopened soda can down and runs over to him.

I let out a breath, finally alone. Lucas still lingers with everyone under the hood, Mace leaning her ass on the edge and looking over her shoulder at him.

He wouldn't take her home, would he? To my parents' house? And I don't think she lives on her own. There's always his car, but...

Suddenly, someone straddles my back, and I look over, recognizing Aro's high-top Chucks. She starts tugging at my plaid button-down that I wear over my white tank top.

"What are you doing?" I yell, not giving a shit who hears me.

My arms flop out of the sleeves as she rips the shirt off me and then sinks her fingers into my hair, fluffing and teasing.

"Aro!" I growl.

She slaps a tube of lipstick in front of me, instructing, "Just a little dusting."

"Why?"

"You let me know if he looks at your mouth," she whispers, leaning into my ear, "and later, I'll tell you exactly what he was thinking."

Huh?

I pick up the tube and uncap it, seeing it's a fire engine red. It's not my color.

She must notice me hesitating because she adds, "Don't you want to know if I'm right?"

Right about what? Lucas not being able to take his eyes off my mouth? What do I care—

She pushes me over, so I'm on my back, and takes the lipstick from me. Brushing it over my lips, she smiles as if unwrapping a present.

"Now, fluff your tits."

I dig in my eyebrows.

"Do it!" she growls.

Quickly, I reach into my shelf bra and shift my breasts back into place as I rub my lips together. "Now get off me!"

But instead, she tickles my stomach, and I squeeze my eyes shut, laughing. "Stop!"

I'm laughing so hard, though, and I can barely breathe with her weight on my gut.

"You got a good blush on your cheeks now," she tells me, leaning in. "Here he comes."

I pop my eyes open. "Huh?"

In a moment, she's gone, walking away, and I'm rolling back onto my stomach. Lucas stands at the edge of the track, looking over at me, a lightness in his eyes.

Where did Mace go? Farrow, Dylan, my brothers...everyone is invisible except him.

He strides over, his hands in his pockets.

I try to write the next recipe instruction, but my train of thought is gone.

"It's good to see you having fun," I hear him say over me.

I look up, returning his small smile as he takes a seat on the ground next to me. For some reason, everyone has disappeared, Codi and the rest of Dylan's friends having walked off.

"Dylan and Hunter seem in love," he says, his arms hung over his bent knees. "They were always a pair, I guess."

Following his gaze, I see Hunter standing behind Dylan, his arms wrapped around her as she tips her head back and looks at him. Her lips move, the blush on her cheeks meaning she's saying things only meant for him.

"It used to be Hawke and Kade," Lucas muses. "Now it's Hawke and Aro. Who's Kade with?"

"Everybody."

He laughs, looking down at me. And his eyes drop to my mouth.

I part my lips as the air leaves my lungs.

One...two...thr—

He clears his throat and glances to the ground beneath me and then back up to my eyes.

I have to turn away a little so he won't see the corners of my mouth lift in excitement. *Okay, Aro. You were right.*

"That, um..." he stammers. "That looks like the notebook you left the last time we were here."

"I dug it out." I continue drawing my dessert bars. "Wanted to look back on how silly I was."

The last time I saw him here, I was thirteen. He gave me the hat, and I gave him the compass. I dart my eyes over to it, making sure it still sits on the grass next to me.

I'd left the notebook here that night, and I was heartbroken to find out he'd dropped it off at my house while I'd been asleep. No one woke me up so I could tell him thank you.

I fan the crinkled pages. "I continued making notes over the years. Recipes, lists, questions I wanted answers to."

This journal kind of grew with me.

He grabs for it. "Can I see?"

I throw my arms over it. "No."

He grins and déjà vu hits, the teasing feeling like the old us.

The rumble of engines fills the air, horns honk, and the thunder of feet hit the bleachers.

"Everyone's leaving," he tells me. "Can I take you home?"

Something swims in my stomach, the idea of being alone with him tonight enticing. We have a pool, couches, showers... So many beds.

And then what? I would fantasize and wait, and as usual, it never happens?

Or worse, it would happen, and he'd just push me away later when whatever he was so scared of grabbed him by the throat again.

I've been right where he could find me for years.

"I'm...not going home," I say quietly.

I can't believe the words coming out of my mouth. Even if nothing happened, I could have him to myself just this one night, but I'm not taking my shot. Why the fuck now?

But then he surprises me by saying, "I can take you to your new home. In Weston."

I shoot my head up. How did—

And then I realize. Farrow. He's the only one who knows so far. Why did he tell him?

"I won't say anything," Lucas assures me.

Why? Is he trying to be my friend again?

There was a time when I trusted Lucas wholeheartedly, but since he's been home, his motives have been hard to gauge.

Finally, I nod. If he tattles, I'll deal with it. I'll have no choice. It would be nice to have a few days to get settled before the storm hits, but it's not like my brothers—or my parents—can stop me.

They will try, though.

Thunder cracks overhead, and we both rise as the traffic picks up. People run to their cars, headlights beaming as the crowd trails out of the stands.

Carrying my notebook, I pick up the compass and slip it into my pocket. When I look up, Lucas is watching me put it away. He slides his hands into his pockets, and for some reason, it feels like I'm taking something that belongs to him. He had it for years, and he didn't seem to want to give it back. He lied about leaving it in Dubai. Why?

I stare at the balled fist in his pocket. Did he carry it often?

No. It's possible it never even went to Dubai. Maybe he found it in his bedroom closet before he put the house up for sale.

I follow him to his car, but he doesn't go left, to the parking lots. Instead, he moves toward the track and pulls open the door of a '67 Camaro convertible. I climb in and put my seatbelt on as he slides in the driver's side.

Wind whips through my hair, lightning flashing across the sky.

"This is one of Jax's cars," I point out.

I thought he was driving Jared's old Boss.

Reaching over, he unsnaps my seatbelt and takes it off me just before starting the engine.

I slip my arm out of the belt. "What are you doing?"

"Swing your legs up to my lap and lie back, flat on your seat."

With the top of my head touching my door? It's a bench seat, so there's no console to get in the way.

"It's okay." He breaks into a smile. "Trust me."

I'm not putting my legs on him. I didn't shave today. Or yesterday.

I heave a sigh, dropping my head into his lap, instead, and setting my ankles on the door. My shoes hang out of the car.

His brow arches, and I do a shitty job of holding back my smile. "Trust me," I say.

The sky opens up over his head, clouds covering the stars, and I feel a couple of sprinkles of rain. But when I look up, all I see is him as the warmth of his body cradles my neck.

"Now, close your eyes." He swallows. "And keep them closed."

"Why?"

"You'll see."

Fine. Closing my eyes, I feel the world tilt a little, and I don't know if it's the cool air or the engine rumbling underneath me. Or being this close to him. All I know is he better get the top up before Jax has a fit over rain getting on his black leather seats. My brother is probably still in the tower, watching as cars exit the track.

Lucas shifts, the muscles in his leg flexing underneath me as he hits the gas. The car vaults, and my heart leaps into my throat. I gasp.

He races, kicking it up a gear, then another, and I grip the seats at my sides, a drop of rain hitting me. Barreling around the first corner, he makes the tires skid, and I press one foot into the door to keep myself stable. My hair flies across my face, my stomach swims, and I breathe hard as the wind gets faster and faster when he speeds up. My chest rises and falls, water touching my lips, and I don't open my eyes, but I feel his watching me.

His leg muscles pump again, hitting the gas, then flex once more, slowing just slightly for a turn. Speeding up again, it's like I'm floating, and I smile just as he wraps an arm over my stomach to hold me as he rounds another fast turn.

Oh, God.

I want to turn my face into his stomach, curl up into him, and feel his arm get tighter.

The car slows, and I wait for him to finally stop before I open my eyes.

He stares down at me, so much satisfaction written across his face. "You like going fast."

Rain falls harder now, and I blink up at him, feeling his hand still gripping my waist. "I like *you* going fast."

Maybe I like speed. I don't know.

I like roller coasters and roller skates. I like pedaling fast and cruising down a hill on my bike.

And I like *his* driving. Madoc taught him just as well as he taught his sons.

"It's settled then," he says. "I'll just have to drive your lazy butt around all summer."

I laugh, beaming up at him. His eyes drop to my mouth again, and for a second—maybe less—I swear they drop farther before he quickly looks away and takes his hand off of me.

My blood runs hot. *Look at me again.*

But his phone rings, and he pulls it out of his pocket, answering it.

I can hear my brother's growl in Lucas's ear. "Why the fuck doesn't she have a seatbelt on?"

Lucas hangs up, wincing at Jax's scolding. Jax is usually the calm one.

But I was right. He's in the watchtower, keeping an eye on me.

"Well..." I clear my throat. "At the very least, they won't put up a fuss if you're giving me rides. They're not threatened by you."

Neither am I. Unfortunately.

If I weren't Quinn, he would've held me tighter.

He props his elbow up on his door, leaning his head on his hand and making no move to raise the top. "Did you ever have a relationship they ruined?" he asks me.

I stay in his lap. "No. No one I was very interested in anyway."

"Any long-term relationships?"

It feels weird he's asking me these things. They're not the kind of conversations we had when I was thirteen.

"I went out a bit," I tell him. "Just didn't feel like I thought it would feel."

"What?"

"Kissing."

He doesn't move, and I don't stop.

"Or their hands," I add. "I'd be cold, or it felt foreign, or like I was bored or something. I didn't really understand foreplay."

I stare at nothing off to the side, remembering Notre Dame. I went to parties with roommates my first year, and I met guys in class and various social clubs, but I knew pretty early on that there was no point in wasting time being that uncomfortable to make a relationship happen that, if successful, would take me away from Shelburne Falls.

I was coming home after I graduated. No exceptions.

"Now that I'm home," I announce, "maybe I can get to know someone to where it feels close and warm and exciting."

But he tells me, "I think that comes when you really know someone and know that what you're about to feel is an escape."

My pulse thrums in my neck as he gazes down at me.

"Their scent," he goes on, "their skin, the feel of their mouth on your stomach. It happens in the middle of the night when she rolls into your arms, and it becomes like food, Quinn. Like shelter."

"Did you ever feel like that?" I inquire, but it comes out as a whisper as I hold my breath.

"No."

Then how does he know that's what it's like?

I lie there, resisting the urge to rub the place over my heart where it hurts. But I never want to leave, no matter how much it rains.

"Why aren't you married?" I ask him. "And don't say it's because you haven't found the right person."

He stares off, trying to find the words. He's probably had several relationships. He's successful, handsome, and probably financially well off—building skyscrapers in one of the wealthiest cities in the world with no family to support.

"I like to be left alone," he whispers.

I narrow my eyes. The words are harsh, but his tone was an apology.

"Why did you stay?" I ask next.

He frowns a little. "I don't know."

Another apology.

"That's good to hear," I tell him.

I like it when the people older than me, who care about me, don't pretend they have all the answers. It rarely happens.

The rain feels fresh on my skin, and I don't want to get out of it yet. "I'm going to ride my bike home."

Sitting up, I get out of the car, and turn around, seeing concern on his face.

"I'll be fine," I tell him.

Yes, it's unsafe, and I'll get drenched, but having a mind of my own feels too good, I guess.

Plus, he doesn't know where my new home is exactly yet, and I like to be left alone sometimes too. Especially when I know what I still want from him, and don't trust him enough to let myself have it.

I set off to grab my bike.

Rain spills down my arms, plastering the thin, plaid shirt to my arms. My legs shine in the moonlight as I pedal, my tiny purse hanging over my body with my phone safely tucked inside.

I dig into the coin pocket and pull out some denomination that might be a nickel and fling it over the side of the bridge. There might be a car down there, but I'll either be leaving too early and coming home too late to see anything in the dark. If I do get the chance, though, I'll have to stop and look. The river isn't that deep in most areas, and Farrow says it's visible on a calm day.

There's no body down there, though. I think she got out of the car and no one knows.

But still... Tradition and all.

Standing up, I pump the pedals uphill, climbing to Knock Hill and checking behind me every so often. There's no one there—no one on the road—but I keep feeling something at my back. Paranoia, I suppose. That creepy, black Dodge still lurks in my mind, and I'm very surprised Lucas or one of my brothers isn't following me to ensure my safety.

Looking over my shoulder, I gaze down the dark road. *Very surprised, actually.*

The odd light will illuminate as I pass a warehouse. Security measures activated by motion, and at one point, the hill elevates so steeply, I have to dismount my bike and walk a little.

When I arrive on my lane, there are two houses on the right with a light on somewhere in their brownstones. And Farrow's is on the left, every room lit up. I smile, walking along. From the small amount of time I've been around the last couple of days, there are people coming and going from his place all the time.

My house sits to the left of his, a glow shining through the living room window.

I halt.

But just for a moment.

Hunter's car sits at the curb, and my stomach sinks. Maybe he and Dylan left something at the house from when they used to spend time there?

Or maybe it's just Dylan, and she's determined to get answers to the questions I ignored when we were at the track.

In any case, my secret is blown. There's no way I can keep this from my family for even twelve hours.

I carry my bike up the steps, turning the knob and hearing voices as soon as I open the door.

"Shut it off," Hunter growls.

"It's research!" Kade shouts, but I can hear the laughter in his voice.

Stepping inside, I quietly close the door and peer into the living room where Hawke stands solemnly as Hunter grabs for the remote that Kade keeps just out of reach.

"I'm gonna do that someday." He points at the TV. "I need to know where all the legs go."

I set my bike inside and glance at the flatscreen Farrow donated to my new place last night, three bodies writhing and sweating on the screen. One man thrusts into a blonde from behind while she takes another guy in her mouth.

"What did you download onto my TV?!" I bark.

Kade spins around. "Jesus..."

Hawke snatches the remote from him and switches the TV off, throwing it down on the green velvet couch that was here before I was.

Hawke approaches me. "We need to talk."

"How did you know I'd be here?"

"There are cameras all over town," he blurts out. "It was only a matter of time before your budding friendship with Farrow Kelly paid off for him."

"He's been lonely without Dylan living here," Hunter adds. "He passes this house out to whoever would be good company if they want to crash."

So, they don't know I bought it. Hawke hacked into the town's traffic cams and noticed me making trips over the bridge. They think I'm hanging out for a little freedom?

I blow out a breath of relief, even though I know it won't last long. They'll certainly know what's going on when Farrow's truck is loaded with my furniture.

"You found Carnival Tower," he states.

I don't move or glance at my other nephews. I won't ask how he found out it was me. Maybe he's got a camera in the alley behind my bakery and saw me retrieving my bike chain the night the hatch in the roof was locked.

Or maybe he hacked into a business's security camera across the street and saw me through the windows climbing through the mirror.

It was only a matter of time before he figured it out.

I sigh. "I'm not scared of you."

Hawke's voice softens as if he's dealing with a child. "That's not what I want," he tells me. "But you don't understand what you're dealing with."

Hunter advances. "Quinn—"

"No." I turn my gaze from Hawke and look at Hunter dead-on. "Carnival Tower is my property. You guys can find a million other places to get laid."

"The urban legends are true," Hawke points out. "Manas and Deacon Doran have been sneaking in for two decades. They're—"

"I know who they are."

He pauses, studying me. If I have access, he must know I've read the murder map on the wall.

Thankfully, he doesn't decide to rehash the whole story. He simply continues. "We don't know why they come," Hawke goes on, "but us being there gives you some measure of protection."

I would agree with that, but...

"Just back off," I say. "You've let Dylan and Aro spend time there. It's my turn."

"Quinn..."

But I'm done talking tonight. Moving in behind Kade, I start shuffling them out of my house. They're talking sense and making good points, but what if they weren't around? What if I were on my own? What would I do then?

Hawke digs in his heels, resisting. "No, we're talking about this."

"He won't hurt me," I tell them. "He hasn't hurt any of you. He just likes being a part of things or something."

"Who?"

"Deacon." Planting my hands on Kade's back, I shove them toward the front door. "If I get concerned, I'll find you guys. I'm not stupid. But he doesn't sound threatening. Not yet anyway."

"Sound?" Hawke whips around. "You talked to him?"

"You haven't?" I stop, all three of my nephews gaping at me. "He called my phone yesterday."

"What did he say?" Hawke gasps.

Followed by Hunter, "How did he sound?"

"What?" Kade breathes out.

They've never spoken to the brothers. I'm the only one they've called.

"Quinn," Hawke says in a stern voice. "We think he hurt... Well, her name was Winslet."

"The car in the river?" I nod. "Yeah, it's empty."

"How do you know that?"

"The diary." Again, they look at me like I'm pointing a gun at them. "Really? You guys have had years. I put that together in minutes."

If the diary is authentic, it wasn't hard to piece together that she either made it out, or it was all a ruse in the first place.

I push Hunter and Kade out the door, then push Hawke, but he stops me. "Wait, what diary?"

All three of them stare at me, confused. They never saw a diary.

I put my hand on my waist. "You never thought of springing a trap for these guys instead of waiting for them to dole out clues at their leisure?"

I mean, they've been researching these brothers for years. They know they're coming into the tower.

I push them out.

"Quinn…"

"I'll let you know what happens."

"Quinn!"

"Goodnight!" I yell, watching Hunter and Kade jog down the steps.

I start to shut the door in Hawke's face, but I stop, grabbing him by the T-shirt and pulling him back. "When Aro wears red lipstick," I ask, "what do you think when you look at her mouth?"

"Huh?"

He blinks at me for several moments, his mouth opening and closing and looking flustered.

"Just say it," I growl.

He tsks, acting just like his father. Like he's not a completely different guy in a bedroom with his girl.

"I'm thinking," he grumbles, "how…good those lips would look wrapped around my…"

I pinch my brows together.

"You know…" he gruffs. "My cock. Jesus, Quinn."

That's what Lucas was thinking? I fold my lips between my teeth, still tasting the lipstick.

"Weirdo," Hawke mumbles.

And I don't have to shove him anymore. He practically runs down the stairs to get away from me.

To my surprise, I laugh as I close the door and lock it. Lucas looked at my mouth four times.

In the living room, I remove the notebook from the waistline of my pants and drop it to the table before pulling out the diary I'd stashed in the bureau. I fan the pages to find the next entry. There are several blank sheets after the initial passage. Not sure if she—or whoever—meant to come back and add things, or if their attention to organization was as haphazard as their writing.

Gone
Alone

Can't go home

Eight days since I felt you

Gone
Alone
Can't go home

Did it to me, now I'll do it to you

Drawings fill the page around the words. The bridge. A car under the water. The warehouses of Weston, his hand, her neck...

I flip the page and stare at the headlights of the '72 Dodge.

Do it to me, now I'll do it to you.

Atta girl.

Light from the TV flashes in the corner of my eyes, and I walk over to the couch, picking up the remote the boys left. The TV must've come back on when Hawke threw down the remote.

QUIET ONES

I stare at the screen, a blush rising to my cheeks. What the hell were they watching? The woman is on the bed, one man under her and the other one behind her, and I crane my neck, trying to figure out whose legs are whose.

SHELBURNE FALLS

CHAPTER FIFTEEN

Lucas

Noah and I hop out of the back of a JT Racing truck, each of us grabbing a few flags already strewn on poles to slide into the lamppost slots along High Street. The Fourth of July parade is in less than three days, so everyone is pitching in to decorate.

"Thanks for paying for the drinks the other night," Noah says.

I fit the end of a pole into a bracket. "I needed them more than you did," I reply. "I guess I wasn't much for company. Sorry."

We barely talked, some local fans of his gathered around as soon as we got there to fawn over him. I was grateful, though. I didn't want to drink alone, but I knew I wasn't going to talk much, either.

"It was fine," he says. "Kind of like drinking with my brother."

"You hang out at that bar much?"

"Never." He moves to the next lamppost, throwing me a smile. "I usually take a bottle out to the river, or sneak into Eagle Point Park. Somewhere I can be alone," he tells me. "And hear the sounds of home that I'll never admit to my dad that I kind of miss."

I get the impression he couldn't wait to get away from his family and Colorado, but he seems to miss them too. He's just like everyone else with a story, and has complications and feelings he doesn't know what to do with.

He's not the guy I thought he was, and I know from watching Madoc that men with constant smiles are hiding things too.

"You need a girl." I toss him the last pole and he slips it in the bracket. "Or a guy?"

He chuckles, and we both hop back into the truck bed that one of Jared's techs drives while we decorate. "Can I have that one?" He points to Quinn's shop, and I look, recognizing her figure delivering a coffee to a table. Her hair is down, tucked behind one ear, and I like the baker's coat she wears.

I cock an eyebrow, throwing the little shit a glare. "And compete with Farrow Kelly?" I force a tease.

Noah is definitely a threat, but I don't know… It's like surface charm. He hides behind it. Something tells me Quinn will see through it too.

He shrugs. "Farrow will just suggest we share her."

My heart drops like a hammer.

We stop and Noah jumps down with my flags. I follow him, sliding a pole in, but my hand shakes. "Quinn isn't like that," I tell him.

"They're all like that."

I drop my arms, the remaining flags draping on the ground. *Son of a bitch.*

Noah meets my eyes, moving to the next pole. "People love to be desired, especially good girls who haven't experienced much attention," he tells me in his confident, piece-of-shit tone. "They're kind of dumb. Hot hands coming at them from two men, they unravel, and all they can do is hang on for the ride."

Who does he think he's talking to? I swipe the flag poles off the ground, ready to lunge.

"Every girl has two sides," he explains. "Sunday best and doggy-style-fuck-fest."

I snarl, throwing the flags into the bed of the truck as I charge for him. I wrap one hand around his fucking throat and pin him to the lamppost. He just smiles, pulling up a hundred-dollar bill from his pocket. "How about a bet?" he taunts.

"How about a lesson, you little shit?"

But he just goes on. "You'll say you don't think about her like that, and I say you want her *exactly* like that."

Quinn's face looking up at me last night floats through my head, and God...

I could've driven with her like that forever. Fuck, I wanted to take her somewhere. Is it obvious?

"If I'm wrong, you win." He stuffs the money into my jeans pocket. "If I'm right, you owe me."

I breathe hard, shoving the little prick away. He's not worth the energy.

"I'll be waiting," he says, jumping into the back of the truck and throwing me the rest of the flags.

I can't swallow. My mouth is parched.

I take the money back out of the pocket and throw it at him. "She's a kid."

"She's not."

He tosses the bill back, and it lands on the ground.

"She's practically family," I growl.

"But she's not."

Brooks, one of Jared's mechanics, starts to drive.

"She's too young!" I bark at Noah.

"Fine!" he shouts. "Let her fuck around with a few boyfriends, and then when you're forty and Farrow Kelly and I have doubly-penetrated her, you can put her heart back together."

Two ladies on the sidewalk stop short, their mouths hanging open, and I blink long and hard.

Fuck.

Noah howls with laughter. "I dub thee my new older brother!" he shouts. "I miss him. You can fill in. Gym tonight. Seven o'clock."

I would yell expletives at him, but he's too far away now even if I can still make out his stupid fucking grin from here. Brooks is taking him to the park to set up tables and chairs.

Plus, I'm the adult.

Images of him, Farrow, and Quinn assault my brain, and I don't know if Quinn would let something like that happen, but they certainly would never say no. And she's the inexperienced one. Someone needs to be keeping an eye on her.

And I'm not clear in my head right now. Watching her the other night on the bed, and last night with her head in my lap, is messing with me. I could bond with her when we were younger and it was safe, but I'm bonding with her now and it's different. My body is reacting. It's not okay.

Quickly, I hang the rest of the flags and pull out my phone, dialing Isobel.

"Good morning, sir," she answers.

It's almost nine-thirty at night there.

"Tell me I'm needed." I sound like I'm daring her. "Tell me to come home."

I hear her tinkling laugh. "You're handling everything just fine via phone and computer for now," she says. "Take a few more days."

I figured she'd say that. She likes being in charge of my office.

"Are you in the mood for some research?" I ask instead.

"Ohhh, what's up?"

I turn in a slow circle, making sure no one is walking up on me as I scan the street for that Traverse.

I spot Kade pulling up to the curb in his truck, a couple of friends in the cab with him. Jax stands up on the hill, in front of the historical society, setting up the sound system.

"Take these names down," I tell her. "Hugo Navarre, Drew Reeves, Noah Van der Berg—V-A-N-D-E-R-B-E-R-G, and Farrow Kelly. F-A-R-R-O-W." I give her a few seconds, hearing her type. "Also..." I swallow, lowering my voice. "Madoc Caruthers, Jared Trent, and Jaxon Trent."

I look around me again for any listening ears.

"I want dossiers that rival that one you keep on that girl who destroyed the curve in your high school calculus class."

Kade rounds the front of his truck as his friends climb out. I watch him hold his arm out and flip the middle finger to some guy passing by on a motorcycle. A young girl with a white-blonde ponytail and red tips hangs on behind him.

"How did you know about that?" Isobel gasps.

I chuckle. "It came up in the background check."

"You did a background check on me?"

"Haven't you done one on me?" I shoot back.

She's nosy and overbearing. Of course she did.

She avoids the question. "Psh."

The guy and girl on the motorcycle pass by me, and I notice he's quite a bit older than her with graying hair and a scruffy beard. I do a double-take, recognizing him.

Is that...?

He looks at me, and I look away. *Shit, that's Nate Dietrich.* He was a rival of Madoc's in school. Or of Jared's. I guess Kade is keeping the legacy alive.

"Oh," Isobel remarks before letting me go. "You have a date tonight. Do you want to cancel it yourself?"

I cut off my groan before it becomes audible. "I'll take care of it."

It's tempting to let Isobel cancel what's just become an appointment for two overworked people who need to blow off some steam, but it's not a situation a good person puts their assistant in.

"I'll get back to you when I have the files," she tells me.

"Thanks."

We hang up, and I walk toward Jax. Across the street, taking the steps up the hill to where he has electronics spread out under a tent.

"Hey," I say, warm wind breezing through my hair.

He looks up. "Hi."

"Need any help?"

"Nah, about done," he tells me.

I nod, letting my eyes roam over the equipment and cords on the table, cases of drones underneath. I can't go back to the Caruthers' place. It's too quiet.

I could go to Fallon's shop, but Madoc's car was there earlier, and I don't have answers for questions he desperately wants to ask.

"You want to talk about it?" Jax offers.

I run my hand over the blade of a drone. "No." I pause, then continue. "Just tell me I'm welcome in the Falls no matter what happens."

"Why me?"

I meet his eyes. "Because you've been the worst places and you're still here."

I'm not supposed to know that he was severely abused as a child or that he killed his father's girlfriend and their friend when he'd had enough. Madoc didn't keep things from me, though, and he wanted me to understand that nothing is as it seems. It's impossible to be aware of everything about every person, and we should always give the benefit of the doubt.

And there's only one person we ever really know. If we're lucky.

"Sometimes I was carried." Jax gives me a soft smile. "Jared, Madoc... And by her."

I don't have to ask to know he's talking about his wife.

"When my heart couldn't stand me anymore, I just gave it to her," he states.

I clench my jaw, watching him close a case, and I move my hand off a box of security cameras as he covers the table with a tarp.

Who do I give my shit to?

I'm a bad guy, and I'm putting everyone around me in danger. Who do I let see that?

Hours later, Jared and Jax take the front line while Madoc slams the racquetball, and I try to keep my eye on the damn game.

"Senator?" I shout.

"I think I can do it!" Madoc boasts back at me.

The ball bounces, echoing in the big chamber. Jax dives to slap it with his racket.

"'Think you can?'" Jared growls, pulling off his shirt and tossing it. "You're not climbing a mountain. You'd be altering your life!" He hits the ball next. "Your family's lives. Our lives!"

We've only been playing for fifteen minutes, but everyone is sweating already. I was thankful they showed up, though. Working out with Noah Van der Berg by myself was the last thing I wanted tonight. He found a girl he's presently spotting on the weight bench anyway.

Jax picks up the ball, tosses it in the air, and whips it at the wall. "Don't senators spend much of the year in D.C.?"

"And there are no term limits," Jared adds to Madoc. "You could be gone for the rest of your life. Is that what you want?"

"I feel our relationship can endure this challenge," Madoc says sweetly.

Jared scowls. "Fuck you."

I rumble with a laugh as I slap an overhand. Jared's embellishing. Madoc wouldn't be gone the rest of his life. But he would be gone a lot, and Jared would miss him. Of course, he's not going to admit that to Madoc.

"We got everything," Jared pants. "And getting greedy is a good way to lose it. Can't you just be content?"

The ball comes for Madoc, but it's lost behind him as he turns to Jared.

"There's no stopping," he tells his stepbrother. "Like you said, we have everything. Now it's time to serve."

"No politician actually thinks like that."

"They should," Madoc retorts. "When life is good, you can help. When life is bad, you can still help. No matter what happens to us, we can always focus on others first. It's that purpose that keeps us connected to the world. Do you know how many people don't know that?"

Jared's eyebrows are etched in a deep V, but he doesn't say anything.

He loves his life. No matter how much he pouts or grumbles or bitches, he loves everything exactly as it is, and is desperate to keep it that way, because he and Jax know how bad life *can* get. They're grateful and don't want to tempt fate.

Madoc's childhood was different. He doesn't really know darkness. He has enough dreams to share with those who don't have any.

A senator, though... People will dig into his life.

And the lives of those he loves. I almost shrink, my past still forefront in my mind.

The air is still, and no one moves.

Suddenly, Jax asks, "Is your dick still pierced?"

Jared actually breaks into laughter, and I snort, going to pick up the ball.

"Really?" Madoc gripes.

I serve the ball. "That might look bad in the press."

"It's the least of what could look bad." Madoc slams the ball back. "There are pictures of things."

Jared spins around, Jax quirks an eyebrow.

Madoc shrugs. "Fallon likes to tie me up for sex."

Everyone reels with joy, laughing so hard we're damn near crying. *Of course, she does.*

We volley for another minute, and I relish this. It's not like I'm his kid anymore. It's like I'm one of his brothers.

Jax slams the ball too hard for anyone to respond. "It's getting late."

"Did Quinn make it home safely?" Madoc asks, his eyes moving around to all of us as he collects the ball.

"I didn't get a call for a ride," Jared breathes out.

"That Farrow Kelly kid is pissing me off," Madoc grumbles. "He keeps hanging around her."

Jax moves for the door. "He's not that bad."

"He's a criminal."

"So was I."

We trail out, Madoc bringing up the rear. "And do you want him doing to Quinn what you did to Juliet?"

I pull on my hoodie, catching the corner of Jax's grin as he no doubt reminisces over his and his wife's volatile early days together.

A brick settles into the pit of my stomach. I'm not so worried about Farrow now. Or Noah. But they won't resist her if she's interested. Not for a second.

"Find her someone we like then," Jared chimes in. "Otherwise, she's just going to end up with one of these guys simply for a lack of options."

I open my mouth to shut them up. She's twenty-one goddamn years old. What's the hurry?

But I'm afraid my irritation will reek of jealousy. I feel like it's burned into my forehead for everyone to see.

Jax tosses his racket to Jared. "I got to get back to the summer camp. Can you stop by the bakery and check on her?"

"I got it." I wipe off my forehead with my sleeve. "I wanted to see if I could steal some leftovers for Fallon's workshop in the morning anyway."

Jared gives me a nod of thanks as I move to grab my bag and water.

Madoc slaps me on the back. "Give her a hug from us."

Yeah. I don't tell him that I'm a criminal, too, but the irony isn't lost on me.

I leave the treadmill area, hearing Jax behind me. "Is she on birth control?"

Jesus. I shake my head too little for anyone to see.

"We're her birth control," Jared replies.

I exit the gym, leaving them behind and climbing into my car. Something about how they talk about her bugs me, and it shouldn't because I hover and talk down to her, same as them. As if I have more of a right to be invasive than they do.

But maybe I do. I want to be her friend. I want her to be happy.

And they do, too, as long as that path includes celibacy.

I lay on the pedal faster than I wish, hating that I'm anxious to see her. Is she still at work? Did she get a ride? I nearly hold my breath, waiting to make a left, and then another, until the shop comes into view.

Parking in the alley behind the bakery, I leave the car running and knock on the back door.

We're friends...

I want the world for her.

"Who is it?"

I lean in. "Lucas."

She unlocks the door, greeting me without a smile, but her eyes are soft and wide. She just wears her black pants and sneakers, with a T-shirt. Her baker's jacket is gone.

"Missed you at the gym," I tell her.

"I know." She turns and walks back into the bakery.

I follow.

"I'm overloaded with orders in red, white, and blue." She laughs, turning back around and slipping her purse over her head. "I have to be back in seven hours."

Locks of hair spill out of her ponytail, and she doesn't look the least bit overworked. Her big, brown eyes gleam fresh and happy.

I clear my throat. "Want a...a ride?" I jerk my thumb to the door and my car parked on the other side of it.

She hesitates. "I'm going to Weston."

My gaze falters, but I nod to hide it. If she had a crush, like she said she did that night on my bed, then wouldn't she like to be where I am? I'm in her damn house, for Christ's sake.

"It's okay," I say instead. "I could use the drive."

She tosses a cloth into the laundry bag. "Thanks."

Walking back out the door, I head for the driver's side while she locks up.

Climbing into the passenger's seat, she buckles up. Her scent fills her brother's car, and I can't help but look at her.

"Don't tell me I look tired, okay?" she says, meeting my eyes.

I tear my gaze away, starting the car. "You look content."

Backing out of the alley, I head to Weston and roll down the windows. She tilts her head back, her eyes turned outside, watching the houses and businesses give way to trees.

Her hair blows across her neck, and I keep glancing at how pretty she looks.

"So," I say, trying to think about anything else. "Did you know Farrow Kelly bought my house?"

Her gaze flashes to mine, and I see the amusement on her face. "You thought I bought it."

"And you let me think it."

She squeezes her eyes shut, laughing. "It bought me time," she muses. "I did think about it. For a few seconds. But I needed space. Real space."

"Yeah, I know." I concede. "You don't have to explain."

I get it. Her family will show up in Weston uninvited and unexpected just as much as they would in the Falls, but it's not about getting away from them. It's about finding something new. An unfamiliar environment is what everyone needs.

Before all they want is to come back home.

Quinn opens the glove compartment, finding some tissues, but I watch a string of condoms spill out.

I widen my eyes.

She holds them up, and I debate for a second.

This is Jared's car. He wouldn't still be using condoms with his wife, would he? Why does he have them in here?

She smirks, stuffing them back in the glove compartment. "I think Hawke used the car last," she jokes. "I'm told he lost his virginity in here, actually."

"Good."

She casts her surprised eyes on me.

"I just didn't want you to think they were mine," I admit.

She breathes out a laugh and stares at her clasped hands in her lap. The wheels in her head turn.

"You know, I used to have a crush on you," she says in a low voice. "Did you know that?"

"Well, yeah." I swallow. "You said you were going to marry me when you were eight."

I grin, remembering her always being around me.

But then she replies, "I don't mean when I was eight. I mean, I did then, but also later too."

I don't look at her now. The lines on the road rush underneath my car, one after the other.

"When I was thirteen and you left," she tells me, "and still at fifteen and sixteen."

We cross the bridge, and I watch her pull out a penny and let her arm whip out into the night, tossing the coin over the side.

I guess I should've known about the crush, but I just thought she was a bit lonely, like me.

She fills her lungs with fresh air and exhales. "I shouldn't have put pressure on you to be here, or to be someone I imagined as a kid." Her eyes soften. "It was unfair."

It's not.

I want to matter to her.

"Friends?" she says.

I can't look at her, the ceiling of the car seeming to come down on my head. I want to be who she imagined. Exactly who she imagined.

It's like she's woken up from a dream to the disappointment of reality.

My eyelids flutter, searching for something to say. "Unless your favorite movie is still *The Shawshank Redemption*," I grumble over the needles in my throat.

"Oh, okay, *Fast & Furious*," she teases.

"*The Matrix*, thank you."

We smile at each other as she points for me to take the hill, and we cruise through Weston, bypassing Green Street down the road on the right.

Yes, her film preferences are a little more sophisticated than mine, but her choices produce far too many emotions for me to go through more than once a year. I guess my taste was shaped by her brothers. Jax raised me on *Mission Impossible*. Jared loved martial arts films. And Madoc loved old school action.

"In fact," I tell her, "You need to see both franchises again. Got a TV yet?"

She directs me right and points to the house on the left. "Yes."

I park, looking up at one of the many massive brownstone townhouses of Knock Hill. I drove around this town many times in college, but I didn't think anyone lived here anymore. Three stories, worn wooden door, ornate stairwell up to the front door.

It must've been beautiful back in the day.

I follow her up to the house. "I'm going to log you into my streaming accounts."

"Fix the settings in there while you're at it," she fires back. "I don't like that TruMotion, or whatever it's called."

She unlocks the door and steps inside. I start to follow her, but something catches my attention, and I see Farrow Kelly standing at the window of the brownstone next door, shirtless and smoking a cigarette.

He lives next door?

I turn away. *Great*.

"I'll be back," she calls out, heading up the steps.

Drifting through the door and into the foyer, I let my eyes roll around the entire space, taking in all the disrepair—the damaged floors, the broken walls, the ancient electrical running across the ceiling to the chandelier. The house creaks when I walk, and as she moves upstairs, immediately making my heart palpitate. Can her bedroom floor even support proper furniture? She couldn't have had this place inspected because it wouldn't have passed. I can already see that. Everything needs to be gutted.

I could start a fight and bring her home.

Or maybe she'll let me help her. I am an architect, after all.

I see her flatscreen and dip down for the remote on the coffee table. Her old notebook lays open, a pen discarded on top as if she was in the middle of writing, and just as I look away, I notice the page titled *Birthday Presents*.

I don't mean to read it, but after the first one, I just keep going.

1. Blow him while he's on the phone.
2. Have sex with him while my brothers are in the house.
3. Flash him while he's in a meeting.
4. Read erotica to him.
5. Feel what it's like to have my panties ripped off.

6. Let him make me come with a rose or a feather.
7. Wear a collar.
8. Perform for him.
9. Wash him.
10. Be *really* loud. So loud, I

So loud, she what?

She stopped writing mid-sentence. Breathless, I rise, squeezing the muscles in the back of my neck and feeling sweat. What the fuck?

I see her on my bed again. I'm behind her. Number five...

My cock swells in my pants, and I groan.

I reach over to close the book in case she thinks I read it, but I stop myself. If I touch it, she might know then.

I rise with the remote in my hand. She could've made this list years ago. She said she recently dug it out to review it.

But no, she was adding to it. *Oh, Quinn.*

Flipping on the TV, the moaning hits my ears before the images, and in a moment, I'm staring at two men pumping their fucking dicks into a young woman.

I fumble with the remote. What the hell?!

Quinn!

But I don't shout. I can't even catch my breath.

I flip off the television. I don't tell her I'm leaving. I don't say goodbye.

In fifteen minutes, I'm back in Shelburne Falls, on High Street.

I climb the stairs to the historical society, whip back the tarp covering Jax's set up, and snatch the case of small security cameras.

She needs more fucking supervision.

WESTON

CHAPTER SIXTEEN

Quinn

"Have a good day tomorrow!" I shout to the back of the bakery. "Stay safe!"

"Bye!" Hailey calls out, followed by the others out the alley door. We should be all set for the Fourth of July the day after tomorrow—pre-orders are ready, cupcakes and tarts baked and chilling, and the booth is set up in the park. The shop will be closed tomorrow to give everyone who volunteered to work the holiday the day off before, and I'm looking forward to it. Maybe I can get some groceries and do some online furniture shopping for my new place. I do have a little money left.

"Codi, do you have a phone?" I ask my remaining employee who finishes cleaning the display case.

She stands up straight. "Yes."

I take out mine. "Can I get your number?"

I'm not sure if she's more than a summer employee yet. Somewhere I picked up the impression that she might not be able to commit to a long-term schedule, so we're taking it a few days at a time. I've just been paying her under the table, but I need to get her on payroll. Taxes and such...

"We'll be all over the place for the holiday," I warn her. "It'll make it easier to find each other." I hand her my phone. "Wanna put your number in?"

Keeping her eyes down, she takes the phone and starts punching in digits.

I take it back and add her as a contact. "Doing anything fun tomorrow for your day off?"

"I have to clean Farrow's house."

Her voice is nearly a whisper, but I'm getting used to it.

What does she mean she *has* to clean Farrow's house?

"As a...a job?" I ask.

She hesitates, as if thinking, before she nods.

Which makes me doubt he's paying her. Is she returning a favor or something? Does he help her out in return?

Farrow's been kind to me, but I haven't known him long.

I step in closer. "He's nice to you, right?"

Again, she nods, but I knew before I asked that she would never say he wasn't. She's afraid of him.

The question is, should she be, or is she just afraid of everyone?

"Call me if you ever need anything," I tell her. "I'm always here."

She presses her lips together before turning and leaving.

I don't stay long. I finish up scheduling, and my lineup for next week's new additions to the menu, as well as carving out time after the holiday to work on the ice cream stand. It would've been ideal to have it for the Fourth of July, but the hottest days are yet to come.

I climb on my bike and ride to my parents' house. The multi-day backpack I got in high school during that phase where I thought I was going to hike the Appalachian Trail is still buried in my closet, I think. Perfect for transporting more of my stuff.

In six minutes, I'm home. Walking inside, I head upstairs and dive into my bedroom, so full of energy even though I've been working for twelve hours. Tonight, I'll be in Weston. In *my* house. Sitting at *my* table, eating something from *my* kitchen. I don't even care if it's cereal or croque monsieur. It's mine.

Finding my pack, I stuff in essential shoes, clothes, extra chargers, and snatch framed photos of my family off my wall. I'll hang them in my new house.

I hesitate for only a moment. It would be smart to wait for the loan to go through before moving all of this in. What if there's a problem?

But I can't wait. I've got the keys. It's as good as mine.

Mentally, I make a list of things to do after the holiday, like getting the utilities in my name, setting up Wi-Fi, and doing a proper scrub down. The place isn't filthy, but it's far from comfortable.

Dashing into the hallway, I open the closet and steal some of my parents' linens. Luckily, there's a twin bed in one of the upstairs rooms of my new house, and Mom keeps twin sheets for anyone crashing on the couch when we're overbooked for the holidays.

Snatching them, I carry the bundle back down the hall. A bathroom door opens, and I stop short, watching Lucas turn off the light. He steps out in black lounge pants, steam pouring around him as he dries his hair with a dark blue towel.

He sees me and slows, water dripping down his chest. The sheets weigh as much as a truck, but I can't take my eyes off his chest. My gaze descends to a toned stomach and trim waist. He's so long and lean…

I look away, blinking. "It's midday," I gripe. "You just getting up?"

"I've been up since the same time as you probably," he retorts, taking the sheets out of my hands and following me to my room. "Work calls in Dubai, and then I helped Fallon at the workshop until I came back and swam some laps in the pool."

I open my pack and grab a handful from him, stuffing the sheets inside.

My pulse races. I wanted to ask him why he just disappeared last night, but he's in my room. Half-naked.

I just packed my bikini. Would he get back in the pool with me?

I lick my lips, grabbing the blanket out of his hands and packing that too.

"What are you doing?" he inquires, running the towel over his dripping hair.

"Taking another load over."

I toss in a few books, some lotions and cuticle oil, and a candle from my night stand. I add *Renting a Moving Truck* to my mental list. I can't keep packing up backpacks as if I'm on an extended sleepover. I have shelves of books, boxes with old keepsakes, and I'm sure my parents would let me have my bedroom set. I'll ask before I take it, though.

Digging in my drawer, I pull out a handful of underwear and some silky sleep shorts, stuffing them in the pack. He drifts back a couple of steps, but looms like a giant in my periphery. Orange and vanilla swirls into the air from his body. *My bodywash.* He used my bodywash. Something tightens between my thighs, and I whip around, gathering more clothes.

"That place could use a lot of renovations," he points out. "Might be a good idea to stay at home till it's more livable."

I tell him softly, "I like it how it is."

"What's it like?"

He looks amused, like I'm telling him about a croissant again, but I don't know...

I don't know how to describe it. The house is bare, raw, and a little dirty, completely unlike me.

"Quinn?"

Joy lifts the corners of my mouth, possibility the only thing coming to mind when I think of 01 Knock Hill. Possibility.

"Like things are going to happen to me there," I tell him.

That's what it's like. Stormy nights and misty mornings, and maybe I won't be alone for all of them.

His eyebrows nosedive, his voice sounding curt, and I almost snort. That was definitely the wrong thing to say.

"What does that mean?" he asks.

I lift up the pack and slide my arms in, strapping it to my back. "See you in a couple days," I reply, keeping my secrets to myself that I seem to have trouble containing.

Leaving him in my room, I exit the house, climb on my bike, and start pedaling for home as thunder cracks across the sky.

The air grows thick, the clouds bearing down, and the wind whips over my body.

There are a million reasons that I'm scared about buying a house I can barely afford in an area where I'm not sure I'm safe, but it's like every minute that takes me deeper into this mistake, the better I feel about myself. I've never done anything on my own, except the bakery. I don't have my own friends. I don't travel without my family. I don't have a past. Hell, Dylan has more of a past than I do.

My parents will have every right to be concerned, but I'm starting to understand that it's okay. My brothers can fight and yell as much as they want. In the end, though, I'm an adult.

And I can't believe I just left Lucas—again—when we could be in my parents' house alone together. If it were the Lucas from eight or ten years ago, I would've stayed. He's changed.

The only part that's an immediate concern is the car situation.

I'm miles away now, Uber doesn't come to Weston, and it's not a good look to still bum rides off family if I'm trying to maintain that I'm an independent adult. It's time to invest in a company vehicle.

I roll my shoulders, the weight of the pack getting heavier every mile as I cross the bridge. I pat my leg, but I think I stuffed my purse in the backpack, and I don't have any spare change in my pocket.

I grunt, breezing by the sunken car far underneath me. "I'll get you next time," I mutter.

Riding through the warehouse district, I look up at empty windows, darkened doorways, and abandoned alleys, but I feel the eyes all the same. As if the ghosts never ran from the flood.

There are still people residing in Weston. Enough to keep the schools running. It was the poorer neighborhoods that proved the most resilient.

The river flows from a higher elevation, and Knock Hill—the more affluent area that looks like it's modeled after the Upper West Side of New York City—took the hardest hit. The streets were consumed, businesses ruined, and most of those who evacuated never came back. Thankfully, the main living areas of the brownstones—which are more black than brown now—were salvaged, only the basement levels really flooding.

I cruise up to my house, taking the sidewalk, because cars block both ends of the street. Tables line the curbs on both sides as Farrow stacks cinderblocks, placing a grate on top. It takes me a moment to figure out what he's doing, but it looks like a homemade barbecue pit.

"What are you up to?" I call out to him as I park my bike.

People surround him—some men I haven't met, and a few familiar-looking faces among the girls. Friends of Dylan's.

He jogs over. "Block party. You coming?"

Tonight?

I climb my steps. "Why not wait till the Fourth?"

"Because we're crashing the Falls on the Fourth."

I throw him a look, shimmying out of my backpack and digging my house key out of my pocket. "You mess up my brother's celebration, we can't be friends."

I don't care how much we might get along. Madoc works too hard.

I start to move through the door, but Farrow comes up to my right and leans into my ear, stopping me. "Behind me, on the window frame, is a camera," he says in a low voice.

I lift my eyes, seeing just past him. A small lens is posted on the exterior of one of my living room windows.

Was that there when I bought the place?

"Two more on the side of the house," he continues, "and one at the rear. Morrow installed them while you were at work this morning."

Lucas?

I dart my gaze between Farrow and the camera and back again. He put cameras outside my house this morning while I was at work?

"They'll feed to a device, probably his phone," Farrow tells me.

That dick! He said he helped Fallon at her workshop, took some work calls… Conveniently left out that he installed security on my house, footage for which I have no access!

I grit my teeth. "Thanks."

He gives me a nod and goes back to his crew. I head inside, locking the door.

I drop my bag on the floor, ready to tear every camera off my damn house. Did my brothers tell him to put them up? Are they watching me too?

But no, they would've freaked first if they knew I bought a house. Jared wouldn't have been able to resist melting down.

I slide my phone out of the backpack and start to call Lucas. Or text him. How dare he take it upon himself to make a decision like this about *my* home, and let's not pretend for a minute it's because he's actually worried about my safety! It's for him and my brothers—and my father, for that matter—to know whether or not I'm staying out too late, having men over, or not coming home at all some nights. I could scream at him. What does he think he's going to see, and what would he do about it? Piss me off some more?

I squeeze the phone in my hand, pacing back and forth, about to rail at him.

But he expects that. Even if I didn't see the cameras, he would assume someone saw him installing them, and instead of warning me when I saw him earlier, he decided to let me come home while he tried to get away with it.

I don't want another fight.

I want revenge.

Crossing the living room, I grab the Cubs cap off the couch and lift the window, wincing at the squeaks the rusted, old metal makes. Sticking my head out, I hear Farrow's music playing from car speakers as everyone sets up for the party, and look up at the camera focused on my porch.

When he checks his app, he'll see footage of Farrow talking to me just a minute ago. Reaching up and staying out of view, I throw the hat over the front of the camera before tilting it on its ball joint to face inside my house.

Right on the living room. It's no doubt motion-activated, but he might assume it's from the wind or a glitch.

Pulling the hat back off, I close the window and have a seat on the couch. Taking out my phone, I call Dylan. I don't have the patience to have this discussion over text.

"Hey," she answers.

"Can you guys get away for a while tonight?" I ask her.

They stay pretty booked at the summer camp, but since she and Aro's boyfriends also work there, they don't want to be anywhere other than with them.

"Can who get away?"

"All of you," I reply.

Hunter, Kade, Hawke…everyone.

She pauses, crunching something in my ear as she eats. "I can work it out, sure."

I spot my notebook on the coffee table, my pen still laying discarded from when I read through it the other night and had another idea to add to the list. I flush with heat, remembering Lucas was down here alone last night. Did he see it?

My lungs empty. That's why he left without a word last night. And probably why he decided I needed more supervision.

I slam the book shut.

"Come to that house you stayed in during Rivalry Week." I clear my throat. "8 p.m."

"Will there be alcohol?"

I roll my eyes the tiniest bit. I should've known it would be expected. No party without it.

"Yesss."

"Quinn!" she exclaims, shocked. "Yay!"

"Shut up."

And I hang up, shaking my head at how everyone underestimates me.

But I'd love to see the look on Lucas's face when the notifications start rolling in.

A few hours later, Hawke is growling at me. "You bought this place?"

"Music's too loud!" I shout over Mace's playlist blasting on my Bluetooth speaker. "I can't hear you!"

He scowls as I lean my ass against the column between the foyer and the living room, clutching a plastic cup full of something Dylan made.

Hawke is exactly like Jax. They don't like surprises. Luckily, I know they've been keeping that hideout for years, so if they want their secret safe with me, then mine better be safe with them. At least for a few days.

Dylan steps in, dragging Hunter from where they were dancing. She nudges Hawke away from me. "Take Aro up to the attic and explore."

Kade hands him a shot, and Hawke gulps it down, those azure blue eyes unrelenting on me. They're not suspicious really; although, I am sure he's wondering if I have anything else up my sleeve, but they're more aggravated than anything. As if he failed in his duty to be the all-seeing eye.

Aro takes his hand and leads him up the stairs. The lights lower, but the crowd is too thick to tell who hit the switch. Farrow leans into a girl by the window, while his boys are probably still in the kitchen, judging from the noise of their laughter.

Codi, Mace, and a few others spread out on the couches and chairs. Codi leans back against the arm, hugging one knee, and she smiles, but it's guarded. As always. I thought she might be different on her turf, but it seems she's quiet everywhere.

Kade pops a cheeseball into the air and catches it with his mouth as some pissed-off kid argues with him about football or something, and Hunter hugs Dylan from behind, the three of us watching more people pile in through the front door.

It was supposed to just be Farrow, my family, and maybe Mace. If I knew I was supplying alcohol to a bunch of minors I don't know, I would've chickened out. Luckily Mace has someone at the door, collecting keys.

I tuck my hair behind my ear, glancing at the window where one of the cameras sits outside. I stare at it as it stares back at me.

Are you watching?

I'll bet he is. If his notifications are on, then he's getting one every time movement is detected. And there's a lot of movement in here.

"My dad is going to freak," Dylan says over the music.

"Eventually," I add. "Here's to you guys being just as good about keeping this secret as you did Carnival Tower."

She winces but taps my cup when I offer it. I'm sure the guys brought her up to speed.

I examine the list of people who know I bought a house, and to be honest, no one is a weak link. Lucas might spill the beans in a moment of reaction, but as much as Hawke hovers, or Dylan sometimes just word vomits all over the place, they're both tight ships when it comes to parents.

"So you talked to Deacon," Hunter says.

I dart my eyes up to him, his skin already golden from the summer and his blond hair laying in different directions as usual.

"What was he like?" he asks.

That eerily calm voice through the phone coils into my ear again, kicking up my heartbeat. *What was he like?*

I shrug. He felt like he was on a timer. An image of a fuse burning quickly drifts through my head.

When I don't reply, Dylan tells me, "This was their house." Her eyes do a circle around the room. "He and Manas hosted Winslet here for the prisoner exchange more than two decades ago. No one has seen her since."

I guess I knew all of that from the murder map they built in Carnival Tower, but the history of the house weighs down, and I think about him. That voice. The man, much younger than he is now, in here with her. Was she talking about him in her diary? Or was she referring to the other one? Manas.

Which one did she love? And which one did she not?

I notice Dylan and Hunter are still looking at me. Do they think I'm not concerned enough?

I am concerned. One of the brothers, at least, is calling me. I have an old car stalking me, and I'm in possession of, not one, but two places that used to belong to the men who quite possibly were the last people to ever see Winslet MacCreary alive.

Do they still think this house belongs to them? I drop my gaze for a moment. I anticipated buyer's remorse, but I kept pressing forward, the desperation for freedom winning out. But I may have bitten off more than I can chew.

I look behind Dylan, seeing Noah toss Kade a beer. "Noah?" I call.

He glances at me.

I joke, "I think Dylan would feel better if you checked my bedroom for ghosts."

"*Her* room, you mean," Dylan taunts.

Winslet's.

I take my drink, jogging up the stairs, aware that Lucas' security camera can see me disappearing around the corner with Noah on my tail.

I enter my bedroom, glad to find it empty. I half-suspected someone would've snuck up here to fool around. The curtains billow with the wind coming through the window I'd left open. Peering out, I crane my neck, seeing people in the street to the right. White hair blows in the breeze coming from a girl sitting on the trunk of an abandoned car at the curb. She drinks from a Hydro Flask.

The hair reminds me of Tommy Dietrich, but I can't tell for sure.

"You don't have much of a bed," Noah says, trailing in.

"But smell that breeze." The wind caresses my scalp. "I'm going to make it smell even better by next summer after I revamp the kitchen and bake something good."

Squeezing in next to me, Noah leans his hands on the sill and looks out into the small path between mine and Farrow's houses. The bigger bedroom only had the twin bed—big enough for one person—but I didn't expect any furnishings, so I'm grateful for it until I can get my own moved in.

I'm anxious to get that couch downstairs replaced too. The kitchen table is some mid-century Ethan Allen. I'll keep that. I like it.

Another camera sits perched above my window, facing the street.

Noah turns to me. "Couldn't use a roommate, could you?"

I straighten, pulling myself back inside. Huh?

He ponders, his blue eyes dancing with a little alcohol. "Your brother is a steady paycheck, and I'm gone a lot, so it would almost be like free rent money for you."

Not a bad proposition, especially since I need to get a business vehicle, and I don't want to take anything more from my parents. They paid for college and gave me the bakery for a damn good deal on money my mother gifted me when I was seventeen. The irony doesn't escape me. Is it really independence if I used money I didn't make on my own to get it?

The rest is up to me now.

But I don't think I want to live with anyone. For someone who's always been lonely, I'm not in a hurry to have another adult presence looming. At least one that's not romantic.

I tease, "I don't think I want to be having coffee with your love life every other morning."

He scoffs, taking my drink. "Like they would still be here in the morning."

I roll my eyes as he gulps down, swallows, and I take it back, partaking of some.

"It's got potential," he says, "the neighborhood."

I think so too. The little voice in my head is thinking about little things, like fifteen-year-old Tommy outside drinking around older guys, or how to pry into Codi's life and what she does when she's not working for me...

Or Farrow and what he's hiding behind his closed doors and clever quips. All of it a responsibility, at least to some extent. Am I trading one set of obligations for another?

But I love the view out my window.

"I just got out on my own," I say quietly. "I think I'm gonna try it for a while."

I look back at him, seeing him nod. He doesn't need it explained.

"But..." I broach. "There are other houses for sale on the block."

He chuckles, coming back to the window next to me. We gaze out at the three-story brownstones, falling apart after so many years of neglect. Looters destroyed the interiors, and broken windows let decades of snow, rain, and wind inside. My house is one of the nicer ones as the history of the place made it more of a shrine than a target.

Not many people want to move to a failing neighborhood with low property value, and spend thousands of dollars to renovate.

But Noah might.

"Farrow probably wouldn't give you permission, though," I tell him.

Noah's eyes flicker with amusement as he stares down at the narrow alleyway between mine and Farrow's houses. "Is that so?"

But he says it like it's a challenge.

Something tells me that Farrow doesn't let anything happen on Knock Hill that he doesn't like, and I'm not sure if he doesn't like Noah Van der Berg, but he will certainly be in his face here.

The music downstairs cuts off, the vibrations through my floor suddenly ceasing.

A piece of furniture moves, someone shouts.

I stand up straight. "Something's up."

Noah follows me out of my bedroom, a growl stopping me in my tracks at the top of the stairs.

"Everyone out!"

I look to Noah.

"Cops?" he says.

I take a step just as Lucas charges from the living room, back into the foyer, and whips open the door.

Turning to Hawke, he tells my brother's son, "Go. She's going to be in a hell of a lot of trouble already. Don't make it worse."

I'm going to be in trouble? Is he serious?

I expected him to call and berate me. Or maybe slip in unnoticed when he saw the party on his cameras.

But he's charging in here like it's his damn house.

"Now!" Lucas shouts when no one moves.

What the hell is he doing?

One of Farrow's friends steps into view. "Who the fuck are you, man?"

But Lucas doesn't hesitate. Whipping his T-shirt off over his head, he spins around. "Out!" he yells.

And I see it. The same thing everyone sees. The tattoo down his right shoulder, curving around the shoulder blade, and fading as it descends to the ribs and waist.

"Oh, shit!" someone exclaims.

The room silences, and I grab the banister, craning my neck to study the design, but he moves too fast.

"Move!" Lucas whips his arm, gesturing to the door.

And just like that, everyone floods out of the house.

Not walking.

Running.

"Let's go!" I hear someone say.

"You heard him," Mace calls out. "Everyone out now!"

Confusion freezes me. Why are they listening to him?

Bodies collide, pushing each other as they try to fit out the door.

"Oh my God," one of Aro's Weston friends bursts out. "Did you see that?"

"That was a real fucking tat," someone else says.

My eyes zone in on Lucas, burning so hard they hurt.

QUIET ONES

I jerk my head to Noah, telling him to follow everyone and get out. I don't want him in Lucas's path.

He holds back, but I stand aside, silently urging him as I tip my head to the door. As the place empties, Lucas glares up at me and I hold his eyes without blinking.

That tattoo. I'd forgotten about it. He had it that day at the camp lodge when I was a kid.

The door slams shut behind the last of the guests, and I barrel down the stairs, charging up to him.

"What the hell was that?" I bark.

I jet around him, trying to get a look at the ink on his back, but he turns, keeping us face to face.

His blue eyes spit fire as he gazes down at me. Heat pours off his body, and he breathes like he's dying to hurt me, and I'm not sure that scares me at all.

"Why..." I swallow, wetting my parched throat. "Why did it seem like they knew you?"

They obeyed him as soon as they saw the ink.

But he ignores my question. "You're not old enough to live on your own." He digs in his eyebrows. "Did you think any of this was going to fly?"

"You're not my father!"

He rakes a hand through his hair, fucking losing his mind. "A condemned house in a decrepit neighborhood," he rambles, "living right next door to a career criminal with any one of a dozen little shits coming and going from his house who would love to slip something in your drink!" He gets in my face. "You failed to mention that! Or was it deliberate?"

My ears sting at his blaring voice, and my heart races, but I don't shout again. I can't tell what's radiating off from him—energy, warmth, passion—but I want him to keep going. This is the first time since he's been home that it feels like he's close to being honest.

He goes on, under his breath, "Serving minors, and who knows how many of them had drugs on them." Then, he turns back to me. "And what the fuck were you doing upstairs with Noah Van der Berg?"

"You noticed all that just walking in the door?" I ask in a calm voice, standing in front of him. "Did you know I was having a party? Is that why you're here?"

Come on. Admit you're spying on me with security cameras you also failed to mention.

He just shakes his head and charges to the coffee table, grabbing the notebook. He flips it open to where it was when he was here last night, my writing visible in blue ink as he squeezes the folded book in his fist.

The list of birthday presents I really wanted the past few years. I dart my eyes to his.

"Yeah, I know what's on your mind." His barely contained growl scares me more than his shouting a moment ago. "You're not capable of making a responsible decision." He throws the notebook onto the entryway table next to us. "Your hormones are all over the place, and you're coming home."

Why? Because I'm normal? Because I want to feel things? Because I have physical desires, the same as almost everyone? It doesn't make sense. Nothing he's doing or saying is making sense.

But to my surprise, I don't argue back. The sweat on his neck. The heat on his cheeks. His eyes piercing me like bullets.

I'm driving him crazy.

I extend my hand and slide it around his waist, to his back. "May I see it?"

My voice is barely above a whisper as his eyes hold mine. His body is frozen, but I catch the falter in his gaze.

And I seize it, softly circling him and letting my eyes fall down the length of his back and the same tattoo I saw all those years ago.

Pressing my fingers to his skin, I feel him tense as I trace the black branches with my thumb. They wind from above his shoulder blade, down the right side of his back, and over his ribs, disappearing below the waist of his jeans.

I hesitate, something familiar about the lines. Something off about the shoots coming out of the branch.

"It's…"

It's not a branch.

"It's the river," I murmur. "The river between Shelburne Falls and Weston."

And I'm the only one in Weston who doesn't know that this tattoo means something. They were more scared of it than anyone in the Falls is scared when they see the Green Street tattoo.

I step back around, stopping in front of him. "You can't keep me to yourself forever." I reach over to the table and start to pull my notebook back. "Someday—"

But he slams his hand down on mine, and I force out my finger, dragging it down the list as he tries to take the notebook away.

"—someone is going to give me all the birthday presents I really want," I say in a low voice.

I look over, seeing my finger pointing to number five. *Panties ripped off.*

Looking him dead in the eye, I unfasten my black shorts. My chest aches, because I expect him to stop me, but I'm too quick for him.

Or he's that paralyzed that he doesn't know what's happening.

I drop my shorts to the floor and stand there in my underwear and little, white blouse that only falls just below my belly button.

His hard gaze doesn't leave mine, and I don't shrink, even though I know he's going to shout. Or he's going to grab me, throw me in my room, and lock me there until I behave.

I barely notice the lights go out or hear the commotion outside as the neighborhood blacks out.

I smirk, shaking my head as I back away. "You can leave."

He has no place in my life anymore.

Turning, I head through the living room and feel his hands before I make it to the kitchen. He spins me around and backs me into the wall.

I barely react, simply lifting my chin. I kind of expected it. He's exactly like the stories I heard about my brothers when they were pursuing women. He's exactly like them.

But as I stare up at him, chest to chest with his hands gripping my upper arms, I can't stop the déjà vu feeling. The last time we were like this was under a dock at the lake, and my nose was right under his chin, just like now. Except then, it was because he was crouched down.

"You just want to keep me the same," I whisper to him.

I don't have any illusions about him making a move, touching me, or kissing me. He won't.

"Quinn?" Farrow says from somewhere behind Lucas. "Neighborhood blackout. It happens. Are you okay in here?"

He must be just inside my front door, but I don't break away from Lucas's gaze.

"I'm okay." I smile a little, taunting. "*Always* perfectly safe with Lucas."

I try to get my body out from between him and the wall, but Lucas locks my wrists in each of his fists and spins me around, pressing my body into the plaster with his own at my back.

I dig in my eyebrows, the breath knocked out of me. What is he doing?

"Farrow?" I pant.

I twist my wrists, sweat breaking out on my forehead as I try to get loose.

But I can't get away.

I can't fucking get away.

I crane my neck, trying to get Farrow to help, but all I catch is the front door closing.

Farrow leaves me.

Lucas releases my hands, his body still pressed into the back of mine as his fingers graze my temple. He tucks my hair behind my ear.

I whisper, realization dawning. "They know you."

"Better than you do," he mocks in my ear.

My eyes go wide, his voice suddenly sounding like someone different. A stranger.

It makes my stomach stir with heat.

All of it—his absence for all of those years, his secrets—has to do with Weston.

They knew him—or of him—before they knew me.

His nose nudges my ear, his breath caressing my cheek, and I feel his hand glide down my back to my underwear.

I stop breathing for a second, not blinking, as he threads his finger under the lace trim, and I think he's going to tear them clean off like I wanted for my birthday when I was eighteen.

Leaning into my back, his wet mouth on my ear, he tugs them down with both hands, and I go still as he drops with my panties.

Looking behind me, I see him squat, dragging my underwear down my legs to the floor. I step out of them, my pussy flooding with warmth and throbbing as he fingers the cotton and then looks up at me as he slides my panties into his pocket.

My mouth falls open.

I turn around, watching his eyes drop to the strip of hair between my thighs. His chest caves, and he rises, pressing his forehead to mine as his hand slides between my legs.

Grazing his fingers up my slit, he spreads my wetness over my skin until his jaw is hard and tight. He grabs my ass, squeezing.

My body shakes, my breathing shallow as he kisses my forehead and holds his mouth there. I untie the lace on my peasant blouse, opening it and dropping one side down my arm. He pulls back just a little, covering my skin with his eyes, and it feels like every drop of blood in my body is low in my belly right now. God...

Hands on my waist, he pulls me in and wraps his arms around me, and I do the same, both of us burying our lips in the other's neck.

"Touch me," I beg.

He clenches his fists in my hair, opening his mouth as if he's going to eat me up, but then...

He shoves away from me, breathing out hard. "Oh, fuck," he growls, rubbing his eyes.

Cold covers my skin, and it hurts between my legs.

No.

The long, thick ridge presses against the inside of his jeans, and right now, I don't give a shit what comes out of his mouth. He can't hide what I know he wants. I tremble, and I don't know if it's from desire or fear. *Don't leave. Please don't fucking leave.*

Standing up straight, he backs away, and I don't cover myself. *Damn him, no!*

He walks to the foyer, picks up his shirt and comes back, tossing it to me. I catch it as it slaps against my body.

"No one will touch you now." He glares at me. "No one except me."

Because they think I'm his. And whoever he really is, they're scared of it.

He starts to leave, and I won't chase him, but he's not off the hook, either. "You missed eight birthdays," I remind him. "Eight presents."

I still want my panties ripped off and everything else, and he's running out of time.

He rips the sheet out of the notebook, folds it, and stuffs it into his pocket as if I'm going to forget what's on it. He whips open the door, glancing back at me, his eyes softening.

"Lock the door…" he says.

…*baby*. Just say it. *Lock the door, baby*.

The pulse in my neck hammers against my skin, sweat cooling my back.

But he leaves, closing the door tightly behind him, and I throw my blouse.

Son of a bitch.

I pull his shirt over my head, his scent covering my body as I walk to the door and lock it. Goosebumps spread up my arms.

The floor upstairs creaks, branches scrape against a window, and music vibrates across the walls from outside.

"You think you have everything under control," I mouth after him as the heat between my legs makes my eyelids flutter. "We'll see."

SHELBURNE FALLS

CHAPTER SEVENTEEN

Lucas

Fuck, I could be inside of her right now. Buried to the hilt in all that soft, tight skin with my mouth sucking on a body that felt like a goddamn cloud.

Her breasts, her stomach, her thighs... Smooth, like silk, and smelling better than heaven. No idea what the hell heaven smells like, but if it's anything other than that, I don't want it. I've never touched anyone who sent a simultaneous current of electricity to my dick *and* to my brain. I mean, what the fuck? I was jacked, and it was Quinn.

Quinn.

Just the thought of what I could be having right now—her, alone, hidden, and in my hands—brings my body temp up so high, I'm still sweating even though it's seventy-two outside and the air conditioning is on.

What the hell am I going to do? I love her too much to just throw her down like she's anyone else. I would open a vein if she needed me to.

But I can't make love to her. I'll lose her completely then.

Kicking the car into a higher gear, I race through the night, away from her, like I have a monkey on my back. And I go to the one place that will recalibrate my perspective.

The train tunnel, Hugo had said.

Images had flooded back when he said it, and I suddenly saw myself there all those years ago. Outside my body. Hazy, like everything was that night, because all I'd felt was small. Something small inside of a man's body, hidden deep in a head that I didn't recognize anymore.

It was as if I was looking through my own eyes with binoculars from far away.

How the hell did I forget about the tunnel?

I knew that the body was in the forest off the highway.

I even remembered it was before Camp Blackhawk, not after.

But I wasn't aware of much else that night.

Parking, I walk, rain pummeling my bare shoulders and chest. I stare down at the old leaves covering the dark earth as I drift and drag my hand over the smooth stone.

Leave, Drew had said. *Or I'll have twenty people back me up when I tell the cops what you did. And Madoc Caruthers will ruin his reputation, buried in a legal battle for you for the next five years.*

Gazing down at the soft mound of earth, I ball my fists to stop them from shaking. "I'm sorry."

My chin trembles and tears fill my eyes.

"I did the right thing," I whisper, rain spilling off my lips. "I couldn't do anything fucking good back then, but I could protect them."

Who knows what Drew would've done to target the Trents and Caruthers? He had a fucking gang.

But in my heart, I *wanted* to run. It was easier than having to face anyone who loved me. My mom and what she'd already been through, losing my father, and Madoc and Fallon and their world of everything so beautiful and perfect.

I was sick. I hated myself.

However, there's nothing noble in letting a soul rot in a grave no one will ever visit.

Quinn deserves better than me.

I gave up everything, so I wouldn't have to do the hardest thing. *What a piece of shit...*

I leave the grave and climb back into my car, racing through Shelburne Falls and back to Quinn's parents' house.

Closing the garage, I shut off the light and step into the house, locking the door behind me. I kick off my muddy shoes and throw them in the mudroom sink. I should grab a towel to dry off my chest and back, but my ire is still up, and it's cooling me down.

Climbing the back stairs, I head to the guest room, close the door, and sit on the edge of the bed.

"What the fuck am I gonna do?" I mouth to myself.

What if Isobel doesn't come up with anything in her research? I have her scouring for any info on the Trents and Caruthers, so I can be ahead of it if Hugo has an ace up his sleeve. Not that I think Jared, Jax, or Madoc have anything to hide, but it's best to be sure.

But what if she can't come up with something I can use as leverage on Reeves or Navarre? What's my next step?

The man deserves a proper burial, certainly. And I won't leave until he has it. But I need to stop Green Street first. If I don't, and I'm arrested, I won't be able to protect my family. Or Quinn.

I stayed because the rumor of the land being developed forces me to face this. I stayed because Green Street has grown, and they're a danger. I stayed because I love the Falls and I'm nothing without the people here in my life.

But really, it was Quinn. I stayed because I can't walk away from her.

She hurts me when she's angry, and she hurts me when she's soft.

I have tunnel-vision with her.

Fucking tunnels. Long, and dark, and the only way out is through.

I shake my head, clenching my teeth. God, I wanted to fuck her tonight. I loved being back in that town and knowing that the tattoo would empty that room in an instant. I loved the power, and I hate that I loved it. She's turning me into that man again.

I may as well have fucked her, given that Jared, Madoc, and Jax won't see any difference between me being inside of her and me taking off her clothes tonight.

I reach into my pocket and pull out her panties, staring at the white cotton. Pulling back my comforter, then my sheet, I lay them in my bed, the fantasy that she's there, naked and ready, making every single muscle hard. Every one.

I should've brought her home to the Falls with the blackout in Weston. I just didn't want another fucking fight.

Taking out my phone, I open the app and check the solar cameras, still not detecting any lights. Front door is closed and better be locked.

Maybe I should go back. What if the blackout was on purpose? I don't trust anyone over there.

But as I check the one near her bedroom window, I see her on her bed inside her room. What looks like a camping lamp sits on the bedside table, and she wears my dark gray T-shirt as she sits alone, staring at her lap.

My throat tightens, but I can't tear my eyes away. I didn't point the camera at her bedroom, nor did I point the one on the front of the house into the living room. Maybe it was wind. Maybe it was her, but as soon as I saw she was having a party earlier with Noah and Farrow in attendance, I didn't care. I kept watching.

And when I saw her head upstairs with Noah, I slammed on the gas, lucky I didn't get pulled over with how badly I was speeding to get there.

She was doing it on purpose, but I wasn't entirely sure how far she would go to prove how grown up she was, so I let her fucking have it. I'm not sorry.

My chest warms at the sight of her bare legs crossed in front of her, her light-colored panties peeking out between her thighs.

Then, I see it. So quick, I almost missed it, but it's unmistakable. The little swipe of her fingers across her face, and then immediately under her nose, before she puts her hand back down on the bed.

Why is she crying?

Tapping the Call button, I dial her and put her on speaker, so I can watch her. My line rings, and a moment later, she's turning and patting the bed to find her phone. She looks at the screen and answers, holding it to her ear.

Her breath curls into my head.

"Still up?" I ask before she says 'hello.'

"No."

"Liar."

She straightens one of her legs, drawing in a breath. "You're watching me?"

She glances to the camera maybe twenty feet away outside her window.

"I can't stop, it seems," I whisper.

I knew she'd find out about the cameras. If she didn't notice them, someone in the neighborhood would've seen me installing them this morning and warned her.

"What's wrong?" I ask in a low voice.

She drops her head, and I can't tell her facial features clearly enough to see if she's still crying.

"I'm so hot," she pants.

Hot?

"You...don't have AC?" I ask.

"That's not what I mean." I hear her swallow as she places her hand on the inside of her thigh. "It hurts."

I close my eyes, my cock twitching. "I know."

My groin throbs, warm blood flooding my legs, and I should hang up. For both our sakes.

I sit back down on the edge of the bed again, my elbows on my knees as I stare at her.

"I loved everything you did earlier," she tells me in the smallest voice, cracking with tears. "You've felt that with other women. I never have, and I feel like I'm sinking to the ocean floor, farther and farther from air. You just made it worse."

We could argue about whose fault it was earlier when I was there, but I don't blame her.

She's feeling things whether I stand in her way or not, and maybe I expected her to ease her pain on her own like what I was planning to do once I left her, but apparently, she didn't.

"Keep going," I whisper.

Uncrossing her other leg, she bends them slightly and leans back on one hand. "What if I said I hated you?" she gasps, rolling her hips. "What if I said that you're not the man I thought you were, and we don't get along anymore, and whatever bond we had is just gone?"

My dick presses against my jeans. Does she hate me?

The tips of my fingers hum, feeling her dripping all over again. I lift my hand to my nose, still smelling her.

"What if I said I'm going to let myself meet someone now?"

I press my teeth together so hard my jaw aches.

"What if I said the man in my bed is the only one I'll let protect me now?" she goes on. "And he won't like anyone else stepping on his fucking turf."

My heart aches, and I wince. *Fuck.* If someone else comes into her life, he will establish boundaries. If he's worth his salt. I knew that, but now she does too.

"It will only feel good with a good man," I growl, straining to keep control. "Don't go wasting it on assholes."

"I haven't met any."

"Quinn..." I warn.

You've met plenty.

But she looks right up to the camera. "Lucas."

Her chest rises and falls, her heated breaths drifting into my ear and making my eyes nearly fall closed.

"Where are my panties?" she asks.

Sweat dampens the back of my neck, and I look over, picturing her in them with my mouth on the triangle of fabric.

"In my bed," I tell her.

"Why?"

I unclench my jaw, unable to stop myself. "Because I want to feel them on my dick tonight."

I hear her suck in a breath.

Reaching over, I place my hand on her panties and curl my fingers, bunching them in my fist.

Fuck this.

Fuck it.

I love her more than Farrow Kelly and Noah Van der Berg ever could. If it's someone tonight, it's me.

"Quinn," I whisper. "Pull up your shirt."

My voice is almost choked, my cock straining to grow under my clothes as I watch her on my screen.

Keeping one hand on the phone at her ear, she lowers her eyes and watches herself tug my T-shirt up, baring her stomach and then her breasts. Dark pink nipples point at me, the perfect shape of her soft skin. Plump and flawless. Leaving the shirt just above her tits, she leans back, looking up at me.

I can't fucking think anymore. "Open your legs..."

She spreads her bent knees, my mouth going dry and dying for the smooth skin inside her thighs.

I groan, "Wider, baby."

She tucks her bottom lip between her teeth and opens her legs more.

"Wider."

And she opens them so wide, one foot drops off the side of the bed, the other leg still bent. Her body sits in full view, spread eagle with her breasts making me so goddamn hungry.

"You know what to do," I pant. "I'm watching you."

Setting her phone on the bed, she leans back on one hand and slides the other inside her panties, and within a minute, her head is falling back and she's rolling her hips into her fingers.

She doesn't know that I've already seen her do this, but I could watch it a million times.

"Where are you?" she calls out, and I can tell she has me on speaker.

Rising, I gaze at her as I unfasten my jeans. "In the guest room."

"Tell me what you look like."

We could video chat, but I love having this view of her. As if I'm sneaking a peek at something she thinks she's alone for.

I wrap my hand around my cock, stroking the long, hard length. "Just muscle, baby. I look like muscle right now. Everything is hard for you. My whole body."

I want to drive into her so goddamn much—my fingers, my tongue, my cock...

Taking her panties, I drop down onto the bed and slide them inside my pants, the cool cotton touching my dick.

I moan, slowly and gently stroking them up and down my length.

"Do they feel good?" she asks, rubbing herself.

"They feel like trouble."

She lets out a little laugh. "Do you have any idea how I would feel?"

"I'll never know," I maintain, and I mean it. "I'm not the one for you, Quinn."

To my surprise, she says, "I know."

She does? I try to ignore the disappointment—or the aggravation—that she's so easily put off.

I want her to forget me.

I need her to forget me.

"You can't quit life in a city like that," she goes on, "and come back here to Friday nights at the Loop, bake sales, and Fourth of July picnics." She moans. "And my brothers would never look at you the same, would they?"

I look down, my pre-cum wetting her panties. Fire starts to spill off my skin as my muscles burn.

Would they tell me I couldn't fucking have her? I know they would. They'll kill me. But to hear her say it makes it more real.

"I wouldn't want Madoc to resent you," she tells me. "I know it won't be you. It'll be someone else."

I shake my head slowly.

"Can I show you what I want it to be like with him, whoever he'll be?"

She rolls her hips, her back arching and her waist rising up again and again.

If I'd stayed, I wouldn't be able to stop myself from tasting her until she screamed.

I hold my phone over my head, looking up at her as I lie back on the bed. "I'm watching."

She slips her panties off her ass and slides them down her legs. "Good," she taunts, "because that's what I want. I want him obsessed with watching me, and I want to see you at family gatherings someday, knowing you loved watching me too."

She pulls a rope out of her bedside drawer, but as she wraps it around the post on her footboard, I see it's not a rope at all. It's a long string of pearls—about two feet. The kind women loop around their neck two or three times.

I can barely breathe as I watch her remove the T-shirt and kneel on the bed, securing the string of beads.

Straddling the rope with one knee on the bed and one foot on the ground, she places a hand behind her, pulling the pearls taut as she takes the bed post in her other hand and starts riding them.

"Quinn..." I breathe out.

What the fuck? She slides her pussy up and down the tight necklace, each little pearl tickling her clit. A moan escapes her, then a whimper, getting louder and louder.

Where did she learn this?

"He digs his fingers into my hips," she says, fucking her imaginary man, "staring up at me like he wants it to go all night."

I look up at her on the screen like she's sitting on me now.

"His breath is heavy, pumping his hips up and pressing himself deeper..." She coos. "...and deeper inside me."

I squeeze my dick, rubbing her panties over the drip seeping out.

"The room is dark." Her voice shakes. "The air is thick, and he sticks his thumb in my mouth so all of his friends in the next room don't hear me coming."

I thrust my hips, pumping my dick into my hand. *So all of her brothers in the next room don't hear her...*

Jerking her hips, she rides faster, her breasts bobbing.

"But he just stops caring," I tell her, joining in, "because he pulls you forward and covers your breast with his mouth."

She follows my lead, leaning forward, and I feel my arm around her waist, pressing her flesh between my lips.

"He glides his tongue over your nipple," I say.

She whimpers. "It feels good."

"What does he feel like?"

"Hard." She starts crying out. "And thick, like a rod pumping into me."

"Fuck him," I beg. "Fuck him, baby."

I fucking wish I was him.

"I'm dripping down his cock."

"Fuck him harder," I growl.

"I will."

Her ass bounces back and forth, and I'm mesmerized. Her lush hips moving as beautifully as a feather riding the wind. She's done this before.

She won't be so quiet in her own house, I'm guessing.

"Harder," I gasp.

I'm so lost in watching Quinn, her hair spread around her arms and in her face as I feel myself under her and behind her and in five other positions, that I don't realize I've stopped stroking.

All I wanna do is watch her. If I can't touch her...

Sweat covers my chest. "You're so beautiful." And I can feel her between my teeth. "He'll clean you up with his fucking tongue."

I know, because I would.

She shoots up, straightening her spine, and throws her head back, crying out.

What is she thinking about?

Is she thinking about me?

Who's she fucking?

Her orgasm spreads through her body, first paralyzing her breath and making the thrusts turn to a steady rocking.

Then...she slows to a stop.

I don't realize my mouth is open, like I'm going through it with her, until my throat is as dry as the desert.

I stare up at her, dying to hold her. I don't think I can do this again.

I need to smell her skin.

"You still there?" I hear her ask softly.

She's so wet by now. I know it.

"Quinn..." I breathe out.

That was number eight on her birthday list. *Perform for someone*.

"Do you think he'll like it?" she asks.

"He better. He should be so lucky." I swallow a couple of times to wet my mouth. "No one is good enough to have you."

She climbs off the pearls and kneels on the bed, sitting on her feet. Her breasts still point at me. "I won't fall in love with Farrow or Noah. Promise." She looks up at the camera, to me. "If it's this good with the right person, then I'll wait for *him*."

Yeah.

I'll be at her wedding someday, and this will just be some awakening secret we'll never tell her brothers about.

But I can't help the spark in my heart that she would see written all over my face if she could see me. I love to look at her. "Put some clothes on."

"'Kay." She grins, picking up the phone and holding it to her ear. "Goodnight."

"Goodnight."

I end the call and close the camera app. My dick is as hard as a rock, and I should just finish myself off, but a pickax is driving into my brain. I'm not sure if it's because I'm so fucking horny, or because I'm a piece of shit, but I know I won't be able to sleep.

In three minutes, I'm in my gym clothes and in Jared's car, speeding out of the driveway.

It's after ten, the gym will be empty, and it'll be a blessing if I don't get any sleep tonight. I'm counting on my exhaustion to keep me away from her tomorrow.

Jacking up the music, I cruise into town, park, and charge inside, heading straight upstairs. Sticking in my earbuds, the song I had playing in my car continues in my ears—"Hats Off to the Bull"—and I jump onto the track. I just go, not pacing myself as I dig in my heels and race so hard that I hope I hurt myself. It's what I deserve.

Even if my mistakes weren't hanging over my head like a dagger, I'm too old for her. I mean, she's a damn kid. I remember being that age. I was an idiot, and worse than most, but no one wants the same things they thought they wanted at that age once they get older. What's the part of the brain that handles good decision-making? The pre-frontal cortex? It's the last part of our minds to mature, and it doesn't happen till our late twenties. I should be ashamed of myself. It's one thing if a guy her age is taking advantage of her, but me? Fuck!

I do four miles on the track, not the slightest bit tired, because the more I run, the more I think. And the more pissed I get. One more fucking thing that I can't undo or take back.

I move to the weights as my phone buzzes, a call from Lance coming in.

I skip the call. Another male, separate from the family, might be pretty amazing to talk to right now, but being around him just makes me want the life he has. It makes me think being in love with someone younger isn't a bad idea when I see how happy he is, and he's no help. He wants me to have a woman here. To fall in love and stay.

I lift a dumbbell, curling my arm over and over again.

Don't touch her again. Don't touch her. Don't watch her.

She's beautiful and gentle and bright, and she notices the little things as if they're all wrapped in chocolate.

She's a sanctuary, and I'm desperate for it. Desperate for everything she is, but I'm making shitty decisions as if I'm her age.

Because she makes me hope for the future.

She makes me think nothing else matters.

I bite down, the memory of her tonight warming my body.

Don't fucking touch her again. I don't want to end up a bad memory for her.

I curl my arm up with too much power and the dumbbell goes flying over my shoulder. Whipping around, I see it crash to the carpeted floor, a man yanking his leg out of the way just before it lands on his foot.

"Shit," I blurt out, rushing over to where he stands at the lat machine. "Sorry." I pick up the dumbbell. "You okay?"

The gentleman, gray dusting the sides of his brown hair, doesn't miss a beat in his reps. He continues pulling down the bar, smirking at me over his shoulder.

"Should I be flattered?" he asks.

Huh?

Then his eyes drop to my pants, and I look, seeing the fucking hard-on thinking of Quinn started stirring again.

I turn. Son of a bitch.

"Kidding," he calls out. "I know who that's probably for. I saw you the other night, working out with her."

"With who?"

"Quinn Caruthers," he says. "The local baker."

I twist back around. Who is this guy? Green eyes sparkle from behind slightly weathered skin and a five o'clock shadow. Maybe ten years older than me, but he's in shape. I don't recognize him. Madoc must know him. He knows everybody.

Did he notice something between Quinn and me? "This isn't..." I stammer. "It's not—"

"It's nice, working out in here so late, isn't it?" he cuts me off. "Empty, quiet, no eyes watching—"

I narrow my brow.

He smiles at me again. "When you got a special place, you want to keep it to yourself. Am I right?"

I go still. It doesn't feel like we're talking about the gym.

He lets the bar go and picks up his towel, walking up to me.

"I don't mind sharing this place with you, though," he tells me, gesturing to my pants. "As long as you keep that thing out of the fucking showers."

I have no idea what the hell he's on about, but I force a laugh at his last joke. I offer my hand before I go. "Lucas Morrow," I tell him.

"Deacon," he says, taking it. "Doran."

I nod. *Never heard of him.* Maybe he doesn't know Quinn's family, after all.

"See you around." And I jump on the treadmill, determined to stay there until I'm too tired to think about breathing, much less the panties still in my bed.

WESTON

CHAPTER EIGHTEEN

Quinn

Sitting at the worktable in my shop's kitchen, I flip through Winslet's diary, trying to concentrate on something other than Lucas.

I won't tell him, but I liked last night for more than just the orgasm. He felt close to me again—like he still belonged to me in the way that I grew up with.

Different, but still a pair. Him looking out for me. Indulging my curiosity and my need to learn and to keep it a secret, except now we're adults, and I need other things.

Oh, God. I don't hate him like I said I did.

I just wish his attention didn't give me whiplash. Half the time, I'm walking into a wall, and the other half, he's as gentle as a breeze.

Blowing out a long breath, I blink my eyes back into focus and train them on the diary. I'll see him later and "think" about him tonight when I'm alone.

I flip through the pages, trying to discern some sort of timeline from the clues.

Her entries are similar to the ones in my journals, whereas they're not arranged as a narrative, so to speak. Neither of us tell stories.

I make lists.

And she rages in single-word thoughts, as if she's trapped deep inside her head and doesn't even know her own language.

Clusters of blank pages appear in between scribbles, notes, and hand-drawn maps. A blue pen running out of ink would disappear in favor of pencil or Sharpie or a fountain pen, but then reappear later in the book.

It's all the same writing, though. I turn a page, seeing the upside-down script and pinch my brow as I turn it around to read. It's like she just grabbed the book in fits, flipped it open, and spit out emotions wherever she could find space.

The only times she displays any semblance of control are when she draws. Cars are a common theme. Illustrations, only in black and white, of a vehicle underwater. Another of a scarf hanging out of a trunk as a hand pries open the lid. The Shelburne Falls High School black pirate flag adorns the end of the fabric just before the tassels. Is the scarf hers? Or is she trying to say the car belonged to a Pirate? If they were planning on shoving someone, especially one of their own, into the river, they wouldn't have left evidence in the car.

There are drawings of a second vehicle too. I turn the page, widening my eyes at the sketch of the '72 black Dodge that followed me the other night.

Rain crashes onto the windshield as it races down a deserted road in the forest, looking like something out of a comic strip in simple black ink. Words float around the scene.

*parents
*clock
*firewood
*clothes
*food
*scream

Is it a to-do list?

I do kind of understand these short, one-word thoughts more now. In my house with Lucas last night, and later on the phone, all I could think were in feelings.

He's not satiating me. I just want more.

Winslet's not so different.

I glance at the clock on the wall, seeing it's after six. I've been here for twelve hours, working alone, but I'm finally ready for the holiday. Everything is baked, frosted, and stored until tomorrow when we transport it all to our booth in the park. In twelve more hours.

Still have to get through tonight.

I fan the pages, reading various entries written in no intelligible order and studying drawings. Fists gripping a steering wheel. A boy running away from a car. Blackhawk Lake and the waterfalls our town is named after.

Death Falls reads the title above the drawing of water pouring down over a mountain.

*Took them from me, took them from me, took them from me...*she scrawled on another page.

I shake my head as I run my finger over the deep indentation of the letters, carved into the paper. Maniacal and desperate.

*dark
*water in the air
*scent of earth
*keys like claws
*headlights
*now
*now
*now

*now
*now
*now!

My heart beats faster, like I'm her. Like I'm feeling the keys between my knuckles. Like claws.

Vengeance.

It starts to come together. Winslet MacCreary went missing, and everyone thought it was Weston. Hawke, Dylan, and everyone surmised it was specifically the Doran brothers.

But this notebook makes it sound like it wasn't.

She was taken. Someone else tried to murder her.

And when she survived, she hid. Possibly at the summer camp, which was abandoned in those years, as she planned revenge.

Why did Manas push her away, though? And what does she mean by "took them from me?"

I flip the page, reading.

My heart never hurt when it was empty.
You make me wanna die.

Needles prick the back of my throat, tears rising to my eyes. I don't know what an empty heart feels like. I've always had love of some sort.

I get it, though. The longing when you can't have who you want.

Memories of Lucas watching me last night wash over me. *You'll never be able to act like I'm your friends' little sister again.* When he looks at me, he'll remember what he saw, and when I look at him, I'll wonder if he wants to see it again.

The backdoor opens, and I hide the diary before even looking up.

Aro strolls in. "Hi."

"Hey."

She stops and heaves a sigh, looking around.

I bow my head, going back to jotting down my to-do list for tomorrow. "In the cooler."

I hear the spring in her step as she dives into the walk-in refrigerator. She emerges with two pink lemonade cupcakes, half of one already in her mouth. A summer staple I quickly learned that she loves.

"Hawke thinks we're going to skinny dip tomorrow," she says, taking a seat across from me. "But I'll be too sugared up to stay awake."

Skinny-dipping. I should add that to my list. If Lucas still has it. It occurred to me somewhere in the middle of the night last night that we checked one thing off. *Performing*.

I keep my smirk to myself, but it's hard.

"Here to talk me into letting you in the tower?" I ask her.

"I'm here for the cupcakes."

I toss her a glance, but keep from reminding her that I'm not stupid. Hunter might feel like he owes me conversation for stealing treats, but Aro isn't chatty.

But while she's here...

I stop writing, resting my chin on my hand. "What do you know about the Legend of the Night Ride?"

She shrugs. "It's your legend, not Weston's." She licks the frosting and then clears her throat. "Hawke says that there's a rider out there," she tells me. "Just searching."

I think of the black car that followed me in the dark. No headlights. "Searching for what?"

She shakes her head. "He just follows you with his headlights off," she goes on. "One night, he saw a young guy at a gas station. It was late, dark. When the kid finished fueling, the rider drove out in his car from just behind the building."

It had been waiting for him?

She continues, "It followed him, and when he was on Blackhawk Road, he noticed the vehicle in his rearview mirror. He turned, it turned. He sped up, it kept up." She peels the wrapper off the second cupcake. "He raced home, dashed up his porch steps, and turned. Headlights blinded him."

Never lead danger home. Never lead it to you when you're alone.

An ancient memory from when I was a kid surfaces. My parents' basement. Flashlights. Dylan, Hawke, Kade, Hunter, and me telling ghost stories. Another urban legend lesson.

"He can't see the figure emerging from the car." She sets the cupcake down and leans in. "They say he was killed by whoever was driving, but Hawke and I never found a record of it. But the locals started having fun with the story anyway, and that part is well-documented. Just slightly before your brothers' time in high school, locals copycatted the Night Ride story. Some high school kids would follow a girl they liked, or sorority girls would follow a teacher," she explains.

"What would they do?"

She picks up the cupcake again. "Whatever manifested, I guess. Scaring each other." She takes a bite. "Maybe some foreplay."

Realization hits me. "Like the Marauders back in the day in Weston."

"Mm." She nods. "But sometimes, it wasn't fun. Sometimes the person being chased realized too late that it was him instead—the real rider—and not some friend playing a joke. It got bad, so they stopped."

So the rider attacked several people.

"If you see him," she says in a teasing voice, "don't lead him back to your house. Drive to a safe place. Or...just keep driving."

"How do they know it was a *he*?" I ask.

"Because it always is."

And she takes another bite.

Winslet's diary is like a voodoo doll. Filled with scratches and screams and tears and written in a way that maintains no clear thought other than what her senses are picking up or the deterioration of her mind.

But the feeling is obvious. She's talking and drawing about the Night Ride. The car in her illustrations is the same one I'm seeing. The one Aro told me belongs to the auto shop at Weston High School.

So the questions are; who was driving then, and who's driving now?

My voice comes out as a whisper, "What do you think the rider was looking for?"

Aro is quiet as she slowly chews. "Whatever it was, he must've found it."

Because he—or she—stopped.

To us, the legend was always just that. No one we know has ever come into contact with the rider. If it ever really happened.

A knock rattles the back door, and I jump, watching Lucas enter from the alleyway.

Aro laughs under her breath at me, but she'd jump, too, if she was alone here late at night with a secret hideout just feet away.

Lucas steps in, dressed in a suit, and I stop breathing for a moment. His crisp white shirt stands out against his dark suit, and our eyes meet, the memory of last night making me almost shiver. His dark blond hair is pushed over to one side as if he raked through it with his fingers, and I can't help but linger on his sun-kissed skin that's the same tone as I now know his naked chest and back are.

He glances to Aro and then back to me, lingering and hiding a smile, and I try not to be obvious when I strip off my baker's jacket. Laying it across the table, I turn back to him, seeing his attention drawn low to my tank top before he inhales a heavy breath and eyes me as if he knows exactly what I'm doing. "Ready?" he taunts back.

I stare at him. Are my panties still in his bed, I wonder?

"Yeah." And I look to Aro. "I'm not allowed to ride my bike to Weston."

She chuckles. "Hi," she tells Lucas.

He nods back to her.

I need a change of clothes, so he's taking me home before we head back to the gym. Will we talk at all? Will my brothers be there to make him nervous? What will he do if Farrow is there and offers me a ride home instead? We're neighbors, after all.

Aro dusts off her hands and tosses the empty cupcake wrappers into the garbage. "Can I join you?" she asks both of us. "I wanted to check in on some friends. Hawke will come grab me after lights out."

Lucas's eyes dart to me as if I might have a problem with it, but I pop up off my chair. "Sure."

We tuck in our chairs, and I double-check the front doors, throwing a glance at the closed mirror before I take my bag and phone. We drift into the alley, and I lock the back door, jogging around the passenger side.

"You can get in front," I blurt out to Aro.

But she pushes the front seat forward and climbs into the back. "Nah, that's okay."

Great. Lucas and I are going to look like a thing, sitting in the front together, and if she doesn't allude to that with Hawke, she'll tell Dylan.

I put my seatbelt on as Lucas turns the key and starts the car. I avoid his eyes but glance at his hand fisting the stick shift as he punches it into reverse. My clit throbs once.

I blink long and hard, turning my eyes out the window as he backs us out into the street. In a few seconds, we're on High Street, making our way to Weston.

I left the diary under the laptop on the worktable in the kitchen. I'm sure it's fine, but I should've grabbed it. I have the utmost faith in Hawke to get into the bakery, even though I changed the locks, and I don't want him confiscating it yet.

I lift my eyes, watching the trees in my side mirror flying past in the darkness.

"That's an interesting tattoo," Lucas says.

I look over, seeing him eye Aro in the rearview mirror.

"Yours is better." She smirks.

Headlights are reflected in my side mirror, and I watch the car far behind us.

"Born and raised in Weston?" he asks her.

"Yeah."

"Which part?"

"The shitty part."

He breathes out a weak laugh, and he's either impressed with her retorts or finds it funny that she's inferring there's a non-shitty part of Weston.

I tilt my mirror to get rid of the glare of the lights growing closer behind us.

"People talk about the glory days," Aro muses. "Bustling population. Traffic. The stands packed at football games and streets lit up with businesses and crowded with pedestrians. It seems like Atlantis, though." Her voice softens. "A myth that we're not sure was ever real."

We cross the bridge, but Aro continues before I have a chance to retrieve a coin.

"I've never seen this town any other way," she tells us. "A ghost town and a breeding ground for...*opportunists*."

Growing up, I don't remember anything good about Weston. We never drove here for a restaurant or an athletic event.

"Not going to ask me any questions?" she presses him. "Like how old I was when they drew me in? Or how much money I stole for them?"

I notice the lights in my side mirror are no longer there and glance over.

The car is still there.

Several lengths behind us but there.

My chest rises and falls a little faster.

"Or," Aro goes on, "how much money I could've made if I'd started saying yes to him?"

It takes a moment to register what Aro's talking about. Green Street? The gang she belongs to that Farrow still belongs to? Why is she talking to Lucas about that?

Tearing my eyes away from the car in my mirror, I look over at him. His tanned jaw is flexed, but he just stares at the road in front of him.

"Drew Reeves," Aro says, the words filling the car. "You've heard of him, right?"

I watch Lucas, since I know it's not me she's asking. I've heard of Reeves. He was a Shelburne Falls cop, but he quit two years ago.

Aro continues, "I wonder if it was his idea to recruit teenagers to steal and deal and hurt people."

I narrow my eyes. Aro's never talked to me about what she went through here. Why is she sharing this now?

"It was smart," she tells us. "Throwing minors to the wolves instead of himself."

"Did he hurt you?" I ask her.

She stares into Lucas's rearview mirror. "He wanted to."

We pull up to Knock Hill, and I take in Lucas's white knuckles, clenched around the steering wheel, and his rigid shoulders. What's going on?

Pieces start to slide into place, conclusions coming more into view. His back tattoo. Everyone at my party immediately recognized it. Farrow just leaving me with him when it wasn't abundantly clear that I was consenting to anything.

Drew Reeves is about Lucas's age, right? Did they know each other?

We stop in front of my house, Farrow's place lit up like a stadium with music pouring out of it and two women on the porch.

I open my door. "I'll be right back."

I want to stay and keep listening, but I'll talk to Lucas when she's gone.

I climb out, leaving it open for Aro as I jog up the stairs to my place.

"Thanks for the ride." I can only just hear her, her tone kind of guarded. Does she know something about him that I don't?

I start to unlock my door, but when I look back, she's still at the car and Lucas is talking to her over the roof.

What is he saying that he couldn't say in the car?

I sweep the street, the car that was following us nowhere to be seen, but I don't relax as their lips continue to move. Why is it easier to talk to someone he barely knows? I don't understand what he keeps trying to protect me from, but I'm now positive that it's not from Farrow Kelly or Noah Van der Berg.

It's nothing that has to do with me.

SHELBURNE FALLS

CHAPTER NINETEEN

Lucas

"Thanks for the ride," Aro calls out, slamming the door of Jared's car.

Quickly, I climb out and ask, "Did he hurt you?"

She stops, and I stare across the roof of the car at her. Drew loved women, and it took a long time to catch on that he liked them young.

Aro turns, and I avoid looking up the steps at Quinn. Wouldn't Drew just love to see me now? Losing my mind over a girl twelve years younger than me.

"He hurt others," Aro tells me.

She struggles to meet my eyes, and I know enough about her in the few interactions we've had to know that she doesn't shy away from saying what needs to be said.

But she doesn't divulge more. She doesn't want to dredge it up, and to be honest, I'm grateful. I'd hate hearing it.

She comes up to the car and lowers her voice as Quinn lingers up at her door, probably wondering what we're doing.

"I know why you left," she says. "Everyone here does, so you better tell her before someone else explains it their way."

I lift my eyes to Quinn. She turns away and starts to unlock her door.

"And I also know you hate what Green Street has become," Aro continues, "so don't even think about leaving again, because you have a responsibility."

"I know."

Green Street has expanded into Shelburne Falls—and into the Trent and Caruthers families—which I didn't consider when I left. I need to get rid of Hugo Navarre and Drew Reeves. When those I love are safe, I'll tell Madoc everything.

She spins back around and heads down the street, waving at Quinn. "See you tomorrow!"

Quinn waves and dives inside to get changed for the gym.

Looking up and down Knock Hill, I see the barber shop across the street that I noticed operating yesterday when I installed the cameras at Quinn's house. Samson Fletcher was working when I was hanging around town, one of the few businesses still operating. Weston has two restaurants, a gas station, a school, and a few other odds and ends, but it doesn't have much else. Not even its own police.

Which is how Drew got away with so much for so long. In fact, he kept the police from coming back here, probably convincing Shelburne Falls to pick up the slack so he could consolidate his vantage point.

I need to talk to Farrow again.

But first, I need a few minutes with Quinn to myself. I gaze up at her front door, warm light glowing from the windows.

She's not going to want to hear an apology, and I never would've dreamed of giving her one last night. It's amazing how differently things look in the light of day. As if guilt takes a back seat when the sun goes down.

I installed cameras at her house without her permission and repeatedly questioned her decisions, not to mention embarrassing her by crashing her party last night. I could claim I was just worried about her, or how old habits are hard to break, but the truth is, I don't want her with anyone else, and I won't claim her for myself. It's fucked up.

A car passes me, and I climb back into my seat, turning the radio up just a bit.

But then I stop, realizing what I just saw.

I spin around, sticking my head out the window and looking behind to where that car just drove. The headlights weren't on.

It comes to the *Stop* sign, the brake lights flash—no taillights—and it slowly turns left. So slowly like it's on the prowl.

Drew. Maybe it's not, but it could be.

I grab the steering wheel, ready to follow, but the passenger door opens, and Quinn takes a seat next to me.

I pause, remembering we're supposed to go to the gym. I can't just drive off on her.

And I can't trail someone with her in the car and put her in danger.

Instead, I shift into first, watching the vehicle disappear in my mirror as I pull away from the curb. I keep an eye on my surroundings as we leave Weston. Did it follow us here?

Maybe it was nothing. I'll have to keep a lookout for it, though, in addition to the Traverse. Just to be safe.

We cruise across the bridge, and as my nerves calm, it occurs to me I haven't heard Quinn so much as breathe since she got in the car. I look over at her, the tendon in her neck taut as she faces the window. I reach out to touch it—run the back of my finger down her nape—but she won't look at me, and I'm afraid she'll pull away. I drop my hand.

"Drive" plays on the radio, the soft, sultry tune filling the air as wind breezes through the flyaways around her face.

I'd texted her earlier to see if she wanted to exercise tonight, and thankfully, she said yes.

"Quinn—"

"I don't want to talk," she says calmly.

Her voice is gentle, steady.

But she couldn't have been clearer.

I shift my gaze back to the road, a little more fucking tortured now. Does she feel like shit about last night? About me touching her? *Fuck*.

Why couldn't I leave three days ago when I was supposed to? I've fucked it up now. Everything. She's resorted to making assumptions because I won't tell her anything. Who knows what she's thinking?

Would I have fucked her last night if she were someone else? If she were just another young woman I'd met with her curious questions, contagious smiles, and little delights she takes in all the small things.

No. I wouldn't have fucked her the first time. The first time I would've gone slow, swallowing every second as if it was food that I could taste, smell, and consume. I would've kissed everything, barely separating my mouth from her body long enough to breathe.

The next time, we would've fucked. On the kitchen counter. On the couch. Against the wall. In the car.

I press my cock down, toss a glare out the window, and shift into fourth. If she were anyone but Quinn, I might feel guilty about the age difference, but not enough to stop.

I pull up to the gym, park across the street, and we climb out of the car, heading to the entrance.

Just give her some space, I tell myself. We'll get inside, blow off some steam on the track, and everything will relax. We'll be back to being friends if I'm patient.

As soon as we walk in, though, I spot all three of her brothers carrying rackets past the front desk. *Goddammit!*

Madoc called me earlier, and I completely blew it off. He was probably inviting me to join them tonight. *Shit.*

I just want her to myself. I watch her check in and get a towel, about to follow myself.

But then Noah, Farrow, Dylan, and Hunter walk across the entryway, as well.

I grit my teeth.

Dylan grabs Quinn in a hug, rocking side to side playfully before releasing her. "Heading into spin class if you want to join us."

Quinn addresses Farrow. "I thought you couldn't do cardio."

"My stamina is what dreams are made of," he taunts, drifting past her with his stupid fucking swagger. "Tomorrow's panties are already wet."

Excuse me? I take a step.

"With sweat," Farrow assures me, taking an extra step back. "That's what I meant."

Yeah, my ass.

He spins around and follows Dylan toward the room, Van der Berg griping at him, "Don't you ever shut the fuck up?"

"When my mouth is full."

Noah shakes his head, and I can imagine Farrow's smirk as they both disappear inside.

Quinn turns to me, her chest rising with a breath. "Well..." She smiles small. "Thank you for the ride."

She turns toward the stairs, probably heading for the track, and I take a step, but Jared is there.

He approaches her, his eyebrow cocked. "We trust your decisions." He grins, Madoc and Jax behind him. "But it's nice to know another adult is on the case."

He tosses me a look, thinking Quinn is at the house with me, and it doesn't even occur to him to worry. I rub the back of my neck.

Jax grabs his sister in a headlock. "You thought you were going to have fun this summer, didn't you?"

Jared and Madoc chuckle as Quinn twists and turns for a second before finally dealing him a blow in the gut.

He growls, releasing her, and everyone laughs again.

She looks at me. "They think you're a priest." She pins me with a pointed stare. "Are you?"

My heart rate jacks up, knowing she's referring to last night, and all that's keeping her from making me the subject of her brothers' attention rather than her is her choice of words.

I maintain a level tone. "As far as you're concerned."

"But *you're* going to have fun this summer?"

My dick twitches, her brothers listening to every word.

They're going to see it in my face. In my breathing.

I keep my tone steady. "That's none of your business."

I'm the adult.

Madoc tugs her close, kissing her head. "Boundaries, kiddo."

She glares at me, and I smile just enough for her to see.

She can tell them what's happened between us, but so can I. Her masturbating on my bed, getting her own apartment next to Farrow Kelly, and supplying drinks to her minor nephews and niece.

She yanks her towel off her shoulder and stomps up the stairs to the second level.

"We leave at nine!" I shout after her.

I want to follow, but it'll look suspicious.

"Thank you for helping," Madoc tells me. "Sorry I haven't been around much. How are you doing?"

I glance up, watching her move out of sight. "I'm fine."

He holds up his racket. "A game?"

"I think I'm gonna run instead."

I start for the stairs, but he pulls me back. "Come on, we need four."

And I actually roll my eyes because I still can't tell this guy no. It's like I'm scared he'll cry or something.

Following the three of them into a court, Madoc and I take the back while Jared and Jax take the front. Madoc serves, the ball slamming against the wall and barreling back to us, echoing through the chamber.

"Is she doing okay?" Madoc asks me, grunting as he hits the ball. "Getting home at a decent hour and getting some sleep?"

"She has a lot of energy." I run for the ball. "Always off somewhere."

"She pissing you off?" Jax jokes.

We volley, Jared catching it, then Madoc slamming it again.

She's definitely pissing me off. But in ways I can't tell them about.

I dive for my shot. "She's still...the same as she always was."

I don't know what to say. Between last night and the car with serious stalker vibes earlier, I can't think.

"Yeah, the parents did a good job." Madoc sucks in air. "She's the best of us. Grew up with everything and took nothing for granted."

His eyes meet mine before he takes another shot.

"She'll never risk what's good in the pursuit of what she thinks might be better," he tells me.

I pause, my shot going over my head. Madoc makes a face and goes to retrieve the ball.

The grass is greener everywhere you're not standing, he means.

Quinn knows how lucky she is. That's a lesson I could've used all those years ago when I went looking for friends that Madoc wouldn't have approved of.

"We don't want her to be alone forever." Jax whips his racket. "We just never want her to know how awful people can be."

I jerk my head left and right, cracking my neck. The people you love the most are the ones who can really hurt you, though. He must know that. She'll suffer in love as much as anything.

"So, what's the agenda for tomorrow?" I ask, swatting the ball and needing a change of subject.

Madoc dives, missing his shot. "Parade at ten," he growls, "barbecue crawl starting at Eagle Point at noon, fireworks at nine."

"What time do I have to be up?" Jared grumbles.

I clench my fist around the racket.

"Five a.m.," Madoc replies.

"Fuck."

Jax laughs.

I don't. I drop my arm, letting the ball fly past me again. "Guys, I'm not in the mood for this today. I'm sorry," I tell Madoc. "I gotta run laps or something."

I have to get out of here and clear my head. I need silence.

"Amen." Jax turns and starts walking past me as if he was thinking the same thing. "I'm going to swim some laps."

Jared follows his brother. "I'm going home for cardio."

I walk out after them, Madoc calling out behind us. "I thought you guys liked racquetball!"

I surprise myself with a smile. I love them; although, I feel bad not one of us are in the mood to indulge him. It finally feels like I'm home.

"See you tomorrow!" I shout back at him.

Bright and early.

Jumping onto the track, I mark the time and start jogging. I keep my pace steady and slow, my stride carrying me lap after lap in no time. Quinn rides a Peloton bike and meets my eyes once.

But not again. Every time I pass, she's lost in her music or her workout, and I leave her alone.

The gym empties more and more as time goes on, and when I pass by again, she's no longer on the bike. I find her at the leg machines, tuning into a cooking show on the TV while she works out.

Still learning. Forever curious. She sits on a leg curl machine, but she's not working, her attention lost in the cake decorating show.

Eyes wide. Lips parted just slightly. I swallow, unable to not look at her as I cruise by. She's beautiful. Just the view of her. And the things she says. It all culminates in this *world according to Quinn* that I like living in.

There's no way I'm fucking leaving her to live in the same town as Hugo Navarre and Green Street. She stays. They go.

"Lucas."

I slow, popping my head up to see a woman just off the track in an Astrophysics black polo and black shorts.

Breathing hard, I reach her and stop, recognition happening almost instantly. "Sarah?"

Auburn hair, beautifully wavy, blue eyes, and freckles—still in shape as she always was. An ex-girlfriend.

She smiles, and I tense, about to move in for a hug, but I don't. The last time we spoke she told me my life would be shit and then threw her milkshake at me where it splattered all over my car.

Glancing at her name tag, I see that she works here.

"I heard you got married," I say, trying to catch my breath.

"I did." She speaks gently. A lot kinder than the last time. "It didn't work out."

"I'm sorry."

"We live and learn." She looks me up and down. "It's good to see you."

I cock my head playfully. "Is it?"

She waves me off. "Oh, a lot's happened since. I've cooled off," she teases. "And I've grown up. You?"

We broke up because of me. I liked her, but I didn't love her. I didn't want to waste her time anymore.

But now...

I breathe out a sad laugh. "We're never where we think we'll be by a certain age, are we?"

She frowns. "No, we're not. They don't tell us that."

Nope.

She was nice. And we had fun. I hurt her, but I knew it was the right decision.

Now, though... We've both been knocked off our high horses.

"Any kids?" she asks.

I shake my head. "No. You?"

"No." She wets her glossy lips, a little orange to match the red in her hair. "Married?"

I shake my head again.

"Are you back for good?" she asks.

"I work abroad now," I tell her. "Just home for some family business."

I glance at Quinn as she changes the channel to another show, her shorts and sports bra showing her glistening skin and every curve of her ass. Some guy stands nearby, stealing glances at her.

"Things on your mind?" Sarah asks.

I look back at her, breaking into a smile. "I was never relaxed."

"I remember."

Yeah, I'll bet she does.

She pulls up her clipboard and writes something on a business card. Handing it to me, she says, "I still remember how much you liked blowing off steam too."

I take the card and see her address on the backside.

"I'm home after ten every night," she tells me. "Key's under the mat."

Something jolts in my heart, and I dart my eyes back up to hers, that easy playfulness in her gaze just like I remember.

She walks away, throwing a smile back at me, and my stomach swims, my mouth like sandpaper.

She didn't ask me out. She didn't give me her number. Just 'here's the key, come after ten.' How many single men wouldn't love the invitation of a good fuck with no strings attached?

I drift to the fountain and gulp down some water.

It would help to have her to go to. I'm still fucked up from last night and haven't had a release.

And we're both older, a little more jaded and willing to take an hour of escapism for what it is. She doesn't care if I love her or not.

I could never use Quinn for an escape.

Oh, Quinn...

My Quinn.

I shoot up, swallowing, but I bump into someone.

"Excuse me," I say.

"Don't mind me."

I rear back, taking in the same dude from last night. What was his name? Deacon?

But he doesn't go for the drinking fountain, just leans back on the wall, gazing at me. I start to walk away, but I only make it two steps when I realize he's staring.

Is he following me?

"What do you want?" I ask.

"To keep watching."

I face him, straightening my spine. "Who the hell are you?"

But he turns his eyes to Quinn, looking lost in thought for a moment, and I don't like it. I move to block his line of sight, but he speaks up. "She looks like someone I used to know," he murmurs. "Someone who's not here anymore."

I glance at Quinn as she sets down a barbell and refastens her ponytail.

"You're going to need to binge her," he tells me.

I narrow my gaze, looking at him.

"No matter where you go," he says, "or who you meet or the time that passes, you will want her when she's with someone else. When she's thirty. When you're in the same room with her... You will want her until you've had your fill of her."

What the fuck?

But my gaze shifts to Quinn again, just for a moment.

Is that true?

She starts jump roping, her ponytail bouncing, and the years ahead of us start piling up. Her career expanding. Mine in Dubai becoming more and more like a prison. Someone climbing into bed next to her at night. Me getting her wedding announcement in the mail.

Standing next to her in a room and watching other people make her happy.

I don't notice when the guy leaves, but when I come back to myself, he's gone.

I look around, seeing him disappear through a door that I don't think is for customers.

Who the fuck is he?

Glancing at the clock, I see it's almost nine. I need to talk to her, and I can't do that here. No one is getting into the car with us when I take her home. No one's dragging me out for a drink. I need to deal with this.

Heading downstairs, I slip into the locker room, grab a towel, and strip, climbing into a shower. Luckily the place is emptying, and I'm alone. I just hope that creep isn't in here. He's weird, and I prefer not to be bothered.

I smooth my hand over the top of my head, rinsing the suds.

He's weird, but he *knows*. And if a stranger can tell, then Madoc, Jax, and Jared don't know yet simply because they don't want to. One of them should take her home tonight. Bingeing her isn't the answer. I need to purge her.

Finishing washing, I shut off the water and rake the towel over my body and head before wrapping it around my waist. I exit the shower and stalk back into the locker room.

As soon as I get to my row, though, I see Quinn digging into my locker.

I start for her. "What are you doing?"

"Taking my brother's car," she snaps. "You can find another ride home."

I charge over and take her wrists, pulling them out of my shit.

But when she fires her eyes up at me, I see the flush in her cheeks and the tension in her jaw.

She's mad.

I draw in a breath, struggling to contain all the shit swelling in my chest. "You saw me with Sarah."

I wasn't trying to make her jealous...

Pinching her brow together, she spits out, "Saw you with who?" And then grabs something out of my locker, flinging the business card at me. "Oh, you mean, that? I don't care."

Sarah's card falls to the floor, and I close my eyes for a moment. Should I piss her off some more and tell her I memorized the address off one glance? I don't need the fucking card.

But, no.

I'm almost elated, unfortunately.

She watches me just as much as I watch her, and we're both fucked.

She searches for Jared's Mustang keys. "I don't want to think about you anymore."

I know.

"I'm done." Her voice is thick with tears she won't let go. "I just want to be free."

And I move. I don't know if I'm thinking with my head or acting from my gut, but I take her in my hands and pull her into my chest.

Gazing down into her dark brown eyes and her pink lips that are puffy from chewing on them, I whisper, "You're all I think about."

I crash down on her mouth, kissing little Quinn for the first time and unable to slow down as I move over her lips. Skin soft enough to eat... *Oh, God.* She moans, and I wrap one arm around her waist, pressing her to my body as my other hand holds her face. I go at her, kissing her again and again before tilting my head to the other side and sinking deeper. Fuck. I dig my fingers into the flesh of her hip and bear down on her, tasting her tongue.

And she matches me, gripping my waist and moving her mouth over mine.

I back her into the lockers, opening my eyes and doing a sweep of the area as we kiss to make sure we're alone. My body stirs with a thousand fucking currents of heat, and any resistance in my head is drowned out.

I tell her, "I can't stop looking at you and wanting to touch you…"

"I wanna feel my skin on yours," she whimpers.

Together, we pull her sports bra over her head, and I palm one of her breasts as she sinks into my body again. "She offered me a roll in bed if I need to blow off steam," I pant between kisses before devouring her neck.

"But you want to blow off steam with me," she says.

Yes. Quinn is the sole reason my body and head are jacked. Only she will do.

I start to peel down her shorts. "Your family is here."

"I don't care."

I'm not fucking her in a men's locker room. But I gotta get off. I need to feel her.

She kicks off her shorts, leaving her nearly naked in her thong, and I lift her up, letting her wrap her legs around me.

She moans again and again, leaving little kisses all over my face.

God, I can't think about anything anymore. She feels so fucking good. Like home.

"I need a shower," she whispers.

I should take her in a shower stall—out of view and shielded by the noise of the water. But she'll be too hard to keep hold of if she's wet. I know what I want.

"Not yet."

Taking a seat on the wide bench in the middle of the row, I let her straddle me as I rip off my towel. Leaning back on my arm, I hold her waist with the other hand as she starts grinding on me. The rock-hard ridge of my cock rubs against her wet panties.

She leans in, riding hard and fast as she kisses me. "I'm safe with you. Show me what you like."

I groan, tipping my head back as she bites my neck. "I like you."

For the first time in nearly a decade, I'm out of my mind with want of something.

And someone wants me. It feels good to have muscles in my arms again. To be scared her family's going to fucking kill me, but I want her more than I fear them.

Heat pools in my stomach, and I punch up a little, pressing my dick into her thin panties.

"Oh, God." She rolls her hips faster, her clit running over my dick over and over again. "Don't stop."

Our foreheads together, she pumps on top of me. "You know what to do," I pant. "Just like that."

Leaning back a little, she thrusts, her orgasm rising as her breathing stutters. I can't take my eyes off her full breasts, taut stomach, and the way her ass rolls on top of me.

"You just move the panties aside and you can be inside me," she teases.

Fuck...

I grunt, feeling my orgasm coming. The mere idea of how tight and hot she'll be sending me reeling.

I shoot back up, squeezing her thighs in both hands and gliding the tip of my tongue over her jaw. *So fucking hot.*

Fire courses up my body, flowing from every limb to my center.

"Oh, God," she cries out. "I want to feel you inside me. Please, Lucas. It feels so good."

I know, baby. I want to fucking fill you too.

But not here.

She throws her head back again, crying out so loudly, and I don't fucking stop her, because I can't. I growl, squeezing my eyes shut, and I pull my dick out from under her and stroke it just as I shoot onto her stomach.

"Oh, baby." I breathe hard. "Oh, God."

She grinds a few more times, her orgasm coursing through her, and I just stare at my cum on her skin, dripping onto her panties.

Goddammit.

Grabbing her, I take her mouth in mine, not an ounce of fucking guilt.

We kiss for a while before she finally mews, pulling back for air. "Thank you," she says.

I kiss her mouth, her nose, and forehead, running a thumb over her nipple.

Binge her.

I feel spent but not sated. We're going to have to do that again. A lot.

Her forehead meets mine again as she smiles at me. "I want frozen yogurt downstairs before you take me back to Weston," she pants. "Or else I'm gonna tell my brothers how good of a summer I'm really having."

I cock a brow. But I smile too. *Well, we can't have that, can we?*

WESTON

CHAPTER TWENTY

Quinn

The heat from yesterday still warms the pavement, filling the early morning air with a sultry breeze that reminds me of the locker room last night. It had been heavy with moisture from his shower, and his skin—especially his neck—was like a blanket of fire. I could taste everything.

I pedal across the bridge, heading into Shelburne Falls in the dark as I let go of the handle bars. I hold out my hands, balancing as I ride with my backpack strapped to my back.

He kissed me.

I let out a breathy laugh, unable to contain it. He *kissed* me like he couldn't stop.

His arms had been so tight, and his hands left bruises on my thighs. I glance down at my left leg, seeing the purple and not minding it at all. I knew he wouldn't hurt me, and I knew he would've stopped if I'd told him to, but I let him squeeze and grip and hold, because it felt like he wanted to glue me to him so he'd never be without me. For a few minutes, it felt like that.

My lips are swollen, and in the hours since he kissed me goodnight and dropped me off at home, it's the kisses I thought of more than how hard he was or how good the orgasm hit.

He'd wiped himself off my stomach, but I hadn't washed the underwear. I'm not sure I will. He'll wake up with guilt this morning and act like the jerk later, but I'll have the panties to remind me that he got off on me, no matter how much he tries to ruin it.

Cruising into the center of town, I peer over my shoulder, the street behind me quiet and misty. Porch lights shine, trees sway in the breeze, and cars sit parked along both curbs, empty and dark. I can't see the clouds above me, but I smell them. It was supposed to be a clear day, so let's hope it holds out.

Barreling down High Street, I'm about to take a left to go around the building, to the back, but someone waits at my front door.

I recognize Mrs. Jamieson. "Morning!" I shout.

She waves, looking relieved to see me.

I slow and jump off my bike, walking it onto the sidewalk and digging out my keys.

"Thanks for being here so early," she says.

"Oh, it's no problem." I unlock the shop. "Lots to do, so I'd be up anyway."

Leaving the *Closed* sign facing outward, I prop the door open so she can carry her order out.

Shelby Jamieson is married to someone my sister-in-law, Tate, used to date. Always a sore subject for Jared, even though Ben is a great guy and tips my staff well. It took him a long time to find someone, but now he and his wife have four kids and they're great customers. I like anyone who keeps Jared nervous.

I park my bike off to the side and let her follow me in.

"Do you have the schedule for the crawl?" she asks.

"Right here." I pat the counter with the schedule of festivities taped to the surface. "Eagle Point, the mayor's house, High Street, Camp Blackhawk, and Fallstown."

I memorized the BBQ Crawl because I'm supplying food to two of the stops. Opening the cooler in the kitchen, I walk inside and reach on a shelf for one of her orders.

"Is your brother bussing the drinkers?" she shouts.

"Of course." I pull out the cupcakes and charcuterie tray filled with little desserts. "Have to make sure the fun goes on."

"Delightful," she coos, coming into the kitchen. "We'll have the kids in bed after the block party here and make it in time for Adult Night Camp."

I chuckle, loving how my brothers plan everything in a way so that the adults can act like perpetual teenagers. Like how Jax schedules the kids' summer camp sessions so the Fourth of July falls between two. The cabins are empty of kids, and the town's adults can come play instead.

"Well, I'll be in bed by then," I call out.

"You're twenty-one now."

I carry the two orders out of the cooler and set them down on the table. "And I can't be drunk when I make coffee for you all in the morning," I tell her.

"Too right."

I lift up the cover for the treat tray.

"Quinn, wow!" She peels it back more and then opens the cupcake box. Her eyes light up, the festive flavors fragrant with fruity smells.

"Wait, there's more," I chirp, running back into the walk-in fridge. "Did you bring help?"

"Oh, Quinn." She continues to gush. "This looks amazing. It's too pretty to eat!"

My heart kicks up speed. I love hearing that tone in a customer's voice.

I bring out another small box of just four cupcakes. "Will Brigit have that friend over today, the one allergic to strawberries?"

"Yes, but don't worry." She can't take her eyes off the fruit kabobs. "I got some alternative snacks."

Setting down the small carton in front of her, I peel back the lid and show her the four identical cupcakes to the ones I already gave her. But these are for her daughter's friend. "No strawberries."

She beams as she inspects the treats. "How did you know?"

"You said she was having a sleepover, so I figured her bestie was coming."

"Thank you." She looks almost in tears. "This will make her night."

As I ring her up, her son pulls up to the curb, and we start securing the treats into her back seat.

"Thank you!" she calls out as they back away.

I wave. "Have fun and see you later!"

Hailey arrives, and we carry trays and boxes of treats to her car parked in the alley. Notifications start pouring in through my phone as the sun comes up and families begin getting excited for the day—tagging me in pics of their decorated patios and spreads of cakes, cookies, and other goodies they bought from me. Hailey takes the last of the Rice Krispies Treats and red, white, and blue macarons, and I smile as I scroll through all the beautiful displays on social media.

Stressful doesn't even begin to cover all the preparation it took to make those dishes and confections and coordinate pickups and deliveries in a narrow window of time. And I'll be dealing with it over every major holiday, if I'm lucky.

The potential of Carnival Tower's extra space makes me breathe easier. More walk-in refrigerators, bigger kitchen, larger dough mixer, more counter space... And the rooftop access! Employees can go out for breaks and fresh air... I could start an herb garden up there.

"Ready!" Hailey shouts from outside.

She starts up her RAV4, and I rush through the kitchen door to go close and lock the front door. Someone steps in from the sidewalk.

"Hi." I smile, grabbing my bank from the register. "I'm sorry we're closed to the public for—"

But my last word drifts off as I see him standing there in the darkened doorway, shrouded in shadow. Standing still.

So still.

I hear my pulse in my ears as I take in his familiar form, the outline of his short, sculpted hair, and the crisp fit of his suit. As if it's not a national holiday for him.

Is it the same suit he wore when he left the phone here?

Is he the one I spoke to on the phone when I was inside the tower?

His frame reminds me of Lucas—his broad, tense stance like armor.

Breathing shallow, I take a step back but halt. I want to know who he is.

Walking around the counter, I inch toward him.

He retreats a foot, and I stop.

An electric current trails up my arms, my neck, and to the top of my scalp. Was he trying to just pop in as a customer and watch me, unnoticed?

Or...

Is he scared? From what I gather from the murder map, these brothers have been living in the shadows for a long time.

I shoot off toward him, he pivots to the right, and then he's gone. I rush to the door, but I hear Hailey's cry. "Quinn! Help! The cupcakes!"

I grab the doorframe, catching myself, and hesitate. I look down the sidewalk, not seeing him.

"Quinn!"

I growl under my breath. *Dammit.*

That was stupid of me, but if he wanted to hurt me, I think he would've done it by now.

Grabbing the door, I slam it closed and lock it before I run back through the kitchen.

It's time to bring in Hawke. I've got a stalker, possibly two if I count the black Dodge, and I don't want to die because I was stubborn.

I'm not letting him take over, though. I'll remind him that I'm older.

Like that will help.

Jogging to Hailey, I catch the box on top of the stack just before it topples and let her resecure the straps holding everything down.

Taking the container, I lock everything else in place, get into the passenger side, and lay the box on my lap as we jet off to the park.

Doing a quick mental check, I remember all the locks I secured. He won't be able to get into the tower.

But still... I take Hailey or Noel back with me over the next couple of hours—just to be safe—as we make several trips to bring food to our booth in the park. Other vendors set up, and a few food trucks arrive.

I gaze longingly at them. A food truck... Great for offsite events like today, or a mobile, second location. It could be at the university. Or off the highway, en route to the summer camp and hiking trails.

I shake my head. I'll never live long enough to make all these dreams come true. Just concentrate on making Frosted a success and my home livable, I tell myself. For a few years, at least.

I have to keep reminding myself that I don't have to rush. I never should've.

Last night drifts through my head again, and I'm breathless.

I liked it.

I loved it.

But it doesn't feel like I thought it would. Or rather, I don't feel like I thought I would. It was no use rushing to be someone he'd want, only to become someone I didn't love. I missed all the milestones I should've had in order to get here, and now that I have my own place, I want more.

For me.

Just for me.

I lock up my shop one last time as Hailey takes her car, and I walk my bike out of the alley and toward the street. It's almost ten in the morning, the sun beating down already. I dig out Lucas's hat and pull it on, weaving my bicycle through the thick crowd lining both sides of High Street.

He could be here. Somewhere.

Deacon.

The parade is just kicking off, the marching band spilling festive notes into the air and everyone is covered in color. Firecrackers go off, a few teenagers jumping around and laughing.

Inching up on my tiptoes, I spot Madoc and Fallon sitting on the back of a classic convertible, my brother beaming, waving, and shouting joyously at friends he sees in the crowd. Fallon, on the other hand, always looks like she's suffering through a calculus class. I laugh to myself. She's a good sport with the whole public profile aspect of her husband being a mayor. She found the trick to survival, though. Focus on the kids. She smiles and waves at all of the little ones, taking balls from a box on the back seat and tossing them to the children.

I see another blond head, my heart skipping a beat, until I realize it's just Hunter. Kade is next to him. They breeze past, walking their dog, Tank, and tossing T-shirts into the crowd to promote their frat, while A.J. rides Dylan's back as she and Aro play rebel soldiers play-fighting Hawke—the British redcoat. They look like the three stooges, antagonizing and fake-kicking each other's butts.

I don't find Lucas in the crowd.

A.J. tosses candy to the spectators, while James does the same from his ATV. Should he be riding that on the street?

I find my way to Jax and Juliet who stand on the sidelines with one of Aro's siblings whom they foster.

"Isn't that like a safety hazard?" I ask, motioning to my ten-year-old nephew on his four-wheeler.

Jax stands behind his wife, his arms around her. "I'm sure."

I sigh, looking at all the phones out filming everything. "Madoc is trying his hardest to get canceled."

Just wait till someone online takes issue with it.

"And yet, everyone just adores him," Jax says with a hint of pride. "What do you think, honey?"

Juliet leans back into Jax's nuzzling. "I think we're about to have a senator in our pocket."

Jax laughs, and I turn my eyes back on Madoc, seeing him shoot one of Fallon's balls like a basketball into an empty stroller, the parents clapping and laughing with the toddler in their arms.

"You don't wrangle him in," I mutter, "you're going to have a *president* in your pocket."

They chuckle.

I don't.

They stop smiling because they realize I'm not kidding. Jax's face falls, followed by Juliet's worrying wide eyes.

"Jared would kill him," Jax says.

"Fallon would kill him first," she replies.

I continue on my way, amused. We could all try to hold Madoc back, but an unhappy Madoc is like a sea monster. You're not sure it exists, and you don't really want to find out, either.

I weave through the parade, cross the street, and jump on my bike. Pedaling hard, I work my way back up to Eagle Point Park, the scent of freshly mown lawns and charcoal barbecues filling the air. Firecrackers and bottle rockets pop and whistle as I ride past houses, and the music from the parade follows me, only fading a little through all the trees that hang over me in the park.

I coast, climbing off the bike and standing on one pedal all the way to my booth. Codi has arrived and helps arrange the treats, while Hailey stocks napkins.

"I'm burning some calories today," I joke as I halt the bike and park it behind the booth.

A few people start to drift down through, while others are still busy setting up nets and lawn games for the kids.

I step up to Codi's side. "Thank you for being here."

She peeks up at me through the hair in her eyes, and I quickly take in her clothes. She wears cut-offs, but the same tattered, dark blue T-shirt hangs over her body.

"The parade will be over soon," I tell both of them. "We'll be swamped."

"That's cool with me," Hailey calls out. "The more tips,

the better my night's going to be."

Codi doesn't add anything. What is she doing tonight? From what Farrow says, Weston might show up, but I haven't seen them yet.

I touch Codi's arm. "Sit down."

I point to the chair, and she hesitates. But she sits.

Pulling my brush out of my backpack, I gently take her long hair and start untangling the ends, lightly at first, in case she gets nervous.

But Codi doesn't fight, and before long, I'm running the brush over her scalp, relaxing when I see her head fall back a little and her eyes close.

Parting it in the middle, I pull it back into two French braids, securing it with the two rubber bands around my wrist. Then I tug at her blue T-shirt. "May I?"

She stiffens, but after a moment, she nods. Lightly, I pull it up, over her head, leaving her in her white tank top that's more blue-gray than white anymore.

Taking off Lucas's blue Cubs cab, I put it on her and dab a little of Aro's red lipstick on her mouth.

"There." I smile. "Red, white, and blue."

I bring up the camera on my phone and try to show her, but she looks away instead.

Is she mad? She swallows, but she looks back up and nods again with a gentle smile. She doesn't look in the camera, though.

I put it away, and she stands for the first customer.

"Codi, cute." Mace bobs her head in approval as she steals a muffin and takes a bite.

Codi shies away, but I see the little smile she holds back.

In an hour, the park is packed, and I spot Dylan and Aro chasing AJ, James, and Aro's brother Matty around. Noah lurks around the booth, devouring two cheese danishes, four cookies, two Rice Krispies Treats, and a whole bag of red, white, and blue chocolate-covered pretzels. He hands Codi money. He looks at her, I look at her, she doesn't look at him, I look at him, he looks at me, he looks away, and I fold my lips between my teeth to stifle the smile. He likes the quiet ones, doesn't he?

"What the hell happened to your leg?"

I hear Jared's voice and inhale a long breath before I face him. Lucas stands just behind him, talking with Madoc and Jax, but everyone's attention is on me now. Lucas's mouth hangs slightly open as he fists a frozen drink. And all of a sudden, the bruises that were a minor tingle earlier now burn. Everyone is staring at the marks left by his fingers last night.

"Oh, um..." I shake my head, trying to think of a lie.

Damn, even Noah is staring at me.

Lucas steps up, about to say something to Jared, but I recover.

"I hooked up with this guy at the gym last night," I joke. "We dry-humped in the locker room."

Dylan, who I didn't realize was that close, bursts into laughter, while Madoc rolls his eyes.

Jared gripes, "I'm not amused."

Heh. They think I'm lying. I'm almost insulted they think I'm not capable.

I restock the paper sleeves, mocking, "Well, are you done then? I'm working."

They drift off, Jax and Madoc taking a free treat, and I risk a glance up at Lucas. He barely breathes.

While nervous a moment ago, his eyes linger on my legs like he's retracing every second of last night, same as me.

He's going to come up to me. He can't stop himself.

He's going to take my ass in his hand and pull me in. In

front of everyone.

Noah would. Farrow would. My brothers would with their wives. Hunter and Hawke would with Dylan and Aro.

Looking like he's got two lungfuls of air locked in his chest, he pivots and follows my brothers, though.

I hood my eyes, sighing.

Whipping around, I'm about to throw the rest of the sleeves back into the box, but Noah stares at me as he stands between my booth and another vendor. His brow damn-near touches his hairline as he no doubt saw the two of us eye-fucking each other. He grins, and I'm sure he knows exactly where I got the bruises now.

When I look back at Lucas, he's leaving. Walking over to Madoc, he downs the rest of his drink, kicks off his shoes, and joins him in the volleyball pit.

"Quinn?" Noah says.

"What?"

He leans against one of the poles that holds up the tent. "I knew it when he crashed your party the other night. He was out of his mind."

Taking tongs, I place the rest of the danishes and cover them with the lid.

Noah plops his ass up on a stack of coolers, gulping down his Solo cup of beer. "He was jealous."

"Nothing happened," I whisper, checking that Codi and Hailey are tending to customers on the other side. "And get down from there."

I give him a little slap on the cheek as I scold.

But he doesn't get off, leaning in to catch my eyes. "Jared is going to kill him."

Looking over, I see Lucas tear off his T-shirt as he glows with sweat already on the volleyball court, the muscles in his arms and chest flexing as he comes in for shots. His damp hair sticks up in places and catches the wind in others, and he looks twenty again. I had my legs wrapped around that body last night. "God, I don't care," I breathe out with a laugh.

I'd rather not admit I'm anything like my brothers, but now I understand. When it comes to wanting someone, I can't stop.

"Good," Noah tells me. "Because the way he's looking at you, he's about ready to kidnap you and take you back to Dubai with him where you two won't be interrupted."

I meet my new friend's eyes, feeling the heat rise in my cheeks as my heart picks up pace. *Is Lucas really looking at me?*

Noah exhales with a longing look. "I miss that feeling."

"What feeling?"

He searches for his words. "You can't think," he says. "Can't see reason. Can't make the responsible decision you know you're supposed to make because you don't want to stop feeling her. You can't."

"How many times have you felt that?"

He's lost in thought for a moment, then shrugs. "Not enough."

"So what do I do next?"

Noah slides off the coolers, walks to the vendor next door, and talks to Brionne Sherwood who's selling wrap skirts, Hawaiian shirts, and dresses. Bringing me a red-and-white-checkered sundress with spaghetti straps, he hands it to me.

I frown. It's the same pattern as a picnic blanket I grew up with.

"Trust me," he says.

I cock my brow. I take the dress off the hanger and start to walk it behind the booth to put into my backpack. I can wear it to Madoc's party.

But Noah has other ideas. "Put it on now," he shouts

after me.

I stop, hesitating. I don't want to be bending over or having the wind blowing up my dress.

I look out, seeing Lucas laughing and hanging his arm around Madoc, my eyes drawn to the V disappearing into his shorts. Moms, sisters, wives, college girls—they all circle the pit, watching the guys. Lucas is the only single man I see playing.

I take the dress behind the booth, pull it on, and remove my shorts and T-shirt underneath it. I let my hair down and pull out the lipstick I used on Codi. I dab a little on, already relishing the cooling breeze riding up my thighs.

Coming out from behind the booth, I notice that Noah is gone. But I feel Lucas's eyes almost immediately.

I don't look, just enjoying the butterflies in my chest.

Trust me, Noah had said.

About what, I'm not sure. But the day is young. I'm sure I'll find out.

"Good job, kiddo."

Madoc yanks me in for a kiss on my head as I try to wipe down the display tables. It's just after four, and many people are still partying in the park, but it's almost time to greet those who'll be moving on to the next celebration at his place. Then, they'll head to High Street, followed by Camp Blackhawk, and Fallstown. He holds up the last Patriotic Parfait I had, the layers of blueberries, rich cream, and strawberries half eaten.

"These were amazing," he muses.

He's not drunk yet, but he's putting his weight on me, which means he's very relaxed. Best get him home so Fallon can get some coffee in him before he faces the rest of the night.

I lay a kiss on his cheek. "I'll bring some to the house in a bit."

I saved a special batch for the family.

I throw off his heavy arm and finish stacking all the empty trays.

"Some shorts under that dress would be a good idea," Jax calls out as he passes by. "It's blowing around a bit."

Madoc scoops out the rest of his parfait. "It's why I don't wear mine on windy days, Quinn."

I laugh.

Jared comes up with Tate and their kids, everyone in my family about to head out. "Can we help before we go?" he asks me.

But Jax cuts him off. "I thought you were heading to Fallstown to start up there so I can go to Madoc's party with my wife."

Jared shoots him a look, and I dip my hands in the water basin, rinsing them off and drying them. "I'm fine," I reply, gesturing to Codi. "We're good here. I'll be along soon. But thank you."

"I'll help," Lucas says suddenly.

I look at him, his neck and chest shiny as he wipes off his face with his shirt.

We could finally be alone.

But just when I'm about to shrug my shoulders oh-so-nonchalantly and say "sure," Farrow finally shows up.

"We got it," he blusters.

He tosses Lucas a look as Noah follows, both of them stepping up to the booth.

Lucas's brow furrows as disappointment hits me. Madoc pats him on the back. "I need you at the house anyway."

I take my trays and walk away, hearing Madoc warn Farrow behind me. "Don't touch my sister, or I'll...annex Weston."

"You can try."

My family leaves, and Codi starts carrying things to his truck with Noah.

Lucas yanks on his shirt as he leaves with Madoc and the rest, and as soon as he looks back at me, I look away. He'll be good and mad by the time I get to Madoc's. Void of reason or control.

Noah stops at my side. "You know why I did that?"

Why he stopped Lucas from helping me clean up, he means?

"Yes." I'm squealing in my head. "Thank you."

We load up the truck with everything left and tear down the tables and tent. Taking everything back to the shop, Codi, Farrow, and Noah help me unload. I hand off some treats to Farrow to take to Madoc's, anxious to get over there, but I force myself to linger at Frosted just a little longer.

Codi stays with me, both of us washing every dish, counting out the register and separating the deposit, prepping for tomorrow. Rivertown next door is already setting up a station on the sidewalk for drinks later tonight, and the police have put up blocks at both ends of the street. Speakers are being set up now.

"Mace is outside somewhere," Codi tells me. "I'll stay here with her."

"Are you sure?" I ask.

She gives one of her nods and fastens the laundry bag for pickup in the morning.

We leave the shop, lock up, and I slide onto my bike, watching her melt into the crowd on High Street. Tossing my phone into the basket with my backpack, I pedal for Madoc's, inhaling the heavy air cooled with the slightest breeze. The wind blows through my hair and dress, and a light layer of sweat dampens my arms, back, and neck as I cruise into my neighborhood.

I close my eyes. Just for a moment.

Then two.

Winslet MacCreary drove this road. I don't know for sure, but it may as well be true. She lived here, and soon, the sun will set, drinks will flow, and monsters will come out to play again. Who would I have been in her day? The quiet one who wasn't involved and never knew what was happening until it was too late? Would I have been her friend?

Or would I have been someone she came after for revenge because I was always a follower and never a leader?

Nevertheless, she's watching me now. Maybe.

I open my eyes, the low rumble of an engine far behind me barely audible in the wind. But it's there.

My heart thrums in my ears as I pass lantern-lit yards and keep going to the next house. Then, the next.

No other lights. No headlights beaming from behind, but the growl of the engine grows louder.

Closer.

The sound of distant thunder rolls, deeper than the engine somewhere behind me, and I comb my hand through my hair.

Every inch of my skin hums as the hair rises. It's that feeling you get when you're a kid and being chased, about to be tagged. Scared, but also thrilled. Like I feel when I'm alone with Lucas.

Closer...

Closer...

Turning down Madoc's driveway, I see kids running around with sparklers on the lawn to the right and stop, listening to the car's engine get louder and louder... I tighten my fists around the handlebars.

Then, the sound starts to fade. As if it's passed by and

is driving away.

I look behind me, the empty road beyond lonely and quiet. I blink, a mix of adrenaline with something like disappointment washing over me. Did I want it to follow me? Like with Deacon, I don't know if I feel fear necessarily anymore. I mean, it's had plenty of opportunity to run me down or chase me off the road, and it hasn't. Maybe it's him. Maybe it's not. But I'm getting braver, hungry for answers now.

Pumping the pedals, I cruise to the front door and park my bike, grabbing the diary out of the backpack, as well as my phone. The driveway is filled with cars, and the party bus pulls out, off to pick up another batch of Shelburne Falls citizens who don't want to drive tonight.

I head around the side, hoping to avoid my brothers for as long as possible. Music blasts from the speakers, several lawn games going on, and Madoc has two bars that I can see spread out on the property. He probably has another one in the house and another by the pool. People dance, the sound of billiards drifts through the open basement doors, and I smell cigar smoke somewhere. Madoc's taken to sucking on one when he's *really* relaxed.

Stopping, I take in the scene for a moment, a familiar sense of love for this town and how everywhere just feels like family.

Everywhere is home.

Everyone knows everyone, and everything is just so happy. I dig in my eyebrows, feeling the sky press down on my shoulders.

Walking up to the pool, I spot Hawke and everyone standing waist-deep, all of them enjoying a drink under their parents' watchful eye. Dylan sees me first, and Hawke follows her gaze. A couple of years ago, I heard he had a party here, complete with soap suds everywhere. I missed it. I stayed at school most of that summer, getting ahead on extra classes. It wasn't their fault I missed it. I did it to myself.

"You gonna let me in my tower yet?" Hawke nags.

"*My* tower."

While it's possible I never would've known it was there without him, he never would've gotten access to it if I didn't own it.

I hand him the diary. "It was on the kitchen counter in Carnival Tower."

He narrows his eyes, setting his drink down and taking the book. Quickly, he opens it, turning pages and then fanning the rest.

He looks up at me, surprised. "I've never seen this."

"Winslet MacCreary didn't die in the river," I tell him, flitting my eyes to Hunter, then Dylan. "And I don't think it was the Doran brothers who put her there."

Kade snatches the book, but Aro steals it from him, Dylan hovering at her side as they look through it.

"I think she made it out of the car," I say to them, "let people believe she was gone, hid out under everyone's noses in Shelburne Falls somewhere, and sought revenge on the Pirates who tried to murder her."

Everyone stops and gapes at me. "Pirates?" Hawke repeats.

I nod. "You read it and tell me what you think. It's...difficult to understand."

I rise, not wanting to get caught up in the third degree right now. They can look through it themselves and get back to me.

I start to walk away but stop. "Stay together tonight," I tell them.

"Why?" Kade asks.

"Something feels weird."

Maybe I'm overthinking, but chaos provides opportunity. And the more the drinks flow, the more poor choices will arise.

I leave them, trying not to scan the area for Lucas. I know he's here, but he'll be cautious with my brothers around. I don't want to be cautious.

Plus, I'm hungry. Starving, actually. Heading to the basement, I slip through the door and to the refrigerator to grab ingredients for pizza. I scarfed down some oatmeal at four this morning before I left Weston, and all I've had since was three spoonfuls of parfait.

Carrying the cheese, sauce, and dough already prepared on a pan out to the patio, I preheat the pizza oven, feeling him close. And the more I try to keep my gaze averted, the more aware I am that I have to force myself not to search for him. Every second. *Don't look for him.*

Every moment. *I'm still not looking for him.*

But I turn around, and he's standing there. Staring at me.

Rounding the little island, he backs me into the corner, out of view, as the scent of his shower and fresh clothes waft off him.

His hand grazes my thigh where my brothers noticed the bruise this morning. "I didn't mean to hurt you last night," he whispers.

His chest presses into mine, and I can barely breathe. I open my mouth, lost in the shape of his lips. And remember how demanding his mouth is when it has a hold of mine.

"What do you want me to say?" I ask, giving the screw one extra twist. "That it's okay?"

I don't feel the bruises. I wouldn't mind more.

He bears down, his head hovering over mine, and my entire body tingles as his fingers drift up my leg, caressing the bruised skin.

"Do you like my dress?" I taunt.

His hand glides up, flattening against my stomach,

coming so close to my breast, and then snaking around my waist, raising my hem. My panties are visible to anyone who might walk by.

I tease him. "Do you like my dress?"

I know he does, and I want to hear him say it. I want to know he's been thinking about how accessible my body has been all day and he hasn't been able to touch me.

But also, I kind of like how it seems he barely notices the question, lost in his desire.

His breath falls on my mouth as he licks his lips, looking down at me like I'm a drug and he's already addicted.

He tugs at the fabric, balling it in his fists tighter and tighter until I hear a tiny tear.

Yes.

"Lucas!" someone shouts.

Farrow?

I blink, feeling the ridge of Lucas's groin press between my legs.

"Someone's here to see you!" Farrow shouts from somewhere.

I pant, and for a moment, he doesn't move. He can't leave me. He can't stop. He's going to lift me up and rip off my clothes...

But he backs away.

And I clench my teeth in anger.

"I'm coming," he calls out.

Holding my eyes, he lets me go, and my body almost leaves the wall as if being pulled as he goes. *Don't leave me.*

Damn him.

Hawke doesn't drop Aro. There's nothing more pressing to him than her.

And it would take an earthquake to get Hunter off Dylan.

I deserve better than this.

I stand there—for one second, then two.

An earthquake.

What if there is one thing more pressing to him than me? Just one thing? The one thing that made him leave eight years ago. Still unresolved.

Taking a step, then another, I follow him, peering around the corner and seeing him climb the small hill toward the front of the house. Slipping behind the tall hedges between the basement and the hill, I crouch down and crawl, following after both of them.

Slowly sinking one hand and knee after another into the black mulch, I hear Winslet, as if those memories in the diary are mine.

*dark
*water in the air
*scent of earth
*keys like claws

I curl my fingers into the dirt, lifting my eyes to find glimpses of him and Farrow through the thistles.

Farrow turns to him, standing close as if he has something private to say, but his body language is cautious. Not confident.

Since when do he and Lucas have shared secrets?

Farrow pants to Lucas, out of breath as the silence stretches.

Then I hear him say, "He knows where the body is."

SHELBURNE FALLS

CHAPTER TWENTY-ONE

Lucas

There's only one way the location of that body is known to anyone but Reeves and me. Reeves told Hugo Navarre.

And he must've told him recently, too, because Hugo didn't seem to know the other day outside of Fallon's shop.

Drew is in the area. I knew it from my second day back in Shelburne Falls, and I will never deny my gut again. I knew it.

Maybe Hugo's bluffing. To get me to leave. To make a mistake. But it's best to assume he's not.

"He'll leave you alone if you give him the building," Farrow tells me. "He wants to meet."

Raking my hand through my hair, I shake my head. So blackmail, it is, then. I'm almost impressed. He could just kill me.

Maybe I should be warier of Farrow. He could do it easily right now.

But then, who knows what happens to the building if I die? They want the deed.

"Where?" I ask.

"He's on Rivertown's roof." He looks away and back again, shifting uncomfortably.

Fucking great. Right here near all the people I care about, shielded by the chaos of the BBQ Crawl.

I walk for my car, Farrow matching my stride. I'm happy that Quinn is safe back there with her family, at least.

"Is there someone buried in River Hill Tunnel?" Farrow asks.

One of the hedges next to us rustles, and I glance down, seeing a bird pop out.

Is there someone buried? Does Farrow even care?

I have no illusions that he saw some shit long before I came along.

"No," I state quickly, surprising myself. I stop next to the Mustang and dig out my keys. "There's someone buried outside of it."

I don't look at him, and I don't know why I told him. Do I trust him? Kind of. But for no good reason, that's for sure. He wants Green Street. That's what he told me the night I found out he bought my house.

He won't want to clean up Weston any more than Hugo, and he could see me as just as much of a threat as his boss.

I'm just worn out on lying. And something tells me he cares about the same people I do.

He studies me. "Why don't you just give him Green Street?"

"Should I?" I ask.

Is that what he wants?

He falls silent and then twists his lips in disgust. "No. Quinn doesn't deserve a coward."

"And why would ridding myself of Green Street make me a coward?"

"Because you'd simply be shifting responsibility from yourself to Madoc Caruthers," he points out. "Hugo will become his problem then."

Exactly. I'm glad he agrees. I can get Green Street off my back in a second, but what then? I'm not leaving the people I care about to face the mess I made.

The hair on the back of my neck rises, feeling like we're being watched. But when I look behind me, there's no one.

Fucking Drew is around somewhere. I know it.

"So..." I face him again, swallowing. "I shut it down then," I announce. "Or sell it."

Farrow looks away. "You do what you want."

I almost fucking smile. I can see right through him.

He wants the building. That was Hugo he was speaking to that night at the gym while Noah and Quinn were jogging. He wants Hugo's position.

Yeah, I trust him. But only a little.

"Do you have to pay?" I clench my teeth. "Or do you get it for free from the girls you turn out?"

He smiles through his sneer. "We supply men too. We've expanded since your day."

I yank open the car door and climb in, and he leans down, peering through the open window.

Staring ahead at Madoc's house, I smell the grill firing up and hear the music.

"I just couldn't...accept what it became," I tell him. "What Drew Reeves turned it into. It was a social club, you know? We found this cheap property, and there were no cops around. I thought we were going to bring in other guys who liked to snowboard in the winter and be lake bums in the summer. We'd drink and have block parties." I meet his eyes. "Maybe network when we all settled into careers. Start businesses in the area and get the town running again. Maybe host a wet T-shirt contest to raise money for the kids or something."

"As you do."

I laugh. "Exactly."

But then my face falls, remembering the fights and the blood and the looks in people's eyes like they were sorry we ever came.

"The girls, the weapons..." I murmur. "Trafficking drugs is no less than a ten-year sentence, kid. For a first offense."

"And murder is life."

Yeah.

"I got in over my head," I admit, "because I had it in my mind that Madoc had filled in as a father long enough, so I tried to make my own family, and I fucked up."

"You only see it that way because you had something better," he retorts.

His words make me pause, guilt creeping in over having all the privileges that others didn't. I get what he's saying. What he has in Green Street is worth saving to him, because to him, it is a family in some ways.

But in the end, it's a downward spiral that leads to nowhere good. Not once. Not ever.

I steady my voice as I plainly state, "Anything else is better for you to the people who love you, Farrow."

There's someone who loves him and doesn't want this for him.

I should've stayed. I could've put all of my energy into finding a way to make amends. I made the wrong choice.

I start the car. "I liked some of it, though," I muse. "I liked feeling tall. I liked girls who wanted a college boy. I liked how dark the town got at night. Cruising the hills. Phalen's Throat. The car graveyard."

We did have some fun.

I grin a little. "I liked that no one I loved knew about my secret life, as if nothing was real. For a while." I fix my eyes on him. "But it was just a fantasy."

Everything ends, and there's always a price.

He stares at me, and I know he's not burdened with the same type of conscience. His father, whoever he is, is a very wealthy man who would never deny him. Farrow doesn't have to be here, but I know why he is. I understand his loyalty.

Still, though, it's a choice. He's a guy with options preying on those who don't have any. Just like Reeves.

I think he's going to reply, but he doesn't, and I shift the car into Reverse.

But he calls out, "It wasn't because you were in college."

I glance at him, seeing the twinkle in his eye.

"They like blonds," he says.

Walking away, he stuffs his own blond head into a helmet, but I can feel the gleam in his eyes from here.

I don't want to like him.

I wish I didn't.

Much the same way I used to like Drew. Until I didn't.

"Someone's going to die," Drew warned.

The hint of excitement in his gaze told me that he was up for the challenge.

I was almost breathless. "Don't worry. I'll save you."

I looked at him, and he looked at me as the old, rusty car rolled into the pond, both of us locked into our seatbelts.

"And if I chicken out first and still don't keep my end of the bargain?"

"Then I'll go to Madoc," I warned him. "After I burn it all down around you."

He could never resist a dare. Maybe I couldn't either. We wouldn't fight. There would be no guns. I simply had to stay in my seat the longest as the car sank to the bottom.

The water fills the space around us, rising up our legs. He turns to me. "You would risk killing me to end Green Street?"

The shock of the cold water made me suck in a breath. "And you thought I was a lamb," I scoffed.

The car started to go bottom-up, plunging, and we planted our hands on the dash, watching each other for any signs of retreat.

The water hit our chest. "I'll miss you," he told me.

I smiled. "Yes, you will."

Drawing in one last breath, I got ready to sink, but then I heard it.

The pounding and screaming coming from the trunk.

I flex my jaw, that familiar roil through my stomach making the bile rise. I could've gotten out of a murder charge. Maybe even a manslaughter charge. But I would never forget what happened. Of that, I was always going to be a prisoner. The horror of the moment when you realize that you're never going to be the same, and you can't undo what you did.

God, Drew knew me so well. I didn't know him at all. How could I not have understood that someone who had boundaries could never beat someone who had none? I still can't believe I was stupid enough to challenge him like that, thinking I would ever win. He didn't follow rules. He would make sure he succeeded, even if he had to cheat.

I speed to town, knowing the police have their hands full elsewhere. Farrow trails me on his motorcycle, and there are a couple of other cars behind him. The traffic tonight will be heavy everywhere as people move from one party to another.

Cruising past High Street, I see the lane blocked up with barriers, tables, vendors, and people slowly filling the space under the street lights. They dance and drink, firecrackers going off as sparklers light up the air. Far off, a firework whistles into the sky. I don't see the pop overhead, but I hear the fizzle as it dissipates somewhere.

I park along a side street and get out of the car, noticing the tail-end of another Mustang, like Dylan's, turning and disappearing down another block.

I shake my head. She was in the pool with her family ten minutes ago. It can't be her.

Farrow strides up to my side, and we turn at Frosted, heading past Rivertown.

"I think they're gonna set off the city fireworks early," Farrow says. "Rain's coming."

All the more reason to make this quick. We won't be in the dark for long. "Where are they again?" I ask him.

"On the roof."

We cut down the next street, pulling down the ladder to the fire escape. Chills prick the back of my neck again, and I look behind me, searching for someone following us. High Street practically vibrates under my shoes, laughter and liquor flowing in equal measure.

No one's looking at me, though.

I shake it off. "How many of them are there?"

"Just Hugo and a couple of his lackeys."

I side-eye him. "Isn't that what you are?"

He could be leading me into a trap, but if there's any chance to settle this on my own, I'm taking it.

But he speaks in a calm, steady tone. "Ciaran Pierce is my father," he tells me.

I freeze, gaping at him. What the hell did he just say?

Tipping his chin up, he adds, "No one knows except Hunter."

No one...

No one except Hunter and me now, he means.

He's Ciaran's son? He's Fallon's brother? And she doesn't know?

Why would Ciaran not tell anyone?

Farrow breathes slowly, stating, "I will never hurt someone Fallon Caruthers loves."

So I'm safe with him. Is that why he told me his secret?

God, Fallon... I clear my throat.

I hope he doesn't expect that I can keep that secret. Not from her. He has to know that.

But I don't have time to hash this out right now.

"In any case..." I nudge him to the ladder. "You go first."

He chuckles, damn near jogging up the ladder as I haul myself up behind him.

We climb three flights and hop over the ledge, onto the roof. Hugo stands near a large air vent, flanked by two of his guys.

"Nicholas and Axel," Farrow informs me under his breath.

Stopping just in front of Navarre, I swallow to wet my throat.

I know he enjoys being someone he imagines I'm scared of. I used to kick him out of Green Street when he was so desperate to be a bad guy for Reeves.

Now I'm the one facing him.

He takes a step toward me. "You haven't tried to evict me," he says, "because you know Green Street is more than a building now. I'll just take the organization and move somewhere else."

True.

"And I haven't taken care of you," he adds, "because..."

"Because what end does that serve?" I fire back. "If you can so easily move, then what hold on you do I really have?"

"Exactly." Light glints in his gelled hair. "I didn't see you as a legitimate threat."

I'm not sure how I feel hearing that. I want to be a threat *to him*.

"That is, until you started throwing your weight around," he goes on. "Showing up in Weston, your little piece of ass taking over sacred ground on Knock Hill, and you ordering my people about as if you're back in charge."

"I was never in charge."

"That's not how they see it," he snarls. "In their eyes, I'm the usurper."

Most of those people have no memory of me there. They just know their lives haven't gotten better under Drew or Hugo, and they think the college boy who owns the building can do better.

I shrug. "You can't be worse for them than Reeves."

"I might be." He shifts his eyes to Farrow, his gaze hardening. "But of course, I don't have the allure of being an original member."

"So, what…" I ask. "I give you Green Street and promise never to go into Weston? It'll never happen."

Not with Quinn living there now.

But he shakes his head. "It's too late for that. The women will follow you. The mothers, sisters, and wives…and my girls."

I go still, noticing the possessive way he says it, but knowing he's not referring to his family or his girlfriends. He's talking about his strippers and escorts and their families. Some might remember me from when they were younger and hanging around, and others might think any change is better than Hugo.

"They would crawl to you if you asked." His jaw twitches. "And without the women, I can't hold it."

"I'm not looking to step into your shoes."

"And I'm not shutting down!"

I pause, only smiling a little. "You will. And soon."

He lunges for me, grabbing my collar just before his fist slams against my jaw. I growl, squeezing my eyes shut as my face whips so far right that pain shoots up my neck. My cheek catches fire as the inside of my mouth cuts against my teeth.

I swallow blood. *Fuck*.

His thugs and Farrow swoop in, trying to push us away from each other, and I fight to stay on my feet as the world tilts around me for a moment.

Curling my fingers around his throat, I shove Hugo back. He stumbles into his guys, both of them straightening him up immediately as Farrow steadies me.

Hugo breathes hard, both of us glaring at each other. "You have twenty-four hours to get your ass back out of the country, or I hunt you down and kill you," he tells me. "And I will reopen that grave and dump you where Reeves should've put you eight years ago."

I get in his face. "Why not do it now?"

Is he bluffing? If he knew where the grave was, why wouldn't he dig up the body himself before I have a chance to get rid of it?

Or maybe Reeves, wherever he is, is still the real boss, and Hugo doesn't trust his own guys. He doesn't want to get caught holding the bag.

Either way, I have to assume the worst.

He closes the distance between us. "There are twenty-thousand breaths in twenty-four hours." He inhales, savoring a long gulp of air. "One down. Make the most of the rest you have left."

Pushing off, he leaves, back down the fire escape and followed by his boys.

Twenty-thousand breaths.

He wants me gone by this time tomorrow night. Would he kill me?

I draw in one and let it leave me.

Quinn...

I inhale another. Then another, picking up a scent.

Farrow steps up to my side. "Lucas..."

"Go take care of your shit."

I don't want to talk to him right now.

Filling my lungs again, I catch a fragrance. Subtle. But close.

He descends the fire escape, and I follow him. Car horns honk, the area floods with lights, and we rush to the street to see the commotion. Sprinkles of rainfall, music blasts from a truck's speakers, and Farrow turns, giving me a grin.

Weston is here.

"Shit," I grunt.

He holds my eyes, backing away, and heads to his crew who just rolled up to make a mess of the Falls tonight. Holding out his hands, he shrugs, and it's amazing how easily he can pretend to have a one-track mind when he's actually quite good at multi-tasking.

I watch Weston bulldoze their way into the crowd, taking over the music and amping up the thunder as rain spills on skin and bodies sway together.

I gaze out at the crowd, now so thick you can't make out individual faces as they hover close, hold each other, and the rain soaks their hair to their faces.

Chaos.

What a perfect opportunity for Hugo to strike. Or Drew.

One breath, then another, and another, and I feel the target branded onto my back, but I weave through the dancers, finding her at the edge, near the sidewalk.

The strap of her dress slides down her arm, and I'm no better than Drew Reeves. Panting after a girl way too young for me.

I knew I smelled her.

I stare at her, she stares at me.

I take a step toward her, and she takes one back.

Did she hear what we said up there? How would she get up there without us seeing? How would she have gotten down so fast?

One thing is likely, though. If she followed me here, then she heard what Farrow and I were talking about back at the house.

I move toward her, and she moves away again, holding my eyes. Dylan and Aro dance a few yards behind her, and I softly jerk my head, telling them to leave.

This is what it would've felt like to embrace Green Street. To be the villain and take what I want.

They stop moving, looking to her for direction, but she's unaware of anything else but me.

Tears fill her eyes, even as she clenches her fists.

I'm not the best choice for her. I'm not a choice at all.

But twenty-thousand breaths and they're all going to be for her.

Closing the distance, I press my body to hers, holding her waist tightly. When I look over her head again, Dylan and Aro are sinking into the crowd, giving us privacy.

"Who are you?" Quinn chokes out.

Yeah, she heard everything.

Lifting her up by the backs of her thighs, I slip my fingers under her dress, close enough to feel the heat pouring out of her.

She lets out a groan, squeezing my shirt in her fists as rain pours down her arms.

"You've got ass at your beck and call, I hear," she grits out. "Call one of *your girls*."

I love the flush of anger in her cheeks.

She jerks her chin to the crowd, the two of us just figures in the mass. "They all want you."

But I want you.

Sliding my fingers into her panties, I rock with her to the music as I lick her mouth, coaxing her fucking tongue out. I don't care who sees us, who's watching, or about the cameras all over the street.

Everything is about to end anyway, one way or another.

Wrapping my arm around her waist, I sink into her mouth.

Twenty-thousand breaths.

How many will I last inside of her?

WESTON

CHAPTER TWENTY-TWO

Quinn

I can barely catch my breath as he moves down my neck.

My mind races. He killed somebody?

Or he buried somebody?

Lucas pulls the strap of my dress down, and I stare at him, my eyes welling with tears as now—finally—the son of a bitch wants to touch me in front of everyone.

What I wouldn't have given, for so long, to have him doing what he's doing right now? In full view of people who will tell my family, even as the rain has us all in our own worlds. High Street rocks like a giant parade float around us as people dance, kiss, and coast to their own rhythm.

We could be just another man and woman like them, but now, I wish it was any other man but him. Did I *ever* know him?

I grip his shirt on his shoulders. "Look at me," I tell him.

He exhales hard, pressing a finger between my legs, underneath my underwear. I squirm in his hold. *No.*

"Farrow knows the truth, and I don't?" I bite out. "Is that really why you hid from us? Because of Drew Reeves?"

Someone who never knew him like we do or loved him like I do? He surrendered everything for fear of *him*?!

His chest shakes, and he tips his head back, letting the rain fall on his face. I jerk him, forcing his gaze to me again. The whites of his eyes are now red.

"Talk to me," I say.

He searches my face as if looking for a way out, but there isn't one.

If he ever spoke to me like I deserved to know the damn truth, I'd understand almost anything. Doesn't he know that?

When he left me at the house earlier, I followed, because I couldn't stand it anymore. I listened in the bushes and then dove into Carnival Tower and snuck up to the hatch in the roof.

He covered up a crime.

And he owns Green Street.

And Hugo gave him an ultimatum because he sees Lucas as a threat.

That's all I know. Did he leave because he was forced to? Or because of the guilt?

"Out with it, Lucas." Enough already.

His lids fall closed.

But just for a moment.

"Life is a force in itself," he tells me, his tone soft and calm. "One way or another, the bill comes due. More than ever, when you finally figure out the one thing you want most of all in the world."

He holds me tightly, eyes only for me as the party bounces around us. Aro and Dylan are somewhere, but I barely move, afraid he'll stop. *Am I the one thing he wants?*

"Life always makes sure it gets paid," he muses, a sad smile on his face. "I did what I thought was best for Madoc and for you and for..." He stops breathing. "...and for me."

I shake my head, my throat swelling with a sob I don't let out. I don't understand. He might've lost his freedom, and maybe even a few people's respect if he'd stayed and dealt with whatever happened, but didn't he lose those things anyway? He's not free.

He hasn't been free. Not really. He gave up *everything*.

Gripping my ass in both of his hands, he holds me close, exhaling over my mouth.

"I don't want to make another mistake," he whispers. "Not tonight. I want to take you back to my old house and make love to you in my old room and not stop touching you once until the sun comes up." Chest tight, he gazes at my mouth. "For once, I know exactly where I'm supposed to be, Quinn."

My heart feels like it's melting in a way that hurts. I close my eyes as his mouth captures mine and he tugs at my lips, sucking and devouring like he's starving. Moving one hand to my hair, he presses us together, and I feel everything. The beat in his chest against mine. The cut of his teeth on my lip, my chin, my jaw...

And I feel everything that's missing too. The happiness he used to have on his face when he talked to me when we were younger. The way I always felt safe with him. The calm and ease—and the trust—he inspired, just being close.

His teeth grab my skin through the dress, and I suck in air.

Twenty-thousand breaths. That's what Hugo said.

What happens after twenty-thousand breaths?

"Lucas..." I pant, trying to pry myself out of his hold.

What about tomorrow? In the morning when he has to face everything again? Is he thinking about that at all right now? Is he even really thinking about me?

Planting my hands on his chest, I shove him back. "Lucas."

I clench my teeth, feeling his chest rise and fall hard under my palms. "What happens tomorrow?" I ask.

His eyebrows pinch together, but he doesn't say anything.

For one second. Then two. Then five.

God, he has no idea.

"Why do you want me now?" I press.

He didn't make love to me the other night at my house, or last night in the locker room. Why now?

Is it because he thinks he's going to be arrested or killed? Would he be doing this without a threat hanging over his head? He isn't thinking clearly. Does he really want me, or am I just the final nail in the coffin?

Fuck this.

I squirm out of his hold, planting my feet back on the ground. "I don't want you like this." I shake my head. "It doesn't feel good."

He should sit down, pull me into his arms, and talk to me, and I shouldn't have to tell him that.

I back up, and he advances. "Come here," he pants.

"No." I swallow through the lump in my throat. "I want more."

This is about him, and it needs to be about *us*.

I start to look for Aro and Dylan—my ride to get out of here while I still want to—but shouting draws our attention.

"She said no!" Farrow barks.

Lucas jerks his head over his shoulder, both of us seeing Farrow pull Codi away from Noah.

I retreat another step while Lucas is distracted.

Noah gets in Farrow's face. No one around them is dancing anymore, everyone giving them a wide berth.

I look at Codi, deciding if I should grab her while I can. She just stands behind Farrow, where he put her, her eyes downcast and her expression blank. As usual.

"She didn't say no," Noah retorts. "She barely speaks, thanks to you!"

"*I* said no." Farrow cocks his head, challenging him. "Hawke bought Aro with a tattoo. You want to fuck one of us, then you know what to do."

"You're pissing me off."

Farrow's eyes gleam at Noah's anger. "Well, whatever will you do with me, then?"

Some of Noah's racing buddies pull him away; although, the threat stretches between his and Farrow's gazes, and more dumb shit is going to hit the fan sooner or later.

The dancing resumes, Farrow and Codi lost in the throngs of people, and I almost think I see the Dodge far beyond Lucas, cruising to the next block. Everything's foggy. My heart thumps against my chest.

I can't keep my voice from cracking as I address Lucas, "I'm not your suicide note."

He twists back to me and digs in his brows, breathless with sweat on his neck.

I won't be his last dance on his way to self-destruct.

"Why do I feel like I don't know you all of a sudden?" I ask more to myself. "I want someone who will fight for me. Who will *always* fight for me."

Whipping around, I slip through the crowd, searching for Aro and Dylan.

"Quinn!" Lucas growls behind me.

I glance back, seeing his six-three form squeezing through the partiers.

Halting in front of Dylan, I hold out my hand. "Give me your keys."

She stops dancing and narrows her eyes, absently pulling them out of her pocket. "What are you up to?"

I snatch them, hearing Lucas behind me. "Quinn!"

I flinch, his bark turning into a bite.

"Quinn?" Dylan prompts next.

I turn back to her, but before I can reply, I blink, seeing it again. Far behind her head, on the street.

"The black Dodge," I murmur.

Aro and Dylan turn, catching a glimpse of it as it disappears down the cross street.

"Quinn!" Lucas bellows again.

I shake my head clear. I need to get out of here.

I bolt, twisting my head around as I go to see Lucas staring me dead in the eyes as he shoves some guy out of his way. Firecrackers pop and sizzle over our heads, and he's beautiful. His wet shirt sticks to every dip and ridge of his torso and stomach, and his jaw has a day of scruff on it. I've waited for this night with him practically my whole life, but it's not him anymore. He's hiding, he's afraid, and he's lying.

I run, pounding the pavement in my sneakers to where Dylan parked one of my brother's Mustangs, both she and Aro hot on my heels.

"Quinn!" Lucas shouts.

I suck in a breath as I glance up the street, catching the Dodge's taillights disappearing around a right-hand turn.

"What are we doing?" Aro bursts out as all of us climb into the car.

I stick the key into the ignition. "I don't know." I tremble. "Maybe follow that Dodge for a change."

"Ohhh," Dylan coos excitedly.

I don't know why I'm doing this, but everything under my skin burns, and I ball my fist, nearly slamming it down on the damn dash.

Damn him.

I need a distraction. I check the rearview mirror, then glance over my shoulder to make sure no cars are coming, and pull away from the curb, not even bothering to put on my seatbelt.

A thud lands on Dylan's trunk as I speed off. "Quinn!" Farrow shouts as I drive.

I spot him and Lucas in my side mirror, Lucas's furrowed brow fading as I escape.

Spinning the wheel, I curve a right, then another, heading back after the Dodge. Aro taps away on her phone.

I'm squeezing the wheel so hard, my thumbnails press onto the tops of my fingers. "Who are you texting?"

I don't want any interference.

"Hawke."

Dylan hangs over the back of my seat.

"Why?" I blurt out.

"Because he's my boyfriend."

Yeah, he's also invasive and domineering, and he'll tell Lucas or my brothers what we're doing.

But then...

I think better of it. "Tell him to scan the traffic cams."

No harm in him being useful before he scolds us.

Taking another right, I keep my eyes peeled for pedestrians, but mostly for the car as we pass Astrophysics. I lock my gaze ahead on two red taillights cutting left. "There it is."

Stepping on the gas, I race to catch up and close the distance between us and the Dodge.

No one speaks. The old black car coasts right ahead of us, making no move to outrun us.

"What do we do?" Dylan whispers as if it can hear us.

Out of the corner of my eye, I see Aro look over at me. I grind the wheel in my fists.

I'm not used to making decisions for other people. Especially out of this group.

My pulse quickens, and I'm afraid to talk or loosen my grip, because I'm shaking.

But I keep going. Following. Daring him—or her—to lead me.

Dylan's phone connects to the car, and the next track from her playlist starts—"You Stupid Girl." I hold back my laugh. If that isn't a sign for me to retreat, I don't know what is.

Staring at the lone figure in the vehicle ahead, I catch the slight movement in their rearview mirror.

They're watching us too.

Reaching over, I switch off the headlights, my heart skipping every other beat.

"Quinn?" Aro prompts, alarmed.

The car accelerates. So do I.

What would I do if they stopped?

But they keep going, leading me away from the parties and the lights. Taking us somewhere private.

I hear fingers tap on screens and know Dylan and Aro are tattling on me. "Oh, come on, guys," I tease under my breath. "It's my turn."

Dylan expels a sigh with a little growl, knowing she and Aro have done their fair share of stupid things. I might be too old for it now, but I guess that's a matter of who I'm comparing myself against. My brothers still do stupid stuff all the time.

The Dodge vaults forward, and I press the gas.

"Faster," Dylan urges.

"Pedestrians," I retort.

I've got this, but I'm not going to risk hitting someone.

The Dodge turns, and I follow, the hair on my arms rising as I push the envelope. I don't like speed, and I don't like recklessness, but every moment sinks me further into danger, and I feel like someone new. Anticipation of all the possibilities for tomorrow, and the next day, and the next starts to fill my chest, and I'm taking in more and more air.

The Dodge jets off, propelling forward, and the girls start yelling.

"Go, go!" Dylan screams.

Followed by Aro, "Don't lose 'em!"

I punch the gas, rounding another turn. My tires screech as the Dodge cuts right, then left, and I skid around after it.

But when I turn again, it's gone.

I gape. "What…?"

We coast down the street, all of us pinned to the windows and scanning the side streets. Where the hell did it go?

And where is Lucas? He would've followed me.

Approaching Jared's shop, I see the lights are all off, no one in sight, and the fireworks have stopped. The black night presses against the car on all sides, and I barely breathe as I scan for any sign of movement. Or headlights.

Shit.

"What should we do?" Aro searches out her window, through the streaks of rain. "Go back to the parties?"

"It's here," I tell them.

I know it is.

I'll drop them off if they really don't want any part of this, but the Night Rider is around. They're playing with me.

Aro's phone buzzes, lighting up her face as she looks down. "Hawke," she tells us. She opens it and reads the text, "'Behind you.'"

She and Dylan jerk their heads over their shoulders, and I lift my eyes to the rearview mirror.

Shrouded in the dark night, far behind us, it's there. No headlights. The old grill. The bent license plate. The blackened windows.

I hold back the thrill bubbling in my chest, whispering, "There you are."

My scalp feels like the head on a glass of soda. A million delightful little pops as the chase ensues. I shift and press the gas, the car vaulting forward.

"Quinn?" Aro plants one hand on her door and the other on the back of my seat, holding on.

A trickle of sweat glides down my temple. I stop breathing, pressing the gas a little more.

Come on.

"Quinn?" Dylan says behind me.

The *Stop* sign ahead grows bigger. I glance in the rearview mirror again. A set of headlights appears far behind the Dodge.

Lucas.

Aro chimes in again. "Quinn?"

I slam on the brakes, halting the car at the sign. Darkness looms at my left and right as we sit just before the highway.

Behind me, the vehicle crawls closer. No lights. No movement inside.

"Quinn?"

But I don't answer Dylan. Sucking in a breath, I spin the wheel right and punch my foot so hard on the gas, I hit the floor. Tires screech under us, Dylan and Aro gasp, and we shoot off, picking up speed so fast, a gust of wind whips through the windows and into my hair.

"Quinn!" Aro shouts.

The car roars, slicing through the darkness.

Aro checks the window behind us, while Dylan's phone rings.

"Dad?" she answers.

Uh-oh. Did Lucas call him?

No, he wouldn't have. If my brothers are around, he can't deal with me.

"No..." she stammers to her father. "We're—"

She falls silent as my brother yells, and I jerk the wheel, slicing to the left, the tires grinding underneath us. Gravel kicks up under the car, and I twist the wheel right. I speed down another empty country road.

Aro rocks in her seat with the uneven path, grunting as I hit potholes.

"Oh my God. Calm down," Dylan tells her dad. "Wh—Hello?"

Great. He hung up. Everyone will be coming.

The Dodge appears in my rearview mirror—closer.

And closer.

I dart my eyes. *And closer*.

It races up on my ass—one, two, three sets of headlights behind them.

"When I stop, we get out of the car and run," I tell Aro and Dylan.

"Where?" Dylan chokes out.

But Aro replies before me. "Wherever you want Hunter to come find you."

We toss each other a look, my grateful smile met with a wink. Everyone worries about me. Aro's decided to play along.

Cabins peek out of the trees up ahead, the soft glow of the camp lights illuminating porches and docks. The whole place is empty until next week when the next session starts, but Jax and Juliet keep security lighting almost year-round.

Except in the dead of winter when the camp is deserted.

The car is right on me. I couldn't see its lights even if they were on.

"You guys ready?" I blurt out.

"Yeah."

Dylan whimpers, "Sure."

I speed ahead, gaining distance, then slam on the brakes as I veer right. We skid to a halt, I turn off the car, and all of us leap out.

I spin around, the Dodge twenty feet away, but I can't see inside because the headlights are on now. Blinding me.

I squint, holding my hand up against the glare. Is that the Dodge?

I mean, it was, but...

"Quinn?" Aro shouts.

I glance at them both. "Go!"

It can't chase three of us.

I slam the door shut, making it look like I'm following as they bolt into the camp and all the other buildings and hiding places to choose from.

But I don't run. Not yet. I glance behind the Dodge. Where are the other cars?

Where's Lucas?

Just then, Farrow's motorcycle rolls up behind the Night Rider, the Dodge's headlights immediately dim, and Farrow's lights spill over the scene in front of me.

And I see that it's not a Dodge at all.

It was, but through the trees and the dark road here, it must've turned off. I don't know...

Instead, Lucas opens the door of my brother's Boss and steps out, rising up from his seat and facing me. Chin raised and not looking amused at all.

My face falls, an electric current shooting up to the top of my head.

Oh, shit.

And just like that, I'm taken back to the last time we were here together—at this camp. Only now, he's hunting me, not helping me.

What about the Night Rider? Where did the old black car go? If Lucas saw them turn off, he decided to pursue me instead.

Twisting on the ball of my foot, I run, digging the heel of my sneakers into the damp soil. I dive into the forest, pushing away branches as I leap and race over old leaves and toward the empty cabins. Immediately, I skid around a rack of canoes and crouch down, peeking between the stacks of boats.

Training my ears, I listen for Aro or Dylan.

But they don't call out. They could be anywhere. The astronomy tower, the archery range, the barn, the dining hall, in one of the cabins...

The showers...

Lucas appears out of the trees, not running, and somehow that's scarier.

Farrow is nowhere to be seen.

I watch Lucas scan the area, looking right toward the main lodge and left toward the lake. He doesn't see me in front of him, about fifty feet away.

He grabs the hem of his soaked T-shirt and pulls it over his head, tossing it to the ground.

His shoulders square as he moves in my direction, and I clamp my mouth shut as his gaze passes over me. I force my breathing to slow down, afraid he'll see my chest rising and falling between the canoes. I don't want to be found. This isn't foreplay. If he catches me, I might say something I'll regret. Or worse, let him finish what he started when he was holding me.

Light droplets of rain mat my hair and make his chest glow under the single overhead light at the top of the electrical pole. I've never run from him before. I never wanted to.

But he's not who he used to be, and that's who I loved. What happens tomorrow?

Looking my way, he doesn't seem to see me, exhaling a long breath. I think he's going to keep going, heading through the camp to keep looking, but instead, he turns. Leaving.

I open my mouth, but I stop myself at the same time he pauses in his steps.

I want him to leave. The Dodge is here somewhere. I'm on my own adventure.

Just go.

I watch him bow his head, and all I can see is the side of his face. His pinched brow is aimed at the ground as if he's in pain. Maybe he's wondering if he should just let me go? That way he doesn't have to explain anything, right?

Just leave me alone.

Needles prick my throat, a picture of him getting back into his car forming in my head. Maybe, on the way home, he visits that woman Sarah whom he used to date. Perhaps he goes to bed with her tonight to forget me.

A lump rises up my throat, tears sting my eyes, and the Quinn who never wanted to be away from him wants to run to him and jump in his arms and tell him he can have me instead.

But I don't run to him. Not this time.

He starts to leave, and I suck in a breath.

And then...

He spins back around and charges deeper into the camp, his brow stern as he pursues me, disappearing between the cabins.

"Shit," I murmur.

He looks pissed.

Luckily, this works for me, though. The farther into the camp he goes to search, the farther he gets from the cars.

I can get back on the road.

Stepping quietly, heel to toe, I head back to Dylan's car,

fisting the hem of my dress as rain cascades down my arms and legs. The black car is out there somewhere. It's looking for me, in any case, and my chest swells up as I traipse through the wet grass, my head filling with memories that aren't mine.

The way the wind tickles my scalp. The pressure of every toe pressing through my shoe to the ground. The trees crowding in around me like walls, a pair of eyes—or two—peering at me from the dark forest.

It's like I'm in her skin for a moment.

It's her shoes walking across the soft earth. Her ears pricking at the sound of fireworks whistling in the distance. Her lungs drawing in the misty air on a night like this so many years ago, and maybe even here, long before it was a summer camp. Voices curl into my ear from somewhere, and I jerk my head, finding no one there. The flap of a bird's wings sound like wind hitting a sail, and I shake my head.

I know it's just the adrenaline. It makes me hear every bug buzzing and feel every hair on my arms rising from the skin. Is this what she felt?

Or what her victims felt?

Emerging from behind the main lodge, I check the vast lawn in front of me, my gaze tracing the path I ran with Dylan all those years ago, straight to the dock on the lake. Keeping my eyes peeled, I quicken my pace, coming up on the cars we ran from minutes ago.

Hunter's '67 Camaro sits behind Farrow's motorcycle, and I halt, making sure I don't see anyone through the windows. Aro talked to Hawke on the way here. He might've been with Hunter, both of them probably off hunting down their girlfriends.

I run to Dylan's Mustang. *They can take Dylan and Aro home.* I'll steal her car. Reaching for the handle, I yank open the door, but the empty space behind the Mustang finally registers. Lucas's car is gone.

I pause, checking my memory. He pulled up behind me, Farrow behind him. Lucas got out and chased me.

He didn't double back. I would've seen him.

Hugo Navarre could've taken it. Lucas probably left the keys inside when he ran after me. Without transportation, he could be in danger.

I start to get in the car. Lucas doesn't want help. I'm not forcing myself on him anymore. Farrow is here. He'll make sure he gets home.

But then, headlights break through the darkness down the road. Bouncing over uneven terrain, two cars race closer, and I remain still, not recognizing them until they hit fifty yards out.

Jared's Dark Horse growls like a bear charging.

"Shit," I hiss, slamming my door closed and backing away. *Fuck!*

I could just face them. Make up something, jump in the car, and promise to get home right away. And I should warn Madoc that Lucas needs him. I wouldn't have to tell him what I overheard on Frosted's roof earlier—that's Lucas's job—but Madoc should know he's being threatened.

The prospect of getting a clean getaway is short-lived, though. Jared won't let me take Dylan's car until he finds her, and even then, he or Madoc might insist on seeing me to my parents' house themselves.

Every muscle in my legs tenses, and I ponder for only another second before I race away from the car. *Dammit.*

Bolting back toward the main lodge, I escape between buildings, covering myself in the darkness, under the trees. I'll jump onto Arrowhead Trail and circle back around. By the time I make it to the cars again, they should be deep in the camp.

Horns honk behind me, my brothers probably trying to get our attention so they don't have to interrupt something they don't want to see. I can imagine Aro and Hawke are oblivious in the Astronomy Tower, and where do Dylan and Hunter prefer to have their little meetups? The barn? I'm sure, with all four of them spending their summers here, they know where they'll be well-hidden.

Still, though. They won't make Jared tear apart the summer camp looking for them. Because he would.

They'll come to him, so I don't have much time. Digging in my heels, I fly past the canoes I just hid behind and take a left before the showers, dashing onto the dirt trail the campers use for nature walks or to connect to Hedge Trail, which takes hikers up to the top of the falls. Pounding the thin mud, I lick the water off my lips, the rain almost a mist. Winding through the cabins and the field house, I keep my eyes moving, ready for anyone.

"Quinn!" Madoc shouts far off in the distance.

I whip my head around, but I'm alone. Dylan and Aro must still be hidden in a building, my brothers are back at the main lodge, and Lucas is gone.

I exhale, turning around.

But Farrow stands there, in my path, and I suck in a breath. *Shit.* I try to stop, but it's too late. He sweeps me up. My feet leave the ground, I'm thrown over his shoulder, and in a second, I'm upside down.

"Farrow!" I cry.

I kick and try to push off his back, but he's walking before I can get stabilized.

"Shhh." He pats the back of my thigh. "You really want your brothers to find you? I've got the perfect hiding spot."

Like hell.

He's on Lucas's side.

He stalks back up the small hill, taking us deeper into the forest as the rain finally stops. I twist my head side to side to see where we're going, but my hair just sticks to my face.

"I didn't know you were such a good friend of his," I spit out.

I feel the laugh leave his chest before I hear it. "It may not seem like it, but I'm being your friend now too."

Yeah, right.

Every male in my life thinks he knows what's best for me. The bane of my existence.

Shooting upright, I plant a hand on the side of his face and shove, flailing so hard, he loses hold.

"Ah!" he growls.

I tumble out of his arms and to the ground, a small branch poking me in the ass. But I don't wait. Flipping over, I scramble to my feet and jet off. Swinging my arms and pushing as hard as I can, I escape around trees, off-path, and between bushes.

"Oh, you better run!" he shouts after me.

I leap over a rock, whipping my head everywhere, because Lucas is somewhere, but I'm not even sure where I am exactly. I've lost the trail, and I never spent much time here. Where's the damn lake? There will be people down the beach, outside the boundaries of the camp, to watch the fireworks show. If it's still happening after the rain. I can find my car then. It's not parked far from the camp dock.

Springing up onto a log, I jump down, continuing to bolt, but someone moves ahead.

Noah walks toward me, holding his hands up to stop me. I grind my heels into the dirt. He cocks his head, a smile playing on his face.

He's not helping Lucas, too, is he?

Spinning around, I try to escape another way, but Farrow is there. He followed.

I turn, seeing Noah inch closer, and back away, keeping them both in my eyesight as they close in.

"The summer camp is supposed to be empty," Noah chides both of us like he's speaking to children.

I can't catch my breath, my chest rising and falling quickly.

He locks eyes with Farrow and vice versa, the rivalry evident. Noah's not here to help him or Lucas. He's here with my brothers.

"Come on," he says, gesturing with his hand for me to come. "Jared is so pissed he's forgotten his words."

I almost laugh. Is he trying to wrangle me like a horse?

But Farrow speaks up before I do.

"Are you getting paid for this?" he teases Noah. "Maybe you should come work for me."

Noah moves toward me, and I start to escape, but he takes my hand. "You don't like me," he reminds Farrow as he holds me.

Farrow grins, eyeing Noah like he's found a new toy. "But I *love* that you always do what you're told." He thins his gaze, target acquired. "Such a good boy."

I try to pry my hand out of Noah's.

"For the right people," Noah whispers.

I stop at Noah's taunt. I feel like I'm missing something. Is Farrow going to hurt him? I thought it was friendly banter, but I don't like their tones.

Glancing at Farrow, I watch his smile fall, and the moment of silence stretches.

Noah laughs, beaming, and I don't want to be here for some showdown. I'm losing time.

"Dylan!" Jared bellows into the night followed quickly by Madoc, "Quinn!"

Noah's hold tightens, and he pulls me, running. A gust of wind sweeps through my hair and dress, and I stumble over the uneven terrain as I twist my wrist, trying to free myself. "I don't want to go home," I tell him in a quiet but firm voice. I tug, fighting to stop him.

But a high-pitched whistle slices through the air, and Noah and I whip around just in time to see Farrow charge him.

He flies in, Noah releases my hand to catch him, and I jump back just as Farrow takes Noah to the ground.

Noah hits hard, the cords in his arms popping out of his skin as he clenches Farrow's shirt.

I stumble as they roll toward me, my heart in my throat. "Stop!" I whisper.

I don't want them to hurt each other. Jesus!

But Farrow looks up at me, Noah holding him down now. "Run!" he growls.

My chest caves, and I watch him shove Noah back over, grunting as he pins him to the ground.

I know I should stop them, but I just bolt. They can take care of themselves, and so can everyone else, for that matter.

Racing through the forest, I pull the straps of my dress back up over my shoulders.

"Quinn!" someone roars, but the wind is flying through my ears too fast to tell who.

Scanning the area, I look for anything I recognize. A trail. A sign. A road maybe? If I can make it back to the car before my brothers find me, it'll be a miracle.

I see a clearing ahead, maybe a parking lot for a trailhead. Twigs snap under my steps, and I whip my head left to right, speeding as fast as I can. Branches fly by, the night envelops me, and a man stands there...

Chills cover my skin, and I gasp.

What...?

I blink, breathing hard as I keep running.

A man. Standing still and dressed in a navy-blue suit, watching me fly by.

I look back, but the space where he stood next to the tree is now empty.

I exhale hard. *What the hell was that?*

I...

I slow to a jog, turning around and searching the brush around the area.

Where did he go? He was right there.

Did I recognize him? I search faces in my brain—friends of my brothers and my parents, customers, business owners in town... Dark hair, graying a little, but handsome. Tan with well-manicured stubble on his face. Around Jared and Madoc's age, maybe a little older. He wasn't dressed for hiking. What the hell?

I feel like I'm never going to get out of this forest.

Twisting around, I slam into a wall, and my head is still reeling so much that I don't fight as someone lifts me off my feet. One hand under my ass and another guiding my thigh around his waist, he raises me up, his hot breath caressing my jaw as I let out a little cry.

Fireworks whistle in the night, lighting up the earth underneath us, and I look down into Lucas's face as the reds and golds from above flicker in his eyes.

Sweat mats the hair at his temples, the vein in his neck throbs, and his chest falls hard under my hands. I try to swallow and wet my mouth, but as if he just came home from work and has been thinking about me all day, he doesn't take his eyes off me. I gaze into his blue pools. Wasn't there something I was running from? Something weird just happened behind me. What was it?

Quick footsteps pound the ground at my back, and Lucas doesn't even break our gaze to see who it is.

"Into the woods," he tells whoever it is. "Don't watch, and make sure no one comes this way."

Don't watch?

I jerk my head, Noah and Farrow meeting my eyes for a moment. Then, throwing each other a scowl, they go separate ways into the woods like Lucas instructed.

Farrow knew I'd run into Lucas. And Noah might work for my brother, but he's obviously not going to stand in Lucas's way. I'll remember this the next time they need me.

Lucas turns with me in his arms, and I notice the car just before he spins us around to walk toward it. Farrow probably moved it when Lucas took off to chase me earlier. He doesn't want to explain to anyone else why his car is here, does he?

"Quinn," Lucas whispers, staring at my mouth.

The heat of his stomach presses between my legs, his hard body making me throb. I expected him to be pissed. He looked angry when he set off to pursue me before. But his fingers are gentle, his breathing calm.

Nudging my chin up with his nose, he sinks into my neck, brushing his lips against my skin.

I shiver, but still...

"No." I push him back and jump out of his arms.

Landing on my feet, I step back. And keep going.

He pinches his eyebrows together, and I look at his fingers balling into fists.

"You're lying," he says in a deep voice.

Am I? My body aches, and I can't calm my fucking heart, but I'm not going to let him use me to avoid what he has to face.

"I'm not lying," I reply. "I'm not like you."

I'm not afraid to tell him things he doesn't want to hear.

His jaw flexes, and he steps toward me as I back away.

"I know you're lying," he bites out, continuing to advance on me as I move. "What was your plan when I finally came home, huh?"

I narrow my eyes. My plan?

He quirks a smile, tilting his head to the side. "Come on, Quinn," he taunts. "I know you thought about how it would go."

I jerk my chin up, watching his eyes gleam. *He doesn't know me as well as he thinks he does.*

But his voice drops to a whisper, almost pleading, "Tell me."

I stumble on a rock, quickly righting myself.

I didn't have "plans." Fantasies, maybe.

He peers down at me. "Did you think about me sneaking you into my arms when your brothers weren't looking?" he asks me. "Behind a door? In a dark corner? In a far-off bedroom?"

I force the lump down my throat, images of all the stupid scenarios and shit I used to dream up pushing to the surface of my mind.

"Or maybe you thoughzt I'd see you in a beautiful gown at one of your mother's fundraisers," he continues, advancing on me as I keep backing up, circling the car, "and not be able to take my eyes off of you. Is that it?"

I harden my eyes, spitting fire.

He just thinks I was wasting away my days, pining for him.

What a waste of time that would've been.

He keeps stalking me. "Or perhaps you're walking home from the bakery one day. You get caught in the rain and climb in my car when I drive by." Lucas holds my eyes, and I know the scene is playing in his head too. "We laugh and talk, just like old times, and then...I park somewhere."

I back into the edge of the trunk, hissing as pain shoots through my ass. Sidestepping the vehicle, I meet his gaze again, glaring.

"In a secluded wood," he goes on. "And you slide into my lap, and after a while, we can't tell if we're wet from the rain anymore or from the sweat."

I breathe hard, seething. I can't help seeing the fantasy play in my head though, hearing the rain on his car roof as we make out inside. His hands under my dress. His tongue on my breast.

Pushing the images away, I scurry back a few steps, increasing the distance between us. "You're making fun of me."

I wanted him.

I care about him. I'm worried about him.

But I'm damn-well telling him no.

"It must've been a double-edged sword," he tells me. "You wanted me home but not too soon, otherwise you would've been too young."

Screw you…

"But not too late, either," he adds, "otherwise I might marry someone else."

I shake my head.

But I know everything he says is true even if I won't admit it to him. Except the part where he snuck me into his arms in a dark corner. It was Madoc's basement, actually. And it wasn't a hot afternoon in his car. It was a wintery night in the dead of December.

Where the hell are my brothers? I'd kill for Jax to show up right now. He's the one people are most afraid of.

"You were in a race to grow up." He charges me and grabs my arms. "And this is what it was for."

No!

I shove him away with a scream. "It was for a dream!" I

yell. "For someone who never really existed!"

I was a kid. A stupid kid who wanted an ideal that wasn't real. And I knew it then. I knew it when I was sixteen, when I was eighteen, and now. The more you dream, the less it's going to happen.

He steels his spine, lifting his chin. "Congratulations," he says in a snide tone. "Now you've officially *grown up*."

My mouth falls, and I don't know if I want to growl or cry. How dare he try to get me into bed and then mock me when I reject him.

What the fuck happened to him?

I don't realize I'm tearing up until I blink. "Did you really kill someone?" I ask him.

"All of your careful plans shot to shit," he continues, ignoring me.

I laugh bitterly, letting my eyes fall to the ground. What am I supposed to do? Hugo Navarre is coming after him.

And he just wants to fuck?

Lifting my eyes, I lock on him. "You used to feel like a giant next to me." The words taste like ash in my mouth. "You knew everything, and you never seemed afraid. Strong and steady, and God, so tall."

He seemed so tall to me.

"But a child's brain sees what it wants," I tell him, "and I actually don't like you much at all."

His breathing remains steady as he continues to step toward me.

"All we do is fight," I point out. "We don't mesh well."

Vomit rises up my throat saying the words.

He whispers, "No, we don't."

And he takes another step closer.

I draw in a breath, retreating as he advances.

I swallow. "I was wrong to hold you to an ideal you never were."

He nods.

Another step.

What happens now? Are they coming for him?

What happens tomorrow? Will he go home to Dubai?

"You're different." I pinch my brow together, feeling the sob rising up from my chest. "Like a ghost, fading in and out."

"Yeah."

I don't know him. Not really. Did I ever?

"And I don't think you like me much, either." I harden my tone. "I'm childish to you."

He cocks his head, his eyes never leaving me. They haven't left me since he caught me minutes ago.

Is Hugo going to hurt him? What if he fucking dies?

"I'm childish to you with my little fantasies," I tell him.

His misty eyes follow me as I move and he moves.

"Of you rescuing me from the rain and taking the long way home," I admit. "Of you getting drunk one night, unable to resist anymore and holding me in a dark corner."

His chest rises and falls heavier, his face pained and desperate.

I stop stepping away from him. "Of you teaching me how to come with a man inside of me."

He closes in, taking my face in one hand and pressing his open mouth to my temple. His hot lips blaze a fire over my skin.

I want him. I've always wanted him, and if anything happens, I want to love him for just one night. I want Lucas Morrow to have me first.

Sliding my hands up his chest and around his neck, I press myself into his body. "Teach me how to come with a man inside me," I whisper. "Just once. Just the first time."

"Ah, fuck," he groans, lifting me into his arms again, one hand under my ass and the other behind my knee. My mouth crashes to his, the hair on the back of my neck rising with the heat engulfing us.

Just once…

Walking me backward, he presses me into the door of my brother's car.

I can barely breathe as he crushes me, bearing down and diving into my mouth, taking me over. His tongue flicks mine, sending a current shooting down my body, straight to my clit. I shudder, gasping.

A fire sparks in his eyes, and he covers my lips again, his growl falling down my throat as he thrusts between my legs.

"Ah," I moan.

Shit.

I break the kiss, twisting my neck to search for others who might see us. We can't be here. I'll be too loud.

I wouldn't put it past Noah and Farrow to be watching from where they stand guard in the woods. If they're not killing each other, that is.

And not to mention my brothers and their kids somewhere…

Lucas guides my mouth back to his.

"We should go somewhere else," I whisper between kisses.

But he trails his lips down my body, kneeling and sinking his mouth into my stomach through my dress. He tugs my panties down my legs.

Oh. God.

Lifting his gaze to mine, he lifts my hem, my eyes widening as he covers me with his mouth.

His hot tongue presses against my clit, and he starts sucking, shock racking through me. Gripping the car behind me, I let my head fall back and my eyes close, cool air caressing my upper body.

My worry is forgotten, everything under my skin coming alive as heat builds low in my belly.

"Don't stop," I beg.

He sucks slow but hard, swirling his tongue around my nub, and my smile almost turns into tears because it feels so good. He lifts my leg and hangs it over his shoulder, sinking his fingers into my flesh, and I don't watch him. I don't open my eyes. I'm just in it. Only feeling it and him and loving being kissed this way. For the first time.

Rolling my hips, I grab the back of his neck and fuck his mouth as he alternates between sucking and licking, nibbling my clit and kissing it. He kisses everything. My thighs, my heat, and then, in one quick movement, he's inside me with his tongue.

I cry out. "Oh, God."

Don't stop, don't stop, don't stop...

I hold him to me, grinding into his mouth. Pleasure grows, heat cascading over my skin, and I rock into him, chasing the orgasm.

"Fuck," I whimper, "Lick me, please."

He swirls circles with his tongue over me, shudders racking through me as I watch him.

"Lucas," I pant. "Lucas."

I suck in air, the orgasm splitting me open, lightning shooting through my thighs, and my whole body shakes as I hold onto him for dear life.

For a moment, I don't care about anything. Not my brothers who are looking for us. Not anyone close by who can hear me.

I just want him to fuck me. I want him to feel this too.

Rising, he spins me around and tugs my dress down to my waist, his hands finding my breasts as his mouth brushes my temple.

His cock presses into my ass, and I can't wait anymore. I don't want to go slow. Twisting my chin over my shoulder, I kiss him, moving over his lips and tasting his tongue.

"I've loved you the most," I breathe out, "and you think I know you the least."

His hand slides up the back of my head, his fingers curling into a fist around my hair. "You deserve better than me."

I groan, coming in for another kiss. "I know."

He yanks open the door of his car, pulls the lever, pushes the front seat forward, and locks eyes with me.

"My brothers are coming," I choke, barely able to take in a breath.

He shakes his head. "Fuck 'em."

I smile. And all at once, I fall into the back seat just as he pushes me, clenching the dress in his fist and tearing the top down the middle. I catch him in my arms, our lips melting together, because neither of us care anymore if this *should* happen. We want it, and we don't care why.

Taking my head in his hand, he moves his tongue over mine as the dress—now in rags—hangs from my body. In seconds, his teeth bite my jaw, his tongue blazes a trail down my neck, and his mouth covers a breast, making me arch up to meet it.

"Oh, yes," I moan.

His mouth moves to the next one, sucking and biting.

I grind into him, watching his hand slip down and open his jeans. Sliding his hand inside, he pulls himself out and strokes his already-hard flesh. I blink, trying to focus in the dark. I can almost see it rising up, reaching for me as he pumps his hand—the muscle thick, tight, and glistening. Warm wetness drips out of me.

My legs fall wider apart, aching to be filled.

I sink into his mouth, slipping my tongue inside as I slide my hand down his body and stroke him, feeling him for the first time. The veins pulse under my fingertips, and I soak in everything. The soft skin over the hard muscle. The cum already escaping him. The heat of his body. The way it throbs in my fist.

I'm so wet. "Now," I plead.

I'm not afraid he'll stop because I think he knows if he does, I might kill him.

He doesn't even hesitate, though. Rising up, he grabs my thighs and yanks me down.

I whimper, his rough hands possessive. Pushing his jeans below his ass, he tears open a condom, rolls it on, and my eyes go wide, fully realizing what's about to happen. He comes down on top of me and presses the head of his cock into me, and I hug his waist with my thighs, threading my lips with his just before he thrusts.

I suck in a breath, squeezing my eyes shut as a sharp pain pierces me.

God. That fucking hurt. It stings.

Slowly, he slides in again. Then again, muffling my cry with a kiss and grunting as he sinks all the way inside me.

The pain fades, but the pressure is more than I thought it'd be. He buries himself, stretching me, opening me.

And he doesn't slow down. Lifting himself up just enough to see my face, he rolls his hips in and out, and I can feel how wet I am as he slides easier and easier. The pressure subsides, and his cock hits deep, everything starting to feel good again.

I grab hold of the back of his neck and his waist in my hands, thrusting my hips to meet his rhythm. His lips touch mine, but we don't kiss. Just pant and groan as we fuck, my back sticking to my brother's leather seat.

"Don't you forget this in the morning," I warn him. "You chased *me* down."

The car lights up, fireworks popping overhead, and his only reply is a kiss. He curls his fingers into my hair, my scalp stinging, and his pace quickens, our bodies slapping together. I pull away from his mouth, looking down and watching him move between my thighs.

Fuck, the door is open. Shit.

But I can't help but be turned on as I watch us. *Finally*.

He couldn't stop himself. He couldn't see reason because I wasn't his last goodbye.

No.

He had to have me.

His breathing stutters, he shakes, and then he thrusts, grunting and groaning as his brow etches in surrender. He holds one of my breasts as he spills, and I look up at him, entranced by the look on his face. His closed eyes. His open mouth. The sweat on his forehead. It's what I've been waiting to see ever since he got home. *Passion*.

And thank goodness, it's for me.

I trail my lips along his jaw as his orgasm subsides. "Don't wake up," I whisper. "Not yet."

No regret. No panic. *Don't ruin it, Lucas.*

He opens his eyes and looks down at me, holding me close. "Oh, Quinn."

I beam up at him. "Sit back," I tell him. "I want control of you now."

I want to touch him.

He removes the condom and finds something to clean up with before sitting back in the seat. I straddle him, reach-

ing over and closing the door.
> *Just once or just one night?*

Same thing.

WESTON

CHAPTER TWENTY-THREE

Manas

Sweat trickles down the back of my neck. *Fuck, it's hot.* It's like New Orleans hot.

Music drifts through the trees from a distance, and I train my ears, listening to familiar voices laughing and shouting down at the camp.

Figures lurk in the brush beyond—searching, guarding... But they don't see us. Not yet.

With the syringe in my hand, I step closer.

Then he moves again.

I follow, matching his pace so I can disguise the sound of old leaves crunching under my shoes.

He watches the car buried under the canopy of trees, two tons of steel rocking in the night. The naked body of a girl on top of a man just visible through the fogged-up windows.

He creeps.

I inch closer, the rustle of the weeds under me lost in the sound of his own movements.

He steps again. Then again, approaching the car, and I suck in air, launch forward, and grab him, dragging my brother down to the earth.

He growls behind my hand as the needle sinks into his neck.

Wind sweeps through my hair, bringing the scent of a campfire, and I pin his chest to the ground as he thrashes.

Then, he relaxes, and I withdraw the syringe and flip him over.

His head rolls from side to side as he exhales. "She's here," he breathes out, the drug working fast as his lids slide closed. "The Dodge..."

Watching him sink into blissful oblivion, I shake my head. His ravings, his obsession, his lack of control... Deacon is a fucking full-time job.

I just hope I found him before he did something *really* stupid. What was he going to do here tonight? Why was he going to that car?

Removing a ziptie from my suit pocket, I secure his wrists. "Sometimes," I whisper to him, the whites of his eyes just visible through the slits. "I imagine what life would be like if I'd chosen her instead of you. But you were both out of your damn minds."

Rising up, I scan the area, making sure we haven't been detected. The blond guys—Farrow Kelly and Noah Van der Berg—drift in opposite directions, but they move too slowly, pacing. I dart my eyes between them and the car.

They're keeping a lookout, I finally realize.

Glancing down at Deacon, I squat and check his pulse. "Is that our girl in that Mustang?" I taunt.

I didn't see the couple get into the car, but why else would my brother be interested in their fucking?

"Did you have anything to do with that?" I tease, dusting off the dirt and grass from his face. "I'll bet you did."

I pull duct tape out of my suit jacket. "She'll love him good."

I don't know who she's with, but she'll be devoted to him and never make him question it.

I pull a strip of tape. "Unlike Winslet with us..."

Manas, hold me, her voice curls into my head again.

Her breathless whisper still tickles my ear, and I let my eyes fall closed a moment.

"She never loved us well enough to replace what she took," I murmur, more to myself than Deacon.

He wants her to be alive. I'll never understand why.

I love you... Her voice, her scent—still perfect memories, though.

I plant the tape over his mouth because he'll fight me if he wakes up. This isn't the first time he's run from New Orleans, and not the last time I'll have to chase after him. Sometimes he comes here. Sometimes he goes elsewhere to play.

"She's dead," I tell him.

Manas... I hear her again.

I repeat to myself. "She's dead..."

But still, I understand his reluctance to accept it when we're here. Home. It's hard not to feel her here. It's impossible to forget how right she felt, and how neither of us could get enough of her.

She was never a choice for me, though. It was always going to be my brother.

Lifting my eyes, I see the little island, dark out on the lake in the distance. "She's gone."

Just then, a shuffle hits my ears, and I jerk my head. A young girl stands six feet away, dressed in some colonial soldier costume. One of the Caruthers, I assume. No one in this town knows us anymore, but we know most of them.

She gapes at me, her gaze dropping to the unconscious Deacon with his wrists tied in front of him and his mouth taped shut.

She takes a step back, but when I don't chase, she stops.

"Aren't you gonna…" Her eyes lower to Deacon again and back up to me, "…kill me?"

I hide my amusement. "Aren't you going to run?"

She pinches her brow. "I was going to, but you didn't move. Aren't you scared I'll tell someone?"

I turn back to my brother, picking up the syringe, capping it, and slipping it back into my pocket. "No."

"What does that mean?" she blurts out. "I could tell somebody if I wanted to."

"I know." I soothe her pride. "I'm just not concerned about it."

"Why?"

I heave a sigh and stand up straight. "We're all living on luck, and mine will run out just like yours someday." I spin toward her. "If today's the day, I'm ready."

"Have you killed a lot of people?"

She thinks my brother is dead.

"I've never killed a child," I say, skirting the question. "It's one of the many lines I won't cross. So go tell someone. Whatever happens to me, happens."

She doesn't move, though, leaning to the side so she can see around me. I'm not even disappointed. I can still make people run from me, but I have no interest in scaring a kid.

"What will you do with him?" she asks.

I'm not even sure yet. Take him out of state, most certainly, but I can't take him back to New Orleans right now. Too easy to escape. "I like your costume." I smile instead. "What are you doing out here so late?"

"My dad said to wait in the car."

I chuckle under my breath. Their family seems to breed and nurture independent women. Aro Marquez, Dylan Trent, and even shy, quiet Quinn Caruthers. I move between the kid and the car, so she doesn't catch a glimpse.

I hold out my hand. "Manas Doran."

She moves in closer and shakes it, not the slightest bit timid. "A.J."

I see the resemblance now. "You look like your father," I tell her. "Your brothers look more like your mom."

She tilts her head, quizzical. She's going to ask her dad now if he knows me, and he won't have the slightest clue who she means.

Turning back to my brother, I search the area, making sure we didn't drop anything. "What does A.J. stand for?"

"Adalia Junior," she says. "After my dad's nanny."

"Adalia." I nod. "I like it. You should go by that."

"I tried, but it's hard to retrain people."

I laugh again. "I hear that."

Glancing up, I notice Farrow Kelly moving behind a tree. He's protected my and Deacon's home on Knock Hill from anyone who wanted it, but for some reason he stepped aside for Quinn Caruthers. He was right to.

"Maybe when I leave for college, I'll change it," A.J. tells me. "I want to go to Tulane. My grandma lives in New Orleans."

I stop, lifting my eyes to the island beyond. "Is that right?" I whisper.

I didn't know the Caruthers had family there.

"Interesting."

"She always brings me pralines—a little lagniappe that she doesn't give the boys."

I nod and start to haul my brother up off the ground.

"Are you both from there?" she asks. "Or just you?"

I halt, crouched and still. How the hell did she know—?

"Your suit," she points out. "It's seersucker. It's what southern men wear in the summer."

Pivoting, I meet her eyes, level with mine.

"And you didn't ask me what a lagniappe was." She smirks a little. "Because you already knew and *no one* knows what that means."

Eyes locked on her, I can't move all of a sudden. How old is she? Eleven?

Seven years, and she'll be on her way to college.

"We're from here," I finally admit.

And then I get an idea.

"Can you keep a secret?" I ask her.

She jerks her chin, nodding.

"Do you *want* to keep a secret?" I press.

I know I'll speak to her again, but I don't know when. I want her to be ready.

She tips her chin down once.

I lower my voice. "When your siblings and cousins all show up in New Orleans looking for me someday—whether you're with them or you're already there—you come find me, okay?"

I dig my keys out of my pocket and unhook the keychain, handing it to her. A bronze fleur-de-lis dangles from a bronze chain, and she takes it, studying it. *Chimney Wind* is etched into the back.

She offers me a skeptical look. "What makes you think they'll all go to New Orleans someday?"

I smile, rising, and drawing in a long breath. "Because you're all smarter than I thought."

Spinning back around, I grab my brother off the ground and throw him over my shoulder.

Turning, I bid her farewell. "Until next time, Adalia Junior."

I leave, moving right, and keeping my eyes on the little island out on the lake for as long as I can till I'm too far away.

SHELBURNE FALLS

CHAPTER TWENTY-FOUR

Lucas

Every time she exhales, I take her in.

Hidden back at her parents' house, I move over her mouth as I press her into the shower wall.

I can't stop. Swallowing, tasting, inhaling, eating...

We should've returned to her place, but I wanted the big shower. And the big bed in the guestroom.

I bite her bottom lip, my dick rising with want again. It's like I haven't fucked in a decade.

Twenty-thousand breaths...

I've lost track of how many hours I have left of Hugo's threat.

Grabbing her ass, I hear her whimper as I lift her up and guide her thighs around me.

The sun's not up yet. When it's light, I'll deal with business. Until then...

I dip down and sink my teeth into her tender flesh, her nipple brushing my cheek.

"I need food," she moans.

But then she presses on my shoulder to lift herself higher and feed me her nipple. I suck it into my mouth, tonguing it as the hot water sprays around us.

"God, what have I done?" I gasp.

Digging my fingers into her, I kiss a trail up her chest to her neck, her jaw, and then her mouth, sweating with need to be inside of her again.

Will her family forgive me if I tell them I love her?

Do I?

She trembles. "You only gave me what I was begging for," she replies, reading my thoughts.

She leaves a feathery kiss on my cheek. Then another one higher.

"I could've entertained any other guy," she teases, "but my brothers wouldn't have wanted you to allow that. You saw your duty and did it yourself."

I can't hide my amusement, feeling her mouth spread, too, as she kisses mine. "Yeah, I have no doubt they'll see it that way."

Yeah, man. She needed it bad. It was either me or them. I took care of it.

But she fires back, "They will see it my way." She leans in to my ear. "I once told you I'd choose someone my brothers liked."

And that day at the summer camp when she was hiding in the rafters floods back in again.

My God.

I pull back, looking her dead in the eyes. "Oh, you little brat."

I refuse to believe that she's been planning this, but...

She knew she belonged to me that first, early morning in her bakery. Would it have been the same if I'd stayed eight years ago? Would I still have been as drawn to her—as possessive—being her friend and watching men want her when she became a woman?

We kiss once. Then again, gazing into each other's eyes as we grind and breathe and touch.

Do I love her? Or is she just a place to hide?

I look into her beautiful face, I just want more. That's all I'm sure of.

I think she does too. I know she said she just wanted me for her first time. To show her how to come with someone, but...

She searches my eyes, and I part my lips, both of us needing to say something. I want her to know that I don't want anyone else.

Instead, we kiss again, both of us tightening our arms around each other and not counting the seconds and breaths that pass. What happens next? I can't think right now.

I brush my mouth over hers. "I've never done it three times in one evening."

"We've only done it twice."

I take her hand and slide it down my body, pressing my hard cock into her palm.

Her chest fills with a breath as excitement lights up her face. "What does it feel like?" she asks. "Inside of it, I mean?"

Inside my dick?

I almost laugh. Questions, questions, questions... Will she ever exhaust her curiosity? I'd like to find out.

"What does it feel like inside of *me*?" she pants next against my mouth.

I don't tell her with words. Slipping inside of her, I slide in and out, her slick heat wrapped around me so tightly my eyes fall closed and heaven spreads from my groin to the rest of my body.

I tell her with my face. The way my body quivers at how warm and greedy her body is.

She doesn't stop me. Just tilts her head back and moans, rolling her hips in a rhythm that matches mine.

"What do we do if my parents come home?" she whimpers.

But I kiss her mouth and her forehead. "Shhh." I tremble. "Enough questions."

I'm guessing I only have about thirteen-thousand breaths left.

Every one of them is for her.

Hours later, I let her peel herself away to go to Frosted. I was tempted to hide away with her all day, but more than anything, I need to make her safe.

I get busy, putting my affairs in order in case shit goes down tonight.

My father's dress coat, cap, and framed picture sit in a single box by themselves. I close the lid and slide it into a corner in one of Madoc's storerooms in his basement.

I restack boxes he already had here on top of it and back away, dusting off my hands on my pants.

My stomach aches with hunger, but visions of carrying her to bed just two hours ago—not to sleep—already make my body miss her more than food. Poor thing didn't get any rest before she had to run off to work.

Backing out of the room, I take a picture in my brain, shut off the light, and close the door. If I tell Madoc the truth—and the police—I need to deliver Drew. It's time to lure him out.

I release the handle, memorizing the smooth feel of the knob. Who will open this room next? Kade? Fallon? Maybe the door won't be opened again for a year. I can't imagine they need to sift through old suitcases and yearbooks very often. But at least my father's things are safe and with people I love.

I head down the hall, past Madoc's liquor storage and a bathroom, coming into the main room of the basement. Spinning in a slow circle, I take in the leather couch, the bar long enough for ten stools, and the piano. This was where Madoc taught me to play pool when I was fourteen. Where I helped Fallon build a haunted house for Halloween for the kids when they were little. This was where I got drunk for the first time. I still don't think Madoc knows about that.

I don't know why I feel like I'm saying goodbye, but throughout my life, I've been in rooms I'll never walk into again. I've seen people whose paths I'll never recross. There are movies I've watched for the last time and songs I'll never hear again and foods that life will never give me a chance to retry. Someday, I'm going to talk to Madoc, and I won't even realize it'll be the last time. Maybe today is that day.

Hands trembling, I spin in another slow circle, hearing the music in my memory and feeling the cold can of beer on my mouth from that one summer night ten years ago when I thought life could never get any better.

I felt the worst I've ever felt in my life in this town. And I've also felt the best. Fuck, I love them.

Leaving the empty house—Madoc and Fallon at work and the kids at camp—I roll down the windows in Jared's car and drive. My heart rises into my throat the farther I race away from the house.

Whistles from people's remaining fireworks continue to pierce the air of the otherwise quiet, summer day. Businesses bustle with activity, JT Racing has both bay doors open as they move vehicles in and out, and the public pool swarms with families trying to find some relief in the heat.

What would I be doing today if I didn't have to worry about Hugo Navarre or Drew Reeves? I crack a brief grin, seeing myself helping Jax at Fallstown, or Juliet up at the camp, or working on Quinn's new house. There's so much to do. The floors need to be leveled and the drywall repaired, but I know as soon as I opened the walls, I'd see electrical and plumbing that needed repairing first. Maybe Madoc would be helping me? And Lance? Beers and laughs and friends.

Climbing up Lake Lane, I spot a car parked at the end of a dirt driveway, a For Sale sign taped to the windshield. Hitting the brakes, I stop and put my arm over the back of the seat, looking behind me as I reverse the car.

Jeep Wrangler. Maybe an '06 or '07. Older than I'd like, but a lot cheaper than a new car. She wouldn't throw a fit at me spending the money on her. Hopefully.

It's white and has a soft-top with a little rust, but brand new tires from the looks of it. Seven thousand or best offer.

Shifting the Boss into gear, I punch the gas and race off, away from town. Heat radiates off the pavement, making the air smell like tar and hot leather, but I don't bother turning on the AC because the wind feels too good. For one more minute, I enjoy the idea of just grabbing Quinn and jetting off. Out of town for the rest of the day, somewhere I don't have to be on guard and or worried anyone will see us.

But soon enough, I see the Do Not Enter sign to the left. It's an exit for the drivers traveling a parallel highway on the other side of the trees. They use it to merge onto my highway, into the opposing lane. I jerk the wheel left, the lump swelling in my throat. A car could pop up anytime, heading straight for me, but I take a quick right, down the overgrown, gravel trail, barely big enough for a car.

It doesn't take long. Branches hit the windows as Farrow's truck appears ahead, parked. I pull up behind it.

Getting out, I look up at the black stone of the train tunnel as it emerges from rock, nothing but the sounds of the distant falls and the wind in the trees around me.

Farrow leans against it, smoking a cigarette, but I don't walk to him. Dropping my gaze, I find the lone, rounded gray stone at the bottom of the wall instead. It's a little lighter in color and surrounded by other stones and mortar.

My stomach sinks, looking down at the soil. Flat with weeds like any other patch of land.

"Were you able to arrange the burial?" I ask.

Farrow falls in at my side. "Not a problem."

I reach for the shovel in his hand, seeing the canvas bag I'd asked for on the ground. "Thank you."

But he sweeps the shovel up in both hands and jams it into the soil.

"What are you doing?"

He shakes his head. "Rest assured, it's not my first."

No. I yank the tool away from him.

"I can do this," he grits out.

I'm not sure why he wants to.

"It's my responsibility." I move away a couple feet. "Fallon wouldn't want this, and I can't believe Ciaran would either."

If she knew who he was, she wouldn't want him involved at all.

Slicing into the earth, I pull out a lump of soil and dump it to the side.

"You should wait for dark," Farrow warns me.

But I might not have till then. "I'm doing it now."

Before I forget, I pull a folded envelope out of my back pocket and hand it to him. "For the burial arrangements when the time comes."

And then I send him off. I need to be alone.

I continue digging, pushing the shovel in with my foot and locking my jaw to keep the bile down because eventually, the shovel is going to hit bone. I cringe every time the shovel burrows into the dirt, waiting for it.

The ache of that night returns, and I try to push it away and keep moving, but I know I deserve this. I owe him.

My chin quivers. "I'm sorry," I murmur to David Miller. "I'm sorry I left you here."

I kept staring at Miller's chest, willing it to move. Please.

My chest shook as I knelt at his side, in the mud, not blinking.

"If it makes you feel better," Drew said as he squatted next to me, "he tried to offer up his girlfriend to me to work off his debt."

The thirty-two-year-old man on the ground laid with his eyes half-open.

"I mean," Drew went on, "I'll still fuck her, of course, but—"

I howled, lunging for Drew and digging my fingers into his throat as I squeezed. "You piece of shit!" I cried, bringing my fist down on his face like a hammer. "You lousy, fucking piece of shit." I got in his face. "I hate you!"

Tears quaked in my vision, and I pinned him to the ground. A smile curled his mouth even as I choked him.

His guys grabbed me, dragging me off.

But grief overcame the anger—the pain, regret, and fear—and everything bubbled up from my stomach. I vomited on the bank of the pond.

No, no, no, no, no, no...

Heaving once, then twice, I emptied my body, wishing I could die.

Or just wake up.

Please let me wake up.

I sobbed quietly, the life I had ten minutes ago a dream compared to what I willingly walked into in just as short of a time. I shook my head.

"I thought for sure you'd be the one to jump ship first," Drew mused, standing up and dusting himself off. "All your daddies are fine, upstanding civil servants—I was certain you'd be the one with overwhelming character."

Daddies.

Madoc, Jared, Jax... My father. Why didn't I know better?

"But you weren't." *I heard his lighter snap shut as he lit a cigarette.* "It was Lance who had the character. You knew something was wrong, but unless you have the guts to walk away, what does it matter?"

I squeezed my eyes shut against the shame. Why didn't I leave with Lance?

"You like Green Street," Drew told me. "More than you know you should. When I picked the two of you, I never thought you'd be the last one standing."

I wiped my mouth on the sleeve of my suit coat.

"Thanks for buying the building." *His voice held back glee.* "Luckily, Lance was stupid enough to believe it was his idea."

My heart sank, realization dawning. Fuck...

"I wish it would've worked out, though," he told me. "It would've made everything easier. The women like you."

"My mom thinks he's a good role model," his guy, McCann, joked.

I stared at David Miller—a thug, an addict, and a burden on everyone around him. But he liked the smell of a good fire, and collected old radios, and tomorrow he could've woken up and made himself into a person he liked. He didn't deserve this.

"He was a good role model," Drew replied to McCann. "Until he murdered Miller."

I ball my fists.

"I wouldn't have believed it if I hadn't seen it with my own eyes," *his other lackey, Carlo Shield, mimicked.*

Followed by the third, Luccson. "We tried to stop you."

They just fucking played along with the new story as the walls closed in.

They were framing me.

"We just couldn't hold you back from hurting him," *Shield added.*

Grabbing my phone from where we left ours on the downed tree trunk, I turned to Drew.

"Try it," *I bit out.* "I have a permanent seat at the dinner tables of two of the best lawyers in the state."

Madoc might've been a little more talented than his father, but Jason Caruthers had a bigger network of powerful friends after thirty-five years.

But Drew just shook his head at me. "And I have fifty people willing to swear that Miller wasn't your only victim," *he fired back.*

"You brought in the drugs too," *Luccson chimed in, eyeing me.*

"And the whores," *Shield offered, a sad pinch to his brows.* "You turned those poor, young girls out."

Oh, fuck you. I didn't do any of that shit.

"You do what you want to do," *I growled, opening my phone and dialing.* "I'll do what I have to."

Holding it to my ear, I faced them, ready to repel an attack if they come at me.

The line picked up. "Shelburne Falls Police Department," a woman answered.

I opened my mouth, but not before Drew. "And I even heard his biggest customers were some fine, 'upstanding civil servants,'" he cooed to his crew, telling another lie about me.

My customers?

"Hello?" the officer prompted over the phone.

Fine, upstanding civil servants. *Did he mean Madoc?*

And then it hit me. He wasn't just framing me. He was threatening my family.

My hand fell away from my ear, and I ended the call.

Drew approached. "You brought this on yourself," he said. "You shouldn't have tried to stop me. We could've been partners. Family."

Until he killed me, he means? It was only a matter of time.

"But still..." He took my phone and slipped it inside my breast pocket. "I'll always protect you. We'll go dispose of Mr. Miller together, you can go home, and we'll never speak of tonight, or Green Street, again."

His boys started to drag the body back up to the grass, beyond which their cars were parked.

"I have no interest in the Falls," Drew explained, meeting my eyes. "I like a nice clean town to work in, and maybe set up a wife someday. Madoc can stay. For now. But you will never set foot across the river again, and when we run into each other, you be fucking civil as I pass by."

Like it's so easy, right? Just move on and live my life, and ask others to invest their love and friendship in me when he could turn my life upside down at any time and ruin theirs in the process?

Not to mention leaving a man in some lonely grave without any explanation to the people who loved him?

He fixed my wet collar, and I shoved his hands away. "If you tell Caruthers—or anyone else—" he warned, glancing at the dead body being carried away, "well, I'm capable of more than this. Just so you know."

So many times, I almost broke the silence. My mom knew something was wrong, and so did everyone else. They thought it was a girl. Maybe I'd been cheated on or I got someone pregnant. Jax even asked me if it was gambling at one point. I laughed. *I wish.*

I told myself that I was scared for the family and what he might do to them. That even accusations are taken as truth these days. The taint of a rumor could ruin Madoc's career.

I worried about their safety and Quinn's association with me. What if I were out with her, teaching her how to drive or picking her up from school and we ran into Drew? I can only imagine what he would've tried with her if he'd gotten Madoc or her father under his thumb.

But the truth was, I was simply ashamed. Disgusted with myself for being stupid. For being selfish and greedy for something of my own when I already had so much. Even if I felt that I didn't want to stain Madoc's future with a dead body I'd helped bury, I should've stayed and protected them. I should've figured out a way to make it right, even if it took years. Even if it made me sick every day.

I ran to hide. To pretend that Shelburne Falls and Weston didn't exist.

The shovel hits something hard, the tip grating over a rigid stone. But I know it's not a stone. Nausea roils through me, the feel of the raw, porous material vibrating up the handle and into my hand.

I tighten my jaw and close my eyes. *Oh, Jesus.*

I grip the shovel, the days and the years and the snow storms that raged here flashing through my mind as he faded away under the ground.

Biting the inside of my mouth, I tip the shovel back, peeling up the soil and unearthing his bones.

I know I should leave it for the police, but if Hugo gets to David Miller, his body could disappear forever. Or just indefinitely until Drew decides the best time—maybe two years, or ten years, from now—to use it against Madoc and me.

I may go to prison, and I'm fine with that now because I can't live with it anymore. As long as I take Drew Reeves with me and get him away from everyone I love, like I should've done in the first place.

The moist soil turns up easily, and so gently, I rake my gloved hand through the earth. Closing my fingers around piece after piece, I place each one in an open canvas bag, the tears streamlining down my face of their own accord. Fragments of clothes dangle, and my gut shakes with the need to throw up. I breathe deep, squeezing my eyes shut when I feel the skull.

"I'm sorry," I murmur again as I set it in the bag. *I'm sorry you ended like this. I'm sorry I challenged Drew. I'm sorry I didn't anticipate him. I'm sorry I helped hide you here.*

And I'm sorry I was quiet for too long.

Farrow arrives back at the train tunnel in no time, and I wrap the bones in the bag, letting him put it into the bed of his truck as I take another small envelope from him.

"Are you sure he didn't have family?"

Farrow takes the shovel from me. "Yeah, I double-checked. And the girlfriend left town years ago with her husband."

"Tell them to prepare the grave and headstone." I start to walk away. "Don't bury him yet, though."

The police will want to see the remains.

Digging out my keys, I walk to the car and open the door. I stop and face Farrow once more.

"I know you want Green Street," I explain, "but I can't give it to you."

I just need to clear the air on that.

He just slams the tailgate shut, shrugging. "Then don't. I'll take it."

God, I hope I never have kids. Or sons, at least. He's so fucking annoying.

"Why are you doing this?" I ask, not expecting an answer. "You don't need it."

He has a loving, successful family with connections. If he chooses to make himself known to them. I know now how valuable that is and how stupid it is to risk it. People who don't actually have options would envy him.

I start to climb into the car when I hear his voice behind me.

"My mom was a fling of Ciaran's twenty years ago," he calls out. "She was afraid he would take me away—or both of us, if he knew about me—and she didn't know how to be someone she wasn't."

I look back at him.

"She didn't want to be rich or live anywhere else," he goes on. "She didn't want me seduced by his money and private schools, so she kept me to herself." He pauses. "I went looking for a family too. Same as you."

So we both lost our fathers, in a way. I did the same thing he's doing. I had it all, but I felt pulled to something I didn't need. For him, he got something he never wants to lose.

"Green Street is still what you tried to make it," he points out. "Even just a little."

He found a family there.

He has people he cares about there, or maybe the whole town, but I'm almost grateful to hear it wasn't all a waste. That there is some good there.

We leave the shallow grave open, exposed, for the police when the time comes. Heading back into town in our own cars, I continue to Quinn's shop, watching Farrow fly by, continuing to Weston.

With my eyes peeled, I scan for Hugo. For Reeves. My blood cooks, making the hair on my arms rise. If Hugo is true to his word, he's coming tonight.

Parking on the curb, I see her inside, through the window in the door to the kitchen.

Hugo doesn't have the bones now, but that won't stop him from dealing with me. I'll need time to draw Drew out. Until that happens, Quinn stays with me when it's dark.

She moves around her tables, heading toward the kitchen, and I follow, into the alleyway.

After two knocks, the door opens. She peers up at me with a messy ponytail and flushed cheeks and lips that look like pink gum. And instead of chastising her for answering without asking who it was, I step inside and sweep her up, kissing her as the door closes behind us.

Wrapping my arms around her thighs, I tip my head back, letting her have complete control.

"How are you doing, not running on any sleep?" I almost accuse. She looks bright-eyed as she kisses me like she's not exhausted too.

But she simply grins. "I feel good. High as a kite."

To be honest, I don't feel the same. A weight sits on my shoulders, and I could sleep for a year, but I don't deserve rest. If I can just hold her for one more night...

I set her back on her feet. "I have a present."

"Number seven?"

I cock a brow at her, remembering what number seven was on her birthday wish list.

Instead, I pull out the envelope with the title and the car keys I had Farrow acquire while I was busy at the tunnel.

Handing her the keys, I gesture toward High Street. "It's old, but it has character."

She takes the keys, looking confused. Holding her hand, I lead her to the front of the shop where she can see the old Jeep at the curb. Farrow had the owner drop it here before he gave him a ride back home and then returned to me at the tunnel.

She looks between the keys to the car. "You bought me a car?"

I don't get nervous at the fact that she's not smiling. Even if she doesn't use it, I need her to have options.

"Just a starter one," I tell her, cradling her face in my hands. "You need something for the business, and you can't ride your bike back and forth to Weston in the dark. I'm putting my foot down."

She cocks her head. "Oh, are you?"

I plant a kiss on her mouth. "Be good and drive it." I turn to leave through the kitchen again. "Or I won't do number seven to you tonight."

She might not remember what it was, but I do. *Wear a collar.*

I have no interest in anything but being as gentle as possible with the most precious thing in my life, but...I can do what she wants and still be tortuously sweet.

And I'm not worried about the car. Once she realizes how much easier life will be with a vehicle, she'll drive it.

"Where are you going?" she calls out.

I glance back. "Pet store."

I face forward again before I see her smile appear, but I know it's there. Number seven requires props.

WESTON

CHAPTER TWENTY-FIVE

Quinn

Checking the clock on the wall, I hold my breath for a moment. Time is moving too slowly. After I closed the shop for the day, I sent my crew off early and raced to my parents' house, irresponsibly leaving the dirty dishes, a full register, and overflowing garbage cans.

But Lucas wasn't at the house. He texted and said he'd meet me at Fallstown at eight instead. I'm sure Madoc wrangled him into an outing at the races tonight, but I would've hoped Lucas would just politely decline. I don't want to go to Fallstown.

I want to see my collar.

And we need to talk.

But first, I want to see my collar.

Throwing down the dishcloth onto the worktable, I lock my hands on top of my head and lift my eyes to the ceiling, pacing the kitchen.

What do I know so far? He started Green Street. With Drew Reeves.

He unintentionally killed someone and banished himself over the guilt.

Now, he's being exiled again by Green Street's new leader.

I try to retrace memories from years ago. How he'd come over for dinner but then jet off to see friends. That one time he was taking me to the library and we ran into someone he knew.

He didn't want them talking to me. Was it Drew?

I draw up the image in my head, but I can't get a clear picture.

Then there was that day under the dock when we hid. Was that before or after the killing? He didn't want to see whoever that was.

And now he hates himself.

I drop my arms, putting the cloth in the laundry and sitting down at my open laptop. When he held me in the car, everything was right. He was like Lucas a decade ago. That's the Lucas I want back. That's the one I deserve. He's not a murderer, and he's not a bad man. He let Drew Reeves cost him too much.

I glance at the clock again. I showered, changed into clean clothes, and came back to the bakery, having time to kill yet. Where is he right now? Every second he's not with me, I'm worried. As if Hugo will snatch him off the street.

I'm surprised he doesn't send Farrow to pick me up and bring me to the track.

I let the wheels spin in my head. *Yeah, that is surprising.* He didn't send Farrow because he's *with* Farrow. Dread starts to curl its way through my mind. Are they up to something?

Why is it so hard for Lucas to talk to me?

To hell with it. If he's not at the track, he will be soon.

Closing my laptop, I swing my crossbody over my head and grab my phone, about to head to my bike.

But then I remember...

Doubling back, I swipe my new car keys off the worktable and turn off the bakery lights.

My phone rings as I open the alley door, and I glance at the screen. I answer as I lock the door. "Hi," I chirp.

"Hey, kiddo," Jax replies.

I slip my work keys into my purse and head around the block, toward my new-to-me Jeep.

"Sorry I haven't been around much," he tells me. "This summer is flying by."

"It's okay. We're all busy."

"It's not okay." He pauses, his voice softening. "I miss you."

I toss my purse into the back of the car and hesitate, loving how that feels. When Jared calls, it's not always unpleasant, but he usually has an ulterior motive, and when Madoc reaches out, it's to get me to join in on a picnic or a party. Again, not unpleasant, but it always feels like I'm a baby bird being tucked back under a giant wing.

When Jax calls, I just feel like he wants me to feel loved. Like he didn't growing up.

"You don't miss me?" he blurts out.

I grin, climbing into the car. "I do. I'm just too busy smiling at how sweet you are."

He falls quiet for a moment. "Yeah, well..."

I can just envision the blush on his cheeks.

The youngest of my three brothers is just as formidable as Jared, and just as powerful as Madoc, but he's always a little gentler. Maybe it's in his nature to keep his emotions in check, but I think part of him constantly feels like he doesn't have the right to bark or make demands of me like the other two. Jax and I don't share blood. There's an invisible line he just never seems to cross, and out of the three, I wish he would the most. He is my brother, and I want him to know it.

"I appreciate you, you know that," he says. "Hawke is driving me nuts right now, and I look at you and think maybe I was a good influence on someone. Because, let's be honest, Jared and Madoc weren't."

I laugh a little, but the guilt makes my smile quickly fall. If he knew I was keeping a secret—or a few, actually...

Starting the engine, I put my earbud in and lay my phone in the passenger seat. "What's going on with Hawke?"

I pull away from the curb and make my way down High Street, toward Fallstown.

"Oh, this frat he's started." His tone drips with disdain. "I didn't think I raised a fucking preppie."

I nearly snort. "He's not a preppie."

Hawke, Kade, and Hunter started a fraternity at Clarke University last fall, Sigma-something-or-other. They even renovated a derelict house on campus. So far, it's just the three of them, but they've aligned with a national organization, formed an executive board, and begun the recruiting process.

He goes on, "Even Aro is disgusted she's in love with a frat-bro."

"Or oddly turned on."

If I know anything about Aro—and Dylan—they will relish the challenge of their boyfriends belonging to clubs they can't join. They don't like—

Movement catches my attention, a car in my rearview mirror. I tense, recognizing the now-familiar sight of the black Dodge.

"Where are you?" he asks.

"Almost at Fallstown." I turn left. "Dylan is racing tonight."

I grip the wheel, glancing in my mirror again. That damn car is just pissing me off now. What does it want?

I clear my throat, shifting gears and speeding up. "You know I'm going to make some mistakes sooner or later, right?" I tell him.

"As long as he has a job, a license, no criminal record, and no sexual past, I approve of any of your mistakes." I hear him chew something crunchy. "I'm very proud of the man Aro chose. And the one Dylan chose."

Yeah. Both their guys are family members of his. And virgins, from what Aro told me the other night in the bounce house and Dylan confided about her and Hunter ages ago. I'm choosing someone who will make Jax more nervous because I'm in love with someone a lot older than me. Someone with a past that's causing him a lot of problems.

"Well, thank goodness your criteria weren't in place when Juliet, Tate, and Fallon were falling in love."

"Right?" he retorts.

I chuckle. We all know that he, Jared, and Madoc would've had a hard time getting around those rules.

The car behind me closes in. "Get back to work," I tease. "I gotta go."

"Love ya, kiddo."

We hang up, I press on the gas, shift gears again, and hightail it to Fallstown.

I race down the long lane to the track, keeping an eye in my mirror. "What do you want with me?"

Are you spying on me? Protecting me? Pondering when to strike?

Lights glow up ahead, and cars sit in the makeshift lots off to the right, before the tracks. Picking up my phone, I dial the number Deacon called me from once. I wait for the light of my call to glow inside the Dodge.

But it doesn't.

If it is Deacon, he's not carrying that phone.

Ending the call, I jerk the wheel and bounce over the already-trampled grass to a quick parking spot. Shutting off the engine, I grab my phone and keys and run back over to the main road, the car still stopped in the middle—staring at me.

Come on, I urge them. *Just get out of the car.*

It's just sitting there.

What the hell do they want? I led it to the camp last night, and it ditched me. I don't understand.

Moving toward the car, I watch it suddenly back up. I stop, letting it retreat as I hold back a scream of frustration.

"Hey, you came!" I hear Dylan behind me.

Spinning around, I open my arms just in time for her to barrel into me with a hug. I don't know if she sees the car behind me, but there are vehicles coming in and out of here all night. "I told you all I'd figure out some free time eventually," I tell her.

She rocks me side to side, gleeful. "Wanna race with me?"

She pulls away, and I glance over my shoulder, seeing the car back away down the long road.

"If you still raced cars, then maybe," I say.

"That could be arranged."

She races motorbikes now, and I knew she had no interest in racing anything else anymore.

I walk over to the tracks with her. "Just be safe."

"I'll be the only thing I can be."

I throw her a small smile, but she doesn't see it. I love that she knows who she is. There's never really a fork in her road.

Engines roar in the night, the bleachers are filled, and lines stretch from the food trucks and merch tents. This is the last race before Jared heads out on the road with his team for a whole month. Rumor has it he's stopping in Colorado. Maybe Noah can see his dad.

And I also heard Dylan will be joining them all for her first real circuit. Which he only agreed to if she promises to be home by the time the fall semester starts.

Lucas stands in a group with my brothers, his hands in his pockets. I stop at his side—close—and feel him go instantly still. I hide my amusement.

Jared doesn't even say hi. Just arches an eyebrow at me. "Nice Jeep."

Jared's not a fan of me making any decisions without him.

"Don't give her that look," Lucas teases. "I checked it out and bought it for her as a surprise. It was cheap, but it runs well."

Madoc twists his mouth to the side but keeps it shut.

Lucas continues, "You can talk her into something with higher safety ratings and bulletproof glass after I leave. Just be glad I got her driving."

"Yes, thank you," Madoc grumbles. "As usual, you're the only one she listens to."

Do I listen to Lucas? I almost laugh, remembering how he had to chase me last night.

But wait... *after I leave,* he'd said. Is Lucas not at least considering staying now? I don't know why that surprises me. It shouldn't. I told him I didn't want more than last night anyway.

I reach into my bag and pull out the compass, slipping it into his pocket as my brothers talk to other people. However it goes, I want him to have it.

"Can we go home?" I whisper.

I want him to myself a little while longer.

But he steps behind me, and I feel his breath in my hair as he moves to my other side. "Farrow's going to trail you to your parents' place," he murmurs, "and make sure you're safe. I'll come home as soon as I can."

"What's going on?"

But it's not an actual question. It's a beg. A plea for him to talk.

He holds my gaze, but I know after one moment turns into five, he's not going to tell me.

"Quinn!" Dylan bounces over, grabbing my hands. "I've never seen Noah race a car, so we're gonna do it!" she exclaims. "You riding with him or me?"

I turn away from Lucas, unable to look at him right now.

Dylan starts to pull me away, and I try to latch on to what she said. She and Noah are racing cars instead of bikes? And I'm riding with one of them?

But I don't have time to react before a grip closes around the inside of my elbow and tugs me back.

We both look at Lucas, and he simply shakes his head at Dylan, telling her I'm not going anywhere.

I don't know if it's his silence, his protective hand still on my arm, or the fact that he's not dictating whether or not she can put herself in danger like he is with me, but I see the moment understanding dawns in her eyes. Her storm blue orbs widen and her lips part.

"Oh my God," she breathes out, beaming at me. "Are you serious?"

"Dylan, go sit down," Lucas bites under his breath.

But she damn-near laughs. "Oh, I'm not a kid anymore, so you shut up."

She throws her arms around me, and I go rigid, worried that one of my brothers nearby will ask what's going on.

But after a moment, it all melts away. I hug her back, my chest tightening in a way that makes me break out in goosebumps.

"Was it good?" she asks in my ear.

"Yeah."

Amazing, actually.

I'm trying to hold back my relief so hard I'm shaking. I didn't realize how exhausting the secret had been. Hiding the looks, the conversations, the attraction... But still, I say, "Don't tell anyone, okay?"

"I'm telling Aro." Pulling back, she hoods her gaze. "You can tell my dad."

She whirls around and skips back to her boyfriend, leaving me with that horrific thought. *Yeah, fat chance.*

Lucas releases my arm, but I don't turn. "Are you really still leaving Shelburne Falls?"

If he thinks he's going to try, I might not be able to keep my tone in check. So much so that not only will Jared know how far we've gone, but everyone in Shelburne Falls will too.

But Madoc's voice interrupts us. "Lucas!" he calls.

He steps over. "This is Vanessa Black, a graduate of the University of Chicago." He gestures to the black-haired young woman behind him. "She interns with Barton & Haynes while she pursues her Ph.D."

So? Why should Lucas care about that?

Does he think Lucas will stay and go back to work for Fallon's and his former company?

"Nice to meet you." Lucas reaches for her hand, shaking it. "What's your specialty—commercial, residential..."

"Whatever work they'll give me," she teases, "but I am particularly drawn to conservation."

He looks at her. She looks at him. Madoc looks at them both.

And it's like I'm the camera panning out at max speed, their cozy little circle far away from me.

"She'll be spending the day in Fallon's workshop tomorrow," Madoc tells Lucas. "Maybe you can make her go green."

Then, Madoc winks at him. Why is he winking at him? I want to feel my place at Lucas's side, even if no one else knows I belong there, I do.

But Lucas isn't even looking at me.

"It's hard to get city dwellers to be happy anywhere else," Lucas says, laughing.

"Just takes the right motivation," she flirts. "Will you be there tomorrow?"

I dart my eyes to him. Images of them in the workshop alone, talking about architecture and their interests, making my head constrict.

My heart lodges in my throat, black starts to spill into my vision like I'm in a tunnel, but then…a hand takes mine and pulls me away.

I draw in air, stumbling after Noah as he leads me to the speakers where a group of people dance. "Don't talk." He pulls me into his arms, and I wrap mine around his neck, closing my eyes and trying to get my pulse under control. "Just hang on to something whenever possible," he tells me.

I'm not sure if I'm shaken because I'm upset or angry. Madoc is trying to set him up. He's doing anything to get Lucas to stay.

But Lucas should've looked at me. Or even better, taken my hand and made it obvious how he felt about me.

It's okay, I tell myself.

One night. That was the deal.

Noah and I slow dance even though it's a high-paced Yungblud song, people enjoying themselves all around us. Hunter hugs Dylan from behind as they rock back and forth,

I don't see Kade, Aro, or Hawke anywhere, and Farrow glares over at us as some girl I don't know hangs off him.

"Farrow looks like he's about to kill something," I mutter, trying to distract myself.

Noah looks at me. "If one of us touches you, he wants it to be him." Hugging me again, he taunts, "So I won't be letting you go anytime soon."

We laugh a little, relaxed. I don't think Farrow's aggravation has anything to do with me. He didn't want Noah having anything to do with Codi, either.

Noah tenses under my arms, and I close my eyes, knowing what's about to happen.

"Quinn?" Madoc says, interrupting my dance.

I open my eyes and twist my head, Madoc and Jared approaching, followed by Lucas.

"We're having a little get-together at the house," Madoc tells me. "Would love some pizza. Why don't you take your new car and head over? We'll meet you."

"Not tonight." I turn away. "I'm dancing."

I've never denied them food if they asked me to cook, but he doesn't really want pizza. He wants me to leave and not have any fun with a good-looking guy whom he thinks has lots of fun with lots of girls. Noah relaxes me. So does Farrow, for that matter.

Lucas chimes in next. "Quinn, let me take you home."

"I'm staying." I start moving with Noah again. "And I'm not a child anymore."

"Quinn—"

"Later." We spin around, slowly moving away and into the crowd. "I'm dancing now."

Noah holds me tightly, and I know Lucas probably thinks I'm trying to make him jealous. Honestly, though, there's nowhere I'd rather be than with someone my own age right now.

SHELBURNE FALLS

CHAPTER TWENTY-SIX

Lucas

Everyone piles in around us. All three of Quinn's brothers, their wives, Dylan, Hunter...

Hugo lingers on the other side of the dancing crowd, flanked by two of his men, and every one of them is keeping an eye on me. He'd arrived fifteen minutes ago, and I'd been trying to get Quinn out of here since—behind a locked door on a property with security.

And then I'm going to Jax. He has access to the town's cameras and a good relationship with the police. I'll be able to see if Drew is in the area before I make a move.

"Shouldn't you be suiting up?" Jared barks at Noah.

But Quinn answers for him. "He's busy."

She gives *him* one of her smiles, and I drop my eyes to their stomachs. Touching.

Well, their shirts are touching, but he can certainly feel her body.

"He's about to be fired if he doesn't stop touching you," Jared growls.

Damn straight.

But Tate chimes in. "Like that empty threat would've gotten you off me back in the day."

He snarls at his wife. "It wouldn't have stopped me this morning! What are you trying to say?"

"That this whole "Do as I say and not as I do" act was kind of a turn on for a while, but now you just seem..." She ponders. "What's the word?"

"Misogynistic?" Dylan offers.

"Judgmental?" Fallon spits out.

"Patriarchal," Tate finally adds. "Like you're a teacher or a principal or something. Elderly."

Jared's eyes bug out, his teeth baring.

Madoc snorts, but his wife quickly taps in. "Oh, don't you dare!" she scolds his amusement. "It's spot on. Quinn's an angel compared to you three at that age."

"Let her make some mistakes," Juliet chides.

"You want her to go through everything we went through?" he argues.

"It's her choice."

Fuck this.

I step up. "Actually, it's not." Snapping my fingers, I give Farrow an order he doesn't need explained in words. "Mr. Kelly?"

And I point at Noah.

Everyone quiets, Farrow grins, and he immediately cracks his knuckles. "Absolutely, boss." He locks eyes with Noah Van der Berg. "I've been dying to get my hands on you."

Farrow belts out a whistle, and his crew mobilizes.

He grabs Noah, I wrangle Quinn, and there's a commotion that I don't see as I sweep her into my arms and carry her away.

Screams hit my ears.

"Oh, shit!"

"Don't touch him!"

"Fuck!"

Quinn thrashes in my hold. "Oh my God," she growls over my shoulder. "Farrow, stop!"

Stealing her away, I ignore her struggling, slipping through the trees to the overflow parking lot and people drinking on their tailgates.

"Let me go!" she bellows. "This isn't fair!"

I spot her Jeep ahead, praying I can keep hold of her long enough to stick her inside.

She snaps in my face, "Maybe I should let them know that Noah has always acted like a gentleman and you were the one pumping their little sister last night. Three times."

"Maybe you should." I plant her on the damn ground next to her car door. "They'll keep us apart."

And she doesn't want that. I fucking dare her.

But she just sneers. "Yeah, anything to not have to tell me your big secret."

I jut out my hand. "Give me your keys."

"Screw you."

Oooh, big words.

Ripping open her bag, I find the keys and draw them out. I stuff them in her hand. "Don't go to Weston."

"I'll go where I want."

To my surprise, though, she doesn't demand to stay and climbs in her car. Without another glance in my direction, she drives out of the lot and back on to the road, disappearing around the trees. She may go to Weston, purposely provoking me to follow, but... She better head to Madoc's. She knows better than to risk her safety to prove a point.

Plus, I'd have to leave her alone at her brother's house. Which she appears to want. For now.

Hugo and his guys appear in the lot, eyes zoning in on me, and I move my ass, leading them away from everyone I care about. Jumping into Jared's old Mustang, I race out of the lot, seeing them hurry for their car, as well.

I think I catch sight of Madoc in my rearview mirror, noticing me leave, but I'm gone before I can look twice.

Pedal to the metal, I fly down the road, rushing onto the highway. Cutting a left, I head for Weston and keep an eye behind me, making sure they follow.

But Hugo barrels through the *Stop* sign and pivots right instead. The same way Quinn drove.

I release the gas. *Shit*.

Jerking the wheel, I swing around, probably leaving a hundred dollars' worth of tire on the asphalt. Kicking the stick shift up a notch, I chase Green Street back into the Falls, riding their ass to make sure I don't lose them.

My phone sits in the holder, hooked up to the charger. I dial Quinn.

I arch my neck, trying to see around Hugo's ride and catch her taillights. "Come on, pick up," I beg under my breath.

The call goes to voicemail, and I hang up. Quickly tapping, I send her a text.

Go back to the Loop.

No one calls it that anymore, but Loop was shorter to type than Fallstown.

This time of night, I'm not sure what businesses are still open, and I know Madoc is having people over after the races, so there will be staff at his place, but I don't want to risk her going there. All the estates in that neighborhood are partially secluded.

And fuck me if she tries to go to Weston. That's not my turf anymore, and Farrow isn't there to back me up right now.

Farrow...

Reaching over, I dial him.

Headlights shine in my rearview. I squint, shielding my eyes, but before I can dim my mirror, Hugo's car suddenly halts in front of me.

"Fuck!" I press my brakes and swerve, but not fast enough. I slice the bumper of Hugo's car with Jared's, careen over the side of the road as Hugo's vehicle rolls, tumbling after me. I spot another car ahead of him, but it's not Quinn. A *Traverse?*

My head hits the roof as the Mustang bounces over bumps into the brush, over rocks and protruding tree roots. Something hits my shoulder, a searing pain penetrating down to my bone.

The car rocks right, then settles left, and I finally exhale as the world falls still. "Son of a bitch."

I'm right side up. I didn't roll, but I look around me, finding Hugo's car. It rests upside down, at least one figure inside scrambling to get out.

What the hell happened?

Unwrapping my fingers from the wheel, I grab my phone and open the door, climbing out. Walking over, I lean down to check Axel's pulse, but in a moment, I'm being slammed to the ground instead. My phone flies out of my hand as a weight lands on my back, crushing me into the wet earth.

Hugo still hangs upside down inside of his car, inches from me, his hooded eyes finally noticing me as he fumbles with the seatbelt.

All three guys are still in the car, in fact.

Chills rise on the back of my neck. Who's behind me?

"You been working out," a familiar voice pants in my ear.

I freeze, Drew Reeves pressing his forearms across my shoulder blades and pinning me to the dirt.

He was in the car ahead of Hugo that stopped him short and drove us off the road.

"I'm bigger, too," he taunts.

I heave myself off the ground, scrambling for my phone and checking to make sure Quinn isn't here. Hopefully, she's long gone.

Drew grips the back of my neck, shoving me into last year's fallen leaves. He grinds my head into the open window frame of Hugo's car, my eyes locked on the current leader of Green Street as he tries to reach his gun lodged between the dashboard and the windshield.

"Kill him," Drew whispers to me.

Hugo breathes hard. "Piece of shit…"

"Kill him," my old friend begs me, that smooth edge in his voice still so in control. "Who will stop him if I send you to jail? Who will protect Shelburne Falls if you go back to Dubai?"

Hugo pulls at the seatbelt, growling at how utterly helpless he is. "Axel!" he bellows, trying to wake up his guy. "Nick!"

A moan comes from the back seat.

"He knows about her," Drew eggs me on. "*I* know about her."

I growl, trying to push myself up despite the weight on my back.

Hugo's seatbelt releases, and he drops to the roof.

"Who will stop him from hurting her if *he* kills *you*?" Drew goes on.

No one's going to kill me.

Hugo swipes up his pistol, and I scurry.

"Kill him and end it," Drew breathes in my ear.

His weight comes off me, Hugo points the gun, and I yank his ankles, dragging him out of the car. I twist my neck around, ready for Drew.

But Hugo's firing.

He pulls the trigger, and my heart damn near stops.

There's no shot.

He scrambles to switch off the safety, but I fall on him, shoving his hands above his head as I try to pry the weapon from his grasp.

Where the fuck is Drew? The back of my scalp turns hot, already anticipating his bullet.

Hugo twists to the side, kneeing me in the ribs. Pain shoots through my body as I hear the crack.

I flinch. *Fuck*.

I slam his goddamn hands down on the ground, pounding once, twice, and then three times until a cry escapes him and the gun drops away.

Giving him no time to recover, I rear my fist back and hit him so hard his teeth cut my hand.

And I keep swinging.

I can die. I can be arrested and incarcerated for the rest of my life, but as long as they're here, she isn't safe. This will never end.

I have to do it.

"Axel!" he cries for his crew. "Nicholas!"

I grip the hair on top of his head, hitting him again and again until my arm is on fire with exhaustion.

This will never end. Even if I can get them sent away for twenty years, it's not over forever. They're just leaving others in charge.

I didn't kill David Miller.

And I don't want any of this.

But they're going to hurt people, and I'm doing what I have to do.

Hands bloodied, I grab his neck and squeeze.

I dig my fingers in, flex every muscle in my arms, and cut off every sputter and every gasp coming out of him.

His face contorts, his skin grays, and I'm kneeling over him, looking down into the dead eyes of another man who's here simply because of choices I made years ago.

My chest caves, agony filling my head as I unclench my fingers.

One is a mistake. Two leaves no doubt on whether or not I'm a murderer.

I draw in a breath and nausea climbs my throat until... he sucks in a lungful of air and coughs, alive.

I choke down the lump in my throat and crawl off him, backing away.

I stare at the blood on my hands, none of it mine. Shame covers my skin, the line I almost crossed making my body shake because it's still there. The line right in front of me as if I can still stumble over it before I have a chance to stop myself.

Drew is gone. Hugo gasps and rolls over, the gun forgotten. Axel and Nicholas crawl out of the car.

I dial 911, not because I'm worried anyone is hurt, but because Hugo is too stupid to count his losses. "There's been a non-fatal accident with injuries on Highway 112, mile marker six."

"No, man," Hugo spits out, all of them climbing to their feet. "Shit."

In moments, they're gone, scaling the incline back up to the road and disappearing. Probably back to Weston, or at least to wait for a ride.

I hang up the phone, the line not even connected out here in the woods.

My feet move, ambling through the forest.

What would've happened if I'd killed him tonight? Would I have bribed his two guys to keep quiet? To help me bury him? Would I have had to go back to Green Street?

How many more lies would I have told?

Shortly before my father died, I remember learning that my homelife was a little different than my friends'. It was a realization like a crack of thunder in the sky. My parents didn't scream like one of my friend's parents did. I didn't have to hide birthday money for fear my mom would steal it, or carry my own house key because there was never anyone home. I don't remember exactly how my father explained it, but one day it dawned on him that he had the exact life he always wanted. He didn't wait for the future anymore, or thirst for something else. He got everything he wanted.

I want one thing. I want Quinn running with a smile to the whole life in front of her.

And I'd really love to never have to leave again.

After I deal with Hugo and Drew, I'll unload the firehouse and turn myself in.

Stripping off my filthy shirt, I cross the street and Madoc's property, slipping into the outdoor shower hidden off the side of the house, in the hedges. Starting the water, I use the shirt to wipe off the blood on my face. The silent house looms next to me, and I'm sure there are a couple staff—a caterer and bartender, at least—getting things ready for Madoc, Jared, and Jax's family, friends, and racers when they get here. I can't make myself care, though. Madoc could be home any moment, and I wouldn't hide. I probably wouldn't even be able to disguise my anger and distress.

What does Drew want?

I can imagine. His job back.

And then realization hits as the shower cascades down my scalp and back. He may try to force me into coercing Madoc to get his name cleared and his job reinstated. That has to be why Hugo hasn't hurt me yet, right? Drew interceded and kept him at bay for a reason.

"Lucas, are you okay?" I hear Quinn's voice in front of me.

The world tilts behind my lids, and I don't recognize what I'm feeling, but it's not confusion. Or even fear.

I let my head fall back, warm water covering my head. I'm not a murderer.

I'm in control, and Hugo and Drew aren't on the same side.

I feel her hands on my face. "What happened to you?"

I guess she's not mad anymore. Opening my eyes, I let my forehead fall to hers and take her waist in my hands. She stiffens, her hands dropping to her sides, but she doesn't move away.

"I know I should leave you alone," I say as the water pours down my face. "I know I should find someone else. You know why I don't?"

"You're changing the subject," she retorts. "What happened to you?"

I clench my jaw, swallowing before I say, "Because I know that when I return for someone's wedding, or someone's funeral, in five or ten years, I'll see you across the room with some guy and feel like he's touching someone who doesn't belong to him."

He's touching someone who belongs to me. That's why I can't let her go.

Even now, I know. I'll always feel it between us.

Her brows pinch together. "Lucas..."

I run my knuckles down her cheek as my thumb glides down the bridge of her nose. "And I'll think that even if I have another woman on my arm."

Quinn is mine.

She shakes her head slowly. "Stop—"

"I don't want to," I interject, that particular truth so easy to spill. "I don't want to stop. Believe me, I wish I did."

I wish I could do what was best for her, but for all of my faults, the most prominent seems to be greed. I want her again and again and again and...

I cup her ass in both hands and press us together, eating up her mouth in soft, quick nibbles and kisses. She's so tender, her skin tasting like peaches. Her hands come up to push against my chest, but her mouth still opens for me. She lets me bite and lick and kiss while her eyes close like she's on a roller coaster and has butterflies in her stomach.

God, she's beautiful.

Watching her start to kiss me back, I unbutton her little red shorts and slip a hand in, sliding a finger inside of her.

She jolts, arching her back and gripping my arms. "Oh, God," she moans. "Not here. What are you doing?"

I slip in a second one, pumping them in and out as I look down into her big eyes. Fingers soaked, I swirl them over her clit.

"Getting you out of my system," I nearly choke out. "You want to get me out of yours?"

Her eyes narrow in anger, and she bares her teeth.

And she nods.

"Fuck..." I growl, gathering her in my arms and twisting her around to pin her against the shower wall. Thin strips of light peek through the wood panels on all three sides, and I kick my leg behind me, slamming the door shut. A few birds chirp as they flap their wings overhead, and the showerhead above her splashes water between us.

I massage her tongue with mine as I pull her tank top down her arms, baring her breasts, and push her shorts and panties down her legs and off her feet.

Gazing down into her face, I rub soft circles over her clit, feeling her bend her knee to open up for me a little.

Pushing two fingers inside of her again, I almost shiver at the tight heat. She's tighter than my fucking hand. *Jesus*.

She whimpers, twisting her head away, and I growl in her ear, "I don't want to stop, and you don't want me to."

Crooking my fingers again and again, I coax her gently, making her eyes roll and her lids flutter.

Taking her hand, I guide it to her pussy, watching her fingers take over. Backing up just a foot, I feast on the scene in front of me—Quinn with her top at her waist and the straps down her arms, one hand opening her and the other playing. Her breasts shake with her breathing, wet hair hanging in her eyes. She performs, never taking her eyes from mine.

My cock swells, pumping with blood, and I almost don't give a shit that I don't have protection.

Jutting my hand under one of the dispensers, I pump conditioner into my palm as I unfasten my jeans. Her eyes go wide, watching me pull out my shaft and stroke the length, my fist slow and tight around it. "I don't have a condom again," I tell her.

But I'm fucking coming on her stomach. I'll damn well be her first everything, if not her only.

Leaning my arm on the wall behind her, I pump my cock, thirsty for her taste, and my teeth aching for a bite of her. Her supple breasts look like heaven, and my lips hum with the need to feel them. My memory is clear on how soft she is. Of how I want to run my mouth over every inch, leaving nothing unexplored.

But I hold off, the torture creating this longing that feels like I'm starving more every second. How long can I go before I ravage her?

She watches me stroke, the conditioner making my cock glisten, and she starts to whimper as her hand flicks faster. Her clit rocks back and forth with her fingers.

Her breathing stutters as her chest rises, and I dart my gaze to hers, watching her come, but…

She jerks her hand away. "I want you inside me now." She pulls me into her arms, pressing her body to mine. "Hurry, I'm about to come," she pants.

The skin of my cock stretches like a rubber band, and I feel the cum sweating from my tip.

Fuck, yes.

Burying my mouth in her neck, I back her into the wall and wrap her leg around my waist. Holding her eyes, I thrust, sliding inside of her so easily. She's so wet, and so am I, and in a moment I'm sheathed in fire.

I shudder, groaning. "Ah, fuck…" God, I'm about to spill right now.

"Quinn…" With my mouth hovering over hers, we stare at each other as I roll my hips fast and hard, sending her sliding up and down the wall. I don't want her to lose it. I want her to come more than once, and if I go slow, I'm definitely going to come too soon.

But as we chase her orgasm, a hard thud lands on the other side of the wall. We freeze.

"Madoc, no," a woman says, her voice something between a whimper and a whisper.

I stop, Quinn and I searching each other's eyes for what to do. What the fuck? Is that…?

"The boys are out," we hear Madoc say directly behind Quinn's head, "and A.J.'s at Jasmine's for a sleepover."

Panting and gasping drifts over to us, followed by a woman's moan.

They kiss and coo, and I try to see through the slits, but all I can make out is people moving.

"But we have guests," Fallon hisses.

"Fuck 'em."

I look back down to Quinn, the fright in her eyes so precious I want to smile. *Fuck 'em.*

I said the same thing to her when she was worried that her brothers would find us at the camp. Fallon was right. I do take after him.

Starting slow again, with her big brother on the other side of the wall, I fuck her, sliding my cock out to the tip and driving back in to the hilt. Her eyes close, her face contorting into a cross between pleasure and pain, and I hold her head, flattening my body to hers, and kissing her beautiful lips.

"Don't let them hear me," she whispers as she trembles.

In and out, I move. Slow. Quiet. Holding her tight and wrapping my arm all the way around her neck so my hand covers her mouth while she comes on me.

"Baby," I say in her ear, hearing her brother elicit the same cries and moans from his wife.

Quinn's hot pussy covers me, her body going lax as the pleasure washes over her, but I don't wait.

I start again, kneading her ass and locked in her hooded gaze.

"Gimme a beer!" someone shouts in the distance. And music drifts into the air.

People are here, but we're exactly where we want to be, unable to stop.

She whimpers again, and I move my hand off the wall and into her hair. Wrapping it around my fist, I slowly pull her head back so her eyes meet mine.

"Say you love me," I mouth as Madoc and Fallon do whatever they're doing to make each other grunt and groan over there.

Quinn's hair sticks to her face, and I brush my lips over hers.

"Feel me," I growl under my breath as I stop and hold my cock inside of her. "And say you love me."

She rubs her hands up my chest, rolling her hips and picking up where I left off instead.

I wet my finger in my mouth and then slip it down her behind, using it to circle her tight little ass.

She stops breathing for a moment.

She stops moving altogether, actually, and I grin.

I press the tip inside, grunting as I harden inside of her more than I thought possible. *God, she's so fucking tight.*

"Say you love me," I whisper.

Her little mews turn short and high-pitched as I slip the finger in up to the first joint and leave it there. She contracts around it, and I hope I live long enough to be inside of her this way. All I know is I won't get her out of my system tonight.

Squeezing my finger and with my dick inside her body, she picks up the pace, coming in to tease me with little kisses as she rides me with her legs wrapped around my body.

"Deeper," she begs.

And I press my finger deeper. "Say it."

She moans, letting her head fall back as she rocks in and out, faster and faster. Then, she holds her breath, her entire body tensing like stone as the second orgasm racks through her.

"I love you," she murmurs, only loud enough for me to hear as she squeezes her eyes shut and shudders.

Her pussy clenches, wetter as she rides it out, and I grip her waist with both hands, keeping her moving as I'm ready to come too.

I groan. "Oh, baby." I bite my bottom lip, hearing laughter and voices growing closer. "I love...."

I love you too.

But I can't say it. What if she loses me? It'll be easier to hate me if I never said it.

"Fuck, I love how I can't breathe if I'm more than an arm's length away from you," I gasp instead.

My orgasm rips through me, and I come, grappling her like my fucking life depends on it. I kiss her hard, crushing my lips to hers. "I love..." And I smile. "I love that I'm already hungry for you again."

Her father and brothers and nephews could kill me, and I would still want her.

Devoid of reason. To hell with the rules.

I want her, and God help me when I can no longer hide it.

WESTON

CHAPTER TWENTY-SEVEN

Quinn

I love how I can't breathe if I'm more than an arm's length away from you.

It was nice to hear last night.

And everything was so hot.

I loved that he desired me. That he saw me as a woman and liked what I did for his body.

But I'm ready to hear something different now.

I said it first, which was a mistake. He's just going to think I'm naïve and inexperienced.

Whatever happens next, doesn't he want me to know how he feels?

The empty bridge opens before me, and I cruise across the river on my bike. A quiet ride to work this morning sounded nice. And I wanted the extra time to clear my head. Lucas still slept when I left my parents' earlier, and I'm glad I cleared away any evidence of us there together. Of course, they would've assumed we were there together as they're still unaware of my new house purchase, but I didn't want them arriving back home from their trip to discover we were sleeping together. I left no condom in the downstairs garbage after we got done on the couch, no trail of clothes to his guestroom, and turned back on the indoor and outdoor cameras as I left a couple of hours ago.

I'm surprised I haven't gotten a call from Jax yet. With live feeds everywhere, there's no way anyone who's paying attention hasn't noticed us together around town as much as we have been.

Cameras...

I stop pedaling. Jax might have footage of whoever attacked Lucas last night.

Someone attacked him. I didn't need him to tell me that to notice the cuts and bruises.

Of course, he won't talk to me about it. As if avoiding the truth makes him look any better in my eyes.

Lost in my thoughts, I don't notice the sound of the engine until it's almost on me. Blinking, I swerve for the side of the bridge to let it pass, but when I look over my shoulder, there isn't anything there.

Training my ears, I hear the car, but I can't see it as the fog rolls in like a wave over the bridge. No headlights, no movement... I hop off my bike and look around, unable to even make out the banks of the river, and only one light from Weston. One among all the mills.

The car is gone, but I twist side to side, my skin crawling all the same. Visibility is scarce with the fog, it's still dark, and I'm all alone.

The engine suddenly revs, and I jump, searching for the damn car on Weston's side.

It's so close. Where is it?

It fades away again, drifting off in one long, musical note.

Lightning flashes across the sky, and then a ring pierces my ear.

The hair on my arms shoots up straight. "Shit," I grit out behind my teeth.

Digging it out of my pack, I swipe the screen.

"Where are you?" Lucas demands.

I try to calm my breathing. "I had to run back to my place. My work clothes were there." I climb back on my seat. "I'm crossing the bridge back to the Falls now."

"In the car?"

"On my bike."

"Quinn." He sounds scared. "I don't want you out by yourself. A storm is coming."

More thunder rolls overhead, but I know it's not the rain he's worried about.

"Just get to the bakery," he tells me.

Fumbling in my backpack for some spare change, I throw several coins over the side. I haven't been adhering to the tradition, and Winslet MacCreary may not be dead, but she could still be watching.

"What's wrong?" he asks.

He must hear my hard breathing, and I shiver at the dark road ahead that I can't see.

"I don't know." I pedal fast, cool air sweeping over my legs. "There's fog everywhere. I can't see."

I hear shuffling, keys jingling, doors slamming...

Holding the handlebar with one hand and the phone with the other, I keep my eyes peeled. "Lucas?"

Is he still there?

"I'm coming," he says. "If there's danger, hide."

"Lucas..."

"Get to the bakery!" he shouts. "Stay on the line with me until you get there."

I toss my phone into the basket, leaving the call connected, and pedal hard. No light appears on the road—no light at all—except for the sporadic overhead streetlamps. The thick fog cools my skin, droplets of water wetting my face.

In moments, my thighs burn, and my fingers ache from holding the handles so tightly.

I don't risk a glance behind me.

I can't go any faster, and if there is something or someone there, the fear will make me fall.

The road curves and drops, my bike coasting down the incline under its own momentum. The wind takes my hair, and my stomach swoops at the speed.

But I coast all the way into Shelburne Falls, pumping the pedals again once the street levels out. I don't hear anyone. I don't feel the heat of any headlights, or any change in the breeze, but just in case... I take turns I wouldn't normally take, trying to lose whoever might be following me.

Swinging onto High Street, I round the corner into the alley and see Lucas barreling in behind me in one of my parents' cars. No idea where the Boss is.

Dismounting, I grab my backpack and phone and let the bike fall to the ground. Lucas charges toward me, and I hurriedly unlock the back door, still seeing no one.

Once inside, I lock us in and actually back away from the door as if there was a ghost in the fog.

But there was no one. There probably wasn't anyone near the bridge, on the bridge, or following me here. Just the dark emptiness messing with my imagination.

Lucas, though... He sounded afraid.

Twisting me around, he cups my cheeks, and I can't catch my breath.

I need to know.

"What happened to you?" I pant. "What are you afraid of?"

Staring into my eyes, he opens his mouth, his body shaking. It's on the tip of his tongue. I can tell.

I want to know everything. Every moment. Every detail that got him here.

He's so loved. What brought him here?

"I wish I could shut off the world for an hour," he whispers, "and stop it from spinning around us."

I don't know why he said it, but I do know what he means. Sometimes you need everyone else to stop moving so you can catch up.

I pull his hand away from my face and hold it as I lead him into the shop. Silently, he follows, his fingers laced with mine.

We pause at the mirror, I look back at him, and then I release the latch, pulling open the mirror.

His eyes widen. "What…?"

Stepping through the frame, I still hold his hand. "I'll tell you something and then you tell me something."

Gently, I guide him in, watching his gaze shoot everywhere to examine his new surroundings. Closing the mirror, I walk us down the hallway, silently letting go of him as he drifts around, checking out the bedrooms, the small gym, the office, as well as the great room with its kitchen and door to Rivertown Grill. He doesn't ask a single question as he studies the words on the wall and all the evidence the others collected. He even walks back down the way we came in to see how the mirror is two-way.

I wait for him in the great room until he wanders back in, looking at me like he's almost suspicious of what I've been doing in here.

But I explain, "Hawke and the others knew this was here for years." I pause a moment. "I just found out a week or so ago. They've been researching the link between urban legends in Weston and Shelburne Falls and found this place."

"Years?" He scowls. "Why didn't they tell you this was here?"

I quirk a knowing eyebrow.

He frowns. "Those little shits."

Yeah, I was mad, but Deacon has only spoken to me, so now I have that. "It's fine."

"It's not fine," he fires back. "They shared this with friends, no doubt. Everyone coming and going from your place of business, strangers right under your nose."

I know. I don't reply, though, because I'll just get angry at them again.

"What are you going to do with this?" he asks.

"I don't know yet." I gaze around at the high ceilings and ample floor space. "I want to use it, but I also want them to come back."

"Hawke?"

I shake my head. "Deacon and Manas."

I recount to him what we've learned about the urban legends so far. About this hideout being Carnival Tower, and my new house being where Winslet vanished from during Rivalry Week so long ago.

And about the Night Rides and the car following us both.

His breathing turns shallow, and I see at least three emotions fill his eyes in a single second—confusion, anger, fear...

I continue before he has a chance to react. "I think she's alive," I tell him. "And I think she's in Shelburne Falls."

Shaking his head, he walks over to me. "It's been more than twenty years, Quinn. No one has that kind of patience."

"Maybe it hasn't been that long." She was clearly getting revenge during the Night Rides, but maybe she didn't know where the brothers ran off to and hoped the news of the murders would lure them back. "Maybe when she killed the people who tried to kill her, the brothers heard about it and returned," I tell him. "The trail hasn't gone cold yet. Maybe there's another chapter, after the tower and Rivalry Week and the Night Ride."

Maybe a lot more has happened in the last twenty years.

But Lucas thinks I've drawn the wrong conclusions. "She hasn't been following you," he states.

I continue, "Maybe they learned she was alive and had to come back for her. Maybe they weren't runners."

Like you, I don't add out loud.

We stand there with the rain and thunder kicking up outside and the sky goes from black to gray as the sun tries to break through the clouds but fails.

He thinks, if someone is following us, it's someone else. Who?

"So here we are," I challenge him, keeping my distance. "The world has stopped spinning, nothing else exists but us..."

Why is he so afraid to tell me his story?

He drops his head, breathless. "You don't want to know," he breathes out. "You want to keep your little childhood crush going, so you can keep imagining I'm this idea I never really was."

He lifts his eyes. "And I want you to keep thinking I'm the person you always thought I was because I was only ever a hero to you and no one else."

"If you leave me, you're no hero."

His jaw tightens, and he lowers his gaze again.

"Out with it, Lucas."

He moves to the kitchen island and leans his ass on one of the stools.

"Drew Reeves used to be one of my *best* friends." He clasps his hands in front of him. "That's how awful my judgment was, and how little you saw me for how weak I could be."

He was friends with a dirty cop. I didn't know they were that close, but I'd heard as much already.

He peers over at me. "Did you ever notice that I always looked for you in a room when you were growing up?"

No.

I looked for him.

"You probably thought I was being nice," he goes on, "to make sure you were included in card games or had someone to talk to on road trips or had someone to practice your baking skills on, but the truth is, I felt like we were in the same boat, for some reason."

"Pairs," I murmur. "Everyone else was in a pair."

"Yeah."

Both of us looking for our niche, our spot.

He continues, "I used to see you trying to keep the peace any time there was an argument..."

Trying to be useful. Valuable.

"Or always doing exactly what you were told as if you knew the pain that was wrought to bring you into the world—"

I think back to Madeline, Madoc's mother, and all the pain she was caused because my parents couldn't stay away from each other.

"—and it was like you were trying to earn your right to exist."

My chin trembles. Is that what I was doing?

"Same as me," he adds. "Having you around made me feel like I had a place. Until I decided that I needed to find my own."

I wipe my eye. I had no idea he felt like that. Madoc—and the rest of the family—would be devastated to know that.

"Madoc had fulfilled his duty long enough," he tells me, "and no matter how much I loved him, I couldn't shake the feeling that the responsible thing to do was to not be a burden anymore and leave him alone."

But I protest. "Madoc loves you. He would never—"

"I know." His eyes soften on me. "My insecurities were louder then, though."

I almost smile. I know what that feels like.

He clears his throat. "So I went to college and made new friends, and we wanted some place to hang out, so I bought Green Street."

I listened as he told me everything. The idea of a social club—a place to network and party and, on their better days, use it for community outreach and revitalization in Weston. Young men, looking for business investments, would be able to snatch up property in a town like that cheaply.

Of course, as smart as Lucas is, he mistakenly assumed everyone was as good and as honest as Madoc, and he actually believed that Green Street would be good for the town.

Reeves took over, his friend having a master plan the entire time to foster a criminal enterprise and take advantage of a desperate population. People got hurt, arrested…

"Green Street and predators like Hugo Navarre exist because of me," he explains. "Aro and all those other people were hurt because of what I helped start. It took on a life of its own, and I still don't know how to end it."

I move a little closer, just the couch between us. "Madoc would've helped—"

"One night," he cuts me off, the story still not finished. "I challenged Reeves. We'd drive a junk car into the river. If he bailed first, he'd disband his tawdry little club. If I bailed first, I'd never step foot in Weston again."

And I know the rest because Green Street still exists, and Lucas left the country. "You lost."

"The moment I heard a scream coming from my trunk as water filled the car," he retorts.

My heart sinks.

I knew someone died, but my God… For a second, I can put myself in the trunk. The horror of watching the water gushing in and being trapped, unable to escape.

And I can put myself in Lucas's place, hearing the screams and knowing you can't stop a sinking car.

My stomach knots.

"He was a cop with access to evidence and digital records," he points out. "He could've forged anything, and he had a whole crew of men to say I did it on purpose."

Piece of shit…

Drew made sure, no matter what, he was going to win that night. Son of a bitch.

I almost laugh at myself. Almost.

I understand my parents and brothers a little more now. Lucas made decisions he thought were harmless, not seeing until it was too late how fast your life can change. In one moment, he could've walked away. In the next, someone died. All the people who love me have experienced firsthand how detrimental seemingly easy decisions can turn out.

"I still would've told," he assures me. "Until he threatened Madoc and Fallon and…"

I lift my eyes, Lucas blurry behind my tears.

…and all of us. Reeves threatened everyone he cared about.

If he could frame Lucas, he could frame my brothers too.

"I stayed for a while after that." He starts moving toward me. "As close as I could to make sure you all stayed safe. But months later, I couldn't look in the fucking mirror anymore. Someone was dead, and I wanted to die." He pauses, the rims of his eyes red. "You think you know who you are and what you stand for, and it's all shot to shit with a series of abominable decisions that kill any anticipation for the future. I wanted to go to the cops. I want to right now."

He stands there, his T-shirt stretched over his chest as he slides his hands into his pockets. His eyes hold mine, pain etched on his brow as he stares at me as if waiting.

Does he think I hate him?

My heart aches, looking at him so far away.

"Come here," I whisper.

He stays planted in place, his mouth opening and closing, like he's trying to resist me.

But the only way out is through, and we start now. I could never hate him.

"Come here," I tell him again.

He hesitates, but only for a moment. In two seconds, he's in front of me, brushing my cheek, my hair, and then pulling me close. "I'm going to put everything back together," he says, his voice strained. "But first, I need to make sure you're safe."

I stare at him through watering eyes. "What are you going to do?"

We hug, and he squeezes me so tightly, I can barely breathe.

"I'm going to go after him." He tucks my head into his neck before I can tense. "And then they can put the handcuffs on me, and whatever happens, happens."

I startle, sucking in a breath. "Lucas, no."

I push against his hold, lifting my eyes to his. It could end badly. It *will* end badly. I could lose him forever.

Hasn't he learned anything? He needs his family. We can help. Madoc needs to know everything. Now.

He holds my face, his hard voice steady and sure as he tells me again without hesitation, "I'm going to make you safe."

SHELBURNE FALLS

CHAPTER TWENTY-EIGHT

Lucas

Pulling my phone out of my pocket, I climb back through the mirror, seeing lightning flash across the street outside her shop window.

She chases after me. "No."

Coming around my front, she snakes her arms around my waist, but I gently pull her off. I need to go. I'm going to find Drew before he has a chance to use me against Madoc.

She pleads with me. "Lucas, no."

I move away from her and dial Farrow. He picks up the line. "I'm here."

"Where's Hugo right now?" I ask. If anyone knows where Drew is, it's him.

Farrow sighs, realization dawning. "Ah, shit."

I unlock the front door to go to the car, but Quinn plants a hand on it to stop me.

Farrow grumbles in my ear, "Meet me at Wicked."

The strip club? It's five-thirty in the morning. Hugo must be self-soothing after nearly dying last night. I'd already had a tow truck dig the Mustang out of the woods and bring it back to Mr. and Mrs. Caruthers's place. It looked fine, but I hadn't had a chance to inspect it thoroughly yet. I just hope I have a chance to fix any damages before Jared sees it.

First things first, though.

"I don't need you there," I tell him.

I can do this alone.

But he just laughs like I told a joke and hangs up.

I slide my phone back into my pocket and try to open the door.

"It wasn't your fault," Quinn states in a stern voice. "You couldn't have known how things would go."

I remove her hand and yank the door open before she has a chance to place herself in my way again.

"It is my fault that I didn't stay," I point out. "That Green Street still survives. I should've dug in and gotten to fucking work."

"I'll call Madoc."

"And implicate him?" Fuck, no. Not yet. "I'll tell Madoc. But I need to take care of this. It's my responsibility."

She shoots out an arm, placing it across my chest as she blocks me from leaving. "What if Reeves is watching? What if he's there? What if he kills you? Who will keep me safe then?"

I stare down into her warm, brown eyes. *That's what I'm trying to do. Keep you safe.* The idea of her alone tomorrow, and next week, and a year from now. With Reeves on the loose? Hell no.

Taking her by the back of the neck, I pull her forehead into my lips, but her body is stiff.

"Don't go," she whispers.

I'm coming back. This is something I should've done a long time ago.

"Stay here, lock the doors," I instruct as I walk out. "No business today."

"Lucas!" she cries behind me.

The scent of rain fills the thick air as a breeze sweeps through my hair.

"You're making a mistake!" she shouts.

And running away and ignoring the problem hasn't done me a bit of good, either.

"Don't come back then!"

Her growl hits my back, and I halt in my tracks. What?

Whipping around, I see her standing in the doorway.

"You don't listen," she bites out. "You don't know that your family is your strength, and you'll never get it through your head! Fuck you!"

I almost rear back, my stomach sinking as I watch her slam the door, lock it, and disappear through the kitchen doors.

Did she just tell me to fuck myself? What the hell is she mad for? I'm finally dealing with this! I—

I cut the thought off before it even fully forms and shake my head. *No*. I can't worry about this right now. She hasn't been living with this shit for nearly a decade! She's speaking from a place of fear.

Climbing into one of Jason's older cars—some BMW that's even older than Quinn—I yank the door closed.

My family is my strength... How does that help me?

I try not to speed to the club, but my blood is boiling. She needs to trust me. For the first time, I know I'm doing the right thing.

But I can't shake the look in her eyes.

Is she gonna let me in when I come back? Does she actually believe I'm not better now than I was? This needs to happen. I'll always have the guilt, but this is the first step in starting to make amends.

All I can seem to picture, though, is her seething in her kitchen and closing the door in her heart because I've abandoned her before and she's tired of men who make their decisions *her* problem. I'm just one more she has to handle, and I don't want to be. I want to be there for *her* now.

In no time, I find myself in Wicked's parking lot, sliding into a spot and turning off the engine.

If this meeting turns bad, will that have been the last time she saw me just now? Probably the best fucking thing for her.

Taking my phone, I open the voice recorder and press the microphone icon. I shut the screen off and exit the vehicle.

Farrow waits at the front door, and without a word, falls in behind me as I enter the club to talk to Hugo. I peek at Farrow out of the corner of my eye, though, wondering if he's just another mistake.

I trust what he said. As Ciaran's son, maybe he doesn't have any plans to harm me or cross me, but I know he has a hidden agenda. Why else risk upending the status quo just to help me? I almost warn him that I'm recording on my phone, but I'm not entirely sure he's on my side.

Emerging from the short tunnel into the club, I'm taken back to my time in college. The crisp perfume of carpet shampoo and air freshener mixed with the stench of cigarettes.

The boom of the bass and the music drowning out my thoughts.

The coolness of the air, like being on an empty trail in the forest.

I feel that same assault on the senses that happened just like the only other time I've been here. That sudden darkness stealing you away from the light.

I didn't think this place was open this early in the morning. They could have a Late Hour Liquor License, but that would mean Hugo and his boys have been drinking all night, not to mention whatever else they might be on.

Fuck it.

I find him off to the right of the stage, in a dark alcove, seated at a booth. Two girls dance on stage, but they're barely putting on a show. They look exhausted, dragging their platform stilettos across the glossy floor. A man sits alone at a table, and a couple sits together, whispering. There's a bartender, and a server moves across the floor. No one else.

I motion for Farrow to stand next to the booth where I can see him, and grab a chair, planting it in front of Hugo's table. I clutch my phone in my hand as I sit. "My family is tracking me, so behave, okay?" I tell Hugo.

He laughs under his breath.

"I find that we're at an impasse," I tell him. "I can't implicate you without you implicating me. And I can't offer you anything better."

His arms hang over the back of the half-circle booth as he blows out smoke. There's a cut on his head just visible behind a lock of hair and a bruise on his cheek. At least no one was killed in the accident.

"But I can replace you," I say.

"With yourself?" He grins. "You won't."

I don't want to. But…

"I want it more than I do leaving you in charge," I retort. "How many kids are selling your drugs?"

He pauses, and I take the chance. "What have you done that I don't have the guts to do?"

The guys around him sit still, but wait for his instruction, and I feel the hair on my arms rise as my phone records. *Say something. Just one boast.* I only need one piece of leverage.

But he looks over my head, gesturing someone over. I'm about to turn, but a girl appears at my side a moment later. A young woman with coppery red hair, dressed in a blue-sequined infinity slinga. She's hanging out everywhere, her ass glowing with oil.

"This is Peridot." Hugo blows out another puff of smoke. "Named after her birthstone."

I look away from her but keep my fucking chin up.

"She can give you a black eye with them tits," he taunts, smiling at me.

He's fucking with me. Drew used to do the same thing. Drop a line and see if I'd bite. I always thought it was because he wanted a friend to go down the rabbit hole with. Maybe he'd feel less sleazy if I did it too.

Now I know…he wanted *me* to feel sleazy. He wanted me to look in the mirror and see him. He hated me.

"Let her dance for you," Hugo tells me as my phone vibrates, "and I'll give you anything you want."

"Like Reeves's location?" I fire back, ignoring a call from Isobel.

A slow smile curls his lips, and he shrugs. "Sure." Hugo announces to his crew, "Hear me, boys? My word is gold."

"Yep," one of them concurs.

Yeah, right.

Before I know it, she's in front of me, holding my shoulder for support as she starts to come down into my lap.

Fuck.

I freeze, the moment hitting me like a car. The memory of Quinn's lips over my forehead—like a ghost—cooks my muscles until they're burning, and I shoot up, pushing her off.

No.

I'm not playing these fucking games.

The whole table erupts into laughter as Isobel's name flashes on the screen again, and I do everything to stand tall and not give away that my pulse is racing. The young woman retreats a few steps as my phone vibrates, her eyes flitting between me and her boss.

Hugo chuckles, pleased with himself for calling my bluff as he takes another drag of his cigarette. "This is my family for a reason. You could never replace me."

Yeah, no shit.

I'd never want to be him.

But the word family keeps turning over in my head.

My family, he'd said.

Your family is your strength.

They all stare at me, probably waiting for my next move, but I stare at the call continuing to come in.

My family.

"I'll be in touch," I murmur to them, backing away. "Tonight."

And I spin around, heading out of the club and hearing Farrow on my heels. "I need to check on Quinn," I call back to him.

"Stay in Shelburne Falls," he warns. "River's going to surge tonight."

I nod, not turning back. I don't want to lose my train of thought.

Leaving him behind, I jump into the car and speed away, kicking up gravel as I drive out of the parking lot.

Drew got to me by threatening those close to me. Maybe Hugo isn't the way in. He's only powerful by the grace of those around him. His family is the way in.

I'm going about this the wrong way. Quinn was right.

My cell lights up on the seat next to me. Swiping it up, I answer, but Isobel speaks before I have a chance. "When the call goes to voicemail that fast, then I know you're 'ignoring' it."

"Sorry." I shift into high gear. "I can't talk about work right now."

"It's not about work," she replies. "You told me to do some research."

I go still. *Right.*

"Did you find something?" Equal parts excitement and dread course through me. "Something on Hugo Navarre or Drew Reeves?" I ask, hopeful.

I'd asked her to look up Madoc, Jared, and Jax, as well. I didn't want her to find anything, though.

"Actually," she tells me. "I found something on you."

Oh, what the fuck... What now?

I'm too exhausted with worry at this point to muster much of a reaction. What could she have possibly found?

"Do you have a Ruger?" she asks.

The muscles leave my arms, and the car swerves. I quickly jerk it back into place. "The rifle?" I blurt out. "No."

Guns? Is she saying my name is being mentioned with firearms somewhere?

"Do you have an AR-15?" she presses.

"What the hell are you talking about?"

I don't mean to shout at her, but now I'm worried.

"Yeah, I've never known you to be an enthusiast," she goes on, "so that's what caught my eye. There are six firearms registered in your name at the address 8 Green Street."

"What?!" I shout.

Weapons? Are they just registered, or are they the subject of police investigations?

That son of a bitch! Drew either registered them under me to frame me for something else, or he wanted weapons that wouldn't be confiscated if he was arrested. I knew he had some. I remember the gun cabinet upstairs where he stored them. I just had no idea he put anything in my name. Did he do it before I left?

"I'll get in touch with a lawyer there," she tells me. "They'll want to have you file a police report."

But that black gun cabinet at Green Street lurks in my head, my memory stirring.

The ammo boxes...

"Wait," I say.

There was one green bullet case. It had a black handle. He didn't store bullets in it, though.

And then it all comes back to me.

Shit. It might still be there. In that cabinet. He would believe it was safe there while he was on the run.

I blink, shaking my head. "Yes," I tell her, changing my mind. "Go ahead. Tell them to call me tomorrow."

I need tonight.

"Is there anything else I can do?"

I'm almost at Frosted, but I need to make sure. "They haven't been used in any crimes, right?"

"Not that I know of."

Thank God.

I swallow. "I'll talk to you later."

We hang up, and I coast into the center of town in less than two minutes.

Your family is your strength. Good job, Isobel. Who knows what I could've accomplished if I'd asked for help eight years ago.

Quinn is going to love hearing I was wrong.

Leaves spin in little cyclones in the empty street, and a couple of businesses glow with light. But most are still quiet. My tires screech as I halt in front of her place, and I charge out of the car, across the sidewalk, and grab the door handle. I jiggle it, seeing her moving in the kitchen, unaware of me.

Rounding the building, I walk into the alleyway behind her business and find the back door locked as well.

I pound on the steel. "Quinn!"

"Fuck off!"

I cock my brow. At least she's not ignoring me.

Glancing to my right, I spot a small pile of cinderblocks. Hauling one up, I bring it down like a hammer on her door handle, the small piece loosening from its bolts.

Her frustrated scream carries through the door because she knows what I'm doing.

Slamming down the block again, I watch as the handle nearly pops off, dangling. I'll get someone to fix it in the morning. I won't be leaving her till then anyway.

Dropping the block, I pull off my T-shirt, thread it around the handle, and pull as hard as I can until the damn thing snaps off. Sticking my fingers in the hole, I open the door and barge inside.

"Get out!" she bellows, her whole body rigid.

I walk right up to her, breathing hard. "No," I gasp.

She moves to shove me in the chest, but I circle her waist and pull her in, just holding her to me. Just letting her feel me and my heart beat.

"You were right," I whisper over her lips. "Okay? You were right."

"It's too late," she cries. "I'm tired of you."

I take her into my arms, sliding my hand up the back of her scalp. "I'm nowhere near tired of you yet," I say desperately.

I cut off her whimper with my mouth, kissing her and relishing the feel of her body plastered to mine. My eyes sting behind my lids, every drop of blood under my skin boiling. Every inch of my body hums with the feel of her.

For so long, nothing felt whole. Not me. Not anything. She was always mine, first to protect and now to take, and my only place is with her.

"You were right," I breathe out again.

She moans as I trail my lips down her neck, clenching her hair in my fist, lightly biting and licking her throat, her jaw, her earlobes...

I kiss away her tears, feeling her soften. "Quinn," I beg, pressing my forehead to hers.

In seconds, I have her shirt pulled off, her bra on the floor, and her shorts unbuttoned.

Lifting her, I wrap her legs around my waist and carry her into the shopfront. We quickly draw the blinds, and I tug her panties down below her ass as I suck on a breast.

She digs her nails into my chest. "I hate you," she sighs. "I really do hate you."

I brush my lips over her flesh. "I don't think so, baby." Then, I go for her mouth. "I'm the one you want."

"You're practice," she taunts, the sadness leaving her voice as she gives me the attitude I absolutely deserve. "I want you to be the first to come on my tongue."

I dig my fingers into her ass, peering up at her. *The first? Is that so?*

Dropping her feet to the floor, I hold her eyes as I unfasten my pants, lower my ass to a chair, and tug her down. Pulling my cock out, I watch her stare at it, already hard as I wrap my hand around the shaft.

Lifting her gaze to mine, she drags her tongue up the underside of my cock, and I move my hand, letting my chest cave as she teases me.

I groan, "Fuck."

Warmth covers me, coating my length as her mouth sinks down on me, taking me in slow and tight.

I tremble, letting my head fall back and my eyes close as she fits me almost entirely inside, taking her time and enveloping me in wet heat. Holding her face, I rub my thumb across her cheekbone, my heart nearly stopping when she pulls back, dragging her tongue up the underside once again. She comes down, and back up, down, and back up, wrapping her hand around the base when I grow too big for her mouth.

Sweat dampens my chest, and I run my hand through my hair, opening my eyes again to watch her.

But first, I catch our reflection in the mirror, my chair facing it. On all fours, her knees pressed to the ground as if she's crawling to me, and her panties right where I put them, below her ass. I close my fingers in her hair, craving to have my mouth between her legs too.

I watch her head bob up and down on me, not thinking I can get any harder, but I hear a little moan when I swell more.

My phone rings, both of us jolting, but I don't even think of answering. Nothing is that important.

She takes my cock, holding it in her hand as she licks it up and down, before sucking on the head. "Answer it," she pants.

"Not now."

"Number one," she tells me. "Answer it."

I remember her list, but I can't remember what all the wishes were. Fumbling, I take the phone out of my pocket and see Jared's name.

Oh, fuck no.

"Answer it," she teases.

I grunt, feeling her sink down on my dick, taking me into her mouth again. *Yes, okay. Anything.*

I swipe the screen and hold the phone to my ear. "Let me guess," I say, sounding out of breath but I can't help it. "You want to play racquetball?"

"Wise ass," Jared grumbles. "Have you seen Quinn?"

I start to break out in a full-on sweat as his sister's mischievous eyes hold mine. Her soft, supple lips suck my cock, the tip of her tongue dipping out to play with me.

My eyes roll into the back of my fucking head.

"I...um." I clear my throat. "I think she's at Frosted."

"Do me a favor and check," he says. "My calls aren't going through."

Thank God he didn't just decide to come check himself. Fuck! The back door is wide open.

"Madoc's sending out an advisory today," he tells me. "Everyone should stay in. There'll be flash floods, and I want her home."

She must've left her phone in the hideout.

She kneads my thighs through my pants, her whole body moving in and out as she sucks me. I'm mesmerized, watching her in the mirror.

I close my fist in her hair again. Everyone's staying home today?

I have all day to fuck her now.

"I'll make sure she's safe," I grunt.

And I pull her down on me, thrusting up into her mouth. The zap of an electric current coasts through my body. *Yeah, baby*, I mouth.

"Tell her to call me when she's home," he orders.

I smile. "Will do."

We hang up, and I toss my phone onto the table.

My body blazes. I need more than her mouth. I need her in my hands and her flesh between my teeth.

"You're mine." I force her eyes up to me, even with my dick in her mouth. "I make sure you're safe."

No one else.

She nods. "Yeah."

"Scream it."

"Yes," she calls out.

I grab her, pulling her up. "Be loud, baby. I'm sick of being quiet."

I force her panties down her legs and turn her around.

"Get in my lap."

I pull her ass down, her spine pressed to my chest and turn her mouth to the side so I can kiss her. Looking into the mirror, I can't take my eyes off us. My hand slips between her legs, rubbing her clit, and her nipples are so hard and begging to be touched.

Digging out a condom, I rip open the package and slide it on with my other hand. She sits up and places a hand on the table next to us for leverage. Then, she rises up, and I fit my dick inside of her. She sinks down, sheathing me in her hot little grip, and I pull the rubber band out of her hair. The blonde locks drape down her back, and I place a hand at the curve of her hip, guiding her ass in and out as she starts to fuck me.

"Yes," I gasp. "Oh, God. That feels so good."

I wish I had that fucking collar. But I improvise. Wrapping her hair around my hand like a rope, I gently and slowly tug her back, keeping the other hand on her hip. I pull her again, like a horse on reins, and she smiles, moaning as she amps up the speed, riding me.

"I'm yours." She plays with herself, her reflection in the mirror about to damn-well send me over the edge. "All yours."

Slouching back into the seat, I watch her move, her gorgeous body so beautiful when it's loving me. She won't be in fucking clothes the rest of the day.

Leaning back, she licks the corner of my mouth, and a nerve shoots from my lips to low in my stomach, making me lose control.

In two seconds, I'm on my feet and bending her over one of the tables.

She grips the edge, propped up on her elbows, and both of us watch ourselves in the mirror. There are whole rooms beyond that frame, strangers coming and going, and I don't even care if someone is watching us now.

And she doesn't seem to care, either, loving every bit of this.

She moans and cries out, the table scraping against the floor as I pick up the pace faster and faster. "I'm yours," she groans. "All yours."

I feel my orgasm coming, but I try to hold it off to wait for her.

I squeeze the flesh of her ass, still fisting her hair. "Oh, God. Fuck," I grunt.

"Harder, harder!" she yells.

"Oh, Quinn."

Her pussy squeezes my cock, our two bodies just one muscle, throbbing.

"Yes!" she cries, arching her back and jutting out her ass to take me.

We come, gasping and moaning, her eyes closed tightly as I release.

I shake, struggling to take in air while sweat drips from my body.

Coming down on her back, I rest my forehead on her spine, both of us not moving as we try to calm down.

Opening my mouth, I feel the words there. I want to say it.

Do I love her?

Or is it just post-coital euphoria?

I grab hold of her body, gripping her tightly and never wanting to be off of her.

"I still didn't taste you on my tongue."

Her sweet voice sounds faded, as if that's all the energy she has, and I rumble with a small laugh.

"A little more practice then?" I tease.

How about twenty-thousand more days? Will that be enough?

"Well, we have beds here," she says in a playful tone. "Don't we?"

I look up, meeting her eyes in the mirror to Carnival Tower.

No need to leave. That's for sure.

SHELBURNE FALLS

CHAPTER TWENTY-NINE

Lucas

The candlelight flickers across her face and mussed hair as I hold her in my arms. I don't know how much rest we got—the little moans she makes in her sleep stirring me as much as the ones she makes when she's awake.

Her lips part, she searches my eyes, and I know she wants to say something. But then she kisses me. Her mouth leaves a trail so soft and hot, I feel the goosebumps break out down my arms.

The bedroom is cool and dark, no windows in the hideout except in the great room, making it impossible to feel like it's anything but night. It feels like the world is still asleep. Or like we're the only ones on the planet.

I brush her hair, tucking it behind her ear. "I love you," I tell her.

Her naked chest presses against mine, and she trembles, her mouth opening and then closing. And for a moment, fear makes me pause.

When I was a kid, I used to carry her around as she clung to my leg. Now, she's a woman. Am I good for her?

She breaks into a smile. "Finally."

I chuckle. *Yeah, whatever.* So I'm a slow mover. In everything, I guess.

I close my eyes and tip my head back as she trails kisses across my neck, over my collarbone, and down my chest.

Her tongue darts out and teases my nipple, tugging it with her teeth.

Nerves fire, and I suck in air, laughing.

I pull her up, but as soon as I open my eyes, I spot black writing on her back. Just over her shoulder.

I tilt my head up. "What's this?"

She tries to look over but her eyes don't reach that far.

The writing is jagged and appears to be in marker. "Two-eight-eight-four," I read.

"Huh?" She sits up and tries to look over her shoulder. "What is that? Where did it come from?"

Her worried eyes jerk to me, and I launch up and examine it again.

Black numbers, the little lines looking like quick swipes as if done in a hurry. The four and last eight are slightly smeared.

There's nothing else. No other writing.

Her gaze wanders, the wheels in her head turning. "I thought..." She starts breathing harder. "I thought that was you," she tells me. "I felt fingers on my skin in the middle of the night. Or I thought they were fingers. I thought you were caressing me or something."

The sounds she was making... I thought she was asleep, but she was being touched. *Fuck.*

She chokes back a sob, the realization that someone was here—in this room, while we slept—frightening both of us. They got close enough to touch her. They could've done anything to us.

Instinctively, my fingers close around her arms, squeezing too hard. I immediately release her.

It could've been Dylan or one of the boys.

And I no sooner think it than the bedroom door flies open. Quinn snaps the covers up, and I jerk my head right, putting my arms around her.

Light pours in, Hunter standing right in the doorway.

His eyes widen. "Whoa."

"Out!" I growl.

But he looks to his side, down the hall, tensing.

Ah, shit.

Kade and Hawke rush up to his side. "What the hell?" Hawke bursts out at him.

But then he sees us.

The three of them stand there, taking in the scene, Quinn and I clearly done with whatever we were doing. Bed, a mess. Hair, a mess.

"Get out!" she cries, reaching for her clothes on the chair.

But Kade only advances on us. "You son of a bitch!"

That was directed at me. He glares, and if I weren't naked, I'm pretty sure he would've charged me. I haven't been in these guys's lives hardly at all, but I already know he's the one who's a pain in the ass.

"Kade!" Hawke barks.

I swing my legs over the side of the bed, pulling on my black pants. "Easy," I chide.

Quinn and I pull on clothes, shielded by the sheet, while Kade's the only one too angry to have the consideration to look away.

I rise, sliding my arms into my shirt. "How did you get in here?"

"You forgot to lock the mirror, I guess," Hawke tells us. He looks to Quinn and back to me. "How long has this been going on?"

"Less than two weeks, obviously," Quinn grumbles.

I almost pause to ask them if this is the first time they've been in this room in the past several hours, remembering the writing on Quinn's back.

But judging from their reactions, this is the first time any of them are seeing us in bed together.

"Are you okay?" Hawke asks her, throwing me a suspicious glance.

"I was until you all barged in!" she yelled. "Out!"

"Can't find an adult, huh?" Kade spits out at me. "You have to pick on someone half your age?"

"She's not half my age." I pull the T-shirt over my head. "And I remember seeing you flip off a twelve-year-old girl the other day?"

"She was fifteen." He scowls. "And she's not a girl. She's a little shit hellbent on pissing me off every time I turn around! You've been gone, or you would've known that."

Either way, I still don't think Madoc knows his son is treating an underage girl like a prison rival because I don't think he would like it.

"Quinn, get over here!" Kade barks.

I move, ready to stop him from talking to her like that.

"Enough," Hawke chimes in.

But Kade is a bullet. "Did he buy you that house?" he asks Quinn. "Some place to keep his dirty little secret?"

What the...?

But Hunter clamps a hand over his twin's mouth and pulls Kade back into his body. "I'm really sorry." Hunter laughs nervously. "The, uh, 'little shit' put full cans of beer inside the firewood logs he uses when he takes girls to Chimney Lock Island," he explains to us. "His blowjob turned a little painful last night."

Kade struggles under his brother's hold, fire rising in his cheeks. I drop my head so he can't see my grin.

Okay, so maybe this 'prison rival' of his can take care of herself.

But Quinn walks up. "Oh my God," she tells Kade. "Are you okay?"

He yanks Hunter's hand off his mouth. "No, I'm not okay!"

Hunter clamps his mouth shut again, his chest shaking with laughter. "He's, uh…out of commission for the rest of the summer."

I try to shake the scene out of my head, but I can't get rid of it. Firelight, the summer woods, owls hooting, and then pop! An explosion in the campfire, scaring his date, who instinctively clenches her teeth around him in fright…

I snort as I move around the bed to fan the sheets and tidy up.

"I could've died!" he screams.

But Hawke interjects, "There's no proof she was the one who did that."

Kade shoves away from Hunter, completely distracted with his rekindled anger. "I'm gonna catch her and bust her so hard, her only option to avoid prison is to join the Army!" he growls. "Either way, she leaves. Not even Green Street can protect her."

I straighten up. *Green Street?*

"That kid works for Green Street?" I ask.

The boys look at me, I glance at Quinn, and Hawke nods. "She's one of their most active little earners now."

My stomach sinks.

But Hunter clarifies, "Theft."

I clear my throat, thankful it's not dealing, or something worse.

But then an idea forms. *Theft*.

And I start to smile.

She doesn't know me, but she might enjoy Kade needing her help.

I glance to Hawke. "Call her."

"Why *should* I help you?" she asks me an hour later.

Thomasin Dietrich is her name, I'd learned. Tommy for short. She's the daughter of one of Jared's old high school rivals, Nate Dietrich.

The firehouse sits lit up behind her, across the street with Farrow's bike parked in front, and despite the heat of the night, she's dressed in black jeans, a long-sleeved black turtleneck, and gloves.

I hate that I'm here again. A bad influence to youths. If they find out she helped us...

But for a kid, she's not easy to intimidate. Arms folded over her chest, eyes stern, and not even the slightest fidget. The red tips in her long, white hair dance softly in the breeze.

"What do you want?" I broach instead.

She's a thief. Good ones don't do anything for free.

Lifting her chin, a smile sparks in her eyes. "The hat."

She looks to Quinn, holding out her hand.

My hat?

I gape at Quinn next to me.

Quinn hesitates a moment, but it comes off her head with no discussion. I watch as it floats from Quinn's hands to Tommy's, and I almost say something. It was fine when something I loved belonged to someone I loved, but I might never see it again now.

But I let it go and step toward her. "Okay, just—"

"I'm not done," she interjects as she stuffs the hat into her backpack. "Payment from everyone."

Hawke, Dylan, Hunter, and Aro loom behind me, the air suddenly thickening.

"The compass," Tommy demands without looking at me.

I lock my jaw.

"How the hell did you know about that?" Quinn asks her.

Tommy just fixes us with a bored look until I shove my hand into my pocket and stuff the compass into her palm.

She moves around the group, looking at each and every person.

To Dylan, "The jacket."

"I don't have it anymore."

"Go get it," she retorts. "We both know where it is."

Dylan barely hides her annoyance before finally jogging off down the block, and disappearing around the corner.

The jacket must be here in Weston.

Tommy continues, "Your T-shirt," she commands from Hawke before ordering from Hunter, "and your watch."

They both remove their items, Hunter sacrificing without a problem, but Hawke looks like a father who's disappointed in his kid's behavior or something as he removes his Sigma Tau T-shirt.

She fits everything into her pack, finally turning her eyes on Kade. "Your St. Thomas medal. Now."

I drop my gaze to his neck, seeing a silver piece of chain peeking out of his T-shirt. His smile is almost a snarl, and it's not reaching his eyes.

But to my surprise, he pulls it off over his head and lets it dangle in front of her. "It'll be fun getting this back," he bites out.

The corner of her mouth quirks in amusement, and she takes the medal, holding it up and making a show of admiring her new necklace.

Without moving to Aro, she zips up the backpack and puts it on.

"What do you want me to take?" she asks me.

"Nothing." I shake my head. "Just show me the best way in without getting caught."

There are five entrances—front door, garage door, basement door, side door, and fire escape—to the second level. I have no idea which ones will be the most clear, or might have security cameras at this point.

But she simply states, "It's better if I go."

"Not a chance," I fire back. "I'm not putting you in danger."

She breaks into a laugh, and I'm not sure why.

"This isn't funny," Kade growls at her behind me.

She stops laughing, looking at him like he's pathetic. "I think you're funny."

The group falls silent, and she turns to me again. "Your presence puts her in danger." She gestures to Quinn. "She lives here now, right? I'm welcome in there."

Well, my hope is that after tonight, Green Street won't be a problem for anyone living in Weston.

But…if I get seen before I want to, the plan won't be able to unfold. And then, who knows what will happen tomorrow?

I jerk my chin at the firehouse. "Is there a black metal cabinet still in the upstairs dorm?"

She hesitates a moment. "Yeah."

"There might still be an ammo case on the top shelf."

Without another word, she jets off and crosses the street.

"Wait…" I whisper-yell, and then glance around for anyone noticing. "Shit."

I watch her climb the steel stairs on the left side of the building, to the door on the second floor.

"Meet me where they are inside!" I shout in another whisper to her.

Dammit.

"I don't think we can trust her," Hunter mumbles.

"I could've told you that." Kade spit into the weeds sprouting up on the sidewalk at his side. "What's in the ammo case?" he asks me.

I hand my wallet and phone to Quinn, in case they try to confiscate anything. "Not ammo."

I don't want to get their hopes up in case the box isn't still there. First, I need to see if this works.

Leaning down, I kiss Quinn, feeling the others look away. "Don't come in," I say.

"Lucas..."

"Please just listen to me for once." I cup her face. "It's better not to involve you, and everyone who loves you will agree on this one."

Even Dylan.

"Stay out here," I tell her gently.

It's not that I'm just trying to protect her. I need to be the one to make it right.

Leaving them all shielded under the cover of trees, I cross the street, my heart pounding in my ears. It's been years since I've walked into this place.

Grabbing the same handle I installed a decade ago, now rusty from weather, I pull open the door.

Music fills the large vehicle bay where the firetrucks used to be stored, and I quickly take stock of my area. Couches sit against the walls to my left and right, tables in front of them, and chairs scattered about. The Skee-Ball alley and the basketball net are gone. Only one pool table remains.

A corner bar sits in the far right of the building, men planted on stools. A young woman—a very young woman—tends the bar.

A desk sits in the center of the room. There's plenty of space between it and me, so their crew can line up for job assignments and payments. The floor is still the same cement, and that old, dank and musty smell is only slightly overpowered by the years of cigarettes, spilled beer, and Chinese takeout.

Young people play video games, the men at the bar turn to eye me, and a round of laughter echoes from down the hallway, in the old locker room.

A woman growls. More laughter. I curl my fists.

So many new faces, but so little has changed. I'm sure they're a lot more profitable now, but Weston isn't any better off for it. There's no getting out of a system created to give you just enough to survive, but not enough to leave, and all you have to exchange for it is your reputation, your children, and sometimes, your freedom.

The hair on my arms lifts, and my clothes stick like a second skin. The adrenaline runs, making me hear the footsteps above, and even the exhale of cigarette smoke in the room ahead.

I walk, not pausing when I see a couple of the guys at the bar jump off their stools to follow me. Heading down the dark hallway, I watch it open up into a room still fitted with rusty, red lockers.

"Well, shit." Hugo blows out smoke, leaning back in his chair. "Coming to evict us?"

The men behind me filter in, ready to move on me if he gives the signal.

Three tables positioned in nearly a complete square fill the room. I flit my gaze to Farrow two seats down from Hugo, a black-haired girl standing behind him with her arms draped over his shoulders. Stacks of money cover the tables.

Glancing around, I don't recognize anyone else. Many of them are young, too young to have been around the last time I was here. But drugs are piled in front of one, and scars adorn the face of another. Guns litter the table.

"Thanks for coming to me," Hugo muses. "It makes this so much easier."

The hallway is behind me, but I know I wouldn't make it far.

I swallow. "Is Reeves here?"

He blows out another puff, narrowing his eyes. "Why would he be here?"

"I assumed you were in contact," I tell him. "He almost sacrificed you the other night."

His men glance at him, and I see his uncomfortable shift and chuckle as he drops all four legs of his chair back to the ground. "You must've been dreaming, man."

I tilt my head. If Drew isn't enlisting his aid, then they're not on the same side. Which makes Hugo even weaker.

I square my shoulders. "I know you think there's only one way out for you—death or prison," I tell him, seeing Tommy drift through a door to the left. She holds the ammo case by the handle and my chest swells with hope. "But you can leave. You can leave now with whoever wants to go with you."

I have the deed. The firehouse is mine. I'm not stopping him from vacating.

Tommy goes unnoticed, setting down the ammo box on a side table.

But Hugo just mocks me, "And why would I do that?"

Walking over, I flip open the box Tommy brought down, seeing that she's conveniently disappeared.

The Composition notebook is folded in half and squeezed inside the long box. The words on the outside are faded, but I can make out the word 'Log.'

Pulling out the book, I turn and hold it up. "Reeves kept this on the people who worked for him," I explain. "On everyone."

Farrow watches, tapping his fingers on the tabletop. He knows this threatens him too.

"It's filled with dates, times, receipts, pictures"—I fan the pages, noticing it's a lot more full than the last time I was here,—"leverage he could use on anyone he did business with. Including his employees." I pause, meeting their eyes. "He kept it in the gun cabinet upstairs because he knew you don't look beyond the end of your nose."

Reeves probably has another log somewhere, maybe more. Eight years is a lot of time to collect more dirt. But they don't know what's in this one and what's not.

"There's some really shitty stuff on you in here," I tell Hugo. He was definitely working here by the time I left. "Do you think it will matter that you were so young?"

They stare at me, some of the much older members knowing they're definitely mentioned in this book. Their crimes, but what else? Are there photos? Receipts? Texts? Cell logs? They don't know.

Hugo isn't smiling anymore. "What's to stop us from charging you right now?"

"You mean, do I have a digital copy somewhere?" I taunt.

He could attack me, take the notebook...

Or...

Taking the lighter off the table in front of one of his guys, I flick it and hold it up, letting the flame catch on the corner of the book.

In a moment, it goes up in flames, and I drop it into a waste bin, the glow rising up the sides.

"That was stupid," Hugo remarks.

But I shrug. "I think some of the men around you wouldn't agree because they know you would've taken it and used it to control them."

I wait for anyone to refute me, argue, pronounce their loyalty to Hugo... But the room stays silent.

"I'm not kicking you out," I tell him. "I'm giving Green Street to Farrow." I stop addressing their boss as I order the men instead. "If he leaves right now."

And I point to Hugo.

He shoots up from his seat. "Fuck you."

The real questions come now. Do they like the idea of Farrow more than Hugo? If they know who Farrow's father is, that could work very much in our favor.

"Take him out back," Hugo barks. "Put him in the car."

No one moves.

"I said put him in the car!"

I wait for one of his men to seize me. One of them will. Someone will be too scared to disobey.

But before anyone rises, a woman on my far right, and another seated next to one of the guys...moves to Farrow.

Hugo looks back and forth before one by one, all of his guys continue to stay in their seats, ignoring his orders.

Farrow lowers his eyes, but I see the smile because whoever controls the women controls Weston. Hugo was right about that.

I don't want him to die. I just hope he has the wisdom to know when to cut his losses.

A knock hits the open door behind me, and a kid walks in. "Package at the door."

He holds up a large manila envelope.

"Who left it?" Hugo demands.

"Didn't recognize him." The kid stands next to me.

"Open it."

The kid, maybe fifteen, rips open the envelope. He pulls out a piece of paper and reads silently, his face falling before he stammers out the words:

"To...to Weston,

Do what Lucas Morrow says, and the contents of the locker is yours.

He has the combination.

-Manas Doran."

And he tips the envelope upside down and catches a copper plate. I pry it out of his grip and examine it, seeing that numbers have been sanded off.

Manas Doran. The story Quinn told me. How does he know what's happening right now?

And what combination am I supposed to know? And what locker?

Then, it hits me. The numbers on Quinn's back. *Two-eight-eight-four*. Oh, fuck.

I scan the room behind the tables, seeing all the numbers are in the one thousands. It's not one of these lockers. Maybe a storage unit?

I start to back away, leaving the room.

"Get back here," Hugo shouts and then orders his men, "Grab him! We'll fucking get it out of you."

They don't budge, and I realize they're waiting for Farrow's orders.

"It's not about the money, Hugo," I tell him. "No one here will go against them."

No one here will go against the Doran brothers. I don't know if it's fear or respect, but their history is a central part of Weston's identity.

I look to Farrow as I turn around to leave. "Clean house." I nod once. "You have an hour."

WESTON

CHAPTER THIRTY

Quinn

"It's been too long," Kade says. "I don't like this."

Everyone's eyes are pinned to the firehouse.

I stand a few feet away from them, my hands in front of me as I remind myself to breathe.

If he gets himself killed…

Tears well in my eyes, and I can't even imagine how he's going to come out of this in one piece. Is Farrow in there? Would he back Lucas up? *God, please be okay.*

I stare at the door, waiting for any shadow to pass by the glass block windows. Any commotion. Or a bellow or a gunshot.

I lock my jaw, anger making the heat rise on my cheeks. If he still thinks he doesn't need his family at his back, then what do I care? He hasn't changed. Still just as stubborn and irresponsible and—

Squeezing my eyes shut, I blow out a quiet breath, reeling myself in. He's going to be okay. He has to be.

And just as I open my eyes, Lucas emerges from the firehouse on his own two legs—alive. I suck in a breath, holding back a sob.

Fuck, thank you, God.

With one hand around Tommy's upper arm, he marches her out, glancing behind him and keeping his eyes peeled. He strides across the street as she pries herself out of his hold and charges away. I shift on my feet, and he must see the look on my face because he wraps his arms around me as he buries his face in my neck.

I squeeze him. Fire courses down my arms, and I can't unball my fists, but I'm enjoying hugging him too much to hit him.

Tucking me under his arm, he walks us to the others, Dylan, Aro, Kade, and Hunter crowding around Hawke.

"What happened?" Kade demands.

"It's Farrow's." Lucas nods. "I gave the firehouse to Farrow. We'll have to wait and see if Hugo abides."

"No one even got hit?" Kade gripes.

Well, there's still time, moron. I can't imagine Lucas *or* Farrow can take anything without some force.

I look up at Lucas. "Are we in danger here?"

He places his fingers under my chin. "We stay together for now."

But where? We'd be safest at my parents' or Madoc's, but that might mean alerting them to the trouble.

"Why did you give it to Farrow?"

Glancing at Aro, I see her brow strained as she glowers.

He simply shakes his head. "Because the community relies on it. We need an infrastructure in place before we take away any means they have to support themselves."

But she presses, "You shouldn't have done that."

"It was a gamble."

Definitely.

For Lucas's sake, the ideal thing to do would be to end it, but he's probably right. Transition to phasing it out would be less detrimental to the people who rely on it for income. If it dissolved abruptly, the most vulnerable would suffer.

"One step at a time," he tells her.

But the worried look on Aro's face remains.

Lucas leads us down the curb to our cars. "Did you guys see someone outside the club, dropping off an envelope?" he asks, unlocking the doors of the Mustang.

Hawke replies, "A man handed the doorman something and left."

"Didn't see his face," Dylan adds. "Why?"

Lucas opens my car door for me. "Let's go," he tells everyone, ignoring the question. "We need to check something out."

I climb in as everyone scatters to their cars, and Lucas starts the engine, pulling away. Tommy is gone, and I twist my neck, searching the street for her. If they know she helped us, she might not be safe, either.

Lucas leads the way through the warehouse district, up into the hills, and around Weston High School. He doesn't offer any information, and I don't know why. Are we in danger?

I peer over at him. "Who was the man who dropped off the envelope?"

We didn't think much of some lonely guy on foot, Green Street probably having all sorts of people filtering in and out of the place every day. But now that I think about it, there was something about him. The fit of his brown leather jacket. The cut of his hair peeking out of his hood. As if the clothes were tailored to him. It's not how most people look, except for men like Madoc and only men like Jared and Jax, because their wives pick their clothes.

"I'm not sure," he says in a breathy voice. "I need to see something first."

He drives over the weeds that have sprouted up through the broken road, and it looks like a lot is happening in his head, but I don't give a shit. He can be quiet, just not with me.

"What happened in there?" I demand.

"It's still happening."

I growl, "Lucas."

Dammit. What the hell is going on?

"I transferred control of the building to Farrow," he finally blurts out. "It's not over yet, but I can help him."

"How?"

Why Farrow? Is that safe? And how did Lucas manage that? How are we going to help him?

I'm about to press for details, but we pass through an open, rusty gate hanging off its hinges. Rows of low buildings appear ahead in the darkness, and he pulls up closer, his headlights illuminating the large doors. Where are we?

Headlights from the others' cars reflect in our mirrors. I lean in closer to the windshield, avoiding the glare and taking in the sight before me.

Storage units?

I had no idea these were here. Dark brown structures with burgundy-colored garage-style doors, some of them are open and empty. Others are closed and still locked. Some sit exposed with boxes or pieces of furniture abandoned inside as if they've been raided.

Pulling my collar back, he checks the numbers on the back of my shoulder again and continues around the corner. Everyone follows slowly behind until Lucas stops in front of number twenty-two. My heart pounds harder as I stare up at the stickers of the two twos, faded from years of sun and weather.

I study the back of my shoulder again. *Two-eight-eight-four*. I lock my gaze on the combination padlock still securing the unit's door.

I shiver, thinking about whoever wrote it on me last night.

Lucas swings open his door, and I don't wait, quickly stepping out of the car too.

"What is this?" Hawke asks, everyone piling in to see what's inside.

Without replying, Lucas dials in the numbers, the shackle clicking free, and my breathing speeds up.

Is this his unit?

Wait, no. He would've had the combination already. Two-eight-eight-four adds up to twenty-two, the unit number.

Does it belong to Green Street? My brain swims with all the stuff that could be in there. Are we sure we want to know?

But as Lucas lifts the door, phones start lighting up as everyone brings up their flashlights. We all inch inside, my eyes trying to focus on everything at once.

My gaze registers a wardrobe, then flits to a trunk, tables, lamps, chairs, a piano, carpets, a mirror, books, statues, suitcases, paintings...quickly assessing what's dangerous and what's not. No weapons, no bodies, but plenty of storage for them. Eyeing the wardrobe again, I wander inside the unit, all of us spreading out to investigate the pieces. Turning the handle, I try to pry the door open, but can only get it cracked enough to see a sliver inside. *Dresses*.

Kade climbs onto a chair and checks out behind a tall bed frame, while Dylan and Aro flip through a photo album, and the others inspect various boxes and antiques.

Something feels off. If this belongs to the Dorans—or Winslet—it doesn't seem like it belongs here. The furniture is antique, the art dramatic, and the pieces too ornate. It's not the style of most residents in this region—blue-collar workers, farmers, and middle Americans.

I draw in air through my nose, the scent triggering a memory.

Wet, aged wood, musty like an old building.

I take in more air, noticing a subtle hint of jasmine, gardenias, coffee, rain, and sweet liquor all mixed together to create a scent cooked in humidity that I've only smelled once before in the only place in the world it can be made. *New Orleans.*

"It was Manas Doran," Lucas says, fanning a file folder. "The man who left the envelope at the door."

I come to his side, scanning the ownership documents to several properties, all located in Weston. I grab a picture of one young man and twin boys with a woman, whom I assume is their mother. I look at the back, reading *Conor, Deacon, Manas, and Mom.*

"They're watching," Lucas tells us. "They're listening."

"Why were they following us, though?" I ask. "In the Dodge? Trying to scare us if they're giving all of this to us?"

But he shakes his head, looking at me. "It wasn't them following us."

He still doesn't believe me. He thinks it's someone else. Maybe Reeves.

"And they're giving this to Weston," Lucas clarifies. "Not us, not Farrow, but to be used for the town."

"How much is in here?" Aro asks anyone who has a guess.

Hawke just ponders. "Hard to say. Maybe a few thousand. Maybe a few hundred thousand."

Anything would help Weston, but we need an appraiser to look at the furniture. And the dresses and the paintings. I'm not hopeful, though. If any of this was valuable, they wouldn't have left it in a non-temperature-controlled unit without more security.

"Catalog it." Lucas studies the documents, continuing to tell Hawke and the rest, "Take whatever pictures and keepsakes you want for your research. The rest we sell."

Lucas slips a pile of papers to Hawke that he's pulled from the file. "And we sell these too."

My nephew takes them, and I peer over, noticing they're deeds.

"Why would they own parcels of land up and down the river, in various towns?" he questions, studying the papers. "For farms? A flood wall?"

"Fallon told me that ComVista, Inc. and East Labs wanted land to create a railway corridor," Lucas tells him. "The government was interested too. I think the Doran brothers stockpiled real estate when it had little value to sell as a whole for train tracks."

He blinks. "Shit. That's brilliant."

"That's a hundred grand an acre," Lucas states.

Millions of dollars. That they're giving to rebuild Weston.

"And if one of the hubs on the corridor ends up being here?" Hawke's eyes gleam.

Meaning one of the railway stops?

Lucas grins. "Now you're thinking like them."

The hair on my scalp tries to stand up. It would mean jobs, factories, hotels, restaurants... It would completely resurrect Weston.

And everyone seems to understand the same thing, because no one speaks as we imagine the possibilities.

Lucas holds my hand on the drive back to my house, the convoy behind us splitting off and returning to the Falls, everyone sworn to secrecy. Helping me out of the car, he doesn't let go, looking around at the people on Knock Hill, who are drinking on porches, and we both take notice of another damn party coming from Farrow's place. He must be back already.

Young men tip their chins at Lucas, but he pulls me inside as quickly as possible.

Locking the door, he brings up the app and loads all of the cameras on his phone, but I leave the lights off and hold him.

Dragging my mouth up his neck and grazing his jaw, I exhale hard. I'm so glad he's safe.

He threads his fingers through the back of my hair, fisting them as he hovers over my mouth. "I need to call your father tomorrow. And talk to your brothers."

"I know." I nod, dying for a kiss. "Can you take Noah and Farrow with you? And my nieces and nephews? Jared and Jax have the strength of three men each when they're ready to kill someone, and Madoc could be armed."

He almost laughs. "I'll face them like a damned grown-up, otherwise I don't deserve you."

Sliding my hands up his shirt, I whisper, "I don't want to talk about them tonight."

I just want to curl up into him and catch my breath.

I turn and take his hand, pulling him toward the stairs, but he yanks me back.

I laugh, crashing back into his chest, but just then, a silver chain collar appears, dangling in front of my face. My mouth falls open. Did he have that on him?

"Ready for number seven?" He hooks it around my neck, the long leash cold against my back.

I close my eyes, moaning as he tugs a little and presses his cock into my ass. "Yes," I breathe out.

"What's number seven?"

I pop my eyes open. My spine stiffening, I feel Lucas do the same behind me at the sound of the stern voice.

Madoc strolls around the corner from the kitchen, Jared and Jax following as they cross the living room and enter the foyer with us.

Lucas unhooks the chain and steps in front of me. "Madoc."

I peer around him, seeing Jared's fists balled at his side, his eyes on fire.

"What are you doing here?" I blurt out.

Madoc growls at me, "We're not ready to talk to you yet because you're just going to double-down." Then he steps toe-to-toe with Lucas. "You know why? Because she's twenty-one years old. She's a kid."

I push around Lucas. "I'm not a kid!"

"He can speak for himself!" Madoc turns red.

I suck in a breath, Madoc's howl something I've never really heard before.

"If he dares," Madoc bites out.

I dart my eyes to Lucas, seeing the pain on his face. The pinch between his brows and the...shame in the way he looks down for a moment. He would rather die than have Madoc hate him. How can my brother talk to him like that? My chin trembles.

"Was this your idea?" Madoc charges, glaring at him. "A place of her own where you could seduce her away from her family?"

"Oh, come on, man," Lucas explains. "It's not like that."

"I'll tell you what it is like." Madoc is almost spitting out his words. "She idolized you. Idolized an idea of you so much that she never entertained anyone else. She was in love with a dream!"

I can't help it. The tears spill. If he gets in Lucas's head...

Madoc continues, "And she's going to give her life to you until you realize she's too young and too devoted to someone who's a figment of her imagination. All because you were horny."

"I would never use Quinn like that!"

"You left for eight fucking years because this place wasn't good enough for you!" Madoc rails. "What's changed?"

Lucas's tone turns solemn. "That's not why I left."

But my brothers aren't listening. "I never thought you'd do something like this. You're gonna hurt her," Madoc tells him, "because you have nothing in common with someone just beginning their life."

Lucas falls silent, and I look at him, waiting for him to fight back. Nausea racks my body.

He's not going to hurt me. Lucas knows that. He's not going to leave me.

I frown at Madoc. "Don't talk to him like that."

But my brother doesn't even know I'm here anymore. He tells Lucas, "I have no fucking clue who you are anymore. I'm at a loss."

Pain hits Lucas's eyes, and I'm about to kick them out. Call Farrow and have him get them out of here, I don't know.

But Lucas turns his gaze on me, and I have to hold back the sob in my throat as a crushing feeling hits me. That he thinks there's no way out of this, and Madoc will hate him forever, and everything is ruined.

A knock lands on the front door, and it takes a moment for anyone to move. Jax finally goes over and opens it.

"Is Lucas Morrow here?" a hard voice asks.

We look over, seeing Shelburne Falls police officers standing on my porch. People loiter in the street below, watching.

Jax looks back at us, and the first cop walks in, addressing Lucas. "Mr. Morrow, you're under arrest for the murder of David Miller." Both cops approach. "You need to come with us."

The first one—I think his name is Jesse Stevens—pulls out handcuffs.

I shake my head. "No."

Madoc's eyes shift from anger to confusion. "What the hell's going on?" he barks.

A fist tightens around my lungs as the officer places Lucas's arms behind his back and fits the cuffs on his wrists. "You have the right to remain silent..." the officer reads him his rights as commotion immediately ensues outside. People start yelling for Farrow, and my brothers move, looking like they're not sure if they need to stop this or get on their phones.

"Quinn?" Madoc looks to me, his eyes suddenly filled with worry and fear.

"Sir, please step aside," Stevens tells his mayor as he walks Lucas out.

"Lucas!" I call as he's ripped from my arms.

"What the fuck is going on?" Jared blusters as Jax jumps on his phone.

I run down the steps after Lucas, but he glances back at Madoc. "Take her home." He gestures to me. "It's not safe here."

I shake my head. *Like hell*. I'm not going anywhere with my brothers after what they just did.

"Hey, leave him alone!" someone calls out.

They lead Lucas to their police car.

"He didn't do it," someone else shouts. "I did it."

"Nah, it was me!" another voice chimes in.

The officers stop, looking around at the Rebel crowd.

"Anyone else we need to bring in while we're here?" they ask Lucas.

But he just shakes his head. "No."

Farrow runs up, but a cop holds out his hand, pointing a finger in his face as a warning.

"Quinn won't go with Madoc," Lucas tells him. "Stay close."

"Don't worry about anything," Farrow tells him.

Lucas stops at the open door of the cop car. Tall with his chin up, he peers back at Madoc.

Then, he looks at me.

I love you, he mouths.

And then he disappears into the car, gone in seconds.

SHELBURNE FALLS

CHAPTER THIRTY-ONE

Madoc

The heat that made my brain feel like it was on fire an hour ago has moved into my chest, anger now replaced with fear.

My God, this was why he left eight years ago. I stare at myself in the bathroom mirror, phones ringing out in the police station where damn-near our whole fucking family sits and waits. The water I'd splashed on my face drips off my skin, back into the sink.

How did I not know that something was wrong?

I mean, I knew something was wrong. Why didn't I press him? Chase him down? Stop him from running? Bring him back?

Why was it so easy to believe he was just some kid being rebellious? I did everything I could to escape my house—my pain—when I was younger, how did I not see that he was doing the same damn thing?

Shit, part of me even thought I'd been suffocating him and he just needed space. I wasn't his dad, and I started to wonder if he was sick of us.

"Jared, Jax..." I spit out at myself in the mirror. "Their kids are no trouble. Why don't mine just fucking talk to me?"

Tears spring up, and I bow my head, gripping the sink. Shame replaces the fear. I'm not built for self-pity. I clear my throat and grab some paper towels, wiping my face clean.

"James is definitely going to fuck with Jared someday." I fix my hair, being more realistic now. "Dylan already nearly gave him a heart attack. That was funny. And Hawke is a late bloomer. There's still time for him to be a hassle to Jax."

I won't be the only one trying to wrangle my damn kids.

Balling up the paper towel, I stuff it into the basket and whip open the door. Fallon turns, her arms crossed over her chest, as Tate, Jared, Jax, and Juliet all look up at me. Bypassing them, I head to the counter and pick up Lucas's statement, continuing where I left off.

He made friends...they started Green Street as a social club...Drew Reeves took over and moved in a direction Lucas and Lance couldn't follow...Lucas refused to give him the building...wanted it shut down...

And I get to the part where Lucas gave him a dare that backfired. Reeves hid a half-alive man in the trunk, and Lucas sank the car, not realizing someone was in there.

I skim over why Lucas felt he couldn't come forward. Reeves, with his position in Shelburne Falls, could hurt Lucas and those he loved.

Tracing my memories, I can't figure out what was going on in my life at that time. What was I doing the night this all happened? What the fuck was so important all the months later as he struggled to keep his head above water with the guilt and I didn't notice?

Hands touch my shoulders, and I turn, Fallon's arms circling my neck.

Barry and two other officers are in Weston, questioning Green Street and...collecting the remains.

"Should we call Grace?" Fallon asks in my ear.

"No."

I pull back. Lucas's mother needs to know what the plan is before she hears about the problem. Grace can handle it, but she'll panic. Just like I am now. One thing at a time.

"I need to go talk to him first."

She nods and backs away, and I gesture to Sam Barnes, the officer on duty. She tips her head for me to follow.

I start after her, but Jax stops me. "He's a better man than me," he says as if I need assurances. "They'll never find the bodies I buried in the woods."

I swallow at the reminder of Jax's justice back in the day. It's not even remotely the same thing. For him, it was self-defense, and he didn't owe anyone a proper burial.

I follow Sam back to the cells and pass an empty one before getting to Lucas standing alone in the far corner. Barry hasn't formally charged him. Just holding him until he can question witnesses. Lucas is cooperating.

Sam leaves, closing the door behind her, and I look at the kid I've known for well over half our lives.

Standing tall, his arms crossed over his chest.

Just like Fallon, he doesn't look away.

I close the distance between me and the bars. "Why didn't you tell me?"

He hesitates as he gazes at me. "Because you would've tried to fix it and put yourself in the line of fire instead."

Reeves had his thugs crash my son's party a couple of years ago, looking for my laptop. His enterprise must've been getting massive, and he wanted to ensure he could blackmail me if—when—it spilled over into the Falls and I tried to stop him.

There was nothing to hide, but I'm sure he would've found something to twist to his benefit.

"And when Hawke sent Reeves running from Shelburne Falls two years ago?" I charge. "You must've heard. Why didn't you come back then?"

Lucas flexes his jaw, and I don't know if he's struggling to tell me something, or just doesn't have an answer.

My nose nearly brushes the bars. "You're my family," I huff. "Whether you think of me as yours or not."

He looks away for a moment.

"You're my family," I state again, "and we would've gotten through it. Running is never the answer—"

He squares his shoulders, blurting it out. "I didn't want you to know."

What?

Why? He knew what Jax had done. He knew about mine and Jared's mistakes. Did he think we weren't up for it?

I narrow my eyes. "Lucas—"

"Look, I know, okay?" he cuts me off. "'I was never a job and you never expected me to be perfect…' I know everything you would've said, but you would've said it because you cared about me." The tendon in his neck flexes, and I can tell he's trying to steady his voice. "It wouldn't have changed the fact that dealing with my mistakes could've hurt you, and me not being able to own up to it buried two miles away in the woods was killing me. So I left."

Reeves had him thinking he was trapped.

"My mood was hurting my mother," he continued. "I didn't deserve to be around Quinn. What if the web got bigger? What if I made another serious mistake?" His eyes redden. "I didn't trust myself anymore."

And I didn't know what to say. That feeling is easy to muster when you're young. You haven't made enough mistakes to know there will be a hundred more before your life is over.

"That's why you wanted to leave the moment you got here," I say, my voice gravelly.

He nods slowly. "The new leadership at Green Street wanted me gone. They believed a founding member with a deed to the property threatened them."

He was supposed to be on the plane back to Dubai over a week ago.

I don't blink. "And Quinn was why you stayed."

He can't stop the smile that starts to form as he drops his eyes to the floor. "I just wanted to protect her at first," he tells me. "Noah Van der Berg and Farrow Kelly were pissing me off." He laughs a little. "I remembered how good it was to have her around. And I wasn't about to leave her alone to make all the mistakes she was begging to." He raises his eyes to me. "But the way she looks at the world, Madoc... I was..."

His chin trembles, and I have a lot to unpack right now. Not only his future but hers.

But there's one thing he doesn't have to say out loud. He's in love with her.

"And if you go to jail?" I press. "You covered up a crime. You own a building used for mob business."

I know he handled the arrangements to have the body buried once the police are done, and something happened with Hugo Navarre. The cops got word that his own people ran him out of town this evening. He could be back, but he's gone now. Was that Lucas's doing?

Between that and what Kade told us, Lucas has been getting everything taken care of in case he had to go away.

But his tone is soft and calm. "I love her, and I told her. And now, I just want you to be proud of me again, even if it takes fifty years."

My eyes burn, and I drop my gaze, not sure how to respond. How could he think I wouldn't be proud of him?

But even as I think it, the disappointment of hearing him with Quinn at her house earlier—and then seeing them together—still lingers. I knew all the years I helped raise him that he was a good man, but that threw me.

We would've handled Drew Reeves together. Quinn, though…

God, I love him, but he hid from me for years. Is he going to leave again? Does he really love her, or is she an anchor?

"Drew Reeves is around," he tells me. "You need Hawke and Jax to be monitoring cameras. In Weston, as well." He hesitates, then levels me with a calm stare. "Quinn won't leave her house, but my phone is linked to the cameras installed around her property. The cops have my cell. The code is 1793."

I swallow hard, realization dawning that a lot has been going on that I didn't know about. He put cameras up outside her new house? I wouldn't have thought of that. I need to get his phone back.

"I've already contacted a lawyer," he says. "They're on their way."

WESTON

CHAPTER THIRTY-TWO

Quinn

Lucas seemed so calm. In handcuffs and more relaxed than he's been since he's been home. I guess there's relief in it all being over. No more secrets. No more dread over whether people will find out.

But what happens next has opened a new level of worry.

Everyone stands in my living room, watching me pace across the decrepit foyer. I look at my phone again.

It's only been an hour since he was arrested and all the cops took their bright lights out of our neighborhood and back to the Falls. But it feels like it's been a year. Why isn't someone calling me? Tate, Juliet, Fallon, Jax, Jared, and Madoc are all at the station, I'm sure.

I refused to go back to the Falls like my brothers wanted. After the way they just treated Lucas and me, it felt important to stand my ground. But Madoc did make all their kids stay with me. Farrow, Mace, and Codi hang close too.

I wish they'd all go. They're eyeing me like I'm a timebomb. I'm not dangerous.

But I can't just wait here. I check my phone again. No texts. No calls.

I glance at the time, noting it's after ten.

"Who the hell turned him in?" Dylan asks the room.

A few gazes shift to Farrow, to which he cocks an eyebrow. "It wasn't me," he blurts out.

Aro says, "You're not as innocent as you would like them to think."

He bares his teeth, speaking hard and slow. "It wasn't me." He rakes his hand through his blond hair. "Maybe Hugo thought he could cause one more stir on his way out. I don't know…"

Someone tipped off the police, but it was more than that.

"They wouldn't have taken him in handcuffs without evidence," I point out. "They would've just questioned him here."

The Doran brothers seem to always be one step ahead. Then, there's Drew Reeves. I'm sure he still has a friend at the police station he can leak info to.

And how many people at Green Street know the stories? It could be anyone.

"What was in the locker?" Farrow asks the group.

"It was a little more than a locker," Hunter tells him. "It was a storage unit."

"And it's for rehabilitating the town, not for you," Aro bites out to Farrow.

He folds his arms across this chest. "I am this town, and I have more of a right to it than any of you."

Aro is from Weston, but she no longer lives here. Neither do her siblings.

But she does have friends here, so she's still invested.

"You can duke it out with Lucas." Hawke taps away on his phone, refusing to look at Farrow. "There's a reason the Doran brothers put it in *his* hands and not yours."

I'd gotten enough from Lucas on the way home earlier. Manas left a note at the firehouse. Lucas still had it on him.

I'd spoken to Deacon, but now we know… They're *both* alive, here, and continuing to keep tabs on what's happening.

Just like her.

Whoever had Lucas arrested tonight wanted him out of the way. I need to be able to move fast if there's danger.

"I want my Jeep," I say. I need my own transportation.

"I'll give you a ride," Farrow offers, walking toward me. "Lucas said to stay close to you."

Dylan picks up her crossbody purse. "We're coming with you."

"No." I pick up my keys off the little table by the door. "I'll be right back. Just stay here."

Farrow won't talk the whole time. I need to think right now.

Farrow swings the door open, letting it bang into my table as he stomps out before me. I follow, shutting the door behind me.

I climb into his truck, pulling my hair up into a ponytail as we drive off. I glance in my rearview mirror, knowing the Dodge is there before I even see it.

We coast down the hill, and I almost think no one's inside because it doesn't move from the curb.

But then…it pulls out, headlights still off as it follows us.

I don't know if Farrow sees it, but I'm not going to tell him. It's not following him.

Windows down, I lean my head back, feeling the breeze cool my scalp.

Farrow's tires roll over the drainage vents, telling me we're on the bridge, and I reach over and pick out a penny from the cup holder in Farrow's truck. He watches me fling it out the window.

I'd blown it off several times since I moved to Weston, and I don't believe that's to blame for everything wrong right now, but it certainly hasn't done me any good to ignore the tradition, so... At most, it won't even cost me four dollars a year. I'll grab some for my own supply when I close out the register tonight.

After about eight minutes of speeding, Farrow races past my Jeep sitting at the curb in front of the shop and turns down the side street.

"No!" I blurt out. "Park in the front."

I don't want him going into the alleyway.

He throws me a look.

"I have to come out that way anyway," I explain.

That's where my car is.

Plus, I don't want him to see the broken back door. He'll want to come inside, and I won't be able to get into the hideout if I need.

Making a U-turn, he drives back to High Street and pulls in behind my Jeep. I unbuckle my belt.

"I'll be right back," I tell him, opening the door and jumping out.

"He said to stay with you!"

"The place is locked," I lie, digging out my keys for the front door. "I'll bring you a Monster cookie."

"Three!" he barks.

I unlock the door and slip inside, quickly shielding myself behind the blinds as I watch the windows.

Ten seconds.

Twenty seconds.

Thirty...

The Dodge doesn't appear, and I was too lost in my head to keep an eye on it on the way here. I'm not sure when we lost it, but I know it's close. It always is.

My keys are in the kitchen, and I twist around to go grab them, but the mirror is open.

Again.

Dread coils my stomach, and I try to think. Did we leave it open?

We could have.

Or maybe Hawke came back?

But deep down, I know it's not likely. I always close it because I don't always enter the place alone. I wouldn't want Hailey, Noel, or Codi to know it's there.

And I seriously doubt Hawke would ever be that careless. He kept it a secret from me for years.

I should get Farrow, but I don't want him to know about the hideout. I'm not ready to make that decision.

I could just leave, ignore it for now.

But Manas and Deacon have helped, and they're the only other ones who have access. What if they can help Lucas?

Stepping toward the mirror, I peek inside the dark hallway, the end of it brightened to a dark gray by the faint light from the windows in the Great Room.

There are no sounds, and the smell remains the same. No one is smoking or cooking inside, that I can tell. If someone was here to hurt me, they could've just been waiting in the shop.

I take a step in and walk quietly down the hallway, the place seemingly empty.

My gaze lands on the island and my parents' love story lays open. My heart skips a beat. The book was definitely not open when I left.

Approaching the counter, I see black writing scrawled on a page.

Maybe you had it the hardest.
To be worth the price that was paid.

I understand you now.

I grab the book and flip through the rest of it, looking for more writing.
But that's it.
I study it again. ...*To be worth the price that was paid.*
Is this meant for me?
I had it the hardest? Hardest out of whom?
Pulling my phone out of my bag, I snap a picture and text it to Dylan.
She's read part of this book with me. She'll recognize it.

Found this written inside, I write.

I look around while I wait for a reply. Nothing else is disturbed from what I can see.

Dylan texts back. *We both know that writing.*

I stare at it again, remembering Winslet's diary that I passed on to Hawke.
Could it be her? I wasn't used to her writing in full sentences, but yes, the strokes are similar.
My skin crawls, feeling like I'm being watched again, but to be honest, I feel like that all the time now. If it's not Deacon Doran, it's Lucas or my brothers.

I tap out a reply to her. *Stay close to your phone.*

I want to know who's in the Dodge. If they're a danger, they sure are patient. Could they have been protecting me, maybe?

If it's one of the brothers—or her—they know Weston and Shelburne Falls. Maybe they've seen Drew Reeves too.

Carrying the book with me, I run out of Carnival Tower like someone is chasing me and close the mirror. Farrow has moved to the front of the shop, behind my Jeep, and I race to the kitchen, pulling open a drawer. Bypassing the big butcher knife, I grab a paring knife—small, pointy, efficient.

I double-check the back door is still tied shut, tuck the book under my arm, snatch up my car keys and three Monster cookies, and charge for the front of the shop again, exiting the front door.

Farrow watches me.

"I'll meet you at home!" I call out.

He peers at me through the open passenger side window. "Lucas said to stay with you!"

I toss the little bags of cookies through his window. "I'll be there."

"Lucas said to stay with you," he repeats.

I glance up and down the empty road. He's not going to let me out of his sight. What will the Dodge do if I'm alone? I need to ditch Farrow.

After hesitating a moment, I wipe the sweat above my chin and nod. "Lead the way then," I tell him.

And I walk away just as his lips part to speak, but I'm gone before he has a chance to argue. Climbing into my car, I start the engine and fasten my seatbelt.

Checking my mirrors, I see half-a-dozen cars parked along the curb around me, but none of them look suspicious. Lucas has been arrested, and this is all connected somehow. Whatever the Dodge is going to do, it'll be tonight.

Signaling, I grip the wheel and wait for him to pull out behind me. He drives past, throwing me a look as he goes.

Yeah, he's on to me.

Hitting the gas, I cruise behind him, driving up High Street, taking a right on Woodland, and a left on Fall Away Lane. The wind whips through the Jeep, making my hair fly, and I don't even have to look in my rearview. I know the car is there.

I glance, recognizing the dark windows far behind me. The shape of the car seems different—the height of the vehicle and the position of the grill—but it's too far behind me to see clearly.

But the lights are off, and it's following me. Same as always.

I punch the car up another gear, picking up the pace. I'm sick of this shit.

"Who are you?" I ask the stalker in my mirror. "Are you her?"

The words float through my mind. *Never lead danger home. Never lead it to where you're alone.*

The smell of wet soil and forest surround me, reminding me of a grave, and I look ahead, seeing Farrow turn onto Frontress Road. We speed down the river, toward the bridge, and my heart starts hammering. My pulse knocks against my throat, then down my arms, and I flit my gaze between the darkened headlights behind me and the bright taillights in front of me.

Farrow cuts a sharp right onto the bridge fifty yards ahead, and I flip on my blinker and curl my fingers around the wheel. I let off the gas to slow down for the turn as Farrow reaches the middle of the bridge. I swerve to follow, a lump lodges in my throat, and then...

I jerk the wheel to the left, laying on the gas.

My tires screech under me, and I race away, speeding off into the night before Farrow can follow. He'll have to cross the bridge to have space to turn around, and I'll bet he's cursing me out right now.

Coasting away, I shift into fifth and keep my eyes peeled and my brights on. The car follows, gaining on me, and I turn and turn again, trying to make sure Farrow can't follow like I know he'll try. Speeding deep into the woods, I crawl down back roads and dark lanes, leading him—or her—the long way to the summer camp. It'll be quiet, but there will be admins and counselors in the cabins, preparing for the arrival of the next session in two days.

Maybe the Dodge will finally introduce itself, but I'm still not stupid enough to be completely alone when they do.

My phone rings, lighting up with Farrow's name, but I ignore it. Lucas is unavailable for him to alert, and he's not going to call my family.

I pause. *He might call Dylan or Hunter, though...*

But it's too late to worry about that now. Rain starts hitting my windshield like little bullets, and I flip on my wipers as cool drops land on my arms and thighs.

Barreling over a gravel hill, I start to descend, but orange traffic drums sit below as a barrier, warning of danger. Water rushes over the broken road, and I can't go any farther.

"Shit," I breathe out.

I have a moment to make a decision with really only one option. I swerve sharply to the left, racing down a thin path probably only meant for ATVs. I have no idea where it's taking me. There are all sorts of remote little properties around the lake. I don't even know how to get home from here. Does this road even lead me back to a cross street? Or does it take me to a dead end?

Never lead it to where you're alone beats in my head like a drum now. This didn't work like I thought it would.

I reach over to my phone and try to dial Farrow, but I spot a glow through the streaks of rain in my windshield. I squint as the water streams down my face, and I think I make out a front porch light peeking out of the woods.

Exhaling a little, I race for the house, bouncing over the overgrown lawn, and halt the car in the yard. Standing up, I peer over the windshield. The windows are dark, no sign of life other than the security light... I try to zone in on the front door and a paper sign taped to its surface. I can't read it from here, but my stomach sinks all the same. It could be a seasonal place. They could be out of town for the week and leaving instructions for deliveries. "Fuck," I mutter, my chin trembling.

I want whoever is in the Dodge to make themselves known, but I don't want to be completely alone out here. *Dammit.*

Sitting back down, I shift into first and start to hit the gas, but the Jeep tilts as air hisses out of a rear tire. I whip my head around, seeing a hooded figure move to the passenger side, the tire on mine already flattening.

"No!" I gasp.

He hauls himself up into my empty seat, and I fly out of the car, scrambling for the front door of the house.

Leaping up all of the steps, I bang on the door again and again. "Hello!"

Thunder cracks across the sky, and I jiggle the door handle, but it's locked. I can't focus enough to read the sign clearly, only catching the words "deliveries" and "private property."

Bright lights suddenly illuminate the front of the house, spilling onto the door. I spin around, seeing the headlights of the Dodge nearly blinding me.

But there's no movement.

"What do you want?" I shout.

This is what I wanted. A confrontation.

They haven't hurt me. Maybe they won't.

"Who are you?" I bellow. "Come on!"

And then, my eyes focus enough to see past the light.

It's not a Dodge.

It's bigger, like an SUV. There's no Dodge at all. Who—

But someone swoops in from the side, grabbing me, and I gasp.

"Thank you for ditching Farrow," he says, pulling back the hood of his jacket. "The boy was always as stupid as he was useless."

I stop breathing, gaping at Drew Reeves. He has scruff on his cheeks instead of being clean shaven like I remember from when he was a cop, but his eyes are the same. Blue, like Lucas's.

Lucas...

What have I done?

Reeves turned Lucas in.

His fingers clench around my wrists, holding them behind my back, and I grit my teeth, trying to free myself.

"I tried to talk myself out of hurting you." His whisper falls over my lips, the stench of his sweat making me nauseous. "You have a lot of cumbersome relatives."

He laughs and opens his mouth, like he's going to kiss me.

"But I think I will," he says. "Hurt you, I mean. Lucas will never be able to forget me then."

I hold back my tremble.

"Get in the car nicely, Miss Caruthers," he tells me, "and I won't slit your throat when I'm done." A sickly smile curls his mouth. "But you might want me to by then."

I growl, dropping like dead weight—just like my brothers taught me—and slip through his hold as I fall to the porch.

I scramble, jumping down the steps. My knife is in the car.

But he grabs my hair, yanking me back. I twist around and spit in his face and he shoves me away. "Right here, then," he taunts, pulling off his jacket.

His threat makes me whimper, my heart in my throat, and I look everywhere for any sign of help. I scream, he comes in to kiss me, and I bite his cheek.

We push away from each other, and I know he's about to hit me. Send me flying to the ground, half-unconscious, and God help me then. *Run,* I tell myself.

But I don't have a chance.

Something fast and dark sweeps in between us, and the next thing I know, blood is spurting from Drew's neck. His eyes go wild, and he reaches for me as he holds his wound with the other hand, blood spilling over his fingers.

My mouth sits open, short, shallow gasps coming in as I watch the scene in front of me unfold.

Lucas's enemy—the cause of his pain and separation from everyone he loves—plummets to the wet grass, and I jump back.

What the hell? A pool of red spills out around him.

I can't move for a second. What...what...

What do I do?

What happened? I—

But the figure still stands to my left, watching Drew fade along with me, and I don't know if I'm safe.

Wet hair spills out of her sweatshirt hood, the rest of the woman clad in jeans and sneakers.

Her eyes lift to me, but only for a second.

My chest caves. The eyes...

And as fast as an apparition, she's gone. Running off the porch, past my car and Drew's, and disappearing into the woods.

Horns honk and new headlights speed up on me from beyond the trees, but still, I watch the forest and the black void where she vanished. "Winslet?"

The nerves under my skin fire like little embers.

Lowering my eyes, I see Drew Reeves's hand laying lax against his neck, blood staining his fingers and eyes gazing up at nothing with his mouth hanging open.

"Quinn!" someone shouts.

My stomach churns, the walls closing in…

They shake me. "Quinn!"

I snap my head up, meeting Dylan's eyes.

"Are you okay?" she asks, then drops her gaze, seeing Reeves. "Oh my God."

I stare down at him again.

She had been so fast. *Winslet*. No hesitation.

"Quinn?" Dylan shouts. "Are you hurt at all?"

I can't take my eyes off the body. What would've happened if Winslet hadn't showed up? Dylan and the boys would've come along quickly enough. Farrow rightly suspected that we tracked each other's phones and called her. Reeves might've killed me instantly. Or shoved me in the car and drove away to who-knows-where. He could've hurt one of them if Winslet wasn't here.

I breathe hard. "I didn't…"

Hunter runs up to us, gaping at the body at our feet. "Holy shit, Quinn."

I don't blink. "It wasn't me."

It was her.

SHELBURNE FALLS

CHAPTER THIRTY-THREE

Lucas

A shout fills my ears. "Barry!"

I turn my head toward the hallway. Phones ring, voices are elevated, and shoes squeak against the floor as people move speedily up and down the hallway.

An officer named Heisler picks up the phone, listens, and then hangs up. Bolting out of his seat, he holsters his gun and starts to leave.

"What the hell is going on?" I ask, walking up to my bars.

"Officer Reeves—" Heisler tells the other cop. "Drew Reeves, I mean. He's been killed."

The other officer bolts out of his seat, but I freeze, watching them scramble to the door and swing it open.

What?

I grab the bars in my fists. "Who did it?" I shout.

Where's Quinn? Is she okay?

"Don't know," Heisler calls back.

And he disappears out the door.

"Good riddance to that son of a bitch," the other officer spits out as he secures his belt around his waist and follows.

"Wait!" I call.

But no one comes back. I need to call Quinn. I need a phone!

My heart thumps, and I yank on the bars. I can't be sure this has anything to do with her or the rest of my family, but it's too convenient. I get arrested two hours before he dies? He had to know I was taken into custody. Did he go after her?

Or was it Green Street?

I pace across the empty cell, the commotion outside quieting down. Cruisers race off, their sirens fading away.

Please let her be all right. Please...

Please let them all be safe. Reeves could've gone after anyone to hurt me, not just Quinn. What about Madoc?

I can't stop the dread piling in my stomach.

The door to the room opens again, and Madoc walks in, still dressed in a light blue shirt with a black suit. The tie is gone now.

I rush to the bars as he closes the door. "Is Quinn safe?"

He slides a hand into his pocket, clutching his phone with the other. "She's fine," he tells me. "A little shaken up, but unharmed."

"What happened?"

"Reeves went after her."

I clench my fists around the cell bars. "What?"

"She's okay," he assures me. "She'll tell you the rest. She's outside."

Exhaling, I drop my gaze. *Thank God.*

Madoc approaches me and stops barely a foot away. "Witnesses came forward and corroborated the story you told Quinn."

Witnesses?

The guys on the banks of the river that night. Reeves's crew.

Realization dawns. They work for Farrow now.

"You're blameless in the death of David Miller," he says. "My office feels that your hesitance to come forward was...understandable given the threat from inside our law enforcement."

He keeps his voice low, but there's something else in his tone.

He's guarded, like he's not sure how to handle me.

I must seem like a stranger to him now.

It takes a moment, but I clear my throat. "If you don't prosecute," I point out, "the town will see it as favoritism."

"I agree." He sighs. "If you're amenable to community service, then it's settled. You're free to go."

Pulling keys out of his pocket, he unlocks the cell, and we both open the door.

Standing in front of him, I wait for some signal. I don't want to just walk out, because right now, we don't feel okay.

His mouth opens, closes, then opens again. "I have never not been proud of you." He lifts his eyes. "Between Jared, Jax, and me, we've done worse and more."

Maybe. It didn't feel the same, though.

"I lost Hunter for a while," he tells me, "and then you..."

I had no idea he'd had trouble with the twins.

And with me abandoning him, he must've thought he was doing something wrong.

He almost whispers, "I'm sorry that you didn't feel like you could fall."

I shake my head. "It was nothing you did."

He hugs me, and I feel my chest about to burst.

"Do you understand now?" He pulls back, looking at me. "The only thing that doesn't make you a man is not getting back up."

"I know that now."

"When I was sixteen, you were my little brother," he muses. "I wanted us both to forget our problems and only have fun, like The Lost Boys. But we became family, and I was prepared for it all because Fallon and I love you."

I want to tell him I love him, too, but my throat swells, and I can't talk.

"Don't ever do that again, okay?" he teases.

I chuckle. "Never again," I breathe out.

We start for the door, and I didn't realize how much I had weighing on my shoulders. Drew is gone. Green Street is Farrow's. Quinn is mine, and her brothers know.

I'm home.

I take the door, holding it open. "So does this community service afford time for me to get a job?"

I have money, but I can't ask her father to trust me if I don't have a steady paycheck.

But Madoc's reply comes quickly. "Nope. Sorry," he says. "The community service will be extensive, I'm afraid." He leads the way out into the police station. "Weston needs a lot of help. Repairs and restoration, infrastructure re-established, fundraising, and they need to hire at least one cop, I think."

"That's a lot for one person to handle," I retort.

Is he serious? That's a full-time job.

He tosses a glance back at me. "It's a mayor's job."

I stop dead. "What?"

He turns with a smile and holds out his hand. I take it, still processing. "Congratulations," he tells me. "You'll serve as provisional until the regular election, and then run for a four-year term."

My face falls. "Madoc..."

Whipping back around, he starts to leave. "It's not a discussion."

I chase after him. "I'm not even a resident!"

"Something tells me you're going to be there every night anyway."

I catch Quinn as she leaps into my arms. Everyone stands around, but I only take count of Fallon and Juliet before Quinn is on me. Lost in her kisses and her scent, I almost don't feel the burn of Jared's glare, which I have no doubt is boring a hole into my skull.

I touch her and look her up and down, making sure I don't see a scratch. Kissing her forehead, her temple, and then her hair, I pull her into a hug.

I'll hear about everything as soon as we're alone. I just can't stop holding her.

Someone steps up to our side. "You shouldn't have given Green Street to Farrow," Aro tells me under her breath.

Quinn turns toward her, but I don't let go.

I explain, "Hugo would've just taken the club and moved it somewhere else—"

"Farrow has no interest in turning Green Street into a legitimate business," she fires back, glancing between us both. "You don't know him as well as you think. Neither of you do."

And conscious of listening ears, she takes her leave, walking out of the police station.

I never specified terms to Farrow, but he knows what my position is and... He's practically family. He'll try to cooperate.

Fallon comes over, we hug, and I try not to be hyperaware of knowing Farrow's relationship to her that she's completely oblivious to. She needs to be told.

Madoc wants everyone at his house to decompress—root beer floats for the kids, martinis for the adults—but I can't talk to any more people tonight.

Except one.

Pulling Quinn by the hand, I lead her outside, to her car, and we head home. To Weston.

I pull up in front of her place on Knock Hill and look up at the old brownstone, my mind exploding with renovation ideas even as I process the details she fills me in on of what happened tonight after I was arrested.

She pries my fingers off her thigh, and I didn't realize I was squeezing.

He almost hurt her.

Fucking God. I'm glad he's dead.

We stay in the Jeep, on the street, kissing for a long time. When I can't take it anymore, I open her door and help her out of the car, and we walk up the steps.

"So...you raced a car?" I tease, trying to take her mind off everything she saw tonight.

She beams. "Well, I never said I couldn't."

Yeah, it's in the blood.

We stop at the door, and I take hold of her again. "I'm sorry I wasn't there."

Her gaze softens on me. "You will be next time." Hesitating, she asks, "Right?"

I pick her up, guiding her legs around my body. "Every time."

Taking her keys from her hand, I unlock the door as her mouth covers mine. She kisses me again and again, moving to my face and my eyes. "I love you."

"I love you too," I tell her, slamming the door and locking it. "But we're going to need a bigger bed."

I can't sleep in that single.

Well, I can tonight. We won't be sleeping much anyway.

But she eyes me, feigning confusion as if she doesn't know what I'm getting at. "*We*?"

Yes. We. It's our room, our bed...

But still, I ask, "Do you mind?"

I need to be a resident of Weston. And Madoc already seems to know exactly what's about to happen and is good with it.

She wraps her arms around my neck and brushes her nose against my cheek. "I've waited long enough for you."

And I've waited long enough to start living.

I just hold her in the foyer, and I start rocking us side to side to whatever music is coming from Farrow's place. All the dreams I have come flooding back, and my heart is pumping so hard with excitement to get started. Making this house a home for her and getting this town functional and productive again.

Bustling businesses, lights, thriving families. Enough to keep me busy for the rest of my life.

I'm about to walk her upstairs, but her phone rings.

"Better check it," I tell her, my voice gravelly with desire.

A lot happened tonight. People will need to talk to us again.

But she looks at her phone, her face falling as if she recognizes the number.

Looking to me, she swipes the screen before I can see who's calling.

She puts it on speaker. "Deacon?"

Deacon? I stare at the screen, memorizing the number for Jax to trace.

"He's indisposed right now," another man replies. "But I saw that he called you, Quinn."

Quinn and I exchange looks as she holds up the phone between us.

"Manas?" she guesses.

"Yes," he replies. "Is Lucas with you?"

I take the phone, hesitating a moment. "Thank you for the help earlier." He has to be close, probably still in town. "But why?"

We're not family. He doesn't know me. He's going to want something for coming to my aid.

When he doesn't reply, I press harder. "Why do I feel like we're game pieces you're moving around?"

"That's not my intention." He takes a sip of something, maybe coffee. "I would've preferred Hawke never find the tower, and Quinn and Dylan never sleep in that house, but every cast of players has their role, and I have very little control."

"Winslet didn't die during Rivalry Week," Quinn tells him. "But you knew that."

"A month after the car went into the river, I started hearing stories of home." He pauses. "Three murders—all Pirates. And Winslet can get very angry."

"Did you return to Weston?" Quinn questions. "Did you see her?"

"Yes."

Quinn meets my eyes. Such a quick and simple answer. She was right. Their trail doesn't go cold after the Night Ride. More has happened in the years since.

He adds, "But you're not at that part in the story yet."

"Where did you see her?" Quinn asks. "Just tell me that."

For a moment, I don't think he's going to answer. Then, he says, "Camp Blackhawk."

The summer camp before it was renovated and reopened. She was hiding there after she survived the river.

Her own friends tried to murder her. She couldn't go home.

Or she didn't want to. She wanted her revenge.

"What did you do when you saw her?" I ask him.

"It was a long night, I'll tell you that."

I shake my head.

"Why are you leaving a trail for us?" Quinn begs him. "What do you want?"

But he simply counters with another question. "How did she look?"

How did she look?

Quinn thinks it was Winslet who saved her tonight. He knows she's here?

"Younger than I thought she would," Quinn tells him.

"Because we stop aging when we die," he points out.

"You believe that?" I narrow my eyes in disbelief. "That Quinn saw her ghost tonight?"

I don't mean to mock him, but come on...

"I believe...that I can still taste her on my mouth and smell her on my clothes." His voice seems like mist, a whisper. "And I believe she's still where I buried her. At Blackhawk."

Quinn's eyes widen, but before I can say anything, the line dies.

"Wait!" I growl.

We call back, but it goes straight to voicemail, as if he's turned the phone off. This phone will never be on again. He'll ditch it.

Quinn searches my eyes. "What do we do now?"

I don't know.

But at the very least, we can write everything down while it's fresh and fill everyone else in tomorrow.

And we can add to the murder map at Carnival Tower. Time to focus Hawke's research on a new lead.

WESTON

CHAPTER THIRTY-FOUR

Quinn

I hover outside my father's office, listening with Lucas at my back.

"It's not our fault!" Madoc shouts.

"It is *absolutely* your fault!"

I wince, my dad's voice more of a growl than a bellow. Lucas holds my shoulder, rubbing his thumb over the back of my neck.

My parents got home late last night, and when they found out everything they'd missed, they wouldn't even listen to me. My brothers were summoned. Jared, Madoc, and Jax haven't been in there more than sixty seconds, and there's already shouting. I can just picture them lined up in front of my father's desk like they're back in high school facing the principal.

I don't hear my mother at all. Usually, she can shorten my dad's leash, but if she doesn't, then she must agree with him.

"I have raised her for twenty-one years without incident!" my dad screams. "I leave her with you three for a week, and she moves out, jumps into bed with an older man, and almost gets herself killed!"

I half roll my eyes. He's just as bad as my brothers. As if he wasn't an older man, seducing my mother when she was younger than me.

He keeps railing, my brothers not saying a word, and I turn my head, lifting my eyes to the only man I've ever wanted. As if they couldn't see this coming my entire life.

"He'll come around," I say.

My dad is like him. And like my siblings. He tends to react before he reasons.

"I'll speak to him tonight." Lucas dips his nose to my hair. "I need to talk to Farrow first."

He takes my hand and leads me through the kitchen where Juliet, Hunter, and A.J. make breakfast, and out of the house, around the back. Everyone showed up here this morning to get all the news and the full story from Lucas, but he's avoided talking to anyone until he can see my father. Farrow stands just inside my father's second garage, checking out his boat.

Lucas reaches into his breast pocket and hands Farrow documents in a trifold—the deed to Green Street, I assume.

Farrow lifts the corners of his mouth, looking pleased, but he doesn't smile, and he doesn't say thank you for a free building.

Instead, he holds out his hand, asking, "Your key?"

I shift my eyes to Lucas.

He simply cocks his head. "If you feel it necessary to keep me out, change the locks."

I smile to myself, but I'm not sure why. Not reading the documents shows that Farrow trusts Lucas, but by Lucas still requesting access shows that Lucas doesn't trust him. Not completely. I guess I like that he feels a responsibility to keep an eye on Farrow, and not because he doesn't like him, but because he does.

Serving in Weston's city government is a commitment to serve the citizens, and Farrow knows as well as Lucas does that Green Street serves itself first. They're not in this together. Not one hundred percent.

Farrow sticks the deed into the back pocket of his jeans. "If you keep a key, then you're complicit in what happens there."

"I don't plan on being complicit in anything," my man responds. "No drugs, no arms, no prostitution."

Farrow laughs, but he doesn't look amused. "Does that include weed?" he retorts.

Marijuana is legal in this state, but Farrow isn't seriously asking. Selling weed won't make them the income they're used to making.

"How the fuck do you expect us to make money?" he barks.

"I have some ideas," Lucas replies calmly, as if he expected the pushback. "But ultimately, it can be anything you won't be ashamed to tell Fallon about."

What? I glance between them.

Why would Farrow have to explain anything to Fallon, of all people?

"Let's meet at Breaker's at seven." Lucas offers Farrow his hand. "We have things to discuss."

They shake, and I almost ask if I can come, but Lucas will feel better on his own.

And I have so much to do. Frosted and the house.

We make our way back up to the patio, the trickle of the little waterfall in our pool soothing as the sound of the lawn mower kicks up and the scent of grass hits my nostrils.

Looking up, I see Madoc pushing our old lawn mower that my dad doesn't even use anymore. He keeps it because "kids who can't be trusted don't get to use the riding mower." Jax holds open a canvas bag as Jared swipes a cordless trimmer around the hedges and dumps little branches into it.

I let my mouth fall open, the urge to laugh nearly overtaking me. They're being punished? They're more than forty years old.

"I can't believe they stayed for this."

"They love this family," Lucas states, holding my waist. "They want your dad happy."

I shake my head, blinking a few times to make sure I'm still seeing Jared actually doing yardwork that's not for his own yard.

Maybe he likes having a father, after all.

My eyes start to sting, and I blink it away.

"I'd better help," Lucas says.

He leans in for a kiss, but I pull back. "What did you mean about Fallon? Why would Farrow care about her knowing what he does?"

Lucas just kissed my forehead. "I'll tell you later. Promise."

He starts to move toward my brothers, two of whom haven't completely accepted us yet, but I hold on to him for another minute.

"Can you actually wrangle them for another job?" I offer a shy smile. "Mom says I can have the bed from my room until I get the house renovated and pick out a new one."

His eyes widen, and he inhales a deep breath. "You want me to ask your brothers to help move their sister's bed that I'm going to sleep with her in?"

"You have to." I shrug. "Jared has a truck."

I kiss his cheek, then move to his mouth. "I have to get to the shop. All of my ice cream equipment came in," I breathe over his lips, "and my stand opens this weekend."

And I have to call a plumber, and figure out some more furniture, and get the Jeep registered, and whip up about fifteen gallons of ice cream.

I bolt away, but Lucas hauls me back, and I grin wide as he wraps his arms around me. Sinking his mouth onto mine, I brush his tongue, my body stirring so easily that I could forget the rest of my day if we didn't already have the promise of tonight.

I feel my brothers scowling at us, but I don't look because I'm not going to stop.

"See you in Weston after my meeting with Farrow tonight," he whispers.

I nod, picking out the piece of old, folded notebook paper from my pocket and handing it to him.

"I added number eleven," I tease. "I may or may not be in the attic when you get home."

He opens it as I move away, reading what I wrote this morning.

Home invasion role play.

Like the Marauders from Winslet's day.

Stifling his smile, he quickly refolds it and stuffs it into his pocket.

"Leave the lights off for me," he says with one final kiss.

And I nearly bounce all the way to Frosted.

WESTON

EPILOGUE

Quinn

Six Months Later

I love the winter months, honestly. Later sunrises and more time in bed. Early sunset and early to bed. The blizzard we had last week cut the electricity for two whole days. Lucas and I found how little we needed lights or artificial heat.

Walking up the wooden stairs in Fallon's shop, I smile to myself as I remember a year ago and how much I never thought I'd see him again. Now, here we are, sharing a dinner table. Although, we never eat at it. When we find ourselves at home, and alone, I'm usually sitting on the counter with him standing between my legs, both of us taking bites between conversation and laughing and kisses.

I move toward the small conference room, seeing him through the glass. He sits at an oval table, facing me with Mr. Bassett across from him, his back to me.

"I understand what you're saying," I hear Bassett tell Lucas, "but we've owned those hills for two generations. You understand our hesitance to change something that suits us so well?"

Lucas lifts his eyes to me, and I see a gleam rise.

"I do." He focuses back on his hopeful partner. "And I will not encourage you to sign a contract until it's exactly what you want. I'm interested in doing what it takes to ensure you're not only comfortable, but excited."

Lucas has been helping Fallon here when he can, but Weston has kept him more than occupied. He started off with an office above Samson Fletcher's barber shop, and now he and the town have cleaned up their City Hall enough to where the entire first floor can be used. There's a food bank, a shelter, a small market has reopened downtown, and a bank will open in the spring. Still no police, and I worry Farrow is getting in his way. It's baffling to watch them. They argue, but they do it while working out at the gym together.

There are still months of snow, though, so not much else can be done right now except planning his resort that he wants to build right next to Pine Tree Peak, the local slopes.

"Right now, you've got some hills," Lucas explains, "and a grab-and-go eatery, and locals frequent your place because there are no other options."

I stare at his relaxed posture in his chair, his ankle resting over the other knee. I love him out of clothes, and I love him in clothes. He's just as hot in snow gear as he is in my shower.

I pinch the zipper of my ski jacket.

"When I build Summit Falls," he goes on, "I don't want to take business away from you. My goal is that it will bring in more."

Pulling the zipper down, I watch as his gaze rises and feel the cool air touch the naked skin underneath my jacket. No shirt. No bra. No fear.

His lips part, and I grip the jacket, ready to close it if his guest turns around.

"I..." he stammers and clears his throat. "I understand being apprehensive about change." He darts his eyes to Bassett, then to me, and back to Bassett, trying to fight the smile wanting to escape him. "You're happy with the way things are. But is everyone else? This means more employment, conservation, enrichment for youth, more options for entertainment for local families..."

I open my jacket, flashing him, and his eyes widen. He can't control it. He laughs nervously and bows his head, coughing to try to deflect. I hold it open, chills spreading over my skin every second his guest doesn't turn around.

Lucas rubs his hand across the back of his neck, and my face is hot. My body is hot. Everything is hot.

"All right." Mr. Bassett picks up the VR headset. "Show me this thingy again."

They both stand up, and Lucas throws me a glare like the ones I get when I'm about to be given chores that make me sweat in ways I love.

"Who knew you were going to be the naughtiest?" a voice says next to me.

I slam my jacket closed, turning my head to see Aro on my right side and then Isobel on my left. *Shit*.

"It's always the quiet ones," Isobel muses, popping an almond into her mouth.

Lucas's Dubai assistant has been here for a month, helping him plan the resort and find investors while she studies under Fallon. She heads back to Dubai in six weeks, but I'm hoping she visits often. I can understand this town is a step down from what she's used to, but she's worked with Lucas for years and can anticipate him. It'll just be a hassle for him to train someone else.

Aro's been assisting him in Weston as an "unofficial consultant," meaning she gives him the inside information when Farrow withholds it.

I zip up my jacket, pushing the two of them back down the stairs and leaving him to work in peace.

An hour later, Isobel and Aro sit on a ski lift with Dylan and cruise over my head as I sit in the icy snow on Pine Tree Peak. Looking behind me, I see Lucas ride his snowboard, leaning back and expertly curving over to me where I'd fallen off to the side. Snow flies up as he skids to a halt.

"The only good thing about this is how hot you look doing that," I call out, lifting my goggles up onto my helmet.

It seems I spend an unnecessary fortune on gear every time I snowboard or ski because I only do it once every three or four years and my size changes. Dylan gave me a pair of her white pants, and I was able to reuse the helmet and jacket, but I had to buy new goggles.

Lucas is dressed all in black.

"I thought you liked skiing," he tells me.

"I like the ski lifts."

That ride is always relaxing. Until it's time to get off.

He removes his snowboard and plops down behind me, his legs around me. Tipping my chin back, he kisses my lips.

"And I love après-ski," I whisper.

I love getting everything off and getting warm with him.

"That was not very nice what you pulled in the office," he growls a little.

"I think I'm very nice."

Our family is all around the mountain somewhere. Except James. He's probably in the lodge, whipping up mischief.

Skiers and snowboarders coast by us, having a ball, and I can smell the snow clouding the sky. January has been an eventful month for weather, but I'm not complaining.

I thread my fingers through Lucas's as they snake around my waist.

"Have you had enough skiing?" he asks.

"Yes."

"Wanna go home?"

"Yeah."

He hugs me close. "Okay," he says. "But you gotta get your ass down the hill one last time."

I crash back into him harder. "Ugh."

We sit there for a minute, out of the way, watching Hunter and Kade race by, carving eights into the snow with their boards. I can just make out Juliet on the bunny hill with Aro's brother, teaching him some beginner moves.

Lucas is going to be here or—hopefully—at his resort every winter. He loves the snow. "I'm going to have to learn, aren't I?"

I want him to say "no." Or tell me I don't have to do anything I don't want to do, but instead, he replies, "Yes."

I eye him over my shoulder.

"I can't own a ski resort and my wife not ski," he explains.

Wife?

Butterflies swarm my stomach, and I can't keep the smile at bay.

I know this isn't his actual proposal, but it's the first time he's alluded to our future together.

Is it really going to be Lucas and me? Forever?

He smiles back and lowers his mouth to mine, but I can't even kiss him properly, I'm almost giggling.

"Quinn," he scolds, wanting his kiss.

But I just laugh, shrinking down in his arms under his cocked eyebrow. "I'm sorry!"

He growls and bears down, grabbing my lips with his.

And my chest caves, breathless.

God, I love him. Our quiet talks and our quiet house and our quiet nights.

But it won't be a quiet wedding. I'll be taking over the town that day.

Winslet stands on the balcony of the ski lodge, steam from her breath barely visible. She doesn't breathe. Not really. Manas once called her a creature, not human. Maybe, after all this time, she understands what he meant.

The way she didn't need air to live, but rather absorbed whatever was on his lips when he pressed them to her skin.

And the way he said her cunt was poison. Like a drug that made him think only of her when he couldn't have her.

Lucas helps Quinn to her feet, slowly gliding down the mountain in short stints and waiting for her as she timidly follows.

If she leaves now, she can get into 01 Knock Hill while Lucas and Quinn are out and leave one last present for them.

But it's best to leave it alone. Let Lucas concentrate on rebuilding Weston. She wants it to thrive before both towns burn.

And perhaps, there are other players to mobilize in the meantime.

She scans the slopes, spotting wild little Dylan flying over a ramp and beautiful Aro, still shaky with her new snowboard. They both went searching Camp Blackhawk last summer with Quinn and others, but they didn't find what is certainly there. It's not their fault. It's hidden as well as the memories of when Manas and Deacon found her that summer, after the night rides, when the blood still soaked the ground.

That...was a glorious night.

She moves away from the railing but notices the white-haired girl in black ski pants. She wears a red-and-black-checkered flannel as she sails through the air, spinning, and then landing before skidding to a halt at the base next to some young men. She beams, removing her helmet to reveal a light blue Cubs cab on backward underneath, Farrow Kelly high-fives her.

Winslet toys with the stud in her earlobe and watches the young woman, the Shelburne Falls girl who joined a Weston family. Someone who knows what it's like to not feel love from others and finally feel home somewhere and not want to lose it.

The best thing about thieves is that people think that's all there is to know about them. But their most valuable quality is desperation.

What isn't Thomasin Dietrich capable of?

What would it take to find out?

THE END

Thank you so much for reading *Quiet Ones*!
The next installment will feature Tommy and Kade
and will take place a few years
down the road in the timeline.
It is being planned now.
Hope to see you back for *NIGHT THIEVES*
and the mystery of Camp Blackhawk.

ACKNOWLEDGEMENTS

From book to book, my acknowledgments never really change. I've worked with most of the same people that I did when I started, and what I'm continually grateful for is that they accommodate the way I work. This isn't the norm in this industry. Everyone has a schedule. Everyone has a life of their own. Everyone has other obligations and other clients. I need to get my book done or my order in or I might lose my spot with that designer, formatter, or editor.

Unfortunately, I just can't. I never could. For someone who thrives off routine and being on time, deadlines are my Achilles' heel.

I know when I sit down and start thinking about how the conversations you just read between these characters are going to go that I will get them written down. I know the words *will* come.

I sit there.

See the characters in my head.

I've almost got it.

And then...

Yes. That's what I want her to say, and then he's going to say that next. And then I sit there again, trying to figure out what she says back.

Sure, I could type anything. I can keep the story going, type words, and finish the book, but I know if I think about it just a little bit longer, the heroine will say something that'll make me smile even more.

Some days I sit at my desk for ten hours and actually only type for three of them. Some days, I'll type for five of those hours. Given that, it's impossible to predict when I'll finish until I'm about two-thirds of the way through the book when it's pretty much on auto-pilot from there.

I'm grateful when my formatter says, "Don't worry, I'll squeeze you in." when I tell her I need two more weeks. Or when my editor barely bats an eyelash that I'm late turning in a manuscript. Again.

Of course, everyone's time is valuable, and I do not expect anyone to drop what they're doing when I'm finally ready for them, but it's hard to anticipate needing extra time and having the freedom to take it when needed has made all the difference. I'm thankful that Bekke, Elaine, Chrissy, Ashlee, Marisa, Adrienne, and Lee appreciate that stories are a fucking hassle to write, but the end product is so worth it.

Thank you, as well, to all of the YouTube ambience content creators who play nonstop in my office. Truly unsung heroes, helping us all live an aesthetically pleasing life. You inspire, nurture my mood, and surround me with whatever atmosphere I need to focus me.

Also...

To Dystel, Goderich & Bourret LLC—thank you Jane, Lauren, and Gracie for being so readily available and helping me grow every day. And Nataly! I love getting emails from Nataly! We know why. LOL

To the PenDragons—love you! Excited to hear your theories on what's to come in the series!

To all of the book bloggers, bookstagrammers, and booktok accounts—thank you, thank you, thank you. I've never believed authors are the best people to sell their own books. Readers are. You've changed the game. We can write and make a living, and you're helping the indie community thrive like never before. So much has come in throughout the past year, and I know I haven't nearly acknowledged every tag, but I want you to know you're appreciated. Your beautiful pictures, your beautiful (and funny) TikToks, your time writing reviews... I know it won't last forever, but I'll enjoy it for as long as I can. Thank you!

To every author and aspiring author—thank you for the stories you've shared, many of which have made me a happy reader in search of a wonderful escape and a better writer, trying to live up to your standards. Write and create, and don't ever stop. Your voice is important, and someone out there needs to hear it.